WRATH AND TEARS

THE CONCLUSION

ALAN JANNEY

SPARKLE PRESS

@alanjanney
alan@ChaseTheOutlaw.com

First Edition
Paperback ISBN: 9781730997747

Cover by Damonza
Artwork by Anne Pierson

Sparkle Press

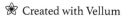 Created with Vellum

This book is dedicated to
the readers
of the Outlaw and Carmine series.

Thank you.
My dream of writing
came true
in large part
because of you.

A bizarre note from the author

Recent events within America prompt me to warn you not to look closely for any hidden political meaning in my novels, especially the one you're about to read. There is no disguised agenda. For example, in 2018 building a wall to keep people out of America is a hot button issue. However, when I first wrote about Blue-Eyes building wall in *Carmine* in early 2016, it wasn't. There's no hidden meaning anywhere, with any character or circumstance. If you think you spot one, dismiss it as coincidence, because it is. This is pure entertainment. Enjoy!

CAST OF CHARACTERS

Infected - **Pure-born Variants**
    Blue-Eyes - President of the former United States
Nuts - mechanical genius
The Outlaw - masked vigilante
PuckDaddy - internet hacker
Samantha - sniper working with the Resistance
Tank - Variant Alpha
Walter - terrorist living in the northwest
Carter- powerful mercenary
China- young girl named Ai, a medical genius
Pacific- ancient woman living on a yacht
Russia- warlord in San Diego (DECEASED)
The Zealot- vagabond, missionary (DECEASED)

KINGDOM VARIANTS
    Becky - scavenger (DECEASED)
Carmine- the former queen of Los Angeles
Kayla - Mistress of Communication
Mason - leader of the Falcons

Travis- leader of the Giants

OTHERS OF NOTE

The Cheerleader - mysterious recluse, girl on fire
Dalton - queen's bodyguard (DECEASED)
General Brown - military commander
The Governess - supervisor of New Los Angeles
The Inheritors- children infected with Hyper Virus
Isaac Anderson - leader of the Resistance
The Priest - traitor to Los Angeles
Andy Babington- strapped to a nuclear bomb

The story thus far...

The Outlaw - Chase Jackson becomes the starting quarterback of his Varsity football team when he throws a football out of the stadium. Soon after he puts on a mask and causes mischief downtown, retrieving Katie Lopez's stolen phone. He earns the ire of local thug and national football freak Tank Ware, resulting in vicious battles on and off the field. Chase's heroics with the mask land him in the news and earns him the nickname Outlaw, a secret he hides from his closest friends, Katie, Cory, and Lee.

Infected - Chase discovers his enhanced body is the result of a disease, and it's about to kill him. A shadowy man named Carter warns that there are others like him, nicknamed the Infected, and that Chase needs to stop gaining national attention. Tank begins dating Katie Lopez, adding to Chase's misery. Soon Special Agent Isaac Anderson and the FBI are hot on the Outlaw's trail, and he's only saved by the intervention of a computer hacker named PuckDaddy and a sniper named Samantha Gear, both of whom are Infected. Chase's girlfriend Hannah Walker is killed in a fiery blast downtown during a confrontation with the Chemist.

The Sanctuary - The Chemist takes over Compton, south of Los Angeles, and unleashes an army of monsters infected with the Hyper Virus, led by Walter. Chase teams up with Carter and Samantha Gear to prevent further destruction. The Outlaw becomes more and more infamous as he dons a flying suit crafted by his best friend Lee. Katie Lopez discovers the truth about Chase's disguise and they begin dating. Despite the Outlaw's help, Los Angeles falls to the Chemist. Tank is captured by the government after being badly burned by the fiery Cheerleader, Hannah Walker, whose body was salvaged by the Chemist.

Outcasts - Los Angeles is a war zone. The Chemist discovers the

Outlaw's identity, forcing Chase and Katie into hiding. He offers a fortune to anyone who captures the Outlaw, so Chase, Katie, Samantha, and Cory seek refuge on a yacht owned by a woman named Pacific. Pacific, however, betrays them—Cory is killed and Katie Lopez captured. Katie is forced to undergo a surgery from which she may not awaken. Chase sacrifices himself to defeat the Chemist, and the gambit works—the madman is thrown off the roof by his henchman and he perishes. Even though the Chemist dies, his army of freaks endures and rampages. Walter and Blue-Eyes begin taking over the world while Chase nurses Katie back to health. She wakes up, enhanced and powerful, but doesn't remember Chase.

Carmine - Katie Lopez has amnesia and she adopts the personality of Carmine, the warrior queen. She ferociously holds Los Angeles together (with aid from Kayla and Mason, two mutants, and General Brown and the Governess). The world falls apart around them as Blue-Eyes and the mutants (or Variants) pull at the seams of society. The United States is divided between the Resistance and the Federal Government. The government calls for the capture of all mutants, unleashing cruel Herders to catch them. In order to withstand Walter's attacks, Carmine grudgingly accepts the help of the Outlaw, whose spine she broke on waking in the hospital. Tank lives nearby, leading a community of giants. Also living nearby is Hannah Walker, the mad cheerleader. Carmine's biggest secret is that she preserved five hundred infants infected with the virus.

Broken Angles - An Infected named Russia nearly kills the Outlaw and Carmine with a bomb. Carmine temporarily goes insane, rampaging with her tigers, until she's rescued by a powerful healer named the Zealot. The Federal government and Russia and Walter all attack Los Angeles, seeking control of the Variants (or Guardians, as Carmine calls them) under Carmine's command, but they're unable to penetrate the defenses. Blue-Eyes begins attacking Carmine through her mind, prompting the Outlaw and Samantha Gear to race to the East Coast to kill the Witch. Tank is enlisted to help defend Los Angeles, and Walter reveals another weapon at his disposal—a man who can control wolves. Carmine and Kayla kill Russia in an explosion which restores Katie's memory. Chase and Samantha grievously wound Blue-Eyes but are unable to eliminate her; however they discover Andy Babington has been strapped to a nuclear bomb with orders to detonate when he gets close to Queen Carmine. Chase's jet is shot down over the Atlantic and Katie goes into hiding to save her friends from the nuke. Each believes the other is dead. Carter and the Priest kidnap Katie/Carmine's secret infected children and take them to Hawaii. Walter and Tank nearly kill one another, forcing Saul the Zealot to save Tank's life, granting him the ability to communicate with animals.

And now, the story continues...

Wrath and Tears
The Conclusion to the Outlaw/Carmine Saga

PART I

Out of the night that covers me
    Black as the pit from pole to pole
    I thank whatever gods may be
    For my unconquerable soul.

In the fell clutch of circumstance
    I have not winced nor cried aloud
    Under the bludgeoning of chance
    My head is bloody, but unbowed.

Beyond this place of wrath and tears
    Looms the horror of the shade,
    And yet the menace of the years
    Finds and shall find me unafraid.

· · ·

It matters not how strait the gate,
How charged with punishments the scroll,
I am the master of my fate,
I am the captain of my soul.

-*Invictus*, by William Ernest Henley

April, 2022
Two years after the televised funeral of Queen Carmine

Carmine, the Warrior Queen, the Red Butcher, the girl once known as Katie Lopez, kneels beneath a budding apple tree on a farm in Idaho and wipes her forehead. Her rich brown hair is tied in a ponytail that falls between her shoulders, but wisps cling to her cheeks and eyelashes.

This tree, the final apple tree in the front row of the orchard, had the least chance of surviving the winter—the bark was ravaged by animals and the limbs hung thin and barren. And the winter was brutal. Yet here it stands, blooming with totemic importance, at least half its branches laden with blossoms.

She smiles and pats the trunk. Why is this particular tree so important? She doesn't know. Somehow it organically came to symbolize something bigger in her eyes. The future, maybe. Happiness.

Apples grow better farther north and west, the books tell her. This far south there's not enough rain. But sometimes life must grow where it's planted, not where it's ideal.

This tree *had* to survive. If it died, so would some of her hope. So she carried buckets of water during the dry January drought. She built fires between the trees to melt February snows, afraid the temperatures would burst the trunks. Last week she personally crawled through the branches and removed every tent worm. And today she spreads compost an inch deep in a five foot radius down the front row of the orchard. Mother Nature needs to get up an hour earlier if it wants to outwork her, she thinks.

Behind her, Sean is coming with another wheelbarrow of the black compost. She points to a spot and the squeaky cart unloads its cargo in a dump within her reach.

"How do you stand the smell," says Sean. Not really a question.

"Smells like success to me. Success and a harvest."

Sean grins at her. "No, it reeks like cow dung."

He's a tall man, approximately twenty-four, undeniably attractive in an athletic and arrogant way. During the long winter, she learned his story. Born and raised not far from here, his family were the only African American loggers within two hundred miles.

"Yes, part of it's cow dung." She tugs on her gloves, the prettiest she could find in the old shed. From her knees she scoops and pushes the stuff into place. "And deteriorating leaves, and rabbit droppings, and leftover food. You know what we've created?"

"A mess."

"Hope, that's what. It's the healthiest soil I can manage."

"Growing up, we used fertilizer. Did the trick," he says. "None of this cattle crap."

"This *is* fertilizer. Homemade. When I was a girl, we'd..." She stops and raises. Her eyes focus on something beyond the orchard. She's clawed back most of her memories. Some are more painful than others. Absently she rubs at an old burn wound on her neck.

"Carmine? Everything good?"

She grins to herself, bittersweet. Joy of the memory, pain at the loss. "My mother. We had flower beds. And yes, we're good."

For a while, she tried to hide her identity from her followers. Queen Carmine died in an explosion, after all. But sooner or later, they all figure it out.

Behind them, a boy her age is standing on the roof of a silver Toyota Tundra. His name is Darren. He grips a spear in his fists and he slowly rotates around it every few minutes, glaring in all directions.

No danger in sight.

Darren stands unnaturally erect, like an animal on high alert. He will follow Carmine all day without saying a word. She found him cowering in a cave a year ago. Darren attacked her and her followers like a feral cat until she pinned him and spoke softly to him for an hour while he raged and wept.

Now? He's one of her devoted protectors. A loyal Guardian,

mostly sane. His mind probes her intermittently but she doesn't let him in.

Finally the compost is spread. Sean hauls Carmine to her feet. She groans and stretches, arms up, then hands pressing against the small of her back. Her joints ache, a constant thunder she can usually ignore. Even so, she'll tie compresses on her knees and shoulders and elbows later.

Sean doesn't back away as she stretches; he enjoys the intimacy. He admires her the way most men his age would.

Carmine is, after all, a sight to behold. Born lovely and forced through a macabre surgery intended to either kill her or perfect her —she survived and emerged as a queen, a natural wielder of beauty and authority; she can tell she's distracting to men like Sean but she doesn't much care.

She's not ready to love. Not even Sean, who professes his affection a hundred ways. He's been a godsend; a survivalist and hard worker with knowledge of the area. He was reluctantly accepted by her followers, which says a lot. Even better, he doesn't worship her like the rest do, at least not rabidly. A serious plus for Sean.

Maybe one day.

But not yet. She's still in love with a man dead for two years. The pinnacle of manhood—the archetype, in her opinion. A man she would have sacrificed herself for a thousand times over...

Carmine shivers. From the rills of sweat, from the chill, and from lonely recollections. She blinks and shakes her head, returns to herself. Tugs the gloves off, finger by finger.

"We need to learn the art of canning fruit," she says. "I never knew how, but I predict a plethora of apples."

"When will they be ripe?" asks Sean.

"Autumn." She picks up the wheelbarrow and shoves it into the Tundra's bed. Sean learned to quit protesting months ago—though he is tall and muscular, his strength is nothing compared to hers. It galls his pride but he lets her do heavy lifting while he gathers her tools. "Drive the truck back, please, Sean."

"And you?"

"I want to walk."

"But—"

She pats Sean's cheek with the cup of her hand and grins. "Thank you, Sean." Without another word, she turns toward the farmhouse and sets off. Darren lands beside her on soft feet and hurries to match her stride for stride.

Sean watches Carmine go. As usual, she's left him frustrated.

Emerging from the orchard onto the grassy hill above, the entirety of the farm comes into her view. The snow-topped mountains of Sawtooth rise to the north. To the south, flatlands. In between, farmland, most of it growing wild. Not enough help to tend it.

Mother Nature returning to her natural state of wilderness. Only where pockets of humanity flourish is the chaos subdued.

Another Guardian stands here, on the crest—Renee. She possesses one of the clear minds and so she acts as an overseer; Carmine's second in command. Cute and short but Carmine has seen her take down a charging brown bear.

Renee smiles and nods her head. She chose this spot because she can keep an eye on the orchard, the fields, and the farmhouse—constant vigilance.

Carmine asks, "Have you eaten?"

"No, Queen Carmine."

"It's noon. Get some food."

Renee smiles at Darren, who returns the greeting with a stoic stare, and then she turns for the house, a quarter-mile march.

Carmine pauses on the brow of the hill and indicates Darren rotate. He does and she retrieves a satellite phone from his backpack.

She mutters, "Would it kill you to be nice to her?"

"My queen?" He doesn't speak much and his voice sounds rough.

"Renee. She smiled at you."

He doesn't answer.

Carmine powers on the phone. "Smile back next time, Darren. At Renee."

"Why?"

She rolls her eyes. "You're a good-looking guy. She's noticed. And Renee's a good-looking girl..."

"...Okay."

"Do you see what I'm getting at?"

"I'm sorry, my queen. I can't."

"You Variants," she grumbles. "Half of you possess the hormone control of buck during rutting season, and the other half..."

"I don't understand."

"Oh hush," she says, pressing buttons on the phone. "Smile at Renee. See what happens. Maybe she'll take pity."

The phone makes contact with one of the thousand satellites orbiting overhead, unconcerned with the world's upheaval. She waits but there are no messages.

That makes her antsy. It always does. But no news is good news. She's given strict instructions on cellphone contact—not unless absolutely necessary. She glares at the phone another minute before powering it off. Shoves it into the backpack.

"Let's go eat."

Darren nods and follows.

"You can sit next to her," says Carmine. "She'd like that."

"Who?"

Another sigh. "Never mind."

The farm is a buzzing hive of activity. The owners of the house, Mr. and Mrs. Barton, are doing their best to direct the workforce of twenty Variants. Getting a hyper and aggressive Variant to milk a cow? Like teaching a dog to talk. But fences are being mended, weeds pulled, fields plowed, chickens fed, seeds sown, water carried, wild game caught, fires stoked, and meals cooked.

The Bartons stayed to tend the farm after their surrounding neighbors fled east to the safety of the wall.

Safety. Carmine snorts when she thinks of the illusions promised by the wall and the Blue-Eyed Witch. There's no safety beyond. The world is hard—no exceptions.

The Bartons stayed and fully expected to die within a few years. Fiercely independent but advancing into their late sixties without any help or medicine or functional stores, they wouldn't last long. Death before dependence, that was their motto.

And then, when the work seemed too great to maintain, Carmine and her gang rolled into view, looking for a temporary home. A symbiotic relationship if there ever was one, going on eight months now.

It's New Los Angeles in miniature.

She sits beyond the house near a copse of evergreens, eating carrots and grilled chicken. The work flows better if she's not in their midst. Her body's biological output disturbs and excites the Variants.

She crunches a carrot and squints thoughtfully at them.

Two years ago she retreated from society, forced into seclusion by the threat of a nuclear bomb with her name on it. Immediately she began drawing wild Variants. An unintentional phenomenon but a welcome one. These were mutants with little control over their impulses; some were tantamount to animals. Connecting with her had soothed them—healed their minds and souls. They ventured into the world as a growing family.

But then the personal growth stalled. The mutants quit maturing. Even after two years, they are still dependent on her. By now she hoped they would need her less. But they don't. She's a crutch.

She eats another carrot.

The Guardians (her term for good-willed Variants) constantly glance her direction. They need the reassurance. It'd be better for them if they could touch her. Contact produces a high and short-lived peace.

"I'm like cocaine," she sighs between bites. "Short-term benefit, long-term disaster."

She blushes slightly. She's never done cocaine and her mama would kill her if she heard the comparison. But it's an accurate analogy.

She doesn't know how to fix their dependence. Surely abandoning them isn't the solution. Sooner or later, though, something has to change.

While she muses, two massive tigers emerge from the copse behind. She smells their arrival and pats the ground beside her without turning. Like her, the tigers know daily farm routines are unsettled if they get too close. The goats and cattle in particular lose their minds. Even her guard Darren, squatting nearby, begins to smell like sweat.

The larger male pads softly to her right. His head lowers to nuzzle hers. He smells rich, like black soil and freshly killed woodland caribou, a heady aroma. The smaller female lays to her left. Carmine examines the pelt for signs of battle damage—the female has taken to attacking entire packs of wolves if they get too close to the farm; she always wins the engagement but emerges with wounds.

With Carmine sitting criss-cross and the animals laying prone beside her, she is forced to reach upward to scratch behind their ears.

"I swear you two are getting bigger. Is that possible?" she wonders.

The male issues a soft chuffing sound.

She leans against him. They both sigh deeply.

Soon all three are asleep.

She wakes an hour later. So do her loyal animals.

Sean is twenty yards distant. His Toyota Tundra idles nearby in case he needs to flee from angry tigers. He's calling.

She yawns and stretches. "Yes, Sean. I'm awake."

"You better come listen to this, Carmine. A scout returned."

At his words, she sits upright.

A scout. And it's urgent.

Not good news. She stands and brushes herself off.

They gather on the porch of the farmhouse—Carmine, Renee, Darren, and the scout.

The scout is a girl who joined Carmine while still battling amnesia. Something the queen sympathizes with. Rather than develop a new name, the girl asked to be called Scout because she's a Runner. She stays out a week at a time, prowling far off mountains and valleys, always watching.

Scout is hungrily eating almonds and meatloaf. Carmine says, "Take your time."

Scout nods. She swallows, wipes her mouth, and says, "My queen. He's here."

He's here. She's been dreading this.

Carmine presses her lips together and the skin around her eyes tighten. "Where?"

"Near Carey. There's some people still living there. A handful," says Scout.

"How far is that? Twenty miles?"

"Closer to fifteen. I don't know how he got so close."

Sean looks between them. "Who's here? Ya'll sound scary."

"How's he look?"

Scout answers, "Like an animal. A wild bear."

Carmine walks away from the little group, her boots thumping on the porch floorboards. He's here. How does he do that? Is there nowhere on the continent she can run and hide? Previously he found them in Kansas.

She doesn't want to give the order. She's been over it a thousand times. But there's no choice.

Carmine takes a deep breath. Turns back. "Renee, start the evacuation. We leave tonight."

Renee snaps a nod and hurries off.

"Evacuation!" Sean looks dumbstruck. "You serious?"

"Darren, get our stuff. Begin loading the Land Cruiser," she says.

He doesn't respond, other than to walk inside.

The radio at Carmine's belt begins squawking.

Sean places both hands on his head. "Carmine, please. What's going on? Who's here? I'm freaked out."

"Andy Babington is here. An old friend of mine."

"So?"

"He's totting a small nuclear bomb. His singular mission is to find me and detonate it. I thought maybe we'd outrun him this time... I can explain more once we're under way. If you're coming with us," says Carmine, formally extending the offer.

Sean indicates the farm. "We're just going to leave all this?"

"We have no choice."

"We could kill him."

"That'll detonate the bomb. I don't have time to argue, Sean. When we roll out, you have a seat. If you like. You've earned it."

"This is why you keep the caravan ready," says Sean. He's looking over her shoulder at the line of hybrid trucks and SUVs. Twelve of them, rugged all-terrain vehicles. "The batteries charged and the tanks full."

Mrs. Barton steps onto the porch, fists on hips. Despite her kind heart and good humor, her face is a constant scowl. "You'll be off then? That what I hear?"

"Yes, Mrs. Barton. I'm very sorry."

"Bah." She waves off the apologies. "Your hard work has give me and Mr. Barton a couple more years, at least. What more can an old woman want."

Sean asks, "We'll leave the Bartons?"

"The bomb will follow me. It's safer for you to remain here, Sean."

"Come," snaps Mrs. Barton. "We have pantries full of food to send you on the way."

Carmine smiles for the first time that afternoon. "I accept."

At midnight, after hours of exhausting labor, Carmine and her followers load themselves into trucks. The batteries and solar panels and water jugs and boxes of food and camping gear and tools and radios and all other things are stowed.

Carmine slides into the quiet of the driver's seat. Grips the wheel until she's close to bending it. Until tears trickle down her cheeks.

She's leaving. Again. She's always repairing the broken and then fleeing. Making forsaken places beautiful, to be appreciated by others while she herself is unable to enjoy the promised land.

Including New Los Angeles, this is the fourth home she's had to abandon in the past two years.

The passenger door opens. Sean wearily pushes himself into the seat. "Okay," he yawns. "Made up my mind. I'm in."

To her great surprise, she experiences a rush of relief. She has a friend.

"You're positive?" she asks. "It's a hard road."

"I'm sure. Whatever road you're on, that's where I wanna be."

She purses her lips to keep from smiling. Queens don't smile at boys. Not even older boys. Not even usurped queens.

One by one, the segments of her caravan flick on their headlights, beasts of burden waking up. They know. Andy Babington is within ten miles by now. Maybe closer.

Her final passenger, Darren, gets in. Doors close. Sudden silence, the night noises sealed off. Her hybrid Land Cruiser drops into gear and eases forward.

"You always drive?" asks Sean.

"Always." She indicates the glove compartment with her chin. "Find the right map. You're navigating."

Sean pops it open and rifles through. "Wow, you got a bunch."

"It's been a long road."

"Which way we heading?"

"Away from Andy. West."

"I guessed that. And then?"

She eyes the glass of water resting in the cupholder. The glass contains a twig snipped from her apple tree—the last tree in the front row of the orchard. The tree that should've died but refused. Her twig bears three small blossoms, indications of life which will fade in the next few days, but at the moment give her hope. Life can go on, with enough work. Maybe not where it's ideal, and maybe not where it's planted, but where hope persists.

Sean clears his throat. "Carmine? Where to?"

"I'm thinking...Alaska," she says, the first time she's uttered the destination out loud, even though the state's been in her mind for months.

"Ahh, damn it." Sean grins at her. It's a good look. "Black people hate the cold, Carmine."

"I've got a premonition fate might have something else in store. But we need a direction." The Land Cruiser rumbles onto Highway 75, past a grazing herd of caribou. A possible repast for her tigers, who'll need the nutrition. "And Sean? Call me Katie."

On days like today on the endless ocean, the shaggy-haired man flies. The Caribbean Sea runs to an infinite horizon and the blue universe stretches beyond the clouds, and when the fickle breeze cooperates the man sets the sail, walks to the front of his boat, grabs a line, and leans out into nothing.

Like flying.

Bending so far his fingertips sizzle across the membrane of the sea.

For hours he does this, rushing with a sweet following breeze. The swell and scent of the ocean bring him peace to an extent he nearly surrenders to the trance. He's been smacked by more than one flying fish, and pods of dolphins often erupt beside him, inspecting the boat and its ludicrous skipper. They cry and shout and laugh, and he returns the favor.

Poseidon himself.

His boat is named *Angel* and she's a catamaran—a majestic vessel, two fiberglass hulls connected by a central cabin, thirty-six feet long, too big for a single man on a long haul in the open sea. Yet he manages. He can outrun and out sail any wind-powered craft in the Caribbean. And he has the winnings to prove it.

On the boat, there is no painful past. No future full of gloom. There is now. There is the struggle to survive and the struggle is enough. And by focusing on the immediate, perched on the bow, he will survive the hurt.

It is on such a day that the man first sees Anna Elizabeth.

He is inclined over the waves, luxuriating in a sky so blue it stings, when he sees her.

A form bobbing to the east.

His keen eyes spot and track the object. It's dead in the water. And small.

He snatches binoculars from the base of the mast and he climbs nimbly to the pinnacle. This high, the boat's motion is exaggerated and he's carried in a twenty-foot oblong oval as the *Angel* crests and dips through gentle waves.

He turns in a circle, glassing the horizon and the intervening vastness. Safety first—who's out there? Any danger? But no, nothing. Maybe a prick to the north, a boat almost lost beyond the curvature of the earth, but that's over fifteen miles away.

There's no threat.

He locates the bobbing form, glares at it, and brings the glasses to his eyes again. The object leaps closer.

It's a body. Probably dead. Or possibly clinging to floating sea garbage.

He grunts. Unhappily—day disrupted.

He releases his hold and slides down the steel mast, careful of the rigging. Replaces the glasses and leaps barefoot to the cockpit located at the stern (back of the boat). He glances at the weathervane and the texture created by the wind on the waves. He's heading south-southwest with the wind, so he releases the foresail line and spins the wheel. Overhead the great mainsail boom sweeps across, catching the wind at a new angle, and he secures the foresail once again. The *Angel* surges with incredible strength, power that once frightened him. He can't intercept the bobbing body directly, but he can ease just to the south of it and then cut north in a zigzag. Of course it'd be easier with a gasoline-powered engine, but those days are past.

The wind is an inexhaustible resource. As long as a sailor knows how to make friends with it. Still it takes him ten minutes to rendezvous with the bobbing form, whereas it wouldn't take two minutes five years ago.

It's a human body, clinging to the broken corner of a wooden pallet. The poor man or woman's back is badly burnt by the unforgiving sun, hair floating in the water like a dead jellyfish's tentacles.

The man releases his sails and the nylon canvas collapses into a heap on the boom and at the bow (front). Coasting under momentum, the starboard (right side) hull bumps the figure, a gentle collision. He crouches on the aft swim platform, takes hold of the sodden wooden pallet, and hauls the body close.

Ironic. Two years ago it was him being fished out of the water. On this very platform.

He gets his hands under the armpits and stands, hauling the body in a deadlift. Drags the form onto the after deck and lays it prone across the wooden slats.

She's a woman. A girl. Maybe his age, twenty-three, maybe a year younger. Her skin is blue where it's not burnt and peeling. Her long brown hair is woven with seaweed. The salt and elements have ravaged away most of her dress.

She groans softly and shifts her shoulders. The deck hurts, he bets.

He releases a blast of air at the horizon. This isn't on his day's agenda. He needs to make another fifty miles south before the sun sets. Time and tide wait for no man.

Or woman.

He crouches and scoops her. It's been a week since he's seen another person. Almost a month since he's seen a girl. She's very pretty, he thinks. Even sodden and sick. It's hard to hide beautiful features.

He knew a girl like that once.

He carries her through the cockpit and steps down into the galley (kitchen), out of the sun. The air is immediately cooler. Once upon a time, this catamaran had three functional cabins. A big boat, it could hold a crew of six with room to spare. Now those spare cabins are stuffed with storage and gear, so he carries her to his own bed—the foreword starboard side.

The shaggy-haired man piles sheets onto her so that she's afforded some modesty as he cuts off the ruined and soaking dress. He wraps a towel around her hair.

She shudders and curls into a ball under the blankets.

The man leans against the bulkhead (wall) and crosses his arms. He's a tall man, unable to stand fully upright below deck.

Huh. How about this.

Water. She's probably dehydrated. And hungry.

He fills his canteen from the cooler's spigot. Gets one arm under her neck and tilts her upwards, closer to the canteen. Cool water trickles between her cracked lips. She moans. Coughs. And finally drinks without opening her eyes.

He read somewhere that too much water will kill a dehydrated person. The girl lies back down, groaning again. Her skin is already less blue.

He leaves her prone and covered, and runs back on deck. His internal clock is ringing, complaining about the lost time. He climbs the mast again with the binoculars dangling from his neck, something he does ten times a day at least. He glasses the horizon twice. Still no danger.

On deck once more, he hauls the lines to raise the mainsail, a task he does by hand instead of utilizing a crank. He does this to maintain strength. Warm wind fills the massive canvas. The entire vessel surges and plows into the coming swell. The sail towers above him and threatens to jerk free but his hands are hard and accustomed to work. He sheets the sail home and sets the jib, causing *Angel* to tilt slightly to port, perhaps her favorite way to sail. Soon she's moving at ten knots and he's able to relax.

The sun is a molten ball hanging over the Gulf of Mexico. Two hours till sundown.

By following a digital signal, the man brings his boat to a large orange buoy. This one's his favorite—always a bounty. He hauls the buoy inboard and attaches one of its two heavy lines to a hand-crank, like a manual winch.

Before beginning, he tosses a weighted net off the port side, opposite the crank. He chucks in leftover bait, wipes his hands, and returns to starboard. Deep breath, and he starts churning with his arms, bringing up the cage.

He's not far from shore, just under ten miles. The cage below rests on a shelf a few hundred feet down. He's seen others try this trick, using a hand-crank—they can't. It's too heavy and they're forced to use a machine.

But not him.

He pauses long enough to tie his hair back with twine he keeps looped around his wrist. Undone, the hair irritates his blue eyes. His hair used to be so dark it looked black, but the sun's bleached it a golden brown, like bronze.

After ten minutes of furious cranking, a large rusty crab trap surfaces. The metal cage is stuffed with prizes—big blue crab, angry at their capture. He pops open the boat's built-in coolers, maneuvers the trap into place above the hatch, and opens the cage. Crabs plunge into the cooler's water, slushy with ice. Another thirty-six hours and the ice will be gone. With enough banging and shaking, the last of the crabs drop in and he slams the lid.

He turns in a circle, inspecting the horizon. Out of habit he glances at the weather vane above.

He tosses the trap back in, releases the first line, attaches the second, and begins hauling up the other cage. The strain is almost too much. By the time it surfaces, the man is sweating and groaning, ample muscles bunched and heavy.

These crabs are dumped into the same cooler, near to overflowing. He releases the line and throws the buoy overboard. A grueling chore, one that requires recuperation. The Bimini provides some shade on a couch so he lounges there and drinks water mixed with lime juice.

Scurvy—not for him.

Soon the internal alarm is angry with him again. Get up. Get moving.

Hand over hand, he hauls in the net tossed off the port side. Usually he comes up empty, but not today—he's caught three snapper and a big tuna. A tuna!

Two of the three coolers on the port side are full of fish and ice. The third is only half full so he deposits his catch inside and seals the lid.

He sets the sail and grins.

Tuna steaks for supper.

Anna Elizabeth wakes twice that day—frantic and febrile until realizing she's no longer bobbing in the ocean. She peers blearily at nothing before collapsing back under safety of the blankets and sleep.

She wakes again, climbing farther out of exhaustion, and experiences a new degree of darkness; the sun has fallen. She's grateful to be on a bed, under the covers. But where? Who...?

A heavy object softly thunks near her head. There's enough ambient light in the cabin to find it—a green canteen hanging from a peg.

Her fingers tremble as she unscrews the top and spills delicious water onto the mattress before getting the nozzle to her lower lip. She gulps and gulps until she gags and coughs. The canteen falls from her unsteady hands.

She reaches for it. Slowly, wincing.

Another hand gets it first. A big hand.

A man is here, in the darkness.

She gasps and closes her eyes. Asleep.

An hour later she surfaces for good. Or at least for longer than two minutes. She smells something...

It's everything. It's all she's ever wanted. It's life. And it's sizzling on a grill.

Should she be afraid? Probably, but she's too hungry. If the owner of the boat wanted to harm her, he could have by now. Or he could have left her in the water.

Or she, or they.

She sits up and there's no awful headache, more of a faint throb. She twists her legs out of bed. Skin across her shoulders and back complains from a ghastly burn. The deck feels alien under her feet and her calves and thighs tremble with the exertion.

Where has her dress gone? That was one of her favorites. She takes a large towel hanging from the door and wraps it around. Not enough coverage so she takes the blanket instead, and unsteadily ventures forth.

A man is sitting in a chair on the back deck of the boat, near a hot grill. She can see him because of the charcoal's red glow. Such a man, she's at a loss for words. He wears khaki shorts and an open blue linen shirt, the sleeves rolled up. Even relaxed in a sitting position, he resembles a big cat, like a tiger, powerful and dark. From what she can tell, his skin is an enriched tan. His shoulders are broad, his chest wide, his forearms and calves knotty with strength. He's tall.

His voice is deep and rich. But soft. "Are you hungry?"

"Famished," she says.

"The tuna is at medium rare. I can leave them over the coals longer, to suit you."

"You took me out of the water. Right?"

"I did. You were disgusting."

"That's..." She frowns. Blushes and clears her throat. "I'll take the tuna now. If you don't mind."

"Sit on that couch," he says and she obeys. He finds a thin metal plate and plucks sizzling hunks of fish off the heat. He places slices of pineapple next to the fish and hands it to her. "Voila."

Her hands quiver and her mouth waters. "I'm very grateful."

He waves her gratitude away and she places a bite of the most delicious pineapple ever grown between her teeth. Her eyes close and she releases a contented sigh.

The man grins and kind of laughs, and looks up at the stars. The sea is calm, the boat barely rocking. Outside the glow of the hot charcoal, there is nothing. Not even the sound of waves.

She watches him watching the sky. His face is handsome and open, his scruffy jaw strong. His hair reaches just past his ears. His eyes hold and reflect the warmth.

Those eyes.

Without knowing why, she envisions him as a dormant volcano. Power unimaginable ready to erupt.

She eats some fish and works it around her mouth to keep from burning. "Where are we?"

"One mile north of the Bahamas." He points to his left, her right. "Not much light this late. No electricity."

"The Bahamas," she repeats.

He nods.

"I'm a long way from home."

"Which is?" asked the man.

"Jacksonville, Florida. I was taken."

"Taken?"

She nods but does not respond.

"Sorry about the sheet," he says. "All my clothes would be too big for you, but..." He holds up a pile of rags that she recognizes as her dress. "I'm working on it."

"You're repairing it?"

"Beyond repair. But salvaging part. Making you a bathing suit. I hope."

"How? Did you measure me? You sew?"

"I sew. A necessity out here. And no, I didn't measure." He casts a critical eye at her legs, the sheet, and her shoulders. "I'm guessing and using elastic. And you can wear one of my t-shirts as a coverup."

"The dress was made out of material passed down to me from my grandmother."

"Then you shouldn't wear it into the ocean."

"I didn't—"

"I could tell it wasn't from Abercrombie. That's why I'm salvaging it."

She presses her lips firmly together. It's just a dress. And she's alive. Stupid for her to get upset about clothing. But when everything else is falling apart, some things take on symbolic importance. "Thank you," she says, frustrated with herself and with the stupid ocean and with everything else too at the moment. "Who are you?"

"No one."

"Nobody is no one. We all matter."

He shrugs, a cagey motion. "I am a simple sailor. Who are you?"

"I am Anna Elizabeth. My father is Willard Washington."

"Great initials," he says. "W.W. Those are elite. Walt Whitman. Woodrow Wilson. Walter White. Willy Wonka."

She speaks in a proper and well-educated manner. "Have you never heard of Willard Washington?"

"I've been out of touch with people a couple years. Should I have?"

"Depends on which side you're on," she says and it occurs to her perhaps she should guard her tongue. She's not thinking clearly and she'll need to sleep again soon.

"Which side." The way he repeats her words is full of meaning and import. An issue as deep as the Atlantic. "Willard Washington is an important man embroiled in the conflict between the Witch and the Resistance, I assume."

A smile hints on her lips. "You call her the Witch and not the President. You know about the conflict, at least."

"I do. An unnecessary, bloody, awful thing."

"Unnecessary?" she says.

"Cooler heads should've prevailed three or four years ago. This is all because of pride and greed."

"You think because it should have been prevented, it should not be fought now? That the Resistance should quit?"

"I don't pretend to know the unknowable. I'm not speaking prescriptively. I'm speaking descriptively. And the conflict is an awful thing," says the man with shaggy hair.

"Yes, well..." She tilts her chin up at him. "That's why some of us resist the Witch. Because she's awful."

"I agree."

"Do you? An insular sailor? Floating around in the ocean by yourself is not any kind of resistance."

"But not all resistance is violent." He arches an eyebrow and she flinches. Anything he does, even small movements, seem to affect the atmosphere enough that she feels it.

"Oh jeez. I apologize," she says, staring at her plate. "That was rude and presumptuous. You deserve better manners."

"You were taken because of who your father is?"

She covers a yawn with her hand. "Yes."

"He must be worried sick."

"I imagine so." Her blinks were becoming longer.

"You were kidnapped, put on a boat, and then dumped in the middle of the Atlantic?"

"I was being taken somewhere. I escaped and jumped overboard," she says with a trace of pride.

"Nice job."

"Thank you." Her eyes partially close and she has a hard time focusing. Her food is half gone.

"The boat, was it motorized? Or a sailboat?"

"Sailboat. Is that important? Hardly anyone has gasoline."

"If they're under sail power, they weren't working for the government. Probably pirates or mercenaries collecting a bounty. We can out-sail them. I'm rendezvousing with some folks tomorrow. After that, I'll take you home."

"That's very generous. Thank..." Another yawn. "Thank you."

"Sure. Not all resistance is violent."

She stands. He reaches out a hand to brace her. She grins, bobs her head sleepily, and returns below. She stumbles through the hatch and falls onto the mattress. Smiling, she curls into a ball and draws the covers around her. Inexplicably this is the safest she's felt in years.

The shaggy-haired man works silently a few more minutes on the fabric in his lap. Then holds it up and inspects his work.

"I'm amazing," he tells the night. "I wish Katie could see this."

Anna Elizabeth wakes up to the sound of voices. Her mind moves sluggishly, piecing together fragments of reality until the world coalesces. Yes, that's right, she's on a boat. Safe. With the man.

Weak light filters in through the dirty portholes. It's morning.

Thirty minutes pass as she listens. She hears the voices of at least four people, some of them feminine. Other vessels nearby? The boat she's inside collides intermittently with...something. Gentle bumps.

She sits up. The man left fruit, water, and stale crusty bread beside the bed. Her mouth waters at the feast. She wolfs it down, abandoning lady-like manners—she's earned the indulgence. As she eats, she inspects the bikini swinging on a hanger in the middle of the cabin. Looks like a tube top that ties in the back, and boy shorts, made from her dress and sewn with elastic. The man did all he could, and it's better than nothing. But she has her doubts.

Her legs feel stronger today and she's able to stand more securely in the cabin. The shaggy-haired man doesn't have a comb or brush so she does her best with her fingers. Her neck is badly burnt. She touches a blister gingerly. It's been treated with aloe. Did the man put medicine on her shoulders while she slept?

She emerges into pure light. Like stepping into the sun. The ocean dances with it and the blue air sings. The boat rises and settles on a sea of emerald and diamond, and the world is so beautiful she aches.

The *Angel* has been lashed against two others, forming a triangle. All three are catamarans, between thirty and forty-five feet. The sails are down. Half a mile distant, green mountains loom over a blue lagoon. The Bahamas, she assumes correctly.

There is another boat here. Larger, flatter, older. The shaggy-haired man is helping transfer enormous coolers onto the flat boat. A crane rises over everything, shooting up from the ocean, anchored into the seabed somehow. As she watches, the crane carefully lifts a secured cooler out of the man's boat and swings it onto the older transport ship. A delicate operation because both boats are rising and falling on the waves, and there's a strong breeze from the east. The shaggy-haired man leaps around, guiding things, making it look easy. When the full cooler has been stowed, the crane returns an empty one to the man's boat. Ready to be filled, with fish, she guesses.

He's a fisherman.

He's working with other fishermen. Or, fisher people, she should say. Two of them are women. And two are men. There's also a man inside the crane's cockpit, and several more on the transport ship. They take turns shouting instructions.

One of the women sees Anna Elizabeth. The woman is breathtaking. She looks like a beautiful wild animal, like a lion. Her thick hair is wild and so blonde it's almost white, held back with a bandana. Golden skin, except the stark green eyes. She's muscular and well balanced. Low body fat. Maybe twenty-five years old, she wears loose khakis and a fancy black athletic top with thin straps going over her shoulders. The other woman has to be her mother, based on the similarities in appearance. She wears white linen and a straw hat, tied under her chin.

"Aye, Chase," calls the younger woman to the shaggy-haired man. "Who's the stowaway?"

The men pause and take second glances at Anna. One releases a low whistle.

The shaggy-haired man looks up from tying supplies on the transport. He spots her and grins. "That's Anna. A friend."

"Yeah?" says the wild and beautiful woman. "And what's she wearing?"

"A bathing suit, Gwen. I made it."

"Yeah I *bet* you did."

"Best I could do and shut up."

The other men laugh.

The shaggy-haired man, his name is Chase? He picks up two satchels of supplies and leaps back to his own boat. It's a long jump.

"Um," says Anna Elizabeth, embarrassed and fidgeting awkwardly. "Chase. May I borrow a shirt?"

"I need to do laundry." He stands and takes off his blue linen shirt, which he'd been wearing unbuttoned. Tossed it to her. "Wear that in the meantime, it's my cleanest. I'll wash you one soon."

"Oh," she says. "Oh. I..."

The man's entire body is deeply tan from the sun. His powerful torso is crisscrossed with old scars, especially his back. She's used to being around pale men, soft like grown boys, and the sight of Chase is arresting.

"Aye Anna," calls the girl named Gwen. "Get yer eyes back in yer head and look sharp." She tosses a hose onto Chase's boat. The nozzle nearly hits Anna. She flinches and ducks. Pulls on Chase's blue shirt, which smells like salt and deodorant, and grabs the hose. Gwen grins without humor. "Stick that in the water tank."

"The what?"

Chase is stowing fresh materials and fruit and foodstuffs, but he pauses long enough to point at a tank in the galley. "There. Open the top. We're taking on fresh water."

Anna Elizabeth barely gets the lid off before lukewarm water gushes from the hose. The tank echoes with the splash. Chase steps inside the galley and smiles at her. "A lot going on, I know."

"You're a fisherman?"

"Kinda. People on the islands aren't doing well. A group of boats I belong with, about ten of us, we provide local villages with fish. In return, they give us fruit and bread and supplies."

She asks, "Is that legal?"

"It is directly against the Witch's orders."

"Nonviolent resistance," says Anna Elizabeth.

He winks. "Exactly."

Despite herself, she blushes. A compliment from Chase should NOT set her heart racing, but it does.

He goes back on deck to complete the transfers. Anna stays with the water but she overhears their conversation.

"Where'd you get her? Out of a magazine?"

Chase laughs. "Think she's pretty?"

"I have eyes, don't I? And so do you."

"I plucked her from the ocean yesterday. She jumped a ship out of Jacksonville."

"Leave her on the island. They'll get her home."

"They can't, no chance. I'm heading north, anyway," says Chase.

One of the men has an accent, some Caribbean descent. He remarks, "Long way Jacksonville, boya. Dangerous waters."

"She needs to go home. Her father has to be worried sick."

"Those the President's waters. Infested with her soldiers."

Anna can tell Chase is smiling. "I'll out-sail them."

"She got gasoline. You? You got wind."

Gwen's voice is husky. The sound of a woman who likes working hard in the sun and storms, so different from the entitled princesses she's used to. "Want company?"

"We'll be fine," replies Chase.

"Just you and her? The girl, Anne? Occur to you, maybe she's after something? After you?"

"Gwen."

"Don't let her seduce you, Chase. We need you here."

Anna Elizabeth peeks her head out of the galley far enough to spy on them, across the rolling water. They stand on the girl's boat. Chase rests a hand on her shoulder and the shoulder of the man with them.

"Thank you for your concern. We'll be fine, and it's important she be returned home quickly."

"She's beautiful, Chase. And it's fogging up yer horizon."

He doesn't respond. He leaps to the transport and picks up sacks of supplies, his face turned in a frown.

She clears her throat and calls, "Do you think that's enough water?"

"No," replies Gwen without looking at her. "She's taking on two hundred gallons. It'll be a while."

"She?"

"Chase's boat," snaps Gwen. "Her name's *Angel*. You land-dwellers don't know anything useful."

Chastised, Anna stays out of the way for the next hour as tons of supplies are transferred. After a while she makes herself useful, finding some of Chase's shirts below and washing them with the fresh water and detergent. Chase calls for one of the other sailors to inspect and repair his ice-making machine. The man hops across, much less spry than Chase, with a bag of tools. He grins at her but doesn't say anything. The shaggy-haired owner of *Angel* makes a thorough inspection of the boat—he plasters a fresh fiberglass concoction to wounds on the forward hulls, he changes out a frayed line, patches a sail, throws out moldy fruit, checks the water tanks for leaks, performs radio tests, re-stows one of the cabins used for cargo, and lastly trades paperbacks with his fellow fishers.

The industrious sailors are sweaty and happy from feverish work. Their ships are lighter, whole, well-provisioned with fruit and vegetables, ready to boldly bear them once again into the deep blues of the sea. Improving their spirits even more, the breeze is fresh and strong.

Temporarily alone on the *Angel*, Chase runs his hand along the top of the cabin and grins at Anna. "She's a great boat. I inherited her from the previous owner. He taught me to sail."

"What happened to him?"

He nods toward the green of the island. "He's ashore, taking it easy. Gave up the life a year ago."

The men on the wide transport call and wave. A sail raises and their ship begins to separate.

"Will you go ashore?"

"No," says Chase. "I stay out here. The others might, tomorrow. You could join them."

"Why don't you?"

He shrugs, his muscular shoulders bunching. "Better this way. I haven't set foot on land in a year."

Anna Elizabeth gasps. "That can't be true."

"The ocean brings me peace."

"What about hurricanes?"

"I monitor the radar." He points inside the boat's cockpit at the displays. "Sail around them, hide in the shelter of shore when I have to."

"But." Anna Elizabeth tries to process his bizarre existence. Where to even begin? "What about your sanity? Your happiness? Your community?"

"Those days," he says, "are long gone. When we meet like this, we make a big raft with our boats and visit. It's like a family. Some others will arrive tonight. We'll ride at anchor and recharge. Get some uninterrupted sleep. That's my community."

"You can't live this austere life forever, Chase," says Anna Elizabeth.

"Not forever."

"Do you even have social media out here?"

"Ahh, no."

"Are you running from something?"

He gives a sad grin. "For a little while longer."

"What is it?"

"Insanity. And grief."

"I don't—"

Tired of questions, the man interrupts her. "I'll take you home in the morning. If the wind holds, we'll reach the coast of Florida tomorrow, and then it's two days sailing north to Jacksonville."

Anna Elizabeth is about to reply when shouts are raised from the transport. The men aboard are pointing east, toward the rising sun. Chase leaps onto the roof of the cabin, the boat's highest point other than the towering mast, and glares.

"Pirates," he says.

Her stomach twists. "The men who took me?"

"No. A local crew. We've tangled with them before. They steal our supplies and traffic them ashore."

Anna joins him and sees boats motor around a rocky outcropping of the island, hidden from view until now, a mile distant. She hears the distant drone of engines.

"Two sails," reports Chase. "And two jet skis."

The other sailors scramble about their ships, unhooking from each other, throwing supplies below.

"What do we do? Do we run?"

"No, they'd catch us."

Chase picks Anna up and sets her down onto Gwen's ship. It's obvious this smaller boat, named *The Defiance*, belongs to her and her mother.

"Stay here," he says.

"What will you do?"

The older woman, Gwen's mother, speaks for the first time.

"Chase deals with pirates, girl. Otherwise, they would slit our throats."

Anna Elizabeth gapes at Chase with wide eyes. "By *yourself*?"

"Aye, get below," snaps Gwen.

"Absolutely not, I'm going with him."

"He doesn't need your help!"

"There are four boats, two of them motorized! He needs all our help."

"Anna," Chase says. "Stay here. We don't have time."

Anna Elizabeth glares defiantly at them and leaps back to the *Angel*. She barely reaches it, and she slips and falls. Gets back up. "You shouldn't do this alone."

Chase shrugs. Before he can join Anna Elizabeth on the *Angel*, Gwen grabs his hand. Holds tight. "We'll head to the cove, boyo."

"Good."

"I know you, Chase. You're gonna have too much adrenaline to come back. No rest for you today. You'll fight the pirates and head north, wont'cha."

Chase shrugs. "Maybe."

"This is goodbye, then."

He doesn't reply. Her mother and the two men in the other sail-boat watch silently. Gwen turns to sneak a peak at the pirates. The jet skis closed half the distance.

"You won't come home from this journey, Chase," says Gwen. "Or at least you won't come back *here*. A girl learns to notice shifting winds."

"There's nothing to notice," he replies. Anna Elizabeth barely hears him.

Gwen takes his face in both hands. Pulls him down and kisses his mouth. Holds it. Releases.

She says, "You like brunettes better. I noticed months ago. So I guess you and I were never gonna float anyway."

Again he says nothing. Gwen is crying.

"Fair winds and following seas, Chase," she says.

The men in the other sailboat repeat the phrase. Must mean goodbye in sailor jargon.

"Stay safe, Gwen. The world needs you," he says.

Chase steps from her boat and onto the the *Angel,* and raises the sails with mighty pulls on the line. The fabric catches the wind and the *Angel* lurches forward, throwing Anna Elizabeth into hammock netting between the hulls. From her vantage point, lying on her back, the mast is a skyscraper above and the mainsail the size of a cloud. Soon the ocean hisses past, the bows tossing shattered water into her face.

"Anna," he calls. He pulls on another shirt but has no time for the buttons. It flaps behind like a cape. "Get back here."

Ahead of them, bouncing on the horizon, come the pirates. The first motor she's heard in days. She crawls aft. Gwen and the other sailors hoist sails and aim for the shore. Scrambling beside Chase, who stands at the wheel, Anna shouts above the wind, "They're leaving!"

"Good. They'll be safe."

"But what about *us*?"

He grins. The maniac seems to enjoy danger. "Not everyone gets to hide. At least not forever."

Two jet skis are almost upon them, tearing through the waves. One of the men, shirtless, wearing silver glasses, has a shotgun. He aims with one hand and fires. A hundred tiny holes rip into the white fabric above.

"They're going to kill us," she whispers.

"Take the wheel."

"What! Chase, no. I can't drive!"

"First of all, one doesn't drive a sailboat. Just steer straight." He takes her hand and places it onto the wheel. "Don't let go." He grabs something out of a cup holder and jumps onto the cabin's roof. The boat is rising and dropping through the swell, but he seems glued to it, in a crouch.

He bounces a small metal object, like a steel ball bearing, in his palm. Draws his arm back.

"We're going to die," mutters Anna Elizabeth. The shotgun roars again, less than twenty yards away. Chase doesn't flinch.

He waits until his boat is perched at the top of a wave and he flings the ball. Anna Elizabeth gasps. As if propelled out of a cannon, the ball tears straight through the jet ski's shell. The engine issues a horrible shriek and belches smoke. The craft noses into a wave, momentum arrested, and the rider is flung head over heels, his shotgun splashing to the side.

"Did you *throw*—"

Chase points to his left. "Steer that way!"

Anna spins the wheel and the craft heels northward. She's nearly thrown overboard. He drops flat and the boom swings over his head.

"Now straight!"

The wind catches the *Angel* at a new angle, pushing the sail out of his way. The second jet ski is in sight now. He also has a gun, trying to aim. Chase throws again and pulverizes the jet ski's bow with two steel ball bearings. This engine catches fire with a whoosh and the man is forced to leap.

The *Angel* rushes by the man bobbing in the water. Chase climbs back to the cockpit, takes the wheel, and aims for the oncoming sailboats.

"Excellent steering," he says. He is flushed, his eyes wild. Surely it's her imagination but she feels heat radiating off him. And...has he grown taller?

"How'd you *do* that?"

"Lucky throws." He hands a pair of binoculars to her. "Tell me what you see."

She raises the glasses to her eyes and the pirates leap closer. "Two boats, smaller than yours." Using her right index finger, she adjusts the focus. "No engines, only sails. Two or maybe three pirates on each boat."

"Three. Anymore jet skis?"

"Not that I notice. But...they have guns. They aren't heading directly for us, though."

"They can't, because of the wind's direction." He looks up and points at the weather vane above. "They've got to zigzag against it."

Sixty seconds pass, a jarring silence after the jet ski motors, and the sailboats approach.

"This is a collision in slow motion," says Anna Elizabeth, watching him. She pushes the hair out of her face. "Do you find the wait unbearable?"

"Anticipation's part of the fun."

"But only if our victory is guaranteed."

He winks. "Let's not lose, then."

The ships close the distance. More details from the pirates' ships become visible. Their vessels are old and battered, the ratty sails a patchwork. Soon they open fire with rifles, bullets slamming into the *Angel*.

Chase grinds his teeth. "I hate repairing bullet holes."

"Will you throw things at them?" she asks, ducking behind the cabin. Her heart is in her throat, pounding a staccato beat.

"No, they don't have engines to break."

"Do you have a gun?"

"I don't," he says. The wind blows hair into his eyes.

"What will you do?"

"Hit them."

"*Hit* them?"

"Hard. Plus, I'll destroy their boat."

"Chase, that won't work! You're going to get us killed. I don't understand."

"What do you think we should do?"

"Run away!" she cries. "Or, I mean, sail away. There's too many."

"But you said we shouldn't just float around the ocean. That awful things need to be resisted."

Her hands ball into fists. "We don't have any hope of victory at the moment."

"Sure we do. There's always hope. That's what wakes me up every day."

"You're insane," she mutters.

"They'll attack from both sides, like the jet skis did. You stay below."

"But I can help," she says, pushing her brown hair out of her face again. Then, frustrated, she tucks it under her shirt collar.

"Can you hit hard?"

"I most certainly can *not*," she says with a fair amount of dignity. "I'll drive. Err, steer."

"Not necessary. Your job is to avoid gunfire."

The three ships become equidistant, forming a triangle, the *Angel* poised to slice between them. The Atlantic foams and rushes beneath.

"Ready?" he says.

"Not at all."

The shaggy-haired man releases two sets of knots and the lines whistle free. The foresail and mainsail both drop into large piles of fabric. Above them, instead of filling and pushing the sails, the wind howls harmlessly past the bare pole, and the *Angel* loses speed immediately.

"We're stopping!" cries Anna Elizabeth, eyeing the pirates' guns. The barrels grow larger. The boats are only thirty yards apart.

"Get below," says Chase. He dives into the water behind the *Angel*, vanishes under the shimmering surface. Anna is suddenly alone.

Gunshots belch from both enemy vessels. Awful noises, and the *Angel* thumps and thuds. Inside the galley, a bullet clangs against a pot and something breaks. Anna wants to flatten herself against the deck but she cannot will herself; partially hidden by the cabin's bulkhead, she peers above to watch.

Chase erupts from the sea as if propelled by a hidden catapult. Somehow he is launched ten feet in the air, an explosion of sparkling blue, surprising the boat from behind. Anna Elizabeth holds her breath. He lands on a man, stomping him into the deck. Takes the second pirate's rifle away and clubs him with it, breaking the wooden stock. He is a man among boys; he's like Poseidon, she thinks. The final pirate he throws overboard—an impossible heave. The pirate splashes down fifteen feet away, extremities flailing. With one furious pull, Chase tears off the ship's wheel and snaps it in half. The whole thing lasted twenty seconds.

The other boat notices the attack and redirects their fire away from the *Angel* and onto Chase.

"Chase!" shouts Anna Elizabeth. "Duck!"

Chase doesn't.

He *Leaps.*

He hurls himself into the sky with such force that Anna involuntarily cowers. The boat he leaped from capsizes. Her wide eyes follow his impossible arc into the blue. He reaches the leap's zenith, gracefully ducks his head and somersaults forward. He falls toward the second enemy vessel, his left foot pointed down. The pirates shout in terror. He lands and the deck splinters. Snaps his arms out to the side, catching a pirate in the face with each and flipping them overboard. One man remains—he screams words Anna Elizabeth doesn't understand and voluntarily jumps into the water.

The closest pirate swims for his rifle before it sinks, raises it and pulls the trigger. Nothing. Gun power ruined.

Chase crouches and wraps his arms around the ship's mast and heaves. He winces and his muscles harden and bunch, and there's a sound of tearing metal. The enormous pole rips free and Chase lets it topple into the Atlantic like a mighty oak, trailing ropes and sails.

Eight total pirates bob in the waves, in various states of discomfort and injury, and they silently watch Chase return to the *Angel*. He swims with calm strokes, as if nothing happened. He grabs the aft deck and hauls himself aboard.

This time, there can be no mistake. The wild, panting, streaming man before her has swollen. Taller and wider. Anna can't get her breath. She feels hot and disoriented, reality spinning beyond her grasp.

"You're..." She gulps. "You're a Variant."

"Yes, but," he says, holding up a placating hand. "I'm not the gross raging drooling kind. I'm the friendly handsome kind."

"I need to sit down," she says. And she does, on the couch opposite the cockpit. Behind them, she notices, Gwen and the others fade into the distance.

Chase glances at the clouds and the waves and the weather vane. He grins and hoists the sails. "We need to make repairs. And then? This is an ideal day for you to learn to fly."

An hour after sundown, the *Angel* lays at anchor off the coast of Jupiter, Florida. Dozens, maybe hundreds, of boats float nearby, a small city lit by solar-powered electric lanterns. Some pay for a berth at the dock, but most hug the shore without an assigned spot. Safety in numbers. The sailors leap from boat to boat, sharing supplies and drink. A floating soiree.

Chase and Anna dropped anchor at a distance. Both are drained, their faces raw by hours flying into the wind, muscles fatigued. Chase reckons they reached fifteen knots at their peak—a terrific speed, he tells her. Not only does each wish to keep their anonymity, they're too tired to join in the merriment of the makeshift community.

Jupiter, like the rest of the East Coast, is still resettling from the dramatic upheaval of the past three years. The population of the United States plummeted due to sickness, wars, and emigration, and those remaining resettled east, inside the Witch's great wall. The small town of Jupiter is constituted by a ninety-five percent newcomer population.

Wanting a night off from fish, Chase takes the *Angel*'s raft around the bay, makes a couple trades, and returns with food. Anna Elizabeth is wearing one of his red t-shirts, slightly stiff from drying in the salty air. She takes the hard cheese and salami and bread and cuts them into slices and they feast.

"You've eaten an extraordinary amount of food today," says Anna around a smile.

"Burned a lot of calories," he replies, "arguing with pirates."

They sit on the after deck, feet dangling in the water, watching the bay dazzle and bob like Christmas.

Anna leans closer to him, squinting in the dark—using the nails of her left hand, she pulls down his collar; with her right hand she pries a piece of metal out of his flesh.

"This is a bullet," she marvels.

"In times of duress, my skin is irascible."

"You Variants are a wonder, you know that?"

"A bigger bullet could get through. That's smaller gauge," he says.

For the hundredth time that day, she takes another look at his eyes. His hair. His jaw and his shoulders. So familiar.

Could it be...?

He says, "What does your father do?"

She selects a pale wedge of cheese. Places it between her teeth and chews silently a moment. Drinks from her water bottle. "The Witch has been after my father for months. He openly defied her on television and became something of a rallying cry. Her minions still search for him, so he's leading as best he can behind the scenes, out of sight."

"Doing what?"

"Organizing minor rebellions. Reconnaissance for the Resistance, that type of thing."

"How goes the war?"

"You honestly don't know?" she asks.

"I turned off my ears. I only hear rumors now and then. When exactly did the Witch become President?"

"Over a year ago. There is essentially a stalemate between the President and the Resistance. She hides on the East Coast behind her wall, and for the moment she's content to stay here, though we aren't producing enough food. She's directionless. It's as if, now that she's in charge, she doesn't know what to do. She leads out of ambition and hedonism, and the rest of us suffer. The cities governed by the Resistance fare much better."

Chase asks, "Which cities?"

"Those which survive in Texas and Mexico and Oklahoma and Colorado...basically middle America, though most of it is abandoned. West of that, it's Variant territory. The Resistance quit patrolling last year. Too much real estate, not enough resources."

"What about Mexico?"

"Like many countries, Mexico floundered. Cartels control a lot, and the remnants of the government threw their power to the Resistance."

He stares at the water, at the mirrored surface of the real world, lights waving and dancing. "Entire countries dissolving."

"The world's population is down to two billion. All the self-sustaining parts of the world survive. But those persons and countries requiring aid? They're gone. Switzerland has barely hiccuped. Countries like Zimbabwe and Haiti are on the verge of extinction. All because of the Chemist and his protege, the Witch."

The shaggy-haired man has a lot of thoughts on that subject but he keeps his mouth clamped for the moment. His mind roils with questions.

She asks, "You're a Variant. Did you know him? The Chemist?"

A muscle in his jaw flexes. "I knew him."

"What was he like?"

He tears a slice of salami into pieces and tosses them into the water. "He lived too long. Lost the ability to reason. It had been a long time since someone loved him, and that takes an enormous toll."

Anna Elizabeth watches the salami bits bob and then disappear under the dark surface, unsure how to respond.

After a minute, he continues, "Also, at the end, he was a bloodthirsty megalomaniac. A tyrant. He hurt everyone I love. And tried to kill me on multiple occasions."

"He tried to murder a Variant?"

"Not all Variants get along. He didn't flinch at murdering even his most trustworthy soldiers."

"But didn't he create you?" she asks.

"More or less."

"Maybe if—"

"What about Los Angeles? Is it still standing?"

"I don't know," says Anna Elizabeth, watching him closely for a reaction. "For a while, we were all obsessed with that city. Carmine seemed like she'd be the savior. But..."

He closes his eyes and drops his head. "But."

She holds her breath. Wishes she could take back the words. "Yeah."

"But she's gone."

Anna Elizabeth doesn't answer.

He says, "Something I've learned—it's foolish for people to put all their hope and trust into a single person. To believe that a person can change things by himself. Or herself. The only thing that matters is holding onto what's good. To hold onto people you love and ideas that matter and to press forward together."

"How can you hold onto people you love from the Atlantic Ocean?"

"I'm not ready to practice what I preach."

"Did...did you know Queen Carmine?"

He nods, eyes still closed. Tears fall freely, dotting his shorts like rain drops. "She was the best of us."

"Chase, this is a stupid question, I know," she says. "But. Are you the Outlaw?"

He chuckles. It's a dark awful sound, full of hurt. "The Outlaw's been dead for two years."

Twenty-four hours later they drop anchor at Playlinda Beach, within sight of Cape Canaveral and NASA's shuttle launching facility. NASA, explains Anna, lost all funding, and most scientists and physicists left to work with the Resistance. They see a couple campfires burning ashore but no other sign of civilization. Anna falls asleep in Chase's bed while he dozes in and out on the hammock netting.

She rises at dawn and comes above deck and squints at the sun rising above the eastern horizon. Chase stands at the wheel, eyes fixed south. She follows his gaze.

"What do you see?"

He says, "A ship. A familiar one, headed our way."

"That speck? It's miles distant. How can you be certain?"

"Because it's a ship I can't forget."

She takes binoculars from the back of his chair and holds them to her eyes. It *is* a ship, a big white one, but that's all she can discern.

He hoists the anchor and raises the foresail, just enough to form a small triangle at the bow. The breeze catches it and lazily points them south.

"Are we intercepting that boat?"

"This is fate. Not mere chance," he says.

She doesn't understand. They drift south on the current for an hour, drawing closer. Soon Anna Elizabeth can see it's a yacht. And then she can see it's a yacht of unimaginable proportions. Five years ago it must've cost a hundred million dollars. She guesses fifty yards long and four stories high, pure and brilliant splendor, like a ship soaring out of the future.

"How does the owner afford the gasoline?" she wonders.

"The owner is ancient and wealthy," he says in a low voice. Almost a growl. He lets the foresail drop.

The yacht towers over them, a haunting and overwhelming sight, and at first Anna thinks it'll steam straight past. Or crush them.

Chase speaks. Not loudly. Certainly not loud enough to be heard aboard the yacht. He says, "You know I'm here. Stop or I'll destroy your boat."

Instantly the yacht's engines die. The wake ceases frothing and a sudden silence envelopes them. A woman leans over the rail, perhaps fifty feet above. Anna cannot make out many details, the brilliant blue blasting her vision. Chase and the woman stare at one another a long time, some kind of elemental communication more powerful than words. Anna inspects the magnificent ship and notes the name —*Amnesia.*

Finally the woman above nods to herself and speaks, not more than a whisper. "There you are, boy, shining like the sun."

"Here I am."

"I've been waiting for you. Through calm and storm."

Chase doesn't reply.

"You're going to kill me, honey?"

"I am."

"Honesty, as is proper in a sailor. Come aboard," she says. Anna barely hears. "And drink wine with me."

Chase tosses his mooring cable around a hook at the rear of the yacht. Ties the vessels fast and helps Anna aboard onto the lowest deck.

"Chase," whispers Anna. "I'm frightened."

"You should be."

"I don't understand. Who is she? Are you truly going to murder her?"

"Her name is Pacific. And she's lived too long."

Anna shivers and her stomach flip-flops. "Should I wait in the *Angel*?"

Chase doesn't reply. His face is stone and he climbs the ladder. Anna follows, pulled by his momentum.

A steward greets the two, a polite man wearing a crimson vest. He places warm, lemon-scented towelettes into their hands.

"Good to see you again, sir," says the man. He watches Chase with a wary, exhausted expression. And maybe with hope, too. He leads them to a sundeck and spreads a large blue Bimini to provide shade. Anna peers into the superstructure, through open sliding doors, and spots a saloon set with overstuffed couches and a sparkling chandelier. She didn't know luxury such as this still existed. The steward says, "Won't you have a seat."

Anna lowers onto the cushions of a deck chair; Chase remains standing. He's barefoot on the rich brown deck slats. The steward gives them each a goblet and goes inside.

Chase sets his drink down.

Anna sips hers—iced punch, wine and fruit. Like drinking heaven.

They don't wait long. The owner of the yacht descends the stern staircase. A strong woman with long gray hair. She's ageless and beautiful, tall and erect, wearing a white sundress. Her skin isn't tan; it's a deep gold.

"The two nastiest sharks in the sea," she says, swirling her own goblet. "And we finally collide."

"Hello Pacific."

"No matter how long I fled, I knew you'd find me. You draw us. You pull me. It's not destiny, boy, it's magnetism. Don't you think?"

Chase watches her the way a cat watches a mouse. She returns the stare, two apex predators. Anna feels wildly out of place, like a lesser species.

The woman named Pacific sets her drink down and places her hands on his cheeks. She inhales and says, "You smell delicious to a starving woman. Power and muscle and fortune."

She kisses him on the mouth and Anna sits up straighter. The kiss isn't romantic or sexual or even friendly. It's something else, alien to her.

Pacific releases and steps back. Touches her mouth with her fingers. "You've gotten more powerful. Of your strong ilk, only you and Carter remain. And perhaps the colossus, though I've never met him. Monsoons ready to crash and kill us."

Anna stands and smiles warily at the woman. Manners are important, and she clears her throat. "Hello, I'm Anna." She inclines her head in a bow. "Your hospitality is very generous."

"Hush, girl, you don't matter." Pacific glances at Anna, a blithe motion. "And don't get your hopes up, sugar, he doesn't return your affection."

"Wha...I..." Anna flounders.

"Somehow, someway, boy, I knew you weren't dead." She backs away from him, picks up her goblet, and folds onto a chair. Crosses her legs.

"Have you radioed anyone?" he asks. "In the last five minutes, about me?"

"I have not."

"**Tell me the truth**," demands Chase, and Anna nearly yelps. Those aren't mere words, more like somehow he issued a spell. Compelling and terrible.

"I told no one!" cries Pacific, the words torn out of her. "I didn't trust my own eyes at first. The world still thinks the mighty Outlaw is dead, trust me."

Anna bolts to her feet. "I *knew* it! I knew it was you! But how? I watched you die, I watched the video a *thousand* times. Where have you been? Don't you understand how much we need you? Don't you—"

"Quiet, girl," snaps Pacific and Anna sits down like she was pushed.

Chase's arms are crossed over his chest. He twists at the waist to look at Anna. His lips are pressed together, his face grim. "I needed time. Still do."

"Too coincidental, I thought," says Pacific and she sips from her goblet of wine. "The legendary Outlaw and his darling queen dying on the same day."

"You're not one for coincidences," says Chase. "You'd prefer to arrange the deaths yourselves, I think."

"Let's get something out of the way. Address the white whale in the room, shall we," replies Pacific. "Yes, I betrayed you and your little girl-friend. Shipped her off to Martin, and he tormented her and put her through his nasty surgery. Awful of me, I know. But I regret nothing."

Chase has become very still, but Anna thinks she might hear his heart pounding.

"Anyway," says Pacific and she waves her hand, as if dismissing the matter. "You killed my husband for it. We're even."

"I didn't kill Martin. He was betrayed by his protege."

"He's dead because of *you*."

"The Chemist is no martyr. He died of self-inflicted wounds, Pacific."

"Don't talk to me of self-inflicted wounds, boy!" she screams suddenly and Anna covers her ears. "Not until you've lived a couple centuries! You cannot *imagine*."

"I know you rigged this boat," says Chase, still calm. "With explosives. And I know your plan is to detonate it, kill us all."

"Surely you don't begrudge an old woman her self-defense."

Anna's head swims. Listening to these two near-immortals casually discuss the most crucial events and people in a millennium boggles her mind. She wants to ask a thousand questions but dares not speak.

"Your steward is upstairs, finger on the button, waiting for your signal?" asks Chase.

Pacific sniffs and sips more of her wine.

"What's his name?"

Pacific says, "He doesn't have a name."

"Tell me."

"Come now, honey, you're above—"

"Tell me."

She says the words as if against her will. "His name is Owen."

Chase calls, "Owen!"

The steward's face appears, two decks above. He leans over the rail and looks down at them. He's sweating profusely, and his hand on the rail quakes. "Sir?"

"You're holding the trigger which will detonate the boat?" says Chase.

"Yes sir."

"Disarm the bomb."

"Pull the trigger, Owen!" cries Pacific with a wild manic laugh, tears pooling in her eyes. "Blast us to the bottom of the sea!"

"Owen, *no*."

The man lowers his head to the rail and groans.

Anna's heart pounds painfully like a drum. These people she's read about are insane.

"You're safe, Owen," says Chase. "Drop the trigger."

"She ordered me, sir..."

"Coward!" Pacific shouts. "Insubordination!"

Without warning, she makes a dash for the stairs. She moves at hyper speed, too fast for Anna's eyes to follow. But she's not quicker than the shaggy-haired man. He meets her at the bottom step and grabs her wrist. The sound of the collision is like a tree breaking. She screams at him and tries to jerk free, but the man is made of steel— he's not even exerting himself.

"Owen," he says. "Pacific is no longer the captain of this ship. Disarm the bomb."

"Yes sir," the man says, and Anna hears a noise; she thinks it's the sound of an exhausted man collapsing with relief onto the deck.

"This isn't your boat," seethes Pacific. "Release me."

"You're a murderer. You destroyed my life and the lives of those I love," says Chase, and with each syllable Pacific's eyes widen further. "You caused harm to this planet beyond imagination."

"Chase, honey, listen—"

"You hurt Katie Lopez, an innocent and perfect girl," he says, voice thickening. "And my friend Cory died resisting you. You preyed on the powerless and for these crimes I convict you."

"No."

"You should have done the honorable thing. You should have sent your steward ashore and voluntarily committed yourself to the deep."

"Stop, please...I can't listen, can't bear it."

"But you didn't. So I'll do it for you," says Chase.

She tugs at him, digging her heels into the deck until the slats break.

"What makes you the moral arbiter?" she says in a whimper.

"My innocence."

"I'm not ready."

"You never will be."

"I admit my guilt. But...the thing about being an elderly woman, I'm terrified of everything." She's weeping now.

"Your mind is already going. I feel it. And before many more decades pass, your blood will be contagious. This is justice. And this is mercy."

"Insolent boy," she cries. "I knew you'd change everything. That's why he feared you."

He doesn't respond. His face is hard and Anna at that moment is terrified of him. He may be beautiful but there is fury inside.

Pacific says, "Kill Owen too. And the rest. We'll go together."

"I will not."

"I don't want to die alone."

He nods. "I'll stay with you."

"The things I've done...are horrible. Beyond what you imagine." Her breath is shaky. "I want to die in the water."

Chase nods again. "Where's your anchor?"

Pacific doesn't answer. She sobbing. She clutches Chase, her face buried in his chest. His grip on her wrist is unwavering and powerful. But his other arm goes around her shoulder—almost a comforting embrace.

"Not yet," she says.

"Now."

The world spins. Anna's stomach lurches and she feels like she has a fever. This can't be real.

Chase moves forward. Having no choice, Pacific goes with him, a doleful death march.

Anna presses the palms of her hands hard to her ears, closes her eyes, curls into a ball, and cries.

Anna's still lying on a couch thirty minutes later when Chase returns. Her eyes never leave his, following him like a spotlight. He sits next to her, takes her hand, and squeezes.

"It's over?" she asks.

"It's over."

"How can you do that? Stay so calm and steady about something so horrid."

"Unfortunately..." he says and he absently stares at the goblet of wine, his mouth a grim line. "I've had a lot of practice."

"Are you inured to violence?"

"No. I didn't enjoy it."

"Who was she?" asks Anna.

"A monster. Born with the Hyper Virus, over a hundred and fifty years old."

"A pure-born."

"Yes." An Infected, he thinks to himself. "Her name was Minnie.

She's been afloat for most of her life. She and the Chemist were loosely attached, and she betrayed us to him."

"She deserved it."

"A hundred times over."

"You're him," she says. "The man in the mask. You're alive."

He nods. "I'm him."

"I want to know everything. But...I'll wait."

He stands. "She was about your size. Find some clothes other than my smelly t-shirt and that ridiculous bikini."

Anna Elizabeth, still struggling with shock, smiles. "It's not ridiculous. I like it. Isn't it disrespectful to raid the dead's belongings?"

"She said you're pretty. Told me she wanted you to have her clothes."

"What will you do?"

"I'm going to look through her stuff. Disrespectfully."

Chase finds the steward sitting on an upper deck, beneath the cockpit. Owen's legs are straight in front of him, and he dabs at his eyes. "Thank you, Master Jackson."

"You're welcome. "

"What now?"

"I'm not sure. The boat is yours."

Owen blinks. And again. "Oh no, sir, I couldn't possibly..."

"Keep it or ditch it, that's up to you. Are you alone?"

"No, there's the cook. And there's Reggie, the captain's mate, but he's in bed with the flu. Should be up soon," says Owen.

"Show me to Minnie's office."

"Of course, sir." Owen climbs to his feet and leads Chase forward. He's lighter of step than he's been in years. Minnie's cabin is near the bow and has an uninterrupted 180-degree view of the ocean—floor-to-ceiling windows. Thick carpet and a king-size canopy bed. Some of the paintings on the walls, Chase assumes, are originally from the Renaissance and worth millions.

Or used to be worth millions.

He passes a full-length dressing mirror and stops. Other than in the water's surface, he hasn't seen himself in over twelve months. A stranger returns the stare. He is deeply tan, giving his blue eyes a stark haunted look. His hair's too long and he needs to shave the scruff on his face. He unbuttons and removes his linen shirt and twists to inspect his back over the shoulder. A mess of scars, from Russia's bomb. He turns again. The stranger in the mirror is shockingly muscular. His abdominals are visible, and his biceps and pectorals flex and relax as he moves. He wonders what Katie would think of him now.

He says, "Owen?"

"Yes sir."

"I've got pretty good shoulders, huh."

"Ah," says the man and he smiles. "The very top, sir."

"Think I should cut my hair?"

"Perhaps ask your lady friend."

"I might get skin cancer, living this way," says Chase, touching his dark face.

"Without a doubt, sir."

"Where's Minnie's office?"

Owen opens a door off the starboard bulkhead and Chase goes into a small room with no windows. A desk is bolted against the wall. On top, there's a fax machine and laptop and cellphone. Stacks of paper held in place with clips.

Chase asks, "The boat receives satellite signal?"

"Satellite and cellular."

"Give me some time, please."

"Certainly, sir. Call if you need anything. I'll order lunch."

Chase lowers into the swivel chair that's attached to the floor. For a long time he simply sits, staring at the desk and its contents, leery of the surprises within. He cut himself off from this world two years ago —an intentional and drastic sequester. The ocean is so much simpler. Exhausting but not complicated. No heartbreak. He doesn't want to wade back into the mire, doesn't want to contend with the waiting monsters. He still feels shattered beyond repair.

Anna Elizabeth finds Minnie's cabin and opens the pocket doors of the walk-in closet. Chase hears her gasp in delight and he smiles.

He takes a deep breath. Grips the tall stack of papers and tugs, inch by inch, until it slides free of the clamp. The papers are dated printouts of emails and faxes, going back two months. Her responses are scrawled on the papers in elegant calligraphy, and then faxed back. A mashup of ancient and modern communication.

An old-fashioned gal.

Chase starts at the bottom and works his way forward.

The first series of notes takes his breath away...

Where are you, dear boy?

>> **none of ur business, crazy woman**

>> **But I see ur off the coast of brazil**

Indeed. Do you know why I send faxes?

>> **duh**

>> **so i cannot intercept them as easily**

>> **its maddening**

Tell me where you are. I'll take you around the world

In my yacht, you magnificent jelly fish

>> **no way crazy bitch**

>> **i hope u drown**

>> **no even better, eaten by sharks**

Chase doubles over. Like he's been struck in the stomach. No names are used, but he recognizes the familiar style of texting. PuckDaddy. On his boat's old satellite phone, Chase has typed out a hundred messages to the infamous hacker, maybe a thousand, but deleted them all. Intentionally walking away from his dearest friends was the most painful of all his sacrifices to stay anonymous, to stay on the ocean.

He reads the back-and-forth again, tears in his eyes.

"Puck," he whispers. "You're the best."

He turns to the next batch of messages. This series is from Mary herself, the Blue-Eyed Witch, the current President of the United States. Mary asks Pacific to come for a visit, as they are two of the last pure-borns. They have so much in common, so much to discuss, she says.

Pacific responded to the request:

Perhaps.

By the way, are you enjoying your chair, darling?

You might prefer life at sea.

Dated two months ago.

Chase heard the rumor that Blue-Eyes is now confined to a wheelchair. Mostly likely from Samantha's bullet.

Water bursts to life in the next room; Anna Elizabeth starting the shower. Soon after, Chase assumes, she'll use the hair dryer—anachronisms from another life.

Chase reads through a long list of updates about the Resistance. Clearly Pacific has spies within the ranks, conveying information. He gets a sense of the current war and stalemate. Both sides were shocked into a ceasefire by the use of a nuclear bomb on American soil. The deaths of the Outlaw, the Warrior Queen, and then the President himself some months after rocked the world. The Federal army and the Resistance returned to their strongholds to lick their wounds.

General Isaac Anderson still runs the show for the Resistance. There are photos of him and printouts of his speeches. Chase smiles fondly, remembering their interactions years ago when Anderson was a special agent for the FBI, tasked with apprehending the Outlaw. The world was a simpler place then.

Chase flips to the next page, an update about wild Variants in the middle states. Cedar Rapids is no more. The mutants descended like a plague of locusts and tore it apart with their bare hands. Unharnessed rage and anarchy. Ripped the tops off buildings like tuna cans. Cities and farms near Cedar Rapids are reinforced with security, but the people know of no good way to stop the horde.

He's still reading updates when Anna Elizabeth walks into the small room. She brings the scent of floral shampoo and expensive perfume. She wears a strappy yellow sundress that reaches the tops of her knees. Her long brown hair shines, held in an updo with silver clips. Diamonds sparkle at her ears and at the hollow of her throat.

She says, "What do you think?"

"I think Minnie bequeathed her closet wisely. You look lovely."

"Thank you." She smiles and a deep patina settles into her cheeks. "What are you reading?"

"Notes about people I used to know."

"Is no one aware you're alive?" she asks.

"I called my father. Told him I'm alive, made him promise to keep it a secret. That's it."

"What about the others? Chase Jackson had friends. I read about them. You and the Resistance's sniper used to make the headlines every few weeks."

"After the explosion in the sky," he says and pauses. Leans back in the swivel chair and stares at something far beyond the wall. Remembers that day in the endless blue, their jet dodging missiles, and then...nothing until waking up to the worst news. "I wasn't in my right mind for several weeks. The world had watched me die. And Katie was dead, and...I couldn't think of a single reason to return. So I didn't."

She places her hands on his shoulders and squeezes. "A single reason? The people who needed you, do we not count?"

"Our country is split in half. Society has been disrupted to the point that millions in America died, billions worldwide. My city was abandoned. My friends are gone. A nuclear bomb was detonated on American soil, wiping Denver off the map. The girl I loved was kidnapped and later killed. My home is destroyed. My enemies are stronger than ever," says the man formerly known as the Outlaw, his shoulder muscles growing more tense with each word. "Anyone depending on me has been let down countless times."

"That's not true."

"Anywhere I go, I leave craters."

"Things would be so much worse without the Outlaw. We're in our nation's darkest hour. The darkest hour in a thousand years, and you're one of the very few bright spots."

He reaches up to pat her hand. "Thank you. But, when I died, it had been a long four years. I took one too many punches, and the

3   61

boat felt like home. I thought about picking up a phone to call the Resistance...but I just couldn't. When Katie died, I died too."

"No. You didn't. You're right here. You're the most amazing thing I've ever seen, Chase," says Anna. "You're coming back to life. I know it." She gives his shoulder one more squeeze and leaves the room, returning to the treasures in Minnie's closet.

Chase flips to a new note, a communication from Minnie to an unknown source:

Where is the boy now?

>> **Unknown. Midwest somewhere. Tracking hardware failed months ago.**

What is he doing? Is he simply a rogue shark cruising the waters of the Mid-American wasteland?

>> **We believe he's insane. Hard to predict what he's doing.**

And will that atomic bomb eventually blow of its own accord?

>> **Also unknown, though we predict a detonation in near future. He dies, it blows. And he's not in a good state to care for himself.**

What a shocking world this has become. Things are so much less complicated on the ocean.

Chase reads it again and again. He thinks they're referencing his old acquaintance Andy Babington.

"Poor guy," he mutters. No one deserves that fate. Just rambling around the middle of America, alone and purposeless, with a nuke bolted into his back? Awful.

The next message is from a physician, reporting on a patient, dated a month ago:

>> **I believe his recovery is as complete as it will ever be. Anyone else would be dead, obviously, but Walter is robust and hale, other than the head injuries.**

Chase wonders, head injuries? He didn't know about those.

In a perfect world, Walter would be long gone by now. He keeps reading...

I don't know why I'm curious, but I am. What are the long-term side effects?

>> That's a good question. The pressure applied to his brain was significant, as was evidenced by the multiple skull fractures. His bone cells are something akin to rock or metal, which gives you some idea of the trauma he endured. When he came under my care, the brain tissue resembled those I see in fatal car wrecks. He could potentially live the rest of his life as if recovering from multiple concussions, to put it in layman's terms. Forgetful, irritable, headaches, sensitivity to sunlight—symptoms like these.

>> He threatens my life on a nearly daily basis. I've almost lost hope of being released from my servitude. He is hellbent on returning to Los Angeles. I will most likely make an escape attempt then and be killed in the process.

Good grief. What on earth had happened to Walter?

Chase keeps turning pages, silently saying a prayer than the captured physician is able to soon get free.

The final messages are dated yesterday. Another communique with Blue-Eyes...

>> I need you here, Pacific. Soon.

>> Diplomacy with Beijing has failed so I'm sending mutants.

I assume, darling and adorable President, you're referring to the pure-born in China?

>> Of course I am, Minnie, don't play games with me.

>> Somedays I think I should just launch a rocket at you.

Pray, madam, be careful. My tolerance of you is not without bounds.

>> You're right, of course, I apologize. But you are not holding up your end of the bargain. So respectfully I request that you get here as soon as possible. And do not force me to do something I'd rather not.

You don't require me to meet with the girl from China. I care not for your world's machinations.

>> I spoke with her, Minnie. She says she has the cure.

>> The cure! Dwell on that before you reply.

Impossible. The disease is as old as our planet. There can be no cure.

>> I strongly believe she's telling the truth.

>> She speaks of the disease mutating and affecting biological structures, like gigantism.

>> Which would explain what we're seeing recently.

>> She's the world's foremost expert, and if she says there is a cure then I trust her.

>> We cannot let her fall into the wrong hands.

>> I hope to capture her within the week, and fly her here.

>> And probably execute her.

>> I'm already laying the groundwork for an upcoming world leader summit, when the rest of the pieces will fall into place.

>> I call them Peace Accords. Isn't that a riot, my dear?

>> Now that Walter is mostly healed, we can secure our future.

>> But I need your guidance.

I will begin heading your direction, dear. But there are no promises.

Chase Jackson lowers the paper. He hasn't blinked in several minutes. He can't focus. Can't think. Can't hear. Can't remember where he is. The fingertips holding the paper tremble and tingle, frissons sparking inside his mind. A thousand voices scream at him, a thousand futures colliding in his vision.

A summit with the world leaders would be disastrous. But even more important than that...

There's a cure for the disease.

There's a *cure!*

And the girl from China has it.

PART II

We shall not cease from exploration
   And the end of all our exploring
   will be to arrive where we started
   and know the place for the first time.
   Through the unknown, unremembered gate
   when the last of earth to discover
   is that which was the beginning.

- *Little Gidding*, by T.S. Eliot

- 1 -
Katie Lopez

Something about staring at a campfire. I could watch it for hours as golden flames devour the wood. The dance and contained destruction erase all other problems from my mind. Even keeps the depression away.

That's a new wrinkle of mine, depression. I'm not prone to it, even during the darkest times. I don't dwell on problems, I solve them. But despondency and melancholy hit me hard the past few days, turning the world a shade of blue. I think it stems from homelessness. I'm living a life of itinerancy and it's left me without a center, without gravity, without purpose. So I float unconnected, no future to drive towards.

Wish I could throw my self-pity into the fire.

I check my watch. Almost midnight. They should be back by now.

I get up from my perch on an old stump and walk circles around the small fire. Our caravan is arranged nearby, and my coterie sleeps inside their vehicles or inside hammocks strung between trees. Sean reclines and snores in the passenger seat of my Land Cruiser. I shouldn't be lonely and depressed—I'm surrounded by friends and followers. Yet...

Winnemucca, Nevada isn't exactly Disneyland. And hiding within the remains of a farm in this abandoned tiny town isn't exactly what I thought I'd be doing with my life at twenty-two years of age.

We might be the only people for a hundred miles in all directions. Maybe farther. The world feels empty, like bellowing black. Void of reasons to go on.

I shove my hands into the back pockets of my jeans and orbit the fire for an hour, scuffing my boots just to make some noise. Part of my emotional funk is that I'm the leader. They still call me Queen. Once one of the most followed and watched people on earth. I cannot help but feel a failure—a leader, supposedly dead, with no place to lead the remnants of her following.

Finally, at one in the morning, I detect our sentries returning. I sent them north and east over a day ago. The enemy has spread haphazardly, as though drifting apart. Where could Walter be? And what about his wolf man? I'd like to head north, but not without more information.

No, that's not true. I don't want to head north. I'm a southern California girl. I want a beach and the sun. I prefer anything other than heading to Alaska. But my choices run thin.

I unwrap some raw mutton and place it on the fire to cook, ready for the scouts' return. Should be within fifteen minutes.

The ocean...how I miss it.

I'm staring at maps when Scout and Darren return. They're both exhausted and exhilarated, worn out and energized by their long trip. Scout moves twice as quickly so I sent her north. Without words they lower next to the fire and take water bottles, and I press the cooked mutton into their hands.

I squat next to them and patiently wait.

Scout grins, licking the sizzling fat off her fingertips. "I think we lost him. He's in Utah, heading south."

I release a breath I didn't realize I was holding. This is life-giving news. Andy Babington, the walking nuclear bomb, is off our trail. At least for the time being. He's a state away, heading in the wrong direction. I wonder what drew his attention? What's south of Utah?

"And to the north?" I ask.

"Nobody. It's empty a long way," she says.

Darren nods his agreement with her.

I tell him, "Use words, Darren. What'd you find?"

"West of us, there's nothing. Wild Variants only. A few. They're excited."

"What excites them?"

He shakes his head and shrugs.

I rise and resume my orbits of the fire. Interesting news. We're safe in all directions. Our enemies are either thrown off the trail or too busy to bother with us. Walter's been missing in action for a long time. I check the news intermittently and he goes months without making an appearance, and usually then gobbles up another city with his force of freaks. Blue-Eyes doesn't know I'm alive or doesn't care.

So which direction do we go?

Does it even matter?

Does anyone care anymore? About us?

About me?

I walk into the woods half a mile. The animals here are abundant and they fall silent as I pass.

I climb into a maple tree, ascend to a thick branch ten feet in the air, and close my eyes. After a few minutes, my pulse slows. Muscles relax. I count backwards until I feel close to to melting, and I cast myself outwards. A way of exploring the world with my senses, an expansion beyond myself. I *Listen*. I *Smell*. I *Feel*.

Animals beyond sight rampage through the bracken. No wolves, though. Birds of prey nest in the trees, and tiny creatures burrow underground.

Soon I feel pricks at my consciousness. Bigger predators—mutants. Barely human. Miles away, drawn to my mind somehow. I experience them the way one does the wind, a general impression of existence and movement. I don't let them in. I examine and investigate them with this extra sense provided by the disease. They're essentially a color to my far-off eyes—scarlet throbbing pain.

Darren's right. They're excited. Like animals verging on a stampede. The cusp of a tsunami.

My eyes snap open.

Something's happening, upsetting the arcane network we diseased souls unwittingly plug into. A burgeoning avalanche.

But I don't know where.

Or why.

At ten in the morning, the Governess shoves open the door into Kayla's suite on the 22nd floor of the 717 Olympic Tower. The door is forced to plow through Givenchy throw pillows and cashmere blankets so thick on the ground that the carpet is hidden. Famous paintings lean against every wall and are stacked on the overstuffed chairs, gathering dust.

A beefy man cooks breakfast in the kitchen on hot plates running on battery power. He's a Devotee, one of the last of his kind—a servant trained to serve pure-born mutants. Most others of his kind quit within the past twelve months.

The man sees her and his shoulders slump. "The mistress is still sleeping."

"It is past time the girl wakes. I have been up since five, as is appropriate."

"But she needs her rest, please let her sleep," says the man, knowing full well the grumpy Governess is not a woman who listens to others. "She was up late talking to the computer man."

"You used to serve the Queen. She got up before the sun. Do you not remember, you thick man?"

"I have bacon almost ready," he says.

"Bacon? You try to distract me with the bacon? You are a pathetic boy," says the Governess in a withering tone. "You need to kill something."

"*Kill* something?"

"Yah. Go into wilderness. Take a knife. Don't come back until you kill many animals. Why do you have so many muscles if you put them to no use."

"But what would—"

"You want to live as servant? Fine. But also you need to know who you are as a human. Find yourself. Stop wearing robes. Get hurt. Right now you are pathetic man-boy." The Governess storms to the

Kayla's door and pauses. "And if you start crying, I pour bacon grease on you." She gives a final sniff and pushes into the bedroom.

Kayla isn't asleep. She lies on her back on the heirloom canopy bed, golden hair splayed perfectly across her luxury pillow. Her legs are pointed in the air and she kicks her toes at the stuffed animals dangling from above.

The Governess gasps. "*That* is what you sleep in?"

Kayla smiles and it's so shockingly beautiful that the Governess nearly trips. "Of course, don't you love it? Tyra Banks wore it to a lingerie fashion event forever ago, and she *signed* it! Note the pink frills! It used to be worth, I dunno, *so* much."

The woman claps her hands twice. "I care not about the fashion. Get up, girl. You were supposed to meet me an hour ago."

"But I don't *wanna*, and ew, you smell like hot tires. Please work on your attitude and return in five minutes. Kay, thanks!"

The Governess glares and sets her fists on her hips. "There is the problem with your Guardians."

"*Sigh*. It's the same problem every day, Governess. That's why I'm staying in bed. It's safe and warm here."

"The boy, Mason, he needs your help."

"Tell him to ask Tank," says Kayla.

"Tank is missing again! You know this."

"*Again?*"

"Of course, again."

"I hate that man. Are you entirely positive this is a problem for me? Remember, I am the Mistress of Communication only. In charge of talking a lot, basically, plus who does—"

"These are mutants, Kayla, silly girl! Your issue!"

"But I don't WANNA!" screams Kayla. She gets to her feet, standing on the memory foam mattress. She throws pillows at the Governess and when she misses they fly out the open french doors, plummeting to the street far below. "Why is it always *me*? It's not fair! I'm so *tired* and this is so *stupid*. Nothing is working right, everything is broken! Why can no one else handle problems, why am I expected to have the answers? I'm not supposed to be the leader, I'm just supposed to handle communications and look pretty and AUGH!"

The Governess, accustomed to these outbursts, makes no reply. Instead she watches Kayla smolder and radiate like a magma flow. She is a breathtaking sight when full of any emotion, and the Governess thinks she smells burning pine.

"I'm just..." Kayla pauses, running out of the energy required for indignation. She stares at her manicured toes and sighs again, while the Governess fetches a robe—women should not wear such night-gowns, not even in private. "I'm just tired."

The Governess grunts understanding. "Did you sleep?"

"An hour, which is plenty, but..."

She throws the silky robe over Kayla's shoulders. "I know. It is hard. Life is hard."

"Queen Carmine made it look so easy," says Kayla.

"That girl, a natural leader. A dozen like her and we would conquer the whole world. That girl had starch, as a woman should."

"Look at it, Governess." Kayla walks out onto the balcony and points at the former City of Angels with a trembling finger, adorned with a diamond once valued over a million dollars. "The city's so beautiful and perfect. And it's dying. Los Angeles falls apart no matter what we do."

"No, the city is surviving," scoffs the Governess. "The world, it drifts to entropy. Just like our city. But we survive and much of the world does not. It is you who falls apart."

Kayla nods and big beautiful tears spill down her face. "I do. I know. I'm sorry. I'm not made for this. I wish...I wish she was here. Or I wish Puck was here. Or the Outlaw, or someone."

"Wishing, wishing, what is the use of wishing? It does no good. We are here. You go meet Mason now. I mean to say, that is, after you change."

Kayla nods and wipes her eyes. She walks into her closet, which used to be the neighboring suite until she knocked the walls down. She stands in the middle of the perfectly organized panoply of fash-ion, entire walls of pink and ivory and sparkles, and she tries to stop crying. Her phone buzzes incessantly with incoming texts but she ignores it—they aren't PuckDaddy's individualized buzz.

The Governess eventually leaves, satisfied Kayla is up and moving. She has no time to deal with tears and there are other people to harangue.

Kayla's Devotee brings her vanilla coffee and bacon and says, "Mistress Kayla, do you require help?"

"I do. I really really do," she says. "But it's nothing that you can assist with."

"What will you do?"

"First things first," she says, holding her chin high. "Dress fabulously and brush my hair. Because if the world is ending, I want to look cute for it."

Kayla's pink convertible Volkswagen Beetle screeches to a stop at Pershing Square, off 6th Street. The park, once a green meeting place for nature lovers, is now home to a small herd of cattle and a chicken coop. Shepherds perk up when they realize who's driving the car— the second most beautiful woman on the planet, according to People magazine, placing her just behind the blue-eyed President of the United States.

Mason McHale—powerful Guardian and the handsome leader of the Falcons—gets off his motorcycle and reluctantly lowers himself into the passenger seat of her car. The seat covers glitter in the sunlight.

"Oh Mason," she laughs, a musical sound which lifts the spirit of all within ear shot. Infected with the Hyper Virus, Kayla possesses extraordinary gifts, causing men and women alike to stop and stare and listen and inhale and enjoy her as one does the sun. "Take off your motorcycle helmet, silly."

"No. One of these days you'll flip this little toy car and I want to survive the crash."

She smiles and pokes him. "You're a stinker."

Mason, like all others, is at least partially in love with Kayla and he savors the poke. It's an unrealistic dream, he knows, being with Kayla, so he keeps his eyes straight ahead. "Just focus on driving, mamita."

Kayla presses the gas pedal and the hybrid car jolts forward with a surprising amount of torque. "Don't you think it's weird you call me 'little mama'? Cause I do and it's a little yikes."

"I think you're the whitest woman on the planet."

They race out of Downtown, passing Cleaners and Engineers and Builders hard at work. The sky is blue and vast, no sign of rain, which means the Gardeners and Farmers will be toting water again.

Kayla points at a cluster of Guardians moping on the corner and says, "Look at those poor babies. No change?"

"If there is, it ain't for the better. Slackers, all of them."

Kayla opens her mouth to reply but changes her mind. There's nothing to say. Call them what you want—mutants, Variants, Guardians, whatever—they're getting worse. She and Mason and some others have recovered from the shock of Queen Carmine's exile. After months of despondency, they rebounded and now function better than ever. But the rest become more feral, more deranged, more disconsolate every day. If they had a proper leader, things might be different.

Mason says, "I don't know what to do about them."

"Me neither," says Kayla and she chews at her lip anxiously.

"We could call Queen Carmine."

"Mason! Only in extreme need can we do that! She's not supposed to exist, remember."

"The Guardians are losing their minds, Kayla. They destroyed most of Montebello last week," responds Mason, shouting to be heard through his motorcycle helmet.

"Does that make it an emergency?"

"I don't know."

"I don't know either. I'm not good at this."

"Eyes on the road!"

Kayla gasps and swerves to miss a goat on the Five, northbound. Then she laughs and says, "Don't you just *love* goats?"

"Where are we going?"

"Tarzana. He's with the giants."

"He wasn't yesterday," says Mason. "I checked."

"He's there today."

"How do you know?"

"I have my sources, silly."

Mason grumbles, "The computer nerd?"

"He is *not* a nerd and you shush."

Twenty minutes later they turn into Redesa Boulevard and park on a private street near Braemar Country Club. This part of the world, without Gardeners or landscaping crews, is dependent on animals to keep the grass and weeds at bay. Which means it smells like dung on hot afternoons.

Mason, peering through the windshield and glaring, says, "This is so creepy."

"It totally is. I wish I'd brought a motorcycle helmet. A pink one with sequins," says Kayla.

She and Mason stay in the Volkswagen several minutes, simply watching the bizarre animal sanctuary this neighborhood has become. They see herds of mule deer, skulks of foxes, packs of dogs, colonies of rabbits, teams of wild horses, dreys of squirrels, and even a sloth of brown bears. Independent cats begin leaping into Kayla's car and curling up on the rear seats.

"Tank is *so* weird," she mutters. "Like, a super freak."

"It's only mammals that love him, you notice that? No lizards."

Kayla points at the oak trees. "Birds too. Ohmigosh, they better not poop on my car."

They talk in whispers, afraid Tank might hear. "He didn't used to be like this. Why'd he go all weird?"

"Who knows. I hate it. Except for those hummingbirds, I *love* the hummingbirds. But other than that...and the rabbits...and those puppies...and those fawns...other than them, I hate it."

They sense the giant before they see him. A seismic vibration felt through the tires. A familiar man, nearly fifteen feet tall, comes around the pool house of the nearby mansion, and roars, "**Kayla! You are heeeere!**" He charges their car, animals fleeing before the clumsy footfalls, and hoists her straight out of the driver's seat.

"Hi Travis!" she cries with no small amount of trepidation. "You're squeezing a *little* tight."

For clothing he only wears a sheet like a kilt around his waist. Better than nothing, which is sometimes the case. "**Look at all the pretty animals, Kaaaayla. As pretty as you.**"

"Travis, where's Tank? And please be careful, this top is by Akris."

"**Helloooo Mason.**"

"Hey big guy, how's it going," replies Mason, getting out of the car and trying not to step on inquisitive chipmunks. A mule deer stands five feet away, regarding Mason and thoughtfully munching grass.

"Travis," says Kayla. "Take me to Tank. Please?"

"**Sure, okaay!**"

He carries Kayla like a baby across the lawn and onto the fairway of an old golf course shared by the mansions. Although Los Angeles is home to hundreds of thousands of people, none live nearby in the once trendy Tarzana. Legend has it that this neighborhood is haunted. Just not with ghosts.

Tank Ware, once perhaps the most famous high school kid in America, sits alone near the pond. He slouches in an overstuffed chair broken by his bulk, and his Timberland boots are crossed on a reading table. The furniture looks alien in the grass, but not as alien as its occupant—he wears designer jeans, a white button-down shirt, and white gloves, a classy outfit spoiled by his half-melted face and scowl. If he tries hard enough he can remember being an attractive and wealthy Hispanic boy. Ages ago. But now the scarred and angry man has no family, no friends, and no reason to smile.

"**Taaaank, Kayla is hereeee.**"

Tank doesn't reply.

The giant sets Kayla down and walks a short distance away, as he knows he ought.

"I'm here too," says Mason. "But not like anybody cares."

Tank makes a sniffing noise. He's staring northward at something far beyond eyesight, unblinking. Animals crowd the golf course, but they keep a minimum distance from their pack leader in the chair—don't anger the alpha. Even the mountain lions respect the circle of space.

Kayla plucks at his dark hair and says, "Yuck, Tank Ware, when was your last shower? Because ew."

Tank's voice is an earthquake. "Don't touch me, bouncy girl. Less you wanna get bit."

"I don't."

"Then go'way. You too, little warrior."

Mason mumbles about not being little.

"Tank," says Kayla. "The Guardians, they're—"

"The freaks, you mean. The mutants."

"Hey, maybe be nice! They can't help it. They need you," she says.

"We been playing this game for two years, Kayla. Two long damn years. Ain't nothing changed. Fact is, the freaks getting freakier."

Mason nods. "Got that right."

"We're all freaks, aren't we?" asks Kayla. She walks in front of Tank and sits on the table, forcing him to look at her. She finds things go her way when people can see her. "We need each other."

"We're not all the same and you know it. I'm not like your pack of..." He vaguely waves a hand over his shoulder, toward the downtown tower cluster. "...of maniacs. My brain works. So does yours. Mostly."

"But they're bonded to you! More or less. If you'd actually pay attention to them, it would help *so* much."

"Doesn't help. You know it. And I'm done babysitting."

"Ugh," groans Kayla and her head drops. "Not this again."

"He's out there."

"The wolf man?" she guesses. Memories flash on her consciousness of that awful night, the wolves so thick they blotted out the crust of the earth, following the orders of the scary man in old rags. "What is it with you and him? We haven't seen him in months."

Tank's lip draws upwards in a snarl. "He's moving. He's north of us but he's heading east. And his pack's gotten big enough to attack again."

"*How* do you know that?"

"Just know."

"What happened to you, Tank? How do you know how to do the freaky stuff like talk to animals? Why do they follow you around, even those icky skunks? Because it's like *wow*."

"Ask the Zealot. I got no idea," says Tank.

Mason looks up from the mountain lion he'd been warily inspecting. "You mean Saul? That old man died two years ago."

"Yeah." Tank nods, his eyes still searching the northern horizon. "Yeah he did."

"Then how—"

"He bought me," says Tank under his breath. Kayla leans forward to hear. "Bought me. Gave me to God. Something like that, I can't remember. But I'm...supposed to do...*something*."

"You're not making any sense," says Kayla.

"I'm leaving."

"*What!* You can't!"

"Can too," says Tank. He closes his eyes and rubs at them with gloved fingers. "Watch me."

"We need you! We're barely hanging on and if you leave then Walter will come back, and that man is YUCK."

"I gotta stop the wolves, Kayla. I think that's why I'm alive."

"But I thought the wolf man was in Vegas."

Tank is whispering. "He's gaining strength. And then he'll come back. There's gotta be a reason for me to exist. Everything else has been taken...so I have to go."

Kayla is so scared her skin is turning pink. "Los Angeles is *important*. The Guardians are *important*. If Walter gets the city, or claims our Variants, the world could fall. Your place is *here*. That's what Queen Carmine says."

"Katie's dead," he growls. "Ain't that right? S'what you told me."

Kayla clamps her mouth shut. There are rumors that the warrior queen lives, the same rumors that circulated about Elvis, Tupac, and

Duchess Anastasia. Most dismiss the conspiracy theories out of hand, and only a small handful know the truth—Carmine staged her death in order to save Los Angeles from a nuclear bomb. Tank's never bought the lie.

"Tank, don't do it," says Mason. "You're the only reason the Guardians haven't gone entirely mad. If you leave, they'll rampage. They'll become like the wild monsters in the midwest being hunted by Herders, until Walter claims them."

"How long we gon' keep this up?" asks Tank. He's angry enough to snatch the attention of the animals. "The Blue-Eyed Witch in the White House ain't going anywhere. The Resistance quit helping us. The freaks in Oregon and Seattle still ready to swoop down. And we just sit here, doin' nothing."

"We're alive. And we're doing what's right, and that matters," says Kayla.

"I ain't built to sit around and wait. Listen, you two. I been sitting here for two years. Two *years*. And I'm tired of it. Help ain't coming, that's for damn sure. Waiting to die is no life."

"Tomorrow!" cries Kayla, bordering on panic. "I'll arrange a meeting tomorrow. Kay? With us and the Governess and General Brown. We'll talk and figure this whole thing out. They'll know what to do."

"No they won't. Nobody don't know what to do. We're stuck, pretty girl. You can smile at me all you want. It's a good one, I admit. But that don't mean we got a leader. Or a plan."

She pats the toe of his boot. "Tomorrow. You'll see. Kay?"

"You know, it's funny," he says. "I almost miss him."

"Miss who?"

Tank only grunts and refuses to speak again.

Kayla and Mason return to the VW Beetle. Mason angrily twirls a knife between his fingers. Kayla's legs feel wobbly and her heart pounds. They shoo cats and two black labs out of the car and close the doors.

She texts with shaky fingers, **Were u listening??**

The reply from PuckDaddy is immediate.

>> of course babe!
>> stupid tank
>> stupid tank and his stupid face
>> but maybe...
>> maybe the giant dumb-head has a point
>> things in los angeles r going down hill

The next day, Kayla returns to Tarzana. This time she drives an enormous Toyota Tundra, far too vast for her, but there's no way she's entrusting her perfect convertible to carry Tank's considerable bulk downtown. She'd rather die.

She eases up the hill toward Tank's mansion and a deep uneasiness envelopes her. At first she can't place her finger on the source. The houses still stand. She sees two giants sitting near a fire, roasting a pig. There's no sign of a fight. All appears normal.

So what's the problem?

She accidentally runs over the curb with the truck's huge tires. Puts it in park and kills the engine. Through the open window she hears nothing. No crying, no screaming, no battle. Yet something nags at her.

She shoves open the door and hops down, careful not to squish mice or chipmunks.

Except there aren't any.

That's it! She snaps her fingers. All the animals are gone. This place used to be an overcrowded zoo, and now...

"Uh oh," she whispers. "Oh yikes. This is super bad."

She already knows what she'll find, but she runs anyway. Runs to the pond. Nothing. Runs through several houses. Empty.

No Tank.

Tank's gone.

She finds Travis in what looks like a salvage yard behind his particular mansion. He's sitting crisscross, surrounded by pipes and old cars, and big fat tears are rolling down his carved cheeks.

"**Kayla**," he sobs. Holds his hands out like a child. She rushes to him and wraps her arms around his neck. Sitting down, he's only a little taller than her.

"Tank left?" she asks, patting his head.

"**He's gooone!**"

"Poor Travis. The animals went with him, I bet."

"**Yes, and some of us.**"

"Some of the giants? How many?"

"**I dunno. Maybe half of us?**"

"It's going to be okay, Travis," she says and she starts crying too. "It's...it'll be..."

It'll be what? She doesn't know. She's out of ideas, out of energy, out of hope.

Her phone is in her left hand, warm from use. She squeezes it like a drowning woman clinging to a raft.

This is an emergency, she thinks.

She needs Carmine.

The Outlaw

"What do I do now?" calls Anna Elizabeth. She's near panic.

I bring the binoculars to my eyes. They don't assist me as much as they would normal eyes, but they help with focusing. Multiple pinpricks dot the northern horizon—I've been watching them the past hour. My guess, those are Federal Navy ships hidden from view by the ocean and the natural curvature of the earth. I can only see the towers, but they look big, the kind that use nuclear reactors to plow the oceans. Looking for Anna? I doubt it. She's not a big enough fish.

"Chase? What should I do?" She's fifty feet below, on deck, while I slowly gyrate at the top of my sailboat's mast. Long waves are passing under our keel, creating a galloping motion.

"Hold your course."

"But we'll run aground soon! What about the land? And the waves?"

"Anna," I say. "Hold your course. Trust me."

She grumbles under her breath. Beside her, Owen says nothing.

I lower the glasses. Why the Federal blockade, I wonder. We're south of Jacksonville, near Sawgrass. Those ships are at the mouth of St. John's River, the watery ingress into the heart of Jacksonville, an odd place to drop anchor. I glance again at our yacht, the *Amnesia,* anchored a mile behind. They shouldn't be able to see her. Except on radar.

Could they have been waiting for Pacific? A trap to destroy the ancient woman? I wouldn't put it past Blue-Eyes. Could the waiting convoy have something to do with the cure? No matter the reason, I'm not sailing farther north.

"Chase..." calls Anna, her hands gripped hard on the wheel.

"It's fine, Miss. There's no danger," says Owen. "I hope."

My boat, the *Angel*, is a hundred feet from the deserted sandy beach and headed ashore at an easy four knots. As I descend the mast, we pass over a sandbar and into the smooth quasi-lagoon beyond. The waves inside the lagoon are minuscule and we level out.

"Drop anchor," I say.

"I don't know how!"

"Here, Miss," says Owen, indicating the release lever. She follows his instructions and my fluke anchor plunges into the water. It catches and we drift to a stop forty feet from the beach, inches off the bottom. Simple.

I walk to our starboard bow and inspect the beach. What a funny place land is, with trees and shrubs and grass shooting straight up out of dirt and hiding everything from sight. On land, roads are necessary to cut through the wilderness and manmade obstacles, very unlike the clean wide-open sea. The air feels heavy, and a thick bouquet of floral aromas wafts on the breeze.

I didn't sleep last night, tossing and turning, unable to calm my brain. Reading about the potential cure to the Hyper Virus set me on fire and I can't extinguish the anxiety. Or the hope. So I tossed and turned and formulated a plan—a stupid, hasty, and foolhardy plan.

On the bright side, it's simple: prevent Blue-Eyes from getting the cure.

How? Hit her in the head. Hard.

The more I think about it, the easier that sounds. I should be able to get close; they aren't looking for me, after all. I'm dead. And even better, I'm forgotten. Plus, I'm already on the East Coast. Practically on her doorstep. She doesn't make public appearances, often refusing to leave the White House, so I know where she is.

Knock knock, hello, bam.

Too easy? Probably.

I don't want to go back. Don't want to plug into the jungle. But if there's a cure then it's the best chance the world has of returning to sanity. I can't let China fall into the grasp of Blue-Eyes—it's that easy.

Anna Elizabeth clumsily navigates to me and takes my hand. "You look like you're far away."

My shoulders are tense and bunched, my brow furrowed. I'm glaring at the land once home to Katie Lopez, and I haven't forgiven it yet. I make a volitional effort to relax. "I haven't set foot in America in two years. My emotions are mixed."

"We've missed you. Welcome home."

"This boat is my home," I say, and I nod at the shore. "That is a battlefield. Where people I love die."

"You'll stay with us." She squeezes my hand. "We're your new home. Jacksonville, the Outlaw's new base of operations."

I pat her hand and pull free. "That's not how it'll work, Anna. I'm not staying here."

"Maybe."

I return to my cabin and pack a bag—change of clothes, food and water. That's it. Doesn't take long.

Owen tentatively knocks on my door and says, "Sir, may I ask what I'm supposed to do?"

"The *Amnesia* belongs to you, as far as I'm concerned, and all the money aboard. You and the other crew. Go wherever you please and start a new life and help rebuild civilization."

He smiles. "That's a tall order, sir."

"No kidding. I do have a request, though. And it's a big one. It'll take you weeks."

"Anything, sir. We owe you our lives."

I pat the bulkhead of the *Angel* with love and affection. I miss her already. "I need you and your yacht to deliver my boat to Los Angeles. Just in case."

Anna Elizabeth has a suitcase full of Pacific's luxurious clothing. I toss it the distance, where it lands with a thud in the sand next to mine. Owen escorts her to shore in the inflatable raft, where she steps into knee-deep ocean, her shoes in one fist, mine in the other, and walks up the sand. Owen returns. I jump into the lagoon, the surface at my neck.

He draws up the anchor, and from the water I slowly spin the *Angel* until she's pointed out to sea.

"Raise the foresail only," I tell Owen. He stands at the wheel, looking nervous. "You'll be fine. Keep her pointed at the yacht. The wind is behind you, so all will be well."

"If you say so, sir. You have my cell number?"

"I got it. Take care of her, Owen. And happy sailing."

"I will, and thank you, Master Jackson."

I turn and swim to shore, slow strokes, enjoying my final dip. There's no hurry. On the sand, I towel off and watch the *Angel* until Owen lowers the sails and attaches her to the yacht. A dull ache uncoils in my chest.

Anna says, "You're quite attached to that sailboat."

"The *Angel* saved my life in a lot of ways. Enough of my blood soaked into it that we're almost related. Being independent and autonomous, with no imperatives except from the weather, was healing."

She indicates the copse of pine trees behind us. "Where are we?"

"Your family lives in Jacksonville Beach. We're fifteen miles south." I pull my shirt on and slip feet into shoes. I pick up my satchel, dust it off, and drop it into her hands. "You carry mine, I'll carry yours."

"You want me to carry *luggage*?"

"Unless you'd prefer to leave yours here."

Hoisting her heavy bag onto my shoulder, I plunge into the woods, high-stepping through the undergrowth toward the road I hear just beyond. She hurries to catch up, smacking at the weeds.

"Should we call for a car?" she asks.

"Got a phone? Or money?"

"No, I was abducted, remember? Don't you?"

"It's only fifteen miles. We'll walk."

But even as I say it, my feet protest. The ground is *so* hard. So firm and unyielding, and I feel clumsy with no roll to anticipate.

We emerge onto a sleepy two-lane highway, cars move in the distance, both directions. Houses are visible to the north, shimmering in the morning sun. A jarring dichotomy, relying on sail power and feeding villages for months and months, and then suddenly walking into a fully functioning civilization with electricity.

"I know this place," says Anna with a cry. "This is Ponte Vedra Boulevard. We can follow it nearly all the way home."

I turn right and begin the trek. Anna is tall but has to hurry to keep up. The highway is well kept, and we're on a strip between beach towns. Sawgrass is maybe a mile ahead. The breeze comes from inland, bringing flying insects, the scent of cut lawns and hot tires, and humidity. Somehow, on the ocean and surrounded by water, the air never felt this thick with water.

"Isn't this surreal? The Outlaw walking up the coast of Florida! So exciting."

"I don't exist. Let's keep it that way."

Anna Elizabeth is beautiful, but in a soft, spoiled way. She's intelligent and has a good heart and she takes care of herself, but next to me she looks frail. Easily broken. And she pouts too much. After a few minutes she's breathing heavy. "Do you worry about being recognized?"

"No. People don't see what they aren't looking for."

"What did you read?" she asks after a burst to catch up. "On the boat, that made you decide to return?"

"A rumor."

"Which rumor? Maybe I could help? Me or my father."

"I could tell you," I say. "But then I'd have to kill you."

"Ha ha."

I grin but say no more.

"You can trust me, you know. We're on the same side."

"I'm a ghost. I'm not on a side."

"Yes you are," she says. "We both hate Blue-Eyes. That's why you returned. We're partners. I want to help."

"It's important you don't tell people who I am, Anna."

"It's Anna *Elizabeth*. That's my full first name."

"Not your parents. Not your friends. Not anyone."

She laughs. "So you'll just live in Jacksonville incognito? That's absurd."

"I'm not staying in Jacksonville."

"Wait until you meet my father. We need the Outlaw. And we can help you."

"I'm taking you home. Then I'm moving on. And no one can know I'm here. No one."

"You'll change your mind. Once you see how determined and committed we are," she says.

I don't respond.

She groans. "This is absurd. Have we even gone a mile? Why are we walking?"

"It's good for you. Builds strength, gives you time to think. I often regret my rushed decisions."

"Well." She sniffs. "I'm going to hitchhike. Get us a ride. The Outlaw shouldn't be walking fifteen miles. Neither should the daughter of Willard Washington."

"We're safe."

"Yes but this is beneath us."

She sticks out her thumb, begging for a ride. Over the next ten minutes, we're passed by five cars going either direction. None slow.

"This is absurd. If only they knew who we *are*. But I'm finished toying around." She's wearing a calf-length sundress taken from Pacific. She hitches it up and ties a knot, until the hem only reaches the middle of her thigh. The dress looks awkward but she's much more eye-catching.

"Think that'll work?"

"Of course, men are idiots," she says.

Sure enough, two minutes later a hybrid Chevy truck slows and the window buzzes down. The man leans across and says, "Ya'll need a lift?"

"Please," she replies prettily.

"I'll ride in the back," I say. "Let you two get acquainted."

Anna stutters, "You'll be in the back? But there's room in the cab."

The driver shakes his head. "Nah, might be tight." He leans over far enough to open the passenger door. "He'll be more comfortable back there. Hop in, pretty lady."

I grin. She glares.

Cheers and shouts erupt when Anna walks into her home in Jacksonville Beach. It's a modest brick ranch, swinging screen door, pool in the backyard, but it sounds like a dozen people are gathered inside. The lost daughter has been found.

I check the sun. A little past noon.

In my head, a clock ticks. Bringing the girl from China ever closer to Blue-Eyes. Now that my cargo has been safely delivered, I'm anxious to be off.

I set her luggage by the front door and move to the driveway, out of sight. Unfortunately I made a mistake—I let Anna Elizabeth take my satchel inside. I don't want to go in, because the family should celebrate without an intruder.

I really like that satchel, though. It was a gift to me from a tribe in the Bahamas, hand stitched, made from shark leather. Plus I need the supplies inside. Maybe I could sneak in...

My decision is taken away; an attractive woman rushes out, hands held toward me. Has to be her mother, a trim and lovely brunette. She looks as though she's normally dignified, when not weeping for joy.

"You! Was it you? You found her? My baby?" she cries. She takes my face in both her hands and kisses my forehead. "Thank you, thank you! Stars above, you're a tall man. I'm so very grateful for you." She cries into my shirt, hugging me.

"You're welcome. I was in the right place at the right time."

"No, no, the good Lord above arranged this. He can't save everyone, but he saved her. Plucked her out of the sea, because of my prayers." At least I think that's what she says. She's weeping pretty hard, getting my shirt wet. I only have three... "Look at me, I'm a mess. Come inside this instant."

"I can't stay, ma'am, I need—"

"Nonsense, don't be absurd. Have you eaten? We'll stuff you full of good southern cooking. Not that you need it, my stars, where'd you get all these muscles?" She pulls me into the house and I'm surrounded and embraced while Anna Elizabeth watches, her eyes shining.

This isn't ideal.

The extended family, which had gathered to pray for Anna Elizabeth's safety, finally begins dispersing near six that evening. I'm so full of sweet tea and fried chicken and peach cobbler that I can barely move. Easily the best I've eaten in two years. Maybe three.

I sit at the wooden table in the small dining room, listening to her aunts talk about the new world they live in, and I'm wondering if my belt buckle will hold. It's pleasant being around a family—reminds me of Katie and her mother. Anna's mother fawns over me, bringing more food, rubbing my shoulders, kissing my head. My temporary mom.

Anna lowers beside me and whispers into my ear, "Are you still threatening to leave soon?"

"I have to."

"When was your last hot shower?"

"I can never remember taking one. So it's been a while."

She says, "Use the shower in the master bedroom. I'll keep everyone out."

I'm ready to reject the idea, politely decline, but I can't. Truthfully that sounds like paradise. Do I have time for untold luxuries such as a shower?

"Go on," she says. "I'll launder your clothes."

"If you insist."

Turns out, the shower is a huge mistake. Because I may never leave. Possibly the best thirty minutes of my life. Clean warm water stridently jetting into my hair, all the soap I could ask for, intoxicating scents, billowing steam, suds swirling at my feet, no salt, pure bliss. The amount of gunk that comes out of my hair is shocking. I shave too, using a small mirror dangling from the shower head. Finally, I force myself to wrench off the water. I stay inside the stall another few minutes and then towel dry and dress.

I'm drowsy when I emerge. The lights are out in the master bedroom, my feet hurt from the hard earth, and there's a soft drone of air conditioning. I haven't slept well recently and exhaustion is accumulating.

"You'll stay in this room," says Anna Elizabeth. We're alone.

"Anna—"

"Just for one night. My father is gone and my mother insists. You're fatigued, I can tell. In the morning we'll make plans."

"I don't have time."

She brings in a chair and pats it. "Sit. I want to cut your hair."

"What a weirdo you are."

She laughs. "Your hair is too long. It's over your ears and in your eyes. I cut my father's frequently. After a trim you'll be much more presentable."

"I'm not being presented."

"Sit," she says.

For reasons I don't fully understand, I sit. She hums while she works, brushing my hair into place with her fingers. She ties a sheet around my neck to catch the clippings. Walks a circle around me twice, examining from all angles, and tells me to stop moving. For the sides, she uses electric clippers. But for the top she has those sharp silver scissors I remember barbers using when I was a kid. The room is dark, and her voice is pleasant, the snipping methodic, and hypnogogia threatens.

I'm drifting in and out of awareness but I catch the words, "I can't believe I'm cutting the Outlaw's hair."

"You're not. I'm just a fisherman."

"You're a fisherman who just gave away a hundred million dollar yacht?"

"Luxuries only slow us. Keep us from reaching our goals," I say.

"Was she right?"

"Was who right about what?"

She sets her tools down. Towels my hair again. Removes the sheet. And then she's in my lap, arms around my neck. "The woman on the boat, Minnie. She told me you don't return my affection."

Oh jeez. This is a fine trap I walked into. I don't know what to do with my hands so I pat her back. A friendly pat, I hope. "I can't, Anna."

"You want to be with me. I know you do."

"Our wants are luxuries. They only slow us—"

She kisses me. Even though I knew it was coming, even though it happened in slow motion, somehow I'm still unprepared.

Chase Jackson, big doofus.

She pulls back. Slow smile, inches apart. "Do you feel nothing?"

She's done everything right. The mood is set, I'm vulnerable, she's beautiful, this should have worked for her. Except that I'm still in love with Katie Lopez.

"I can't, Anna. You're trying to wake a man you think is sleeping, but he's not—he's dead inside. This won't work."

"Because of the blonde girl on the boat? Gwen."

"No, not because of Gwen. You're great, Anna Elizabeth. You're destined to be with someone who deserves you. And that isn't me."

She stands and uses her fingers to shake out nonexistent tangles in her hair. Has trouble meeting my eyes. "You're really going to leave? I thought it might be fate, you finding me in the water."

"Not all stories have happy endings."

She goes to the door. "We'll talk in the morning, after I've made you breakfast. You'll think more clearly after a good night's rest."

"I'm leaving now, Anna."

"Good night." She closes the door.

I get up. Go to the door. I leave the house and head north.

Or at least that's what I try to do.

But somehow I'm on the soft queen mattress.

Sleeping at sea is hit or miss. Mostly miss. I go days at a time without hitting an REM cycle. Occasionally I drop anchor in a sheltered cove and do my best to eliminate the sleep debt I've accrued. But this mattress is soft. The sheets don't smell like salt. The pillow is foam and new.

Just five minutes, I think...

...then I smile, and burrow deep under the blankets, and decide to indulge this once.

Someone softly enters the room the next morning. I'm already awake, having slept an astonishing eleven hours. An unimaginable gulf of time. The sun is about to rise. Normally I'd have a dozen tasks to run through on my boat.

A man at the doorway says, "You're up."

"I am. You're Willard Washington?"

"Yes. Anna Elizabeth told me who you are."

I don't reply.

He says, "For your safety, and for the safety of my family, it's time for you to leave."

"I agree."

"I have supplies for you. Meet me outside."

My clothes are folded at the foot of my bed. They're crisp and clean and smell like soap. I dress, repack my bag, and step into my sneakers.

The man is on the street. He's a tall, handsome guy, reminds me a little of Tom Hanks. Is that guy still around? Do people still make movies?

He shakes my hand. "I'm forever in your debt. Thank you for returning her."

"Who have you told about me?"

"No one. I figured that's your decision."

I nod. "Good. Let's keep it quiet."

He's standing next to a motorcycle and he pats the seat. "I've been pulling strings as fast as I can. This is for you."

I know enough about bikes to recognize a Honda Rebel, one of their street machines, made for cruising. It's a few years old. Black, red, and beautiful.

"There's money in the compartment, and a phone. It's the best I can do on short notice."

I shake his hand again, harder this time. "Mr. Washington, this is perfect. You're a life saver."

He winces and chuckles. "Never thought I'd be shaking your hand. Anna Elizabeth tells me you're out of touch with the world."

"She's right. I know very little."

"Well, here's one piece of information you might not know. Your sword, or staff, or bat, or whatever you want to call it—a private diver found it at the crash site. The Federal government tried to capture the staff but it was sold at a blackmarket auction first. It's out there. Somewhere."

I grin. The first time I've thought about the Thunder Stick in a long time. "Good. I've missed that thing."

"You should go, before you're recognized. I wish I could do more to help."

I get on the bike. "This is all I need, Mr. Washington. You're the best."

"You're headed into danger, aren't you."

"Afraid so."

"Good luck. My family will be praying for you."

"I'll take it." I pull on the helmet—it's made for street bikes and has a face shield. The engine roars, impossibly loud. I'm used to sail power.

He gives me a little salute and walks away.

Gasoline in my engine, adrenaline in my veins, ready to fly. The bike leaps forward, an accidental wheelie. I better relax.

I roll to the stop sign at the end of the street. Which way is north, I wonder...

What I don't know at the time, and what I find out later, is that Anna Elizabeth is awake. Hiding in the garage, spying on us. She's using a phone camera to record me, doing her best to keep her father out of the picture. She gets several seconds of my face before I don the helmet, and then the engine roar and wheelie. Perfectly preserved in her phone.

She whispers to the camera, "It's really him, can you believe it? He came back to save us. Do you like his hair cut? I did it myself."

Katie Lopez

"Carmine? Err, I mean, Katie?" says Sean. "We're ready to roll in five minutes." He's below me, standing in the tall grass, shading his eyes against the morning sun.

I'm sitting crisscross on the roof of my Land Cruiser, thinking.

Ready to roll. If only I knew which direction.

"Thank you, Sean."

"Everything okay up there?"

"Peachy," I say.

He grins. "Want company?"

"No. But thank you."

The Guardians are nearly done breaking camp, and they keep shooting glances my direction. They sense my anticipation. Something is happening, momentum building. I sense the potential energy, almost as if the substrata of the cosmos is tensing, creating ripples. Gears turn...somewhere. But I don't know where.

I hit play on the phone again and fast-forward a couple minutes. Kayla's voice, usually sugary and full of pep, sounds stressed.

"...so yeah," she says in the voicemail. "Tank's gone, and I know I keep saying that, and I know I'm talking too much, but...this is your city, Queen Carmine. It can't run forever without you. You fled to protect us from that bomb, which is *yikes*. You left so we could survive. So brave and heroic of you. And that has more or less worked for two years, but I feel like our time has run out. And also...Mason get your hand *off* me..." Kayla snaps, her mouth removed from the receiver, and I smile. I've missed Mason, the leader of the Falcons. "Sorry about that. Stupid boys. Anyway, we need you back, I think, and we'll figure out solutions to the other problems. Because, truly, Carmine, for real, I don't know what I'm doing and I'm totally *sick* of the Governess. Plus I super duper miss you. Okay, I've talked too much. A million hugs and infinity kisses and please text me to let me know you're alive! Kay byeeee!"

I lower the phone.

Figure out solutions to the other problems, she said. But a nuclear bomb is a massive problem that can't be easily solved. Its payload could wipe out half of Los Angeles, and the other half would be forced to evacuate. But evacuate to where?

I bounce the phone on my lips, thinking. Tank is chasing the wolf man into the desert, she says. But why? And to where? Those two have some kind of pull over the animals and other Variants, and the moving herds of mania are probably what's got everyone so excited.

A funny coincidence. If the wolf man, and Tank, and Andy Babington all maintain their current trajectories, based on what I gather, they'll come close to intersecting in southern Nevada.

That's not funny, actually, that's terrifying.

I'm staring southwest. Towards Los Angeles. Could it be time to go home? Or would that wrench the universe farther into chaos? I'm a double-edged sword, bringing both peace and mayhem. Saul the Zealot told me once that I could help the world most by staying out of it. I'm starting to believe he's correct. For the most part. But maybe not in every situation.

Wish he was still around. I could use the counsel.

Kayla wrung the scantest of details about Saul's death from Tank —only that Walter was involved, and it affected Tank deeply; he refused to divulge more. But Kayla tells me the animals began flocking to him immediately following the Zealot's mysterious demise, so that's related somehow.

So much I don't know.

I unfold from my sitting position and stand on the roof. All eyes swivel my direction—the Queen stirs. I can't pry my gaze from the southwest horizon. My decision's made, I think.

"We're going home," I announce and there's a smattering of applause. Los Angeles isn't everyone's home, I guess. But they'll love it, and it'll be their home soon.

I'm about to hop down when my phone beeps. Incoming text messages. From PuckDaddy.

>> AAAAAAAAAAAAAAAAAAAAAA

>> KATIEKATIEKATIEKATIEKATIE

>> AAAAAAHHHHHHHHH!!!!!!!

>> WHATWHATWHATWHAT!!

Then more messages, these from Kayla.

>> OMGOMGOMGOMG! Are you seeing this??

>> Carmine, sweet wonderful woman, turn ON your phone!

What on earth is happening?

>> He's back, he's back!!!!!

>> Did you

>> I don't even

>> I think I might be dying

>> I'm so happy that my wax candles are melting!!!!!!

>>ASFHGGGGGUUUHHHEEEEE!!!!!!!!

Puck texts again. He's sending me a video.

Good grief, Puck and Kayla are excitable people naturally, but this seems excessive.

>> WATCH WATCH WATCH WATCH!!!

I click the link. It's YouTube. The video registers ten million views. While I stare at the number, it jumps to eleven million. Then thirteen.

I press play.

A guy straddles his motorcycle, pulls on a helmet, revs the engine, and drives away. Twenty seconds long. It ends with a girl whispering. I can't hear her well, something about a haircut.

So? What's the big deal?

The guy's handsome, I admit. Thick head of dark hair, good tan, broad shoulders. Outrageously good body, now that I look again. His blue linen shirtsleeves are rolled up to the elbows, tattoos glint on his arm...

My hand trembles. My biological architecture registers something my mind can't allow.

I hit play again.

And again.

And again. Thumb up the volume.

My screen begins shaking so badly I can barely make out the blue of his eyes. I feel as though I'm being electrocuted. Hot and cold waves radiate from my core.

More incoming text messages. I ignore them.

What am I seeing...?

What am...

How...

When was...?

Dated yesterday.

Teardrops dot my screen.

The girl whispers through my speaker: "It's really him, can you believe it? He's come back to save us."

My emotions are soaked up by the other Variants. An odd noise, similar to a hum, rises from their throats.

More phones beep and buzz around the camp. Like the whole world is wakening to the news.

I try to press play again. Can't. My fingers have mutinied.

The phone slips out of my hand, bounces off the hood.

I scream. Loud enough to blow out the windows of my Land Cruiser. A sound heard for miles.

Loud enough to wake the dead.

The Outlaw

I'm not great with directions and I'm unfamiliar with the East Coast. I take a wrong turn in Savannah, end up in Atlanta, and find my way onto I-81 north. I soon realize the trip, which should have taken twelve hours, will require fifteen. Maybe twenty, because traffic clots the roads and I refuse to speed. Explaining myself to a police officer would be a mess.

I grin. Police officers and speeding tickets. What a world.

I reach Roanoke, Virginia near midnight. A draining day and I can't drive a mile further. I'm exhausted and my butt's sore; a sailboat requires near constant movement, exactly opposite a motorcycle. I had the radio pumping music into my helmet but it sounded like noise, everyone constantly breaking up or falling in love, and I'm done with it.

Roanoke is a charming city. Despite a receding economy, this city flourishes due to it's concentration of medicine and higher education. Hotel Roanoke refuses to give me a room because I don't have identification. So suspicious, these Virginians. The kind receptionist at the Hampton Inn downtown takes pity on me, because I pay the deposit in cash. Also I get the distinct impression she's taken with me, which might have something to do with it. Two years of hard work at sea under the Caribbean sun potentially does wonders for one's love life. I ring for room service and she personally delivers it with a smile. I thank her, take the food, and shut the door again.

I eat a hamburger with bacon and cheddar cheese, plus fries. So delicious I come close to crying. Also a Sprite and a beer. I'm twenty-one, so why not? My father drank beer, and possibly still does. He let me try his occasionally, a lifetime ago.

I sip the beer and spit the foul brew into the sink.

Nope—still gross.

The Sprite on the other hand, I might order a dozen more.

A foam mattress, clean sheets, food delivered to my door, air conditioning, abundant electricity, and a television. It's like I leapt forward in time to a period when people are allowed to grow soft and fat. It's the best. And the worst.

I try a few channels and only find cooking shows, carpenters repairing houses, women with smart phones screaming at each other. This is entertainment now? No thanks.

I set the alarm clock—an alarm clock!—and flip off the lights. I only need four hours. I don't have time for more. Who knows when the girl from China will be captured and delivered to Blue-Eyes. So I need to get there soon.

I remember hearing about the girl from Carter and Puck. We called her China, and none of us knew much about her. We knew she was a genius, a brain on par with Nuts or Puck but geared toward medicine. What kind of cure has she found, I wonder. And how would it be administered?

Several species of mutant roam the earth today. Four subgroups.

First, mutants like me, either born with the Hyper Virus or injected at birth. Carter, Blue-Eyes, China, Tank, Samantha Gear, Saul the Zealot, PuckDaddy, Nuts...? Could that be it? So many have already died. Maybe more, now.

Second, there are mutants like Kayla and Mason. High functioning and powerful. Katie was like this, except she was the strongest. The strongest *and* the most intelligent. The most kind. The most brave. The most beautiful...

I can't think about her long, even still.

Third, mutants with broken minds living in a community, like many of the Variants living in Los Angeles. They function, but not well. They've attached themselves to an Alpha, like Katie or Tank. Or, unfortunately, Walter. The Alpha helps them stabilize.

Finally there are mutants in the wild, terrorizing the midwest. No sanity in sight. Like Andy Babington or Hannah the Cheerleader.

Could the cure heal all of us? Only some? Would the Witch use the cure to reduce the strength of her enemies? Would she try to replicate it? Improve upon it?

The most likely answer is she seeks to destroy it.

Something I refuse to let happen.

I'm staring at my phone as I begin to drift.

Sooner or later, I need to contact Puck.

That'll be a weird conversation...

The alarm clock is wailing.

Someone's knocking at my door.

This early? I sit up. Groggy. Sleeping on a boat, I'm usually alert even in repose. Something about a mattress, though, sends me far under.

Who needs me this early? It's only—I check the clock—it's only...

Two in the afternoon!

I slept *twelve* hours? It was supposed to be four!

I'm no longer a sailor, I'm a landlubber. That happened fast. I'm off mission, succumbing to the temptations of a luxurious life.

I leap out of bed and smack the snooze button. The top of the cheap box breaks, shards flying. Dang it.

"One sec," I call. So bizarre, feeling rushed and shamed by the knocking of some hotel employee. Use the bathroom, change my clothes, pack my bag, tie my shoes, throw open the door.

"Yes sir, sorry to bother you, but..." He pauses, clearly caught off guard. I tower over him. His shoulders droop and he's overweight and pasty. Probably good at video games, though. He clears his throat and adjusts his glasses. "Um, yes, I hope I didn't wake you. Sir."

I pat him on the shoulder. He staggers to the side. "I'm glad you did. I meant to be gone eight hours ago. Leaving now."

"There's no hurry, sir." He clears his throat again and pulls at his tie. Looks like he wants to say more but doesn't.

I say, "In fact there is. I'm off."

"Be sure to check out at the desk, s-sir," he says, faltering slightly when I glance at him.

"You bet."

I take the elevator down—the elevator!—and stop at the bar. Need some food. No time for a leisurely lunch, will eat on the road.

The bartender takes a second glance at me and she says, "Look at you. Just get back from vacation?"

"Kinda, yeah. Can I get a hamburger and fries?"

"Absolutely." She slides a plate of peanuts across the polished surface. "You wanna to try the club sandwich, hon? Our burger isn't very good, my opinion."

"Are you kidding? Your burger tastes like it came from a golden cow, bred and raised for no reason other than to make me supremely happy," I say.

"Wow, okay." She smiles. "One burger, coming up. Anything to drink, sugar?"

"Sprite. Please."

She sets it in front of me, points to the television above the bar and says, "You seen this yet? Crazy, huh?" and moves to help another patron.

I eat a handful of peanuts and drain half the soda. Corn syrup and carbonation! What a combo. Glance at the television, tuned to CNN.

I try to make sense of the headline.

Eat another handful of peanuts...

...and I spill my Sprite across the bar.

"Oh crud," I say, staring at the TV screen.

That's me. Sitting on my bike. A homemade video, playing over and over. The news anchors are delirious. No. No no no no.

I smack a twenty dollar bill on the bar and I run.

Has to be Anna Elizabeth. No one else was close, or at least not that I saw. She recorded me on the bike and somehow the video got out. Or maybe she published it intentionally? Either way, my element of surprise has evaporated.

I fill up my gas tank at exit 283. Twenty-five dollars a gallon. I walk nonchalantly into the gas station to pay with cash, keeping my helmet on. Do people know what I look like? I forget how this works. I purchase a pack of almond M&Ms and beef jerky.

I'm approximately an hour outside Washington D.C. The whole world is talking about the Outlaw. Every channel on the radio. I'm the hot button issue of the day. This would've been easier if I could've busted my way into the Oval Office unannounced.

I veer onto I-66 East as ESPN Radio announces the Outlaw's bike has been spotted headed north on I-81. Rewards are offered for more information. My bike is described, as is my helmet. The descriptions are close enough to make me nervous. Am I being watched right now?

Being on land is hard.

Helicopters lift off like fireflies on the horizon ahead. Television stations and law enforcement. Police cruisers surge onto the interstate with increasing numbers, and it won't be long before I'm spotted—in my ear, the radio keeps relaying the color of my bike, and they offer potential license plate numbers. Chaos accelerates around me.

I swerve onto an exit ramp at Front Royal and strike gold. There's a small car dealership half a mile off the interstate and they have used motorcycles. I cut into the parking lot, braking hard enough to leave a trail of rubber, and I hop off. A clock ticks in my head—I should've been in Washington hours ago.

A muscular man with tattoos on his arms and hands comes out to greet me. His head is shaved.

"I need a bike. In a hurry," I tell him, pulling off my helmet. "I'll give you mine and all the cash I got. Unorthodox, I know."

I'd rather not forcibly steal one, but my options are limited. I don't have time for paperwork or registration or however people purchase automobiles these days.

He regards me, silent and cool. There's an unbearably long pause before he saunters into the glass offices. He's gone a couple minutes. When he comes back, he tosses me a black helmet and a key. Nods at a couple used motorcycles in the grass.

"Take the Yamaha," he says and spits tobacco juice onto the pavement. "The blue YZF-R3. It ain't super powerful but it's light and quick."

"Perfect. How much?"

"Keep your money, Outlaw," he says. "Just glad you're alive. I'll report this bike stolen in a couple days time. Not all of us support the blue-eyed bitch."

Wow.

I say, "I don't want you to get in trouble. We can work a deal—"

He nods toward the interstate. "Get on, boy. Still got fifty miles to Washington. You were never here." He turns to go but calls over his shoulder. "Give my regards to the President."

How about that. Being the Outlaw isn't all bad.

Sixty seconds later, I'm on the interstate again and howling east on a different motorcycle, new license plate, and updated color palette. Anger and adrenaline surge like fever.

The interstates thicken with congestion. The closer I get the slower we go, so I jump into the narrow shoulder between the HOV lane and the barriers. The other cars slow to ten miles per hour but I rev it up to seventy. If someone opens their car door, I'm toast.

The nation's capital is in a frenzy, according to the radio. Could the video of the Outlaw be real? Certainly not. Experts disagree on the validity. And even if it *is* the Outlaw, when was the video taken? Who knows. Could be years ago. Besides, there's no way he could get close to the White House.

The Secret Service is scrambling and every branch of the military gears up—just in case. All for a dead man. Motorcycles are being pulled over, and police barricade the bridges over the Potomac River, but not quick enough. I zip over an HOV interchange and race against traffic—they don't see me coming. I fly across Francis Case Memorial on 395 as workers try manhandling the concrete roadblocks. I streak past their lines and the officers wave their arms and shout. In my side mirror I see them run for their cars, calling into shoulder radios.

Man on bike broke our perimeter, they'll say.

The Outlaw is here, they'll say.

The Outlaw is here indeed. And he's getting angrier by the second. The President's security detail will force her to leave town now. My time runs short.

Red and blue flash behind. More sirens on either side. Feels like the entire world contracts around me, like a noose.

I haven't missed this.

Well, maybe a little.

I know nothing about Washington, D.C. How do I find the White House in this neoclassical labyrinth? It's not a tall building, I know that much. I grind my teeth, swerve around a police horse, and cut north on 12th, nearly destroying a pod of Segway tourists. In my mind's eye, they're wheeling the President toward the Lawn, Marine One inbound and thundering.

There! I know that landmark—the National Mall. A beautiful green field stretching a dozen city blocks. The White House is attached to it, somehow. I think.

Sirens everywhere. At least six helicopters swooping overhead. Can't concentrate. My breath sounds harsh in the helmet.

I jump the curb and jet onto the National Mall, weaving between citizens throwing frisbees and sitting on blankets. My motorcycle is loud and people scream. Others raise their phones to record me.

Which way? Maybe there's still time, but all these government buildings look identical. I need to pick a direction. To the west, the Washington Monument rises stately and thin against the weak blue sky. I gun the engine, rear tire chewing the grass, and aim for the Monument as police cars flood the walkways. They can't follow well because of the pedestrians and potential collateral damage.

The Washington Monument has been defaced. I know enough to realize it doesn't look like the pictures in my history book. A face stares out from all four sides. It's a portrait of Blue-Eyes, etched into the stone. A monument to herself. Cobalt glitters from the irises. She has no shame.

I reach the Monument and follow the Lawn as it turns north.

Bingo! The White House, dead ahead.

I cross Constitution Avenue at sixty miles per hour, nearly

unseated by the jarring collision with the curbs. Hit eighty on the speedometer racing across The Ellipse.

Eighty-five.

Ninety. Engine screaming.

The Secret Service is ready at the black iron fence surrounding the President's Park and Southern Lawn. They kneel behind concrete barriers and bristle with firepower. While I, on the other hand, don't have a single gun. Not any form of defense.

The White House looks grotesque. She's adding floors to the eastern wing, and the trim throughout is painted navy.

Power corrupts. And Blue-Eyes has power overwhelming.

Her guards beyond the barriers open fire. Bright flashes.

My adrenaline is pumping, annealing my skin, slowing the world. I lay the bike down in the turf before reaching E Street. A spectacular eruption of dirt and grass. Looks like I crashed going a hundred miles per hour. Solid diversion.

Everything happens in freeze-frame bursts.

I roll once, twice, across the grass and sidewalk. My helmet is painfully wrenched off, but I decelerate enough to give my feet purchase on the earth. I come out of the tumble sprinting at forty miles per hour. The agents still gape at the tumbling bike and cloud of dirt. I *Leap* over, soaring thirty feet above their heads, moving so quick at least half never see me.

I was right—Marine One crouches on the Southern Lawn, blades churning, shattering nearby plants. It's a Sikorsky White Top. The ramp is down and men with pistols aim at me. My eyes sharpen.

Blue-Eyes.

She's sitting in her wheelchair at the open hatch. Smiling.

Massive doberman pinschers are released from their heavy chains. The canines are the size of brown bears, thick with muscle and they run like Formula One cars. Teeth like cages, barks like gun blasts.

What fresh hell is this? Chernobyl fever dreams. Other creations of the Chemist, like Carmine's tigers were?

I need a weapon.

The Sikorsky tries to throw itself into the ether but it's a heavy machine. It labors upward, too slow. And I move like a lightening strike.

Her inner sentries yank their triggers. Gunpowder bursts, and I watch the incoming bullets. A dog is shot by accident but it doesn't notice.

I *Jump* and vault the dogs and the first volley of bullets. My second jump propels me into the sky.

I connect solidly with the outside of the green chopper. The aircraft rings as if struck. There's no landing struts so my shoes kick wildly, looking for footholds, forty feet in the air. The White House swings dizzily underneath.

Nothing to hold onto. The ramp has retracted but the hatch is open. Before I fall, I get my fingertips inside. Dig them into the metal.

I'm dangling, with a view of the chopper's belly. Inside the cabin, people scream. The helicopter banks sharply to the north.

I haul myself up. Get my chin over the edge of the helicopter's floor.

Blue-Eyes and I meet face to face. She flung herself to the floor, crawling as close as possible—our noses literally touch. Before I know what's happening, she kisses my lips. A playful, cruel tease. Her guards grasp her feet. She's perfect; lovely and appealing, as though I'm mesmerized by a golden dawn. Heart-shaped face, lurid eyes like eternity. Her exotic essence goes straight into my nose, my pores, my ears.

"Hello, beautiful boy. Such a display of bravura, such a leap. I'm so glad you're alive," she says with a sigh and my heart nearly shatters. "For a few more precious seconds."

No...can't listen...

I yank the fingers of my right hand out of the dented metal and reach for her, but the helicopter twirls madly. The force throws me to the side and I can't reach. The pilot watches me through the port window, spinning his aircraft, trying to throw me off. The wind is a hurricane around my ears.

"Give me your hand," I shout. To both our astonishment, she

starts to obey. Her hand stretches my way before she catches herself.

"Well, well," she coos over the noise. "Look who's gotten stronger." Her blonde hair whips in the wash. If only I could grab it, I'd pull her out with me. She kisses my hand, the one still clinging desperately to the metal. "A shame. I'd like to have you for a plaything. Anyway, goodbye again. Now, if you will please—"

I growl, "No," and I grip tighter and try to find another place to hold. I'm so close!

"—*let go.*"

My body responds to her demand. My fingers release and suddenly I'm falling.

"No!"

Marine One hurls upwards and I drop. Free falling for several seconds, as from the tip of a parabola, a sudden quiet after the screaming turbines in my ears. I can't even think about landing safely, so outraged and furious I am at missing her.

I crash into the rooftop of the West Colonnade of the White House, nearly puncturing through. The layers of insulation and substructure don't exactly break my fall, but they do prevent significant injury. For a moment I don't move, sitting up to my shoulders and knees in the crater I created.

Marine One is already vanishing to the north.

There's a Secret Serviceman on the roof with me. Separated from the whomp and wind of the rotors, the world feels small and silent, like he and I are alone. He's wearing body armor and holds an assault rifle. Just a kid, maybe twenty-five, never seen combat. He watches me warily as I groan and climb out, checking for broken ribs.

"This is a little awkward, huh," I tell him, brushing debris off my pants and grunting because moving hurts. "Because I tried to kill your boss."

He doesn't reply. He's listening to radio traffic in his earpiece.

I say, "Sorry about the roof. Nice view up here, though. Never stood on the White House before. That's the Capital Building, right? The big white one? You ever been there? This is my first time in Washington."

"Can't believe you're alive, sir."

I shoot him a thumbs-up. Which hurts. "Right? I'm like Rambo."

"I'm supposed to subdue or eliminate you."

"Give it a shot."

"Nah. I'm from Los Angeles."

"No kidding. Which part?"

He straightens. Listens to his ear piece and then salutes me. "You need to go, sir. Missiles inbound."

"At the White House?"

"President's orders. Good luck, Mr. Outlaw." He jumps over the parapet and lands in a shrub below. Takes off running with a slight limp.

Is she really about to demolish the White House? I can't believe it.

The Apache over the President's Park opens fire, and another levels to the east. The first salvo erupts into the South Portico, and the entire residence shudders and jumps upward. Fire and noise blossom at my feet.

The second salvo shatters the press room offices, chasing me onto the West Wing. I *Leap* the distance to the roof of the Eisenhower Executive Office Building, a hulking and dark structure with columns everywhere. The Apaches have only been ordered to destroy the White House, because the rockets don't follow me, but snipers do. Angry whining bullets snap past as I *Sprint* south.

My phone is in my hand. My thumb punches a number from muscle memory.

A familiar voice picks up.

He says, "You reached the baddest man on the whole damn planet. How can PuckDaddy save your life today, you big dummy?"

"Puck!" I shout, *Leaping* across 17th and landing on a bank. "Get me out of here! I need directions!"

"PuckDaddy's got you, homie," he says. "Head east, gonna get you into the metro. Trust me, a million places to hide down there. Also, now ain't the time, I know that, but Puck's kinda in his feelings about you being alive and all, so prepare for me to kick your ass soon as possible."

- 6 -
Katie Lopez

We make good time and reach Las Vegas by nightfall.

Sean drives. I sit in the passenger seat, wildly out of character for me. Although I am Katie Lopez, girl from Los Angeles, lover of books and flowers, I carry with me vestiges of Carmine and she hates riding shotgun. But I can't tear my eyes off my phone.

The boy I love is alive.

He died two years ago—I even held a funeral for him, burying one of his t-shirts to force myself to let go. I said goodbye a thousand times until I started to believe it...

And now I'm watching video of him leap buildings. Video captured earlier today.

Today!

I press the sleeve of my shirt against my eyes once more. I cry and I smile and I laugh, and I hit play again on the video from Fox News. He is riding a motorcycle across the National Mall, *such* a Chase Jackson thing to do. He is *Leaping* onto the White House Lawn, and then dangling from a helicopter. According to PuckDaddy, he came within inches of killing the Witch. He is jumping buildings and then vanishing underground.

He is amazing, the boy I love.

But he's not a boy, not really. He's a man. He is thunder and lightening, a hurricane and a whisper, unable to be caught by thousands of soldiers in the city. Boyhood was wrenched from him too soon, turning him into the battering ram he is today.

Sean gives me the gifts of silence and privacy, not asking questions even when I came close to hyperventilating earlier. He squeezes my hand or shoulder and keeps us on the road.

I text Puck, **Where is he now?**

>> **rrrrrgh, Katie, stop asking questions**

>> **hes undground, sneaking through the metro**

>> **hes exhausted. running super low on calories**

I *want* to ask questions. A hundred million of them, but I don't. Instead I bring up the audio file Puck sent me. A voice easily identifiable as Chase's bursts through:

"Puck! Get me out of here! I need directions!"

I laugh and start crying again. It's Chase but he's altered. The boyish tease is gone from his voice, replaced with fury. Puck is saying, *"so prepare for me to kick your ass soon as possible."*

"Copy that. Looking forward to it. Now where?"

"Go north on, uhh, ummmm...go north onnnnn..."

"Puck! People are shooting at me!"

"Well whose fault is that? Not PuckDaddy's! Go north on 18th. I'm trying to get you into the metro."

"But I don't wanna go underground."

"Why not?" asks PuckDaddy.

"It's dark and scary under there."

"Are you kidding?"

"No. What's funny about that?"

"You're the Outlaw, dude. You're afraid of the metro?"

"I haven't been underground in...hang on," says Chase, and then I hear noises like combat, except he keeps apologizing. I grin, picturing him disarming and pulverizing his enemies and telling them he's sorry for it. He comes back, panting, and says, *"I haven't been underground in years."*

"For real?"

"For real."

"Where you been, homie?"

"On a...hang on, sorry! Sorry about that! Maybe your insurance will cover it? ...okay, I'm back. I've been on a boat. I see the metro. Farragut Station?"

"A boat? But we thought you were dead! You could have called any time?"

"Focus, Puck."

"Okay okay, fine. Our connection is about to get real bad, so I'll send text directions. Head below and run into the tunnel. You'll take the orange line west. Got it?"

"This sucks."

"Then maybe call ahead next time and we can plan better!"

The audio file comes to the end.

I'm still grinning. Too many tears to wipe.

I'm a mess.

I text Puck, **He needs to eat. Find him food!**

How's he feeling?

Is he hurt?

>> carmine

>> or katie, or whoever u r...

>> the almighty puckdaddy is busy

>> AND HE DOESNT HAVE UR ANSWERS AT THE MOMENT!

Does Chase know I'm alive?

>> we haven't discussed

>> now isn't the time

>> but I get the feeling he doesn't know

TELL HIM, TELL HIM, TELL HIM!!

>> no no no!!

I groan, frustrated, but Puck's right. If he's running for his life, that bombshell needs to wait.

Keep him safe, Puck. Don't let him get caught.

Using my phone's browser, I switch to CNN's coverage to see if they have any video I haven't watched a hundred times.

My goodness, those are big dogs. How's she doing *that*?

"Katie?" Sean says quietly. "We're here."

I look up from my screen and blink. Remember where I am.

We left the desiccated scrubland behind and moved into the torched husk that used to be the neighborhoods to the north of the Las Vegas strip. By now we should see the glittering towers and casinos once famous around the world, but instead the horizon is flat and dark. The city and suburbs are entirely gone, burned to a crisp.

"Don't go any closer," I say. "There are wild Variants and mercenaries and Herders downtown, and I can't deal with them tonight. Find a place to park here."

"Got it," he says. He finds a golf course called the Arroyo Golf Club, long since abandoned but perfect for our needs. Our caravan circles up on the brown overgrown fairway of the 6th hole. Despite the dark, we kill the lights—most of us see fine without aid. My coterie stretches their legs, stiff and irritable after the long day's travel, and they prowl the surrounding area, probing our campsite with their senses.

We have enough water for two more days, so Renee informs me. We'll run out of gasoline tomorrow but should coast the remainder on battery/solar power, reaching Los Angeles around dinner. My home.

We recline car seats, sling hammocks between trees, and lay out inflatable mattresses on the scrubby dry grass. I arrange sentry schedules. The Variants gather and talk quietly, stealing glances my way. The news has reached us all; the Outlaw lives. What will the Queen do?

Cry some more, probably. Hopefully not shatter stuff with my voice.

I'm pacing the perimeter of our camp when I pinpoint what's been nagging at me since we arrived—someone else is here. I catch a scent on the wind. Nearby. Not deodorant or cologne, no smell an ordinary human might detect. It's the disease I smell, coming from a powerful and pungent source. Before I know it, my feet turn and I'm striding into the dark, away from our campsite.

My two tigers do not travel in close proximity to our caravan, yet somehow they appear nearby each evening. Tonight they materialize a quarter mile from camp, ghostly guardians watching me curiously. Concern shines in their eyes—*where do you go?*

I smile. "Going for a walk. Stay here."

They pad closer and push against my head with theirs. The gesture is affectionate and playful but they nearly knock me over. I scratch the tough skin under their jaws and behind their ears, causing them to emit a rhythmic chuffing. Not only do their foreheads press against me, so does some part of their inner spirit. They seek connection.

"Sleep," I say after a good long scratching session. "Stay here and rest."

Silently they pad into the remains of a nearby house, searching for shelter and a comfortable place to lay.

I leave roads behind and hike the dirt. The dry land rises fast, headed toward peaks to the west. This is an ugly arid wasteland; how the heck did Las Vegas spring up here? Red sandstone spires thrust organically from the earth, the only interesting features in sight for miles. Each step I take issues a crunch from brittle rock; the thin crust of the earth breaking into sand. The plants, looking sick and brown, cannot grow high. Has rain ever fallen on this soil?

After several miles I crest a rise and discover a makeshift camp in the vast valley below. Much larger than mine. A dozen pale red fires flicker, but I see no vehicles. Most of the bodies glow green to my eyes. Not a vibrant electric color, more like a festering haze under their epidermis. Bioluminescent Variants. But I see more. I see giants, and what looks like a herd of...something. No, not a single herd, rather multiple herds. Thousands of animals. Maybe tens of thousands. Deer and foxes and mountain lions and...jeez, everything else too, eddying through the camp.

My eyes zero in on a road sign a half mile away—The Calico Basin.

Despite the distance, I'm detected before long. Not by the animals, but by the mutants. They stand and stare, even the giants. I know what's about to happen so I sit down and wait. I'm too tired for this but it's inevitable.

Soon enough the camp's leader emerges and makes his way up the side of the hill. The hike takes him ten minutes. The land is so dry that he slips and slides through several minor avalanches. Finally Tank Ware himself stands over me, blocking out the stars.

"I knew you were alive," he grumbles, so deep I'm surprised there's not another flood of rocks tumbling down the side. I've long held a soft spot for Tank, the angry giant with a bruised heart. Not even his disfigured face changes that. He says, "Never bought the lie that Russia killed you."

"Hello Tank."

"Don't 'Hello Tank' me. Where the hell you been?"

"Running for my life," I say. "And for yours."

"Shoulda told me. I could help."

"Not with this."

"With Andy Babington?" He makes a scoffing noise. "He's a quarterback. That's what I do, kill the QB."

"He's got a nuke, Tank."

"I heard. You think I wouldn't die to keep you safe?"

I'm caught off guard. That's a bold claim from a man whose modus operandi is usually causing problems. "Would you?"

He doesn't respond. He turns and waves his hand at the valley below. Rabbits and squirrels have begun to scamper the hill, staying near Tank. "Look what you stuck me with. A frickin' zoo. Not to mention Kayla, the craziest of them all."

"I'm going to Los Angeles tomorrow. Please come back," I say. "We need your allegiance. This war isn't over."

"No kidding. Why do you think I'm out here?"

"Running away?"

"Don't assume the worst about me. Not after what I've sacrificed. For you. I'm chasing him. He's not far."

"The wolf man?"

"Yeah. The wolf man," he says.

"Has it occurred to you he's headed to the desert to draw you out of Los Angeles? He knew you'd chase him, so the kingdom is left largely unprotected?"

He stiffens. Clearly he hadn't considered it.

"What is it with you two?" I ask. "Where does this bizarre connection come from?"

"Got no idea."

"The animals, right? It's gotta be. Kayla told me you collect them now."

"*Collect* the animals? Hah. I hate'em. Can't make them stop following." He lowers next to me, close enough that our shoulders touch. Well, not exactly. My shoulder touches his elbow. He's *so* big.

"Good to eat, though. They'll start dying tomorrow if they don't find water. Not my fault, I didn't ask them to tag along."

"Head downtown," I say. "Or what used to be downtown. Vegas still has residents so they're getting water somewhere. I see no reason the pipelines would have ceased diverting water from Lake Mead. It's not like the Colorado River quit flowing."

"Colorado river. Lake Mead. How do you know that crap?"

I shrug. "I'm kinda a nerd. Valedictorian and all."

He glares at me suspiciously. His ruined eye socket forms a gruesome visage. "That you in there, Katie? Or still Carmine?"

"It's me. Carmine's here too but I took the wheel."

"Good. Carmine got on my nerves," he says. We sit quietly a minute, lost in thoughts and watching his circus below. "She's kinda hot, though."

I laugh, a rich surprised sound that Carmine never made. "Heck yeah she is. A Los Angeles nine, in my opinion."

"No way, babe. You're a ten across the planet." He elbows me and my cheeks burn. "Your hair's long again."

"About time. Only took three years."

"I was gonna bring you here," he says, and he indicates Las Vegas by jerking his chin over his shoulder. "Back when we were together."

"No you weren't. That wouldn't have advanced your football career or your criminal enterprise. You weren't exactly overflowing with devotion back then."

"Just wasn't good at showing it. I'd never been with a girl I respected more than myself. My family owned a condo here—"

"Of course they did."

"—and we coulda spent weekends at a casino."

I grin. "Shows how little you know me. I'd rather read books on the beach. But I think those days are gone."

"Maybe not. Maybe...maybe..." He hugs me suddenly. Only then do I realize he's dealing with waves of sorrow. Still waters run deep, and even dragons have emotions. I pat his arm. This close, the disease in his body is like a musk. His voice comes out tight and thick. "I'd do it different, you know. If I could."

"What do you mean?"

"This, all this damn mess," he says. He stops to sniff and wipe his eyes. "Part of it's my fault. I know it."

"It's the fault of everyone. We let medicine grow unchecked. The Infected pure-borns hid maniacs like the Chemist for too long. The people still refuse to stand up to Blue-Eyes. Our weapons of war are too deadly. The countries don't cooperate. It's on all of us."

"Look what we did, though. Someday I can't believe it. Wasn't long ago you and I were in my truck, ready to graduate, and now... what the hell happened?" He wipes his eyes again and clears his throat. "Monsters like me...made it worse. Sometimes when I think about how horrible reality is now, I can't sleep."

He doesn't know Chase is alive. The big oaf didn't think about things like electricity for his phone when he left Los Angeles, so he hasn't seen the news. He's out here running on instinct, blind to the world. Where Chase is a focused battering ram, Tank is a wild wrecking ball banging around unchecked.

I give his hand a squeeze. "There's still hope."

"Damn right there is. That's what I'm doing."

"Tell me, Tank. What are you doing? I don't get it."

"I can't sit in Los Angeles one more day. It's about to kill me," he says, and I understand. It's the Hyper Virus and the oceans of adrenaline. To be honest, now that I consider it, I'm surprised he stayed as long as he did. "Can't live with myself, can't live with the guilt. I gotta help fix things."

"The guilt? What do you mean?"

"That old man, the Zealot. Fool saved my life."

"How?"

"Doesn't matter. Said some weird crap, like he bought my soul for good."

I smile and squeeze his hand again. "Did he say you no longer belong to evil, but to good? That he bought your soul and gives it to God?"

"Yeah, that's it. Bizarre, right?"

"Not bizarre. He's quoting one of my favorite books."

He shrugs. "Whatever. It's like he cast a spell on me. I feel things now."

"What kind of things?"

"I dunno. Weird-ass stuff. Right now, it's like the world is speeding up. I feel like we're in a car, all of us, and we're going fast as hell, faster and faster, right? But I can tell, I *feel* it, we're about to crash."

My skin prickles and I shudder. His words terrify me, because I've felt the same augurs. Like the Almighty is preternaturally warning us. I keep my mouth clamped shut for the moment.

"We're about to crash," he says again. "And a lot of us are going to die. And I feel like I need to do more. Something good. For once in my life. Before it's over."

"You've done good, Tank. You tried to save me from Pacific and Walter."

"That was pure selfishness. I love you and didn't want you to die yet. Nor did I want Pajamas to have you," he says. "I gotta do this. There are millions of people trapped in Oregon and Washington state. Hostages of Walter and the wolf man. If I help them, if I get rid of the wolf man, my debts are paid. The old man didn't die for nothing. Maybe the animals will quit following me, and I can die in peace."

"It's not your time to die, Tank."

I hope.

"Not yet." His eyes are far off. At least his good eye is; his damaged eye twitches. I bet his burns cause him constant pain. His blocky hands are balled into fists, the bones protruding at strange angles. I'm prepared to tell Tank how much he has to live for, how bright his future could be, how much his family needs him...but his family is gone, abandoning him years ago. Others with the disease burned and electrocuted him. The government starved him and kept him in a cage. All his possessions are ruined. And now he's alone, except for the charges who follow him around against his will. If Tank wants to sacrifice himself for the greater good, maybe he's earned it. He says, "But soon. I hope."

The Outlaw

I exit the Metro in Tyson's Corner, west of Washington. Trudge the staircase, head down like everyone else. Behind me, ten miles distant, the world rages. I see it on the televisions I pass—the White House is destroyed and the Outlaw escaped. I'm beyond their search radius; they've forgotten how fast I am.

The sun falls toward the horizon, darkness in a few more hours. My body trembles with a tremendous calorie deficit but I left my cash in the motorcycle. I'm hollow inside with no immediate way to fill the maw. My phone buzzes and buzzes but I can only focus on food. Patrons in Wendy's and Starbucks mock me with their excess.

There's an apartment complex off Gosnell. Three stories with a community pool. I stagger to the third-floor landing and listen. Two of the units are occupied, televisions blaring, but I detect nothing in the others. I twist the first doorknob until it breaks, force myself in— vacant. No furniture, no food, nothing. I try the opposite unit— people live here but they're out. I raid the kitchen and steal their orange juice, bread, peanut butter, granola bars, and an apple.

Back to the vacant unit. Close the door and set the chain with shaky fingers. Blood sugar so low I'm nearing unconsciousness. I sit heavily on the carpet and fight light-headedness and nausea. I drink the OJ, spilling it down my neck. Pound two granola bars, and start on a peanut butter sandwich when exhaustion hits too hard. My eyelids meet no resistance and they surrender...

...I miss my boat...

...I miss...

~

"Get up," says Katie. She shakes me. Pats my face and I smile, eyes still closed. "Hey, you big beautiful baby, get up. We gotta go."

She's on the bed with me, sitting by my side. She pushes my hair back, checks my temperature. Pats me again, harder, more of a smack.

I yawn and stretch and try to open my bleary eyes. "Morning."

"It's still evening, dummy. We need to move."

I see her above me, an angel framed by a halo. Sweet wonderful Katie. I grab her face with both hands and kiss her on the mouth. She makes a surprised grunting noise and pushes me back.

"Listen, Chase," she says, wiping her mouth. "Not gonna lie. That was nice for me, and maybe later tonight we can continue. I'm a grown woman and you're a grown man and we're both hot as hell. And I'm digging your new tan. But right now you need to get your ass off the floor."

I raise up. Rub my eyes and blink away the fog.

It's not Katie. The woman kneeling beside me wears a flack vest and an impressive rifle is slung over her shoulder. Her hair is cut short and her green eyes pierce like lasers. She's striking the way a bird of prey is striking.

"Samantha?"

"Okay, fine, one more," she says and kisses my mouth. Hard and quick. "But only because I've missed you. Police are outside, investigating the neighbor's break in. They'll knock on this door any second. Let's move."

She's right—noise on the landing outside, the hard voices of officers. I wasn't subtle during my mad dash for food.

I get to my feet. Shove the apple and two granola bars into my pocket. We go out the sliding glass door onto the wooden deck and jump down. Three floors but the drop is nothing for us. The night is clear but feels thick with humidity. She leads me to a big silver Toyota Tundra and tosses me the keys. "You drive."

I get behind the wheel and slam the door. Sudden quiet. Slip the key into the ignition.

"Where to?" I ask.

She pulls a black pistol from her belt. Thumbs back the hammer and places the barrel firmly against my thigh. In the compacted silence inside our truck cab, the weapon's click sounds enormous.

"Sam?" I gulp.

"I'm going to shoot you," she says through clenched teeth. "Unless you offer a very *very* good reason you haven't called me for two years. Go."

I begin sweating. The pistol looks gigantic all of a sudden. I'm faster than her, but not fast enough to prevent the gunshot. And Samantha Gear is a crazy woman—I know she's not bluffing. She'll shoot me and laugh about it.

I smile and try to diffuse the situation with humor. "It started a long time ago. I was born at a very early age—"

"Bang!" she shouts and my whole body clenches.

"Okay okay! Jeez, don't pull the trigger."

"Puck says you've been on a boat? A *boat*? A stinking boat and you could have called anytime? Use your words, Outlaw. Ten seconds."

"Alright, here's the truth. I was still inside the jet over the Atlantic when the missiles hit. The impacts nearly killed me. I think I was clinically dead for a while, but—"

"Wait!" she orders, a burst of noise so abrupt that I nearly pee my pants. She hasn't released the gun's pressure on my thigh. She hits a button on her phone. It rings and PuckDaddy answers. She says, "Listen up, Puck. The arrogant and selfish jerk is about to explain himself."

The speaker buzzes. "Good. If it's not adequate, shoot him."

"Oh believe me, I'm gonna."

"Right between the legs, you know what I mean?"

I yelp, "What!"

"Eh, might be a little much. So Chase, you were saying?"

"Yes, dummy, you were saying?" says Puck.

I start over. About being inside the plane when the missiles hit, about my heart stopping and me blacking out before the water's impact. I tell them about drifting for days, and then waking up periodically on a boat, half dead, and hearing the news that Queen Carmine had been killed. Samantha shifts uncomfortably during that part. I describe the boat which saved me and the shocking extent of my injuries and about how I couldn't move or function for weeks, too exhausted and heart-broken and damaged. A kind man named Ervin Simms nursed me back to health. My delirium was significant, and when I finally regained myself I couldn't pick up the phone. I tried and tried, but couldn't force it. I tell them about how the world felt like a new place, one that needed me to stay away. About how Katie was dead, and I didn't know if Samantha had survived, and that everything I touched fell apart, and the longer I waited the more certain I became that I needed to stay on the boat, even after Ervin quit fishing. That I'm pretty certain the disease almost got me, nearly broke my mind, and that only the things which preserved me were the wind and the waves and the lack of responsibility.

Somewhere during my story Samantha puts the gun away. She stares straight ahead, through the windshield, her jaw set, arms crossed.

"I should have called," I say at the end. "I know I should have. But by the time my mind was sane and my reasoning sound, months had passed. That's not an excuse. It's just what happened. And I'm sorry."

"What about your father?" she asks. A scolding tone. "Poor guy thinks his son is dead."

"Well, him I actually called. Told Dad I was alive."

She sits up straighter. "You're kidding. You called Richard?"

"Swore him to secrecy."

"No," she says.

"Yes."

Puck makes a groaning noise.

"He knew." Samantha's eyes are enormous. "He knew this whole time?"

I can't tell if Puck is laughing or crying or doing something else, but he's making noises.

"I told him not to say a word," I explain. "He's a cop, good at hiding information."

She pinches the bridge between her eyes. "He knew. This whole thing could have been avoided. He knew."

"How is he, anyway?"

"Dunno. Haven't seen him in over a year. I broke up with him," she says.

"How you gonna dump my dad? You're the worst. And a prostitute."

She laughs, a low and mirthless sound. "Did it for his benefit. The guy's gorgeous. Women all over him, and he didn't need my dead weight. I White Fanged him for his own good."

Puck says, "He's getting married soon, actually."

"What!" I shout.

"What!'" cries Samantha. "That's kinda quick, I think."

Puck says, "Yeah, she's a knockout too. Super pretty."

"She'd have to be," grumbles Samantha. "To replace me."

"He's not gonna tell his own son?" I wonder.

"No fun when people keep important secrets, huh."

I frown. "Shut up."

"Speaking of secrets," says Samantha, watching me from the corner of her eye. She pauses and takes a deep breath.

"Oh dear," says Puck. "Oh man. This is huge. This is HUGE."

"Puck and I need to fill you in on something."

I nod. "Sure."

"Wow. Oh wow," she says and she scrubs a hand through her short hair.

"Oh wow what?"

"Damn, this is a big one, too."

"Puck freaking out a little," the phone rattles. "Can't breathe."

"What's going on," I say, my pulse quickening. "What's the secret? Can't be as bad as what I hid from you."

"Hah," she says.

Puck makes another groaning noise.

"*What?*" I shout. "Stop being weird."

"Okay, I'm just going to say it."

"Good."

"Here goes..."

"Wait! Should we record this?" Puck asks. His voice buzzes through her phone, propped between us in a cupholder.

I shout, "No! Just tell me, you idiots!"

Samantha chews on her lip. "Not sure how to phrase this."

"Immediately, that's how."

"Okay," she says. She's breathing heavy and her face is a little flushed. "Okay."

I groan. "Ohmygosh, I'm so frustrated."

"Okay."

"*Okay*," I repeat.

"Ready?"

"Obviously I'm ready. I'm *so* ready."

Samantha says it in a rush. "Katie didn't die in the blast. She faked her death. She's still alive."

...

...

"Chase? Did you hear me?"

...

...

"Oh crap, Puck, I think he might be fainting."

...

...Turns out, I wasn't ready.

- 8 -

Katie Lopez

I stand on my Land Cruiser's roof so I can see over the crest of a small hill of dust and cracked brown dirt. I don't want to be visible. Beyond the hill, a half mile distant, Tank's long caravan of lunacy moves down highway 159 and into Las Vegas. He's at the head, striding with purpose, and behind him there is a wake of followers—giants and Variants and mountain lions and elk and a thousand other animals.

Saul the Zealot did something to Tank when he died; there's no other viable explanation, even if he won't discuss it. Tank's strength has always drawn followers, but now the influence spreads to wildlife, and it's no coincidence that Saul had some sort of incorporeal connection to animals. Now he's gone and Tank is hounded by them.

I grin. It's funny. And kinda cute.

I dread what'll happen when Tank finds Las Vegas's water source. The flowing pipes will be guarded by mercenaries or criminals or crazy men or wild Variants, or all of the above. They don't stand a chance against Tank, who is the strongest person on earth. I've seen him shrug off gunfire and rip through steel. Most likely the poor souls near the water will be killed or flee or be forced to join his entourage. And then...

And then who knows. Maybe he'll find the wolf man and destroy him, earn himself some relief from the guilt. Some relief for all of us.

But an even bigger concern for me at the moment is, where do I go? Which direction? Kayla needs me in Los Angeles. But Chase is alive in Virginia. And I continue to get rushes of adrenaline, inexplicable premonitions that we're all sprinting at a sheer cliff, about to run over and plummet. The cracks in our stratum of peace are spreading.

Darren, my ever-present guard, squats nearby and pokes holes in the crust of dirt. He's doing his best to ignore Tank, an unimaginable source of power and strength beyond the hill. An alpha even more powerful than me calling.

Speaking of calls, my conference call with Puck starts soon. Me, Chase, Samantha Gear, Kayla, General Brown, Puck himself, and members of the Resistance, probably Isaac Anderson. Fifteen minutes. Apparently Chase has vital information he needs to share with us.

I desperately want to call Chase. I've come close to demanding Puck patch me through to his new cell, but something holds me back. Chase had a long day yesterday, but that's not what stays my fingers.

The truth is, I'm terrified. Like a school girl afraid of the boy she loves. What if he forgot me? Or moved on? Chase thought I was dead; Puck said when they told Chase I was alive, he didn't speak for hours. It's been two years, and he's beautiful. Most likely he has someone else by now.

I'd rather him be furious with me than apathetic. I'd rather him hate me than have forgotten. After all, my ruse cost him immense pain. I wouldn't blame him for being angry.

That's an absurd fear—I am Queen Carmine, the Red Butcher, one of the most respected women on the planet. She does not worry if boys are mad at her. Except...I'm Katie Lopez, girl with insecurities, and the world thinks I'm dead, and he's the boy I love.

My hands tremble with the thought of hearing his voice. What if he says, "Hi Katie," and then moves on? Like I'm simply part of his past? "Oh hey Katie, what's up? Anyway..."

I will die.

I need to call him. Be proactive. That's what a true queen would do. That's it. Need to call him immediately.

No. I need to practice the phone call first. I whisper, "Hello Chase? Hi, it's me Katie. You might have forgotten me, but I'm so glad you're not dead. I love you. I know you probably married some other girl by now, some tramp who doesn't deserve you, who doesn't realize how truly magnificent and perfect you are, and I'm happy for you. Good for you. Good for you and the tramp. But that doesn't change the fact that I love you. Let's try to be grownups about this."

No no no. That's awful.

Darren inspects me curiously. I don't care.

Try again. "Hello Chase? I'm going to kill the tramp you married in the Caribbean so you and I can run away together."

That's better. Queens can kill their competition, right?

"Hello Chase. I'm madly in love with you. And always will be."

I groan and roll my eyes. I'm a mess.

My phone buzzes. A text from Puck.

>> katie katie katie!!!

>> oh man

>> u need 2 see this

>> u know how PuckDaddy can hack phone cameras??

>> i just saw this video through mason's phone

>> happened minutes ago

>> puck might throw up

>> hit play

Mason's the leader of the Falcons, an elite team of Guardians in Los Angeles. A talkative but trustworthy guy. I didn't know Puck spied on him through his camera phone.

I shield the screen from the sun and hit play on the video he sent me. It's grainy, hard to make out details.

Two men are fighting, I can see that. But not much else. If this came from Mason's phone then it has fallen to the floor, and the camera is pointing upwards. The mic catches sounds of struggle. Someone kicks the phone, so the video feed spins off to the side. There's more jostling and then an awful silence.

A man slumps onto the ground. The camera goes fuzzy for an instant but then the face of Mason comes into sharp relief. He doesn't move; his throat is cut.

I gasp. Hand to my mouth.

No! He's dead? Not Mason!

The phone is picked up—the video shakes, blurs, and cuts off. But before it does, the camera shifts focus and a new face is visible, only for an instant. A flash of Walter. Puck has the video pause with the face in view.

Walter, the monster in cornrows from Compton.

"No," I whisper.

Walter killed Mason! Just now? Where?

Inside I hear a whisper. *Mason was a good soldier. And he died bravely.*

Carmine? Are you there?

More texts from PuckDaddy.

>> that video is less than five minutes old!!

>> walter's in Los Angeles

>> right now

>> and puck worries he's gonna kill kayla next!!!!

No. Not if I can help it.

Poor Mason...

I text, **On my way**

Tell Kayla to hide

>> thank u!!

I'll run out of gasoline halfway there. Find me another ride.

I drop from the roof and slide into the driver's seat of my Land Cruiser. The engine roars and I stomp the gas. Darren scrambles in. Dirt and dust erupt behind my tires. I bang and bump my way over the rocks until finding solid purchase on highway 160.

I don't stop for my caravan. Sean waves and shouts. The rest rush to pack and load up. Something's wrong with the queen—they see it with their eyes, feel it with their senses.

Catch me on Interstate 15.

The drive to Los Angeles is two hundred fifty miles. Pedal to the floor. I'll do it in two hours.

The Outlaw

Samantha Gear and I sit inside her truck, parked at a Chik-Fil-A and eating chicken sandwiches. I ordered four, and might be happier than I've ever been.

The man at the drive-thru window gawked at us. He's got a medium build, a thin goatee, losing some of his hair, kinda pale. Like a different species than us. I remember the first time I saw Samantha Gear. On a football field, walking my way. She was the fittest and most striking person I'd ever seen. Immediately I knew she was different. What would I think of her now, seeing her for the first time? She's been hardened by war, purified and strengthened by conflict and sacrifice. Essentially a demigod.

What would I think of myself?

Or of Katie...

"Have you talked with her?" I ask around a mouthful.

"Not much. She keeps her phone off usually."

"Where is she?"

"Last I heard, in Idaho. Puck says she's on the move but I don't know where," says Samantha. "I tracked Andy for weeks, hoping for a long range shot, but he's sneaky. Like a wild animal. I gave up but went back last year. Never even got a glimpse."

"I bet Katie's hair is long now."

"Who cares about hair?"

"Is she with anyone?" I ask.

"You mean dating? Married? Probably. Girl is hot."

"Yeah she is." I grin and finish my second sandwich. We chew thoughtfully in silence for several minutes. "I hope she's still single."

"No way."

"Maybe."

Sam shakes her head. "Not with that body. Or that face."

"Crud. You're probably right."

"I'll shoot him for you. Or them. Probably several."

"Several?" I yelp. "No way."

"Why not? You're dead."

"This makes my heart hurt."

"Don't pretend to be dead next time, idiot, and she won't forget about you."

"*Forget?* Really?"

"Sure, maybe, who knows. Might have a couple kids by now."

Her phone rings. I nearly drop my fourth sandwich. Puck's ten minutes too early. We put him on speaker.

My heart pounds. Is Katie on the line? Maybe her boyfriend is too. Or her husband. I'm going to throw up.

"Okay listen," Puck says in a rush. "I got General Isaac Anderson on the line, but Katie and General Brown won't call in. Got a situation in Los Angeles."

Sam and I bolt upright.

"Is Katie okay?"

"She's racing there now. Walter attacked and killed Mason. Not sure what he's planning to do next."

Samantha growls. "Walter? Haven't seen him in over a year."

"Killed Mason?" I ask. "Katie's righthand man, the Latino kid? Leader of the Falcons?"

"Walter cut his throat. Katie'll be there in two or three hours. Tank abandoned the city so Walter saw his chance. Kayla and General Brown are working on defenses."

I rub at my forehead. "Stupid Tank. Should Samantha and I fly there?"

"Easier said than done. It'll take you until tomorrow to find a plane and land in Los Angeles. My guess is, when Katie shows up then Walter will back down. He thinks the city is defenseless."

Isaac Anderson, my old pal from the FBI and the current leader of the Resistance, speaks for the first time. "I'm sending a squad to help General Brown. I agree with PuckDaddy—Walter is still injured, and the show of force will drive him away."

I ask, "Is Dalton still with her?"

"Dalton died two years ago, homie. Fighting Russia."

I groan and squirm in my seat. This is why I didn't want to come back. Nothing but pain and tears and death.

Samantha swears. We look at each other. Do we just sit here?

Not sure what else to do. Maybe let the queen handle her kingdom, and pray.

"Walter's still in northern Los Angeles," says Puck. "I'm scanning cameras now. I think Katie has time."

I nod, teeth grinding.

"Outlaw," says Anderson. "Good to hear your voice. My world got a little less gray when I learned you're alive. My wife Natalie sends you her best. I hear you have intel?"

"Yeah, we need to talk. But this is difficult, trying to focus while Katie's in danger."

"She has Kayla and General Brown and an army of Variants. She'll be fine," says Puck. "I hope. Probably. Tell us what you know and then we'll worry about Katie."

"Alright. I'll be brief. There's a potential cure for the Hyper Virus."

Samantha makes a small gasping noise and Isaac whistles.

Puck coughs around whatever it was he'd been drinking. "Huh? What? PuckDaddy wasn't paying attention. Did you say *cure?*"

"How do you know?" asks Samantha.

"I read through correspondence between the Blue-Eyed Witch and a woman named Pacific, and they think—"

"Whoa! You did? Pacific, really? Where'd you find her correspondence?" asks Puck.

"In an office on her yacht."

Samantha sniffs. "What'd you do about the woman herself?"

"Pacific is gone."

"Good. She was on my list."

"You have a list?"

General Anderson says, "Ah, should I know who you're talking about?"

"A freak like us," I say. "One of the oldest, living on a boat. Dead now. Here's what I gathered from her notes. There's a girl in China who's Infected and claims she has the cure."

"I know her," exclaims Puck. "That's Ai, codenamed China. She's around the Shooter's age. She's a genius, like Nuts. I remember Carter mentioning her, claiming she worked as a physician."

"Have you spoken with her recently?"

"No, been a while."

I say, "According to the correspondence, Ai developed a cure. Somehow, Blue-Eyes found out and she contacted Pacific, asking for advice. The note says she negotiated with Beijing to get the girl transferred but they refused, so now she plans on using force to extradite the Infected girl."

"Beijing, you say." We hear PuckDaddy's keyboards clicking. "How long ago was this?"

"A couple days. A week by now, maybe."

"Found her. Sounds like she's in jail. Hmmmm."

"A cure," says Isaac Anderson. "As in, it would make you guys normal? Or prevent future outbreaks? Or what?"

"No idea," I say. "You now know everything I do."

Puck mumbles to himself, "PuckDaddy hasn't talked with China since right after the Chemist died."

Samantha absently rubs the palm of her hand against her pistol. "Blue-Eyes isn't interested in a cure. She wants to kill China. Has to be. If there's a cure, we could use it to weaken her forces, and bring peace to the middle states. It could salvage the entire planet."

"Those are my thoughts, too," said Isaac. "This cure could be what we've been waiting and praying for. Our chance to end the war. Or at least, it could be our chance to *begin* ending the war."

Samantha nods. "We can't let Blue-Eyes have China."

"Except," I say. "We don't know where China is, and we lost Blue-Eyes."

Isaac says, "Intel suggests the President has two favorite spots, other than the White House. She goes to Camp David and to a mountain resort named Greenbrier in West Virginia. As it happens, you and Shooter are approximately halfway between them."

"How's this for a plan," says Puck. "Let the almighty PuckDaddy do some digging into China. See if I can pinpoint her exact location. You two stay put, because you might need to dash either direction, depending on what I find out. Meanwhile, during my research, I'll help keep Kayla and Katie alive."

"Just sit here?" I grumble. "That's awful."

"I been doing it for*ever*, Outlaw. Get used to it," says Samantha.

"You two, send me your coordinates." I hear a grin in Isaac Anderson's voice. "I got a care package for you. Trust me, this is good."

Kayla stands on the roof of the H&M Tower, balanced on a large air duct and pressed against the protective parapet. Below her, Los Angeles is a play set, miniature and vast, stretching to the mountains on one side and the sea on the other. There isn't a cloud in the sky, yet the universe doesn't look empty; rather like a heavy ceiling bearing down. Crushing her.

She is crying.

Gone. Her friends are gone. And she feels utterly alone.

Across from her, beyond Interstate 10, stands Walter. On the roof of the fully functional Good Samaritan Hospital. Her eyesight isn't as good as Queen Carmine's but she can make out details. Razors are bolted into the bones of Walter's fingers, and his cornrowed hair is braided with teeth, probably human. He wears silver aviator Ray-Bans and his mouth glints with gold.

Mason's corpse dangles from Walter's raised right hand.

One by one, her friends have fled or died. The Outlaw, Shooter, Saul, Carmine, Tank, and Mason. Now only she is left to face the horrifying Walter and his army of dysgenic goblins.

She can't do it—she understands this with surety. She's not a fighter, not a warrior, not even during her enthrallment with the Chemist so many years ago. She possesses no courage, no anger, no leadership skills, no ability to inflict harm. If Queen Carmine's vestigial army is a body, she is the vocal chords. Maybe the mouth, yet with no way to bite.

PuckDaddy sends her a constant stream of text messages, begging her to hide, but she can't stop staring. The other Variants in Los Angeles, Carmine's Guardians, they feel it too. Bereft of leadership, they're being drawn to Walter's power. They perch on nearby towers or slink closer through the streets, like starving animals willing to drink poisoned water.

Such powerful creatures, capable of leveling cities and bringing the planet to its knees, but unable to function without an alpha. They obeyed her to a point, but that point has passed. Feral animals do not heed the weak.

Walter's voice is the polar opposite of weak. His power and influence broadcasts like a radio frequency. The disease operates beyond normal senses, calling on some other plane.

"Poor Mason," she whispers to herself. There is no one to hear her. She speaks into a thundering absence. "He deserves so much better."

"Your Queen is dead," bellows Walter, a sound heard for miles. He's chosen his location well. Surrounded by an audience, his booming voice caroms through canyons of skyscrapers. "Your giant left for the desert. And this guy? Dead. Now you're alone. You been forgotten." He tosses the body of Mason far into the sky. The crowd of thousands gasps and watches the descent. Mason was a favorite.

Walter is flanked by a hideous creature. The creature was once a man, now a nightmare. Twisted and disfigured with hate, tainted beyond imagination by gorging on Walter's insanity. He is taller than a normal man, shorter than a giant. His eyes don't line up, his hair is gone. His jaw juts out, and his muscles bulge when he moves. He holds a wicked sword and wears only animal skins around his waist. He looks like the other goblins, but he's their king.

Walter and the goblin king stand with impunity—General Brown won't launch rockets at a hospital. And Walter can probably dodge sniper fire.

"This city is mine," he shouts. "You freaks belong to me now. Your sorry ass resisted long enough."

"No." Kayla can only mouth the words. "Outlaw, Queen Carmine, where are you..."

Do something, she should do *something*...

But what? She's only the Minister of Communication.

Communicate, that's what she can do.

She starts sending texts faster than humanly possible. To the various Guardian strings, demanding that they run, get away from Walter's influence. To the Workers, urging them to hide. To the Hospital, get your patients underground. To General Brown...

This won't work. No one's looking at their phones. Her digital influence is muted by the looming physical world.

"Anyone trying to leave," calls Walter. "Be fed to my dogs. We gon' have us a functional city, so stick around, keep raisin' them cows and hogs. General Brown, man to man, run home to your masters in Texas. Take your soldiers. Maybe you still got some time. Won't tell you again. Meantime, I'm looking for someone. Girl named Kayla."

Kayla keeps texting, but she lowers to her knees so Walter won't spot her on the roof.

Walter chuckles, a dark nightmarish sound. "Me and her got some catching up to do. Any of you brings me Kayla..." He stops. Puts a hand to his head. Staggers like he's dizzy. Is he sick? All his knotty muscles flex and bunch. Rumors are Tank nearly killed him and it's taken years to recover. He slowly stands upright, shakes his head and growls. "Bring me Kayla, you get rewarded. Understand?"

Kayla feels the Variant's indecision. Queen Carmine's Guardians are good people and they despise Walter, but their spirit has been leached out for months. They want to fight, want to resist or run, want to do anything but surrender...She *Feels* it. But they don't know how.

History hangs in the balance. Teetering on the edge of a knife. If Walter subsumes all the Variants, Carmine will be a queen without an army. Los Angeles will fall within a day, and soon after the world will too.

Kayla growls and puts her phone away. She doesn't have any courage or fighting ability, but she's loud. That's something. If she's gonna die, at least she'll do it noisily.

She jumps to her feet and cries, "Stop!"

The blast of her voice is a shock to the city. Even Walter takes an involuntary step back. She doesn't speak with a timbre like anyone else—her's has magic. It's too little, too late, but it's all she's got.

"Go away, Walter! This is a good place, and you can't have it!"

Walter laughs again. So awful. "There she is."

"This is Los Angeles! *We* are Los Angeles! We will die to protect our home, if we have to!" She's throwing all of her influence into each syllable. If only she knew better words, or had time to write a speech, maybe she could rouse the troops. "Turn around and go back to your hole, Walter! You aren't welcome!"

The Variants, thousands of them, watch her. Then glance at Walter. Dying for leadership, and they know she isn't it.

"Bring me the blonde girl." He says the words softly but everyone hears them. "She and I can catch up right here on this helicopter pad."

The Variants shudder, being given a direct command. Citizens below cry out. The goblin king snarls something unintelligible, and small pods of his followers begin climbing down the hospital walls. Most of Queen Carmine's Variants—she calls them Guardians, and where *is* she?—sit still. But some turn towards Kayla's aerie, their will already cleaved in half.

"We worked too hard," shouts Kayla. She's panting with fear, lessening the strength of her voice. "We've come too far. We will *not* surrender. We will fight to our last breath. We will *not* give in to a terrorist like Walter who only wants to destroy us."

"Got no choice, little girl," says Walter. "See, I planned ahead. I dammed up your water supply. Los Angeles only has a few days before you run out. And what's better? I got ya boy. Captured him. You call him Nuts, little guy keep this place running. He's mine now. Only way you get water is to surrender. Get it?"

"That's not true." But she experiences a spasm of horror. Without water, they're dead. Without Nuts, they're dead.

"It's true. Don't matter you like it or not."

"We won't surrender. We'll find other water. We will...we will..."

"You'll what? You'll die, what you'll do."

"We..."

Her words falter. Into the awful silence the echoes fade, but there's a new sound. She hears it. Maybe Walter does too, but he ignores the noise, so focused on Kayla. The noise fades, then revamps, and fades again.

It's a gasoline engine. When all the city has stopped, someone approaches. But who? Where? It's not General Brown, he ordered an entire standstill while they decide what to do.

A motorcycle bursts from the Good Samaritan's parking garage, the engine screaming. The upper deck of the garage is nearly equal to the roof of the hospital's main structure. The rider pulls a wheelie, zips up the hood of a Prius, going close to eighty miles per hour. The car's windshield acts as a makeshift ramp, launching the rider a short distance, but it's enough to clear the roof.

Walter is too stunned to react.

The bike and the rider are frozen in Kayla's mind. She feels like the very air is being charged with electricity. It's Queen Carmine, her face a mask of concentration and grit, the most beautiful thing she's ever seen. They are poised over the gulf. Her back is arched, her hands up and to the side, steadying herself mid-flight. The bike's rear wheel howls.

Oh, Kayla thinks to herself. Carmine's hair has gotten so *long!*

Carmine's bike bowls into the goblin king, knocking him from the roof. The queen herself lands against Walter's chest, feet first. A jarring collision that would kill anyone else. The momentum nearly carries the queen off the roof, but she snags the helipad's safety netting.

Walter is ejected clear into the air. He roars, arms flailing, plummets across Wilshire Boulevard and smashes through the glass side of the old Wells Fargo bank.

No one moves. Kayla doesn't breathe or blink.

The queen climbs to her feet.

Inhales.

Carmine roars, an almost alien noise. High-pitched and ferocious. A sound to rattle the planet. Kayla feels it in her bones. It's the enraged howl of an alpha.

Of the queen returned to protect her home.

The Outlaw

Samantha and I motor west on I-66, leaving Washington. Northern Virginia is a mess for fifty miles spiraling away from the capital. Traffic moves slowly, as if unsure which direction to drive. Law and order fractures and civil unrest accumulates. The societal structures were already tenuous at best, and now their mad President is on the run. I am all over the news—protestors march against me, other protestors rally to my defense, governmental bounties are placed on my head; my reappearance is all we hear on the radio.

We know our destination. Based on heat signatures and military traffic, Puck deduced the Witch fled to West Virginia, to a luxury mountain resort called Greenbriar. The military built an underground bunker there for World War II, codenamed Project Greek Island. It'll be a tough nut to crack, and she knows it.

Samantha says we're going to crack the heck out of it.

I want to call Katie, but Puck advises against. Yesterday she drove Walter out of Downtown but he didn't go far. They're searching for him, preparing for the eminent invasion of his oncoming army, and scrambling to solve their water crisis. Puck says it could get ugly soon.

Katie's got her hands full. Too busy for ex-boyfriends.

Ugh, I'm an *ex-boyfriend* to the woman I love. That's the worst. But at least I rose from the dead. I bet whoever she's dating now didn't do that.

But I can't dwell on Katie. Yet. Kill the Witch. Save the world. *Then* win back the girl. The final part of my plan might be the most difficult.

I'm brooding on unhealthy and self-pitying thoughts when Samantha blurts, "What do you think it's like to be ripped in half?"

"Gross, Samy. That's what happens in your head when you're quiet?"

"Ripped in half at the waist. Ever consider that?"

"I have not."

"You're Infected, Chase. Surely you've considered different ways to die."

"Old age," I say. "That's how. I don't dwell on being torn in two."

"You should. Here's what I think—"

But I'm saved from the gruesome discussion by her ringing phone. She presses her screen and puts PuckDaddy on speaker.

"Sup homies. I got Isaac Anderson on the line too. Big news! Ai, the girl from China, was broken out of prison yesterday. The authorities tried to cover it up, but PuckDaddy found reports. The government claims Variants overwhelmed the prison guards and smuggled her to an airport."

I pull thoughtfully at my lower lip. This isn't great news. Gotta be the Witch's Variants. Would've been better if we'd been the ones to release China.

Samantha says, "At least they didn't kill her outright."

General Isaac Anderson asks, "So she's en route to the States now? The East Coast, I assume."

"Puck found the plane. Her jet is refueling now in Hawaii. But there's a problem. They know the omnipotent and omniscient Puck-Daddy can spy on them, so they have no charted flight plan. I can't determine their destination."

Samantha and I reach I-81. We merge south, but I pull over at an exit so we can focus.

I say, "But you can track the jet in realtime."

"Not so much, dude. Satellites aren't what they used to be and the FAA crumbled without funding. As soon as they depart Hawaii, I'll lose them. We *assume* the jet is headed to America, but in reality it could go anywhere. The CDC in Georgia, some research lab in Maine, or maybe South America, who knows."

Isaac says, "That jet won't land at Greenbriar or Camp David, because they anticipate the Outlaw's arrival there soon. In reality, there are few safe places for it to land. The carrier group in the Pacific is now essentially a pirate kingdom unto itself. Latin America is in disarray. Maybe Canada, but I doubt it."

"She's bringing Ai to the East Coast," I say. "Blue-Eyes wants to meet her. She's got a ticking bomb on her hand—she knows if we find out about the cure then we'll move heaven and earth. What happens when the jet flies over California?"

"Assuming it does, the almighty and handsome PuckDaddy will find it again. Most civilian and military radar on the West Coast still operate. But it'll only be a short-term blip. No way to determine final destination."

Samantha asks, "Is there anything the Resistance can do once it pops up on radar again?"

"We could shoot it down. But we don't want to kill the civilians on board. Especially if one of them knows a cure."

"So even if we scramble fighter jets, they'd be helpless," says Samantha. "They could damage her aircraft and force it to land, but Ai's guards would execute the girl instead of surrendering her."

I ask, "Puck, you can't take control remotely?"

"No way. The Federal military disabled those features over a year go, across the board."

"Here's an idea," says Anderson. "I have a few AWACs at my disposal. I'll put them in the sky over California. Once Ai's jet jumps on Puck's radar, our Sentry can monitor it long range."

Samantha nods, her jaw set, green eyes hot. "Good idea. Will buy us time."

"Hey, military knuckleheads," I say. "What on earth is an AWAK? Sounds like a monster on Endor."

"Airborne Warning And Control," replies Anderson. He sounds impressed by the depths of my stupidity. "Radar in the sky. A big Sentry jet that can tail Ai. The Sentry'll follow her as far as the wall, potentially, but then the Federal Air Force will shoot it down. Maybe by that point we'll know her destination."

Samantha grunts. "Maybe or maybe not. And then we'd still need to rescue her. No easy trick."

"So let's do it the easy way," I say. An idea's been percolating in the back of my mind—it's a good one, which means Puck and Anderson will hate it.

Puck says, "The easy way? 'Splain, dummy."

"We'll hijack Ai's airplane."

"PuckDaddy already told you," he growls. "I can't."

"I meant manually."

Puck says, "No chance. Her plane takes off soon. We can't get people there in time."

"Oh," says Samantha. She perks up and her mouth twists in a sinister smile. "You mean, hijack her plane mid-flight."

"Of course. Anything less would be boring."

Isaac says, "I don't follow."

Puck groans. "That's because you aren't accustomed to their lunacy. They're talking about boarding Ai's plane at twenty thousand feet."

"Precisely."

Isaac Anderson says a very bad word.

Puck continues, "Chase did that a few years ago, with the Chemist's cargo plane. It was terrifying and Puck hated it."

"I remember. I was jealous I didn't get invited," says Samantha.

"Gross. Puck hates it. Gross and scary and absurd and terrifying. You two imbeciles have issues."

"If I had a boss," mumbles Isaac, "this would get me fired, no questions asked."

"Anyone have a better idea?" I ask. "We're out of time. If there's a cure, it's worth dying for."

Samantha nods. "My thoughts exactly."

Isaac covers his phone's receiver with his hand, but we still hear his muffled words. He orders AWAC Sentries into the air. And he's using colorful language to do so.

The phone between Sam and me rattles. "Hey dummies! You're not thinking. Her jet will cross over the coast in about five or six hours. You're in frickin' Virginia."

"So we need our own jet. Obviously."

"Ridiculous," he grumbles. We hear his keyboard clicking like gunfire. "You idiots think Puck can just wave a magic wand and make impossible crap happen."

"Then come up with a better solution than mine."

"Shut up," he says.

"Find us a ride. We'll figure out the details en route."

Samantha is zooming around a map on her phone. "Okay, so lemme see. There are landing strips not far from here. Maybe we—"

"Shut up, shut up you feeble minded nitwit with your slow fingers and stupid brain. Puck already found a jet. There's a small functional airport in Front Royal, Warren County. Couple business class jets for rent. Might get you there in time. Sending you directions now."

I gun the truck's engine and turn around, heading the other direction.

"It's important you two dummies realize that PuckDaddy is an absolute magician."

"This is madness," grumbles Isaac.

"C'mon, guys." I laugh, adrenaline leaking into my veins. "Admit it —this is kinda fun."

"Fun? Making plans for you to commit suicide? Helping you leap to your death? ...Yeah, kinda fun."

The airport is in the middle of farm country, miles from anywhere. A mist hangs over the land, obscuring the Shenandoah mountains. Our engine dies and we hear nothing except mooing cows. The pungent aroma of manure creeps into our truck's cabin.

The little airport is in good shape—the grass is mowed and the tarmac intact. I see an ample runway and a separate area for taxiing. A small terminal is situated next to the parking lot, near long hangers. We bypass the terminal and brake near the first hanger.

The airport's owner and operator is a man named Clive and he looks stunned to see us. He pushes his Washington Nationals baseball cap back from his forehead and says, "Repeat that?"

"We're renting the jet in your hanger," I repeat. "The Eclipse. And we'd like to take off in ten minutes."

"How'd you know I got an Eclipse?"

"Magic. How much to rent it?"

"Not rent," calls Sam, rolling aside the tall metal doors. "Buy. It's not coming back. Ah *hah!* Here it is."

"*Buy* it?" Poor Clive's eyes bulge. He's not used to dealing with morons this early.

"Right, that's what I meant. How much?"

"That's the nicest plane I got." He gestures toward the hanger. "Cost me two million, used."

I ask, "Does anyone rent it anymore? Might be a good time to sell."

"Not much. Gasoline is a fortune. Usually I only rent to the military, you understand."

"We know. How much?" I ask again.

"I don't reckon you can afford it. We'd need to write a bill of sale, work the taxes, check your pilot's license—"

"Listen, Farmer Joe," barks Samantha, hauling supplies out of her truck bed. "We're taking the plane. Want some money for it? Or not, your choice."

Clive slowly mouthes the words 'Farmer Joe.'

I send Puck a text, and I say, "Clive, I'm having a few million dollars put into your account."

"Few million? Where'd you get that much? And how can you do that? Who're you people?"

Samantha walks by, arms heaped with gear. She grumbles, "You're an inquisitive guy, Farmer Joe. And thanks for the help, Chase, really nice of you to carry stuff for me."

"Now look," says Clive. "This is illegal. You can't take it."

I place my hand on his shoulder and he flinches. I'm taller than him, broader. He's a grown man, but compared to me he's almost a child. "Clive, let's be honest. Yes we can take it. And we are. But the money should be in your account now."

He whispers, "I'll call the cops."

"We'll be gone before they arrive." I release him and go to the truck to carry supplies. "And if not, we'll take away their guns."

He takes off his cap and rubs his forehead. "Ya'll two are mutants, ain't ya."

"But the best kind."

Samantha fires up a tractor and jockeys the Eclipse into the open. A sleek white and red plane; it's small, only six seats. I toss cargo into the cabin and Samantha climbs into the cockpit to warm the systems.

A couple of the bags are absurdly heavy and they clank and thud. "Jeez, Sam, what the heck's in there."

"Hey, a full tank!" she calls, pleasantly surprised. "Good ol' Farmer Joe."

"Make sure you stir the gasoline," says Clive, looking torn between wanting to help and wanting to fetch his shotgun. "Been setting a while."

"We're wheels-up in five," she shouts as the turbine begin turning.

"Five minutes?" yelps Clive. "Well, I better check the radar. Make sure the skies are clear. Can't imagine they ain't, but better safe than sorry." He half shambles/half jogs to the terminal.

My phone rings.

"What's up, Puck."

He says, "Don't be alarmed, but you have two inbound drones. Remember the care packages Isaac Anderson mentioned? They're here."

"Where?"

"Coming from southwest."

"What are they?"

"A *surprise*, jerk. No hints. Don't you remember how Christmas works?"

Three minutes later, I spot two dots zooming low over the horizon. My ears catch the tinny buzz created by the blades.

"We cut it close," says Puck. "This fog killed their solar batteries. Almost had to stop and recharge."

The futuristic drones are large, the size of bicycles. They hover twelve inches off the tarmac and clips automatically release their packages. Then the machines tilt and drift to the grass, powering down. Fascinating.

"Care packages," I marvel. "How great. Haven't had one of these since middle school camp."

Samantha jogs down the steps and we tear them open.

Fresh cellphones, batteries, bluetooth headsets. Ammo for Sam. But even more importantly...

My Outlaw costume.

The familiar ballistic vest with a parachute sewn into the back. Nylon cargo pants complete with retracting wings to help me fly. Samantha gets one too—hers is black, but mine has red accents. For me, there's even a red mask with properly sewn eyeholes. Attached is a note.

DUDE!! I'M SO FREAKING PUMPED YOU'RE ALIVE!!

Also you're a jerk because I was sad you died.

Here are new Outlaw suits for you and the Shooter.

Tell her I said What's Up girl.

And that I'm still single.

LETS HANG OUT SOON, OUTLAW, AAAUUUGHHH!!!

(I can't tell you where I am. It's top secret)

(Because I'm a big deal now)

(A big awesome deal—tell Samantha Gear that)

I smile so big it hurts and tears leak out. A note from my friend Lee, a buddy from high school I haven't seen in years. I hold the vest out in front of me. It's even North Face brand, just like old times.

The Outlaw is back.

Katie Lopez

Kayla and I sit on top of 717 Olympic. Returning to this tower feels like slipping on a comfortable pair of old sneakers, a sense of belonging; Kayla largely preserved my apartment. Despite the conflict and drama and pain, I fell asleep smiling last night.

We worked for six hours this morning, searching for Walter and his goblin king, and now we break for lunch. Except I can't eat—Kayla's emotional again, hugging me and kissing my head; I can't even use my phone.

Walter's close. I feel the scrim of poison he disgorges into the atmosphere.

I also sense the Variants—my Guardians. They crowd the walls below our perch and hunker in the levels under my feet. They're like plants being fed water after a drought, returning to life. The dependency they have for an alpha is unhealthy, to a elegiac degree. It can't go on, but I don't know how to solve the issue.

In most circumstances, I'd feel tremendously relieved to be home. But instead storm clouds gather in my mind—I have to bury Mason later today; sentries need to be set for the Andy Babington watch; we'll run out of water soon; the Guardians are sick and dependent; Walter is close; I don't know if the Priest is nearby; and I'm weary of death. I don't want to bury Mason. Instead I want to watch him flirt with Kayla, and listen to his stories. I still miss Becky to this day, and now Mason too. Who's next? Not Kayla, please not her.

"Kayla," I say into her shoulder. She's patting my head and cooing over my long brown hair. "This has got to stop."

"I know, I know! I will. I just missed you SO much. And this hair! And these muscles, so impressive Queen Carmine. It's like, pow!"

Kayla, if possible, has grown more beautiful. Being with her causes a kind of exquisite pain; she's impossible to ignore, and it's impossible not to compare myself to her. When she's nearby, I over-correct my posture on instinct and pluck at my clothes. I don't know how men function around her.

She releases me at last, and sits crisscross as I recline in a deck chair. She takes my hand and uses a small metal tool to clean under my fingernails and push back my cuticle.

"If I didn't know better," she says and tsks. "I'd say some of the dirt on you is cow manure."

"No way," I lie. Better to deceive her than risk hysterics. "That'd be ridiculous."

"But when was your last shower, Queen Carmine?"

"Good question. What month is it?"

"Holy moly, never mind. I'm not even sure I can handle giving you a pedicure until you've bathed."

"Kayla—"

"Just kidding, yes I can, it'd be SUPER fun."

"Kayla, would it be weird for you to call me Katie? And not Queen Carmine?"

She pauses with her nail file and looks up. "You've found more of your memories?"

"I found them all." I lean forward and take her face in my hands. "My name is Katie Lopez. The queen you served is part of me, but she was running on survival instincts and fear and hate. Carmine's around, but I've got her under control." I kiss Kayla's forehead. "I know it's strange, and you're wondering who I really am. But I know you. You kept me alive. We're only here because of you, Kayla, a true hero. You have my eternal gratitude."

Her face turns pink, the most perfect patina imaginable, and I feel the Variants hiding out of sight respond to her emotions—their pulses ramp up. They love her.

"It's like you're Queen Carmine, but nicer," she says and she wipes her eyes. "She used to bite me, but I bet you won't."

I laugh. "I'll try not to."

"All my friendship dreams are coming true! I'm so happy I might POP. Now let me have your hand again."

"Only for a minute, while I finish lunch," I say. "We need to meet with the Governess, find Nuts, and figure out our water situation."

"Poor Nuts. I hope he's okay. I like that crazy old man! And poor Mason. I can't believe he's gone. I should've let him touch me more, huh?"

I consume my chicken and carrots quickly with the hand she isn't using. It's time to go. There's too much to do, and not enough hands to get it all done. According to General Brown, the water is dammed somewhere far outside the tower cluster, and he can't get to the reservoir. Nuts and his Engineers would know what to do, but... The Priest is gone and so is Mason—I relied on them to direct our manpower, so I'll need to appoint new Overseers.

Kayla interrupts my thoughts. "Can you even BELIEVE the Outlaw is alive? Isn't it the BEST? And not only because he's gorgeous. I'm not *that* shallow."

I grin and blink away the stupid tears that well up when I think about him. "It's a miracle I haven't fully absorbed yet."

"He's been on a boat this whole time? That's so ew and yuck, but maybe nice? I don't know if I've ever been on a boat, but they smell like fish, right? Or maybe not, maybe it's super romantic. Sailing around the Caribbean for a couple years? Sounds kinda dreamy, now that I think about it. Is he different now?"

"We haven't spoken yet."

"Why not?" She gasps—an honest to goodness gasp. "Oh no, you think he's married now?"

"What! I hope not. Why do you say that?"

Both her hands are at her mouth and her eyes are the size of ponds. "What if he's avoiding you? Oh gosh."

"He's not... PuckDaddy says he's busy doing something with Samantha Gear and Isaac Anderson, and it's very important. I'm sure it's—"

"What could be so important?"

"Puck won't tell me. He says I have enough to worry about right now. Which makes me even more worried," I admit.

"Maybe the important thing is his wedding?"

"No." My shoulders slump. "You think?"

"Probably. He's super hot. I'd marry him. You know, if I was single. I mean, he thought you were dead. A hunk like that on the open market for two years? Oh wow, what if he has a kid?"

I sit up straighter. "A kid! Really?"

"Probably! A daughter? Maybe he named her Katie! Awww, that'd be sweet."

I groan and rub my eyes. "Ugh, this is the worst. I'm rethinking my policy on biting you."

She grabs my other hand. "Well, let's get you gorgeous so his wife'll be jealous."

"No!" I stand up, pulling my hand free. "He's not married. Probably. And we have too much work to do, so c'mon."

"But maybe you take a shower first?" she suggests.

The Guardians around us are already on the move, responding to my intentions. Imagine what would happen if Walter got them—they'd destroy the world at his slightest whim. I've got to figure out what to do about their over-reliance on a leader. And soon.

But first, fix the water. That's more urgent, because dying of thirst is a very real threat.

And then, murder Chase's wife and adopt their daughter as my own.

Wow, I'm a mess. Not handling the stress well.

I bet Carmine was better at this than I am.

The Outlaw

Samantha keeps us low to the earth and we thunder over the Great Wall in Missouri. The stark contrast between sides is apparent—to the east of the wall is civilization and order and Federal protection; to the west, the land is abandoned, the cities are razed, and wild fires burn unchecked. Far to the south, the Resistance thrives but here in the mid-west is lawless country.

The Witch's plan worked—her country is protected and whole. But at what price? The world rages around her, trillions worth of property goes up in flames, millions of people die, but at least she's comfortable and running the show.

I'm dozing when Puck sends a news article to our phones. Samantha, not trusting the ancient autopilot, yells at me to wake up and she keeps her hands on the yoke. I yawn and scan the article.

"The President of the United States just announced the upcoming world summit of leaders will be held in Los Angeles next month," I tell her.

"That's absurd," Samantha scoffs. "What does Blue-Eyes plan on doing about the current residents? Katie and her freaks?"

I wake up quick and my teeth grind. The Witch would only make such an announcement if she was confident of reclaiming the city. Which means she has plans I don't know about. Which means Katie's danger is larger and more eminent than I realized.

"I don't know," I admit. "But this isn't good news for us. She's risking a world-wide embarrassment."

"Unless she believes there isn't much of a risk. Or if the risk's worth it. If she gets all those world leaders under her influence? She'll become the most powerful human to ever live. More dominant than Alexander the Great or Napoleon or any Roman caesar."

We stew silently inside our gloomy thoughts, watching the charred remains of Wichita leap past, until Puck calls. I put him on speaker.

"Bingo! Got Ai's jet. Or, I should say, her captor's jet. They're trying to sneak through between Los Angeles and San Fransisco, but I'm tied into small-time radar systems up there. Where are you two right now? Kansas, looks like. Puck predicts you'll intercept that jet in southern Utah or Nevada."

"Not far from Las Vegas, then," says Samantha.

"Huh, you're right. How about that," he mutters. "Weird coincidence."

"What is?"

"Nothing, just...nothing. Lotta stuff going on. You two focus on not dying. General Anderson's AWAK is hustling into range, tracking the bird long distance. Puck'll keep you apprised. Like that word? Apprised? Puck's so smart. Recommend you ascend to ten thousand feet."

"Roger that, Puck. Keep up the good work, you beautiful nerd," she says and she points out nose at the sky. We rocket into the blue, knifing through clouds. "Ten thousand feet isn't very high. Ai's jet must be keeping low to avoid detection."

I say, "I'll take your word for it. These numbers mean nothing to me."

"Listen, Chase." She pinches the yoke between her knees and arches her back. Stretches her hands above her head and presses against the roof, working her muscles loose. "You should know I've made my peace. If anything happens to me, don't waste any time mourning. I'm ready."

"Ready to die? What an ominous thing to say."

"I'm Infected. You said it best—we're like supernovas; we burn up fast and bright. You feel the urge just like I do, the siren call to leap into our final adventure. I've come close a dozen times during the past two years, with you and Katie either dead or hiding. My life was empty before you two, full of pain and loneliness. I'm glad I waited, because I want you two happily ever after." She ceases the stretching and takes my hand. Squeezes. A very un-Samantha-like thing to do. "If it's my time, I'm ready. Because I'll die helping friends, and what better ending is there?"

"You're freaking me out, Sam. Let go of my hand."

"Turns you on a little, huh."

"You don't have my permission to die. Not anytime soon."

She shrugs and lets go. "I'm just saying. I'm ready."

"Too bad."

"You ever wonder what it'd be like to be eaten by a shark?"

I groan and climb out of the cockpit. The cabin isn't big enough for me to raise upright, so I crouch in the tiny bathroom and pull on my Outlaw gear. The vest has elastic seams because Lee knows my chest and shoulders swell when my adrenaline starts churning. The gloves are a perfect fit and snap easily onto the wings built into my cargo pants. Feels like coming home.

The crimson mask feels nicer than the rags I used in the past. The material is thick but breathable, some kind of moisture-wicking cloth. Lee reinforced the eyeholes and there are straps to keep the bluetooth headsets in position. It wraps around my face from the bridge of my nose up, like a helmet, and ties in the back.

Just like that, staring back at me in the mirror is the Outlaw. The vigilante in black and red. The sight of the masked man jars me, stirring dormant emotions.

I remember pulling into a parking lot six years ago, downtown Los Angeles. Katie's phone had been stolen, and I was hellbent on retrieving it, but didn't want anyone to recognize me so I rooted in my trunk. I settled on an old ski mask and a bandana. Later that night, wearing the ludicrous costume, I bumped into Natalie North in front of an ATM machine and its security camera captured me and the rest is in the history books.

I'd been scrawny, still getting used to football practices. A dog chased me in an alley, and I was so scared I nearly wet myself. That dog seemed monstrous and terrifying at the time.

Now I'm the terrifying monster. The man in the mirror is crisscrossed with scars and his blue eyes are hard stone. Muscles pack my frame like armor, my bones are steel, and I possess the ability to flip cars, haunt the darkness, rip metal, dodge bullets, and command mutants.

Powers I never wanted.

I come out of the bathroom and Samantha glances through the cockpit door at me.

"Hot damn, Outlaw, you look beautiful."

"It's just the tan."

"Probably. Check the bag at your feet. Got a surprise for you," she says.

I lower to my haunches and unzip her satchel, the heavy one.

Inside is a rod, the shape of a baseball bat, slightly longer. Tapered at one end, like a handle. The color is deep midnight, flecked with blue—the metal sucks in light, it's so dense. I heft the rod and enjoy the impossible weight.

"It's beautiful," I whisper. "I missed this."

"Hah! I thought you'd like it. What'd we call it? Staff of Treachery? Rod of Doom?"

I grin. "Thunder Stick?"

"Whatever. Paid ten million for it on the black market. Guy was getting higher offers, but I persuaded him."

"Samantha, I owe you. This is a debt I can never repay."

"Mch, it belongs to you. I tried using it but the stupid thing's too heavy. The diver had to use a private submarine to lift it off the ocean floor."

"I'm going to hit the Witch in the head with it."

Samantha offers a wry smile. One without mirth. "You said that before."

"I know. Maybe my simplistic plans need to evolve."

I buckle the rod onto a chair and return to the cockpit. I take the yoke, which is horrifying, while Samantha changes. For fun I toggle it back and forth and side to side—the plane obeys, but that makes my stomach lurch so I quit.

Jump out an airplane? Sure. Try to fly it? Heck no.

Samantha returns. "How do I look?"

"Super hot."

"Right?"

She makes me keep the stick while she checks and rechecks her ammunition and weapons. A shocking display of firepower—metal and bullets and gun oil. Useless in my hands, but with it Samantha Gear can bring a city to its knees. She smiles and hums and coddles the hardware, the way I imagine young mothers swaddle their infants.

Puck calls.

"Alright homies, you ready to die? PuckDaddy doesn't get scared but if he did then he'd be SUPER frightened right now. Ai is a hundred miles ahead of your position. Change your heading to three ten."

I stare blankly at the blinking instrument panel. "Ha ha."

"Ha ha what?"

"It's funny you think I can do that."

Samantha says, "Use the compass, genius."

"Where's the compass?"

"It's that swiveling ball. Duh. There's also a digital compass on the dash."

I gesture at the myriad of buttons and displays. "Pretend I'm an idiot and be more specific."

"Pretend?"

The speakerphone rattles and Puck cries, "Whoa! Is Chase flying the plane? You two really don't care if you survive, huh."

"Just look at the...ugh," she groans. "Aim north until I tell you to stop."

I nod and obey, pulling the yoke.

"No," she snaps. "That's *up*. Not north."

"Right, I know that, shut up."

"Aim north."

I obey.

"No! That's *south!* Seriously, Chase."

"This is hard!" I shout.

"Didn't you live on a *boat* for two years?"

"The sun's hidden above us! There's no wind! I can't tell which direction we're facing!"

She groans. "We're aiming west. Stupid. Turn to the *right*."

"You mean starboard."

"I will kill you."

"Perhaps," says PuckDaddy and he clears his throat. "Just perhaps, now, at one of the most crucial points in history, we shouldn't teach Chase to fly."

I'm insulted and relieved when Samantha sits in the pilot's chair and takes the yoke. She increases the throttle and effortlessly banks north, the capacious world tilting below.

Puck keeps us updated. Ai's jet turns southeast halfway across California, possibly aiming at the CDC in Georgia. The pilot believes he snuck through undetected—they're past Los Angeles and far from Resistance strongholds, and unaware a Sentry is tracking them a hundred miles away. Samantha swoops south, picking up her tail. Locating Ai's jet is easy—it's humongous, shoveling through the air like a fat bird. Samantha falls through the clouds and slides behind it, matching the pace, two hundred feet above.

"It's a Boeing," muses Samantha. "Looks like a newer version of the C-17. Stripped down to conserve fuel, maybe?"

I don't know much about military aircraft. It's enormous and painted army green, and soon it fills our entire windshield. She inches lower until we're almost sitting on the back of it. The air buffets us, tossing us around our in seats.

"Jeez, this is kinda freaky, even for me. Hopping planes going two hundred and fifty miles per hours," she says. "We're *so* high."

Puck says, "Don't screw up. We don't have a backup plan, other than shoot Ai down. Which would suck."

Samantha nods at the windshield. "We're here, Outlaw. Now what?"

"We board it."

"Roger. How?"

"No idea."

Puck grumbles something about us being idiots. Dead idiots.

"Take the stick," she says. "Keep us level."

She nimbly climbs out of the seat and packs on her gear—pistol on each thigh, assault rifle strapped to her back, knives and ammunition on her belt, grenades clipped to her vest, and another blade in her boot. She uses the empty satchels to create a makeshift autopilot, tying the straps between the yoke and the captain's chair.

"It's not perfect," she says, eyeing the contraption. "But it should hold a few minutes."

I climb out of my chair. My vest and shoes constrict, indications my body swells with adrenaline and wrath. The forward hatch is on the port side of our small jet. I place my hand on the fiberglass surface—it's cold from the air hurtling past.

"Prepared to open?"

"Hell no," she says. Her voice sounds small. We both know madness waits on the other side. "We have to go fast because the change in cabin pressure will make things dicey."

I toggle the hatch's first lock and an alarm sounds. I release the second and shove. A sudden rush of oxygen tugs at our vests. The hatch resists but the torrent of air catches and throws it wide, a portal opening into anarchy. Fifteen feet below, the spine and shoulders of the Boeing provide a wide landing spot; below that, the planet and all of eternity churns.

Sudden depressurization whips the cabin into a madhouse, and tears Samantha's autopilot free. The jet waffles.

Deep breath.

Not much oxygen.

I step into nothing.

I drop, intending to land between the enormous wings. Instead the wall of air slams me backwards, pummeling me toward the aircraft's tail. I bounce and skid and say words Katie doesn't approve of. I flail and catch a protruding antenna housing. Gracelessly jerk to a halt.

The world spins and howls, mad and off-kilter, and I can't get my bearing. Sensory overload. Turbines under the wings thunder and deafen, engines the size of a house.

Samantha tumbles my direction, shouting and using similar terminology. She catches me full in the face, a collision jarring me loose from the antenna housing. I wrap an arm around her and snatch another protrusion, halting our skid.

Dangling outside a military cargo jet at five thousand feet—I miss my boat and the languid lifestyle of a fisherman.

"Look out, Outlaw!"

The private jet above us, freed from its teether, ponderously dips toward the Boeing. Toward us. We'll be crushed between aircraft, a crash in slow motion at two hundred and fifty miles per hour.

She shouts in my ear over the roaring slipstream, "It's going to hit us! Hold tight!"

My left fist grips the Boeing's fuselage hard enough to dent metal and create finger-holds. My right arm locks around her midsection, pinning her.

She lays flat on her back, raises her hands, and *Catches* the private jet's nose before it bumps into the roof of the Boeing. She clenches her eyes and grunts with the effort. The muscles in her arms bunch and flex, her elbows forced to bend. The jet's descent slows and halts, inches from our foreheads.

Wait until I tell Puck that Samantha Gear can bench press a jet.

"It's too strong," she pants. I barely hear her. The smaller private jet's tail wavers mere feet from the tail of the Boeing.

She keeps her arms pushing, and curls into a ball. Gets her knees to her ears, and presses the bottom of her boots into the underside of the private jet's nose. Uses her stronger leg muscles to shove the nose up, up, up, an inch at a time.

The bluetooth headset in my ear rings once, and then somehow Puck forces it to remotely answer. His voice bursts, "You two alive?"

Neither of us answer. Samantha's face is bright red with exertion.

"Oh crap, sounds loud," he says. "Puck'll wait patiently."

All of a sudden, swirling vicissitudes and debris inside the private jet's cabin catch the yoke. The jet pitches upwards, releasing the pressure off Samantha's muscles. It banks to the right, and peels away from us. Instantly blue sky and sunlight erupt above us. We watch the jet glide north in a long curl.

Samantha groans and rubs her wrists.

"See?" I shout. "Boarding a plane is easy!"

"I *can't* see! Or hear!"

"Last time I did this, I think I wore a helmet."

"Damn it, Chase! Not helpful to remember this now," she calls.

"Think the guards inside heard us?"

"Let's find out! I hate it out here!"

There's a hatch under our boots. A roof access panel, but from our tenuous position we can't reach it, not without letting go and sliding into the sky. We need a protrusion closer to the hatch, like a piton to anchor us, but there isn't one. I get my mouth close to Samantha's ear and explain my plan. She nods, grabs my vest, and finds another handhold. Now she's holding me to the fuselage. I slide free my Thunder Stick.

"Ready?"

She nods again.

I raise the bat and *Drive* it into the roof of the military jet, near my knees. The metal sunders, punctured through. A screeching horrible sound, definitely detectable by sentries inside the Boeing, but it provides an anchor. We have to move fast. Samantha releases her hold and we slide several feet closer to the hatch. Each of us get a grip on the Thunder Stick. With my free hand, I punch through the hatch lid and fling it into the sky. She takes a pistol off her thigh and slithers into the open hatch, disappearing from my sight. I slide in halfway, yank the stick loose from the roof, and drop into the sudden silence of the Boeing's interior.

- 14 -
The Outlaw

Samantha has already moved on. I stand alone on a landing at the back of the gargantuan plane, above the long ramp which can lower to allow vehicles to board. Only red bulbs burn, casting the cavernous interior with an eerie glow, a scene from hell.

From my point of view above the cargo bay, the place looks empty of hostiles. Pallets of supplies and gear stand like six-foot statues on either side of the bay. In the dead center, all alone, a single pallet of boxes shines like a crimson beacon. My heart sinks—someone is chained to the center pallet, like a slain animal on the alter.

Where'd Samantha go?

"It's so quiet." A whisper in my ear. "Sorry. PuckDaddy is working on patience."

I hop onto the closest supply pallet and silently move to the center of the cargo bay. I'm scanning everywhere and detecting nothing.

The person in chains is Ai. Puck showed us her photo on the jet. Her arms are stretched wide, like a crucifix, held by thick chains encircling the supply boxes. She watches me, strangely calm. Duct tape wraps around her head, sealing her mouth.

Why is this one pallet in the center of the cargo bay? And why is she strapped to it?

I creep to her and hold my finger to my lips. Quiet.

She doesn't respond.

Again I pause. Inspect the shadows. Listen. Wish I could use my senses like an animal, the way some of Katie's mutants can. The place seems deserted. If the jet was crawling with feral mutants, I'd be able to tell.

I place my Thunder Stick next to her chains, intending to twist them apart or smash them.

She issues a faint grunt and shakes her head.

No?

Shakes her head again.

Something's not right, that's obvious.

Ai is short, clearly of far Eastern descent. Her hair's black, dark almond eyes. She's calm, no emotion, watching me blankly. I slide the stick down the back of my vest, and I pull the tape at her mouth. Adhesive peels away, leaving her skin raw and pink, and I tug the gag lower so she can speak.

She whispers, "It's a trap." Her voice caroms around the bay like a marble in a glass jar.

"Of course it's a trap." Carter steps out of the shadows beyond the pallet. He presses a large silver revolver into my nose. "So predictable, that's what I admire about..." His voice falters, staring at me.

I haven't seen Carter in years. The oldest living Infected, bald as marble and just as hard. He wears his standard getup—tactical gear, trench coat, and boots. An unlit cigarette is pinched at the corner of his mouth. His bottomless eyes glitter.

Once upon a time, he held himself up as my mentor. The guardian into a mystical world I could only imagine, and he offered me his hand. However, time revealed his true intentions—Carter is the shadowy autocrat of his own empire, built on the backs of other mutants. He doesn't seek fame or glory, like his old partner the Chemist, but rather power and autonomy. He fashions himself a deity and he kills those who disagree.

"You," he growls. Most of his faint Australian accent has been ground away during the previous century. "Thought you were in Washington.

"Fools believe what they want to believe, Carter."

"I couldn't fathom the news when I saw it—the infamous Outlaw was back and charging around the East Coast. Good on you, kid, staying hidden as long as you did. The mark of a survivor. Happy to see me?"

"That's an unqualified No. How'd you get on this plane?"

"Who do you think broke China out of prison?" He grins, flashing sharp white teeth. "Think I'd send rookies to do a man's job?"

"Get the gun out of my face."

He presses harder. "A monster with your abilities? Not a chance."

"You were expecting Samantha," I say, wondering where the heck she is.

"Of course. Sam's been playing the hero ever since she met you. Thinks if she saves enough people she'll find purpose in this machine of a world. Delusional."

Ai watches our back and forth without expression.

I say, "So what, you work for Blue-Eyes now? You're her errand boy?"

"It's no use trying to goad me, kid. Won't work. I've been waiting for your Resistance to kill the Witch but they can't, so now I'm looking for other avenues. Took years to find China; she hid herself well."

"Other avenues? Other ways to kill the Witch?"

"Obviously."

"If you're on this plane, you allied with Blue-Eyes. You sold out," I say. His pistol is making me sweat. He's too fast for me to escape. He'll kill me—happily.

"More than one way to skin a cat, mate. And one of them is to befriend it. Plus, fooling the blue-eyed Witch provided certain political connections."

"So you allied with Blue-Eyes to get Ai—" I say.

"And now that I got her, the girl will spill her secrets—"

I finish, "And you'll use them against the Witch."

"Precisely, kid. I wish I was immune to her influence, but I can't guarantee it. Ai here, she's gonna help. Whether she likes it or not."

Without moving my head, I glance at Ai. "Does it work like that? Can you create immunities to Blue-Eyes?"

She mumbles, "No."

"Not yet," he barks. "But with the labs at CDC, who knows."

"Carter, we've got to end this. No more games. This world is breaking."

"You see brokenness, I see opportunity. You're too short sighted, always have been."

"You can't resist her. Imagine what'll happen at the upcoming peace accords. The leaders of the planet will fall into her lap help-lessly. Entire countries will succumb to her hedonism. She'll be the most powerful person to ever live."

"You aren't listening, mate. Not seeing the opportunity. Look harder. What happens if all those world leaders die?"

I shrug. "World War Three."

"Exactly. Or maybe even better."

"Jeez, Carter."

"Men like you and me, we'll rebuild society. We'll be kings. Gods."

"You plan to kill them."

"The summit was my idea. Get them all in one place," he says.

"You're insane."

"Maybe." He winks. "Par for the virus."

"It's not a virus," mumbles Ai.

"Whatever. Shut up."

"Maybe you should just kill Blue-Eyes," I say. "And then slink back into your hole."

"She's too well guarded. Always has been. If Shooter can't get her, no one can. And this is more fun, after all. She's been asking to meet me since the Chemist died, but that'd be a disaster. For me. But now, with China's help, it should be no issue. The Witch won't know I'm immune."

"It doesn't work like that," whispers Ai.

"Not yet. Didn't I tell you to shut up?"

"I'm taking her, Carter," I say.

"The hell you are."

"She and I are going to the Resistance. She'll teach us the cure and we can use it to stabilize the planet." I pause, and glance at Ai. "Can it work like that?"

She whispers, "I hope."

"The long nightmare can finally end."

"Nightmare? That's your problem, Chase. You've been sleeping in cars and hiding and fighting wars you didn't need to. Me? Living in paradise. Crafting the future. To opportunists, this is no nightmare."

"The rest of us don't have the luxury of living in paradise."

"Oh?" He waffles the gun. "I'm curious, then. Where you been the past few years?"

"Working."

"Yeah, me too. But where, kid?"

I stay silent.

He says, "I have a guess. Islands in the Caribbean? Your plane was shot down near there. And look at this tan you got. Maybe you and I aren't that different, mate. We both been biding our time in paradise as the world burns."

"Don't compare us. I've been taking care of people."

He chuckles, a dark sound like echoes in a cave. He raises a lighter, flicks it, and brings the flame to his cigarette. "Me too. And trust me, my work is far more consequential."

"How so?"

"I bet you can guess, mate. Not so hard to figure out."

"How would I know what you've been doing?"

He half squints, giving me a piercing inspection. "Do you really not know?"

"Know what?"

He removes the cigarette and blows blue smoke from the corner of his mouth. "That can't be true."

"What can't? Don't play games with me, Carter."

"I thought they knew. This whole time, I thought they knew," he says. "How about that. Gave the fools at the Resistance too much credit."

"Ugh. I forgot how super dumb and frustrating you are."

He grins, wicked and cold. "This is rich. Too good. I could tell you, kid, but then I'd have to kill you."

"Deal," I say, praying Samantha is close. Cause I'm bluffing—I'd rather not die. "Tell me and kill me. If I'm not dead from boredom by then."

"Back when you and I were trying to eliminate the Chemist, we didn't guess at the depth of his depraved agenda. He did more than create an army of nineteen-year-old freaks," says Carter, leaking smoke from his nostrils, cigarette back in his mouth.

"You're talking about the infants he injected with the Hyper Virus," I say.

"You knew about them."

"Sure. Katie hid the kids and their mothers."

"It's not a virus," Ai whispers.

"Your girlfriend hid them as best she could," says Carter. "But not good enough. I took them."

"No you didn't."

"Yeah. I did."

I close my eyes and groan. "Carter, you're the worst."

In my ear, Puck whispers, "Oh heck."

"They belong to me now. You have to see it to believe it, Chase. These kids are...hard to explain. The Chemist tinkered with the virus or something—"

"It's not a virus."

"—and they already display traits of the disease. They aren't like your girlfriend's mutants, who are powerful enough. These kids will grow up like me. And like you. Over two hundred of them."

"Sounds awful. Hell on earth."

"Sounds like opportunity."

"You stashed them in Hawaii," I guess. "You mentioned paradise."

"You want to help? Truly help? The kids need guidance. And I'm sick of the little bastards. You could train them."

"Into warriors."

"Of course," he says. At his hip, he makes a gun with his thumb and forefinger, and shoots me with it. "Obviously."

"Here's a better idea, Carter; let's train them to be *anything* else. Plumbers, teachers, veterinarians. Something other than world breakers."

"You won't help."

"Train killers? No."

"So I have to execute you," he says.

"Maybe so."

"You still have the power, Chase. I feel it, drawing me. These kids will be *Infected*. Not mindless freaks. Soon they'll learn to despise one another, as all alpha predators do. But they'll follow you."

"Or maybe Ai can cure them," I say.

Ai tugs at her chains. No use; she's stuck fast.

Carter shakes his head and the ash of his cigarette flicks onto the ground. "Where's your vision, boy? Where's your ambition?"

"Those kids aren't means to an end."

"That's why they were *created*. As tools."

"Enough. I'm taking Ai," I tell him. "To the Resistance."

He grins and curls of smoke secrete from his teeth, framing his face. "Fraid not, champ. She's mine."

"I'll go through you, if I have to."

Mocking and derisive, he laughs. "You and I both know, you can't beat me in a fight. You're still an infant."

"But he's not alone," says Samantha Gear, materializing behind Carter. She presses the barrel of her pistol into the back of Carter's head, and she rests her other hand on his shoulder. In that hand, she holds a grenade. The safety pin is already pulled—the spoon's ready to be released, triggering the explosive.

"Ah. There you are, Shooter," says Carter.

With her grenade hand, she pulls him closer and kisses the side of his face. An affectionate gesture, but one full of menace. Friends or enemies, Carter. The kiss or the grenade? You choose. "Good to see you, old man."

He says, "I was hoping you'd show. The fate of the world is being decided in the next few days, Sam. Be easier with you by my side."

"Tell your pilot to turn south. We're heading to Texas."

"Negative," he says. "Time runs short. We're bound for the CDC."

"Carter—"

"I need you, Samantha."

"—don't force me to put you down. I have a round in the chamber that'll go clean through your skull."

He grins. Like a madman. "And the grenade?"

"Just for fun."

"You might get me—I admit it. But not before I kill your boy." He nods at me, in case there's any confusion. Which there isn't.

"Do it," says Samantha. "I don't care. He's gotten fat anyway."

Carter repeats her words, staring me down. "Do it, she says. Hardly a strong alliance."

"Fat?" I blurt. "Did I hear that right? Fat?"

"You've been eating nonstop since you showed up."

"Not *that* much," I say. "Maybe a couple pounds, I put on. At most."

"Yeah. Gross."

"That's...unkind."

"I'm just saying, maybe cool it with the hamburgers before you see Katie," she says. "I bet her new husband doesn't eat five sandwiches every meal."

"You two idiots, shut up," growls Carter.

Speaking for the first time in several minutes, Puck says into my ear, "New husband? Huh? Katie's not *married.*"

My eyebrows rise and my heart skips a beat. "Not married?"

"Of course not, dummy."

"She's single?"

"Absolutely. She's been begging me to give her your new number," he says into my ear.

I smile. I smile to the point it hurts. "Give the girl my digits; what are you waiting for?"

Carter's expression shifts to a glower. "You're communicating with the computer hacker. Another one of my employees you stole."

Puck's voice drops to a whisper. "Oh damn. Don't let him hear PuckDaddy. Carter freaks me out. He cut my legs off, you know. I hate that guy."

I say, "See, Samantha? Katie's single. You're just a punk."

She rolls her eyes.

Enough of this. Buoyed by Katie's sudden availability, the sensation of invincibility rises in my chest. A false and stupid sensation, but it rises anyway.

I *Move*, catching them both off guard. I slam Carter's revolver upwards. The gun fires, puncturing a hole in the jet's fuselage. Ai screams.

He's *so* fast. He spins and puts an elbow into my head. Like being crushed by a sledge hammer. My bluetooth earpiece breaks—Puck's voice crackles and dies, and I'm thrown across the bay.

Samantha yanks her trigger five times, one long explosive blast, but Carter pivots around the pallet and out of sight. She goes after him but finds only shadow.

His voice fills our metal cavity. "Little children shouldn't pick fights with grown monsters."

"You can't beat both of us, Carter," I call, climbing to my feet. "Give us the girl."

"Two on one, hardly even odds," he says, manic laughter in his voice. The sound's originating to our right, deeper in the cargo bay. "You came to take what's mine but I won't let China go. I won her, fair and square. She belongs to me."

Samantha silently gets my attention and waggles the grenade. Now?

I shake my head. No, not yet.

"She's a genius, kiddies," calls Carter. "You'd use her brain to change the world. Trouble is, I like the world now. You can't have her. At least not alive."

He fires. Two muzzle flashes from the dark. Samantha leaps behind cover. I *See* the incoming rounds, glowing in the red light. My Thunder Stick sings, deflecting the rounds quicker than thought.

"You won't win," shouts Samantha. "Tell your pilot to turn south."

Unseen, Carter releases a theatrical sigh. "A lot of planning and hard work is about to be ruined, you two know that?"

"Let her go, Carter," I say.

"As you wish."

The Boeing's all-consuming hum increases. The cargo pallets and fuselage rattle. The metal deck we're standing on begins pitching upward.

Carter's plane is accelerating and aiming for higher sky.

The busted speaker in my ear crackles and I pull it out. Useless now.

Sirens wail. More red lights click on.

"You want the girl?" Carter says from everywhere. "Catch her."

The cargo bay door behind us growls. Light erupts in a horizontal slash. Sunlight pours in, like a great mouth yawning, wider and wider, as the long ramp lowers.

Sirens keep wailing, harsh and grating.

The floor we're standing on jerks to life. It's a conveyor track; Ai's strapped to a hydraulic cart which will move her down the ramp.

Carter's about to dump Ai into the atmosphere, chained to the heavy cargo boxes.

"Oh hell no," mutters Samantha and she rushes to Ai. The chains are thick, too strong for her bare hands, and possibly for mine. "Chase, he's trying to kill her. I need help."

Carter fires his gun twice more. Both rounds catch me in the chest. My flack jacket and inspissated skin absorb the rounds, keeping me alive, but it hurts. I stagger backwards and Carter pounces like a wild animal. We land on the cargo bay floor, him on top. The Thunder Stick digs into my spine.

"Chase!" screams Samantha, tugging at the chains. She's unable to break them so she scrabbles at the heavy military hardshell boxes. They crack and tear off in chunks under her powerful hands. "I can't get her loose!"

The jet roars upward, tilting the floor more and more vertical. Ai's pallet groans and tips forward, pulled by gravity but stayed by the hydraulic cart. Her lips are a tight line, her eyes wide with horror. Her muscles bunch as she works at the shackles.

The cargo door finishes its descent and the ramp locks into place. Below us, the Grand Canyon is swollen and hazy.

"Carter, don't do this!" I roar. He gets his hands around my throat and squeezes. His arms are more dense than steel. My airflow is cut off. My hands pry his thumbs back, but it takes everything I have to keep him from tearing my esophagus open.

"You're a special kid, Chase," he seethes. Smoke and ash spill from his mouth. An angry light shines deep within his irises, the glow of madness. "Far stronger than I was at your age. But I've had a hundred years to ossify into a force unstoppable. You? You're, what, twenty-three?"

"Help! Please!" cries Ai. Her pallet is crawling to the edge. Samantha plants her feet on the side of the hydraulic cart and pulls, screaming, trying to unseat the cargo from the cart. The heavy stack of boxes rocks her way. Too slow. Too late. She doesn't have the strength of Tank or Katie.

"The girl should've been mine. Instead she's about to die. This is your fault!" Carter is so mad he's spitting at me, increasing the pressure around my neck. "You should've stayed gone."

Ai's cart reaches the end of the track. Her hair whips in the wash. Lights at the door switch to green. Ai is tipped forward, face first. Her pallet teeters, pulled inexorably by gravity. She's leaning into space over the vast Nevada desert.

I can only watch.

Carter's plane is pitched too steep. The pallet nosedives, taking Ai with it. She screams but the sound is lost—she's suddenly gone.

"Chase!" Samantha is still gripping the grenade in her right fist. She fires it at me, like a fastball.

She leaps. Frozen in my vision, framed by the open cargo bay. Her silhouette seems to pause at the top of her jump. An eternity in that moment. She bends over, and plummets headfirst, arms pressed out, ankles together. A perfect dive. Vanishes from sight, going after Ai.

My heart nearly stops.

The grenade's safety spoon releases mid-flight, activating the device. We have mere seconds before shrapnel tears us apart.

Samantha's words from earlier flash upon my consciousness.

"You should know I've made my peace, Chase. If anything happens to me, don't waste time mourning...You said it best—we're like supernovas; we burn up fast and bright. If it's my time, I'm ready. Because I'll die helping friends..."

Samantha's vest has a parachute but it's a small one—barely big enough for her. She knows it won't hold their combined weight at this height.

She'll give the chute to Ai.

She's sacrificing herself.

I scream, "No!" but I have no air.

The grenade was thrown true. I release my hold on Carter and catch the device, the firm surface slapping my palm.

Carter sees it and rears back. "No! You'll kill us both!"

"So be it," I snarl. I shove the grenade upward, under his shirt.

He flails, groping at the bulge held against his abdomen. Falls off me.

"Fool! You fool!" he howls, clawing at his jacket. "I'm not ready!"

I'm up and sprinting on instinct to the open cargo bay door. Without thinking, I leap into the void.

My stomach vaults into my throat. Rushing wind rips off my mask and fills my eyes with tears. Arizona's landscape twists and revolves, like the horizon is a drunken gyroscope. I snap my arms back and shoot through the air like a missile, accelerating.

Below me, Samantha battles with the tumbling cargo pallet. She flings hardshell boxes until Ai's chain has nothing more to hold onto. Nothing except the girl herself.

I close the distance as they thrash. I don't know our altitude, but we were flying low and the earth is swelling.

Samantha tugs her vest off. She nearly loses it to the howling gale, catching it by the zipper.

"Wait!" I scream but they can't hear.

Ai's shackles won't come loose from her wrists so Samantha guides her hands and the chain through the arm holes. The metal links snap and crack at the air. Samantha zips the vest over Ai's chest and she shouts in Ai's ear.

I'm close enough to see Ai nod.

Samantha yanks a chord and the chute blossoms like a white flower ten feet below me. I spin to evade Ai, her descent halted. She's safe.

Samantha and I race past her in our dash to the ground. She sees me and her eyes pop. She looks strangely vulnerable without her vest, wearing only a tank top and pants.

"No! Chase, no!"

I'm a rocket and she's waffling in the air like a leaf and I slam into her.

"You stupid jackass, I won't let you do this!" She pushes at me, trying to get away. "There's no time, pull your chute!"

"Take my vest!"

"There's no time!"

She's right. The walls of the Grand Canyon rise up like a mouth to consume us. I won't be able to transfer the vest.

She's fighting, kicking, trying to release my chute. Doesn't want me to die.

"Stop!" I shout.

"Pull your chute!"

"Trust me! I have an idea!"

"We're almost at the ground!" she screams.

I hit her. A solid connection to her temple and she goes woozy. I pull her body to mine. Wrap my legs around her waist.

The ground is *so* close.

I connect my gloves to the wings in my pants. Haul my arms forward. The wing suit fabric fills and rips, but provides a precious few seconds of thrust. I bank left, aiming for the middle of the canyon and the ribbon at the bottom.

The wings tear as we arc, never meant for this weight or speed. But hopefully it's enough.

I pull the parachute cord and snatch at Samantha. I get her before the air catches the chute with a snap. I'm nearly jerked out of the vest, forty feet above the earth. My Thunder Stick shoots free, driving down at the ground like a nail. The parachute strains with the load, slowing us in a hurry, before surrendering to physics. The material rips free over my right shoulder.

We're falling again.

Too fast to survive a collision with dirt. But the wings did their job.

We drop like cannon balls into the raging Colorado River. Viewed from on high, it looked like a ribbon.

Samantha lands in shallower water, close to the shore. I splash down in the middle. The surface impact would kill a normal human. I hit the riverbed hard. The lights dim and I fight to remain conscious, my whole body ringing.

The vest and chute act like an anchor, pulling me downstream. My lungs burn. Need oxygen. I fight the zipper with numb fingers, getting free after an eternity, and kick up.

I reach the surface and blow water and suck air and nearly drown. Far overhead the Boeing belches smoke, heading east. I notice it vaguely in my delirium.

The water's cool. I pull against the current with powerful strokes. Still dizzy, I hope it's the correct direction. Samantha bobs lifelessly, so I grab her and tug.

After the interminable swim, I crawl onto the rocky shore, gasping. She hacks and coughs up water. The stones are firm and cruel against my back, a beautiful life-giving solidity.

Too exhausted and hurt to care at the moment, I watch Ai land a quarter mile upstream, safely on dry land. Alive. That's what matters.

Downstream, my vest snags on an outcropping. Near my head, the Thunder Stick is buried to the hilt in the pebbles and sand. I pant for several minutes, happy to be breathing, listening to Samantha groan. She calls me names and I grin. Both of her legs are broken; serves her right, trying to kill herself.

A red mask flitters out of the sky, like a feather drifting on the winds of chance, finally coming to rest draped over the handle of the Thunder Stick. The empty eyeholes glare at me.

High above Nevada, a lonely plane curves west in an elongated arc. The private jet is a red and white Eclipse and it's empty, the pilots having leapt out long ago. Inside the cockpit, alarms wail. The fuel gauge reads empty.

An hour after pushing across the the old California borderline, the engines quit. There's no coughing or sputtering, only a sudden absence of sound. Momentum keeps the Eclipse moving forward, but the nose drifts lower.

And lower.

The man called Nuts lays on his side in a stuffy tent, using an old boot for a pillow. The Los Angeles sun, without the palliative effect of a breeze, cooks him and thickens the hot air. He'd almost rather not be breathing it, except only a fool would consider such a thing. His hands are bound at the small of his back, tied with rope—quality half-inch cordage, the kind a man can trust. His feet are bound too.

His shelter was erected in a parking lot, alongside a city of other tents—a temporary rallying point for Walter's forces as they arrive from the north. Nuts peers relentlessly through a small vent at the base of the tent, where the flaps don't overlap, watching and cataloging. The man in the tent with him, his sentry, can't stay awake. Lulled by heat and boredom.

Nuts is a prized captive. He's no fool—his chances of escape are grim. Never been a fighter, no sir. Not like the Outlaw. Doesn't have the strength of the Hispanic boy, nor the spirit of the Carmine girl. He's a fixer, simple as that. A builder. At the moment, his eyes are fixed on the Van Norman Reservoir, a project dear to his heart.

Los Angeles—Carmine's kingdom, as he thinks of it—needs water. He could provide water from multiple sources, if he wasn't bound and if his Engineers weren't slain. Walter and his murderous band of fools blocked all the aqueducts, the beginning to his siege. Pipes are going dry and the people will start drawing on reserves and bottles soon.

With no outlet, the Van Norman reservoir is overflowing its banks. The water spills into the bypass reservoir and then into Granada Hills. A potential disaster waiting to happen, the accumulation of destructive forces. The water filtration plant is ruined, and all ability to control the flow mangled; months of work wrecked in one fateful night. The problem worsens by the hour because the rivers cascading down the Sierras never cease, and if Walter's makeshift clogs break then water will tear through the pipes like concentrated hurricanes—the safety valves are most likely destroyed too.

A mess. A damned mess, he thinks. If only they'd let him help.

He's deep within his thoughts on how best to safely release the water pressure when captors outside the tent begin shouting. A jet, they say. A plane. A plane is coming! They haven't seen many of those recently. But this plane is small. Moving too low and dropping fast. Where's the pilot? It's going to hit! Here it comes, they cry.

An explosion rocks the earth. Nuts feels it in the dirt, his bones rattling. The sound of rending metal and splintering wood. Through the tent walls he doesn't see much of a flash, though. Jet must've been out of gasoline, mitigating the eruption. Judging by the sound, it impacted a quarter mile north.

His guard jumps and exits the tent, shouting with the others. Sunlight, pure and heavenly, bursts in—and even better, a brief breeze to stir the air—until the flaps close again. For the moment, Nuts is alone.

He raises in a flash, ignoring cramped muscles. Hops to the nearby table, where he knows he'll find razors. Razors which can be bolted to the end of Walter's fingers. Razors which his goblin king used to poke and prod him recently, ripping open his flesh for fun.

Nuts rotates and leans against the table, getting his hands to the blades. Blindly he gropes until his fingertips connect. Inch by inch, the razor slides off the table into his palm, and he gingerly stuffs it down the back of his pants. Hidden but easily accessible. A tool for use in the near future.

He hopes.

The guard returns to the tent a few minutes later, checking on his captive. He finds Nuts is lying on the ground, face first, staring at the reservoir and pondering the inexplicable plane crash.

- 16 -
The Outlaw

That night, I sit with Samantha and Ai around a dingy campfire that Ai somehow coaxed to life using rocks and scrub brush. Pure sorcery. But it keeps our waning spirits up. Between us we've eaten four granola bars—our entire stash. We're hungry and tired and cold and alone. Sheer cliffs rise to the north and south of our narrow canyon, blocking out the stars except those directly above.

Samantha's vest is wrapped tight around her legs, keeping them compressed and immobile. The rest of her is wrapped in her parachute and she shivers against the night chill.

Ai doesn't seem to feel the falling temperature. She watches me with large eyes, dark except for the fire's glow.

Samantha's phone was in her vest, which Ai wore and saved from water damage. PuckDaddy, practically hyperventilating, was able to determine our coordinates. He says we're not in the Grand Canyon, technically, but rather an Indian Reservation to the west of it. Closer to Lake Mead. Sure does look like the Grand Canyon. A rescue helicopter will find us in a few hours, he says, his tinny voice banging off the canyon walls.

So we sit and wait, knowing we'll need to hike south at first light to reach our transportation. Sleep feels impossible.

Ai breaks the silence. "It's true. What I heard."

"What's that?"

"I feel you. And I like you," she replies. She has a little trouble with English words. She pronounces it as, *An' I rike you.* "I don't like the others. But I like you."

I nod. "Something about the weird composition of my disease. All the pure-borns feel it."

"I don't like her."

Samantha, teeth chattering, says, "Thanks. I don't like me much either right now."

"Even though I don't like you," says Ai and she makes a small bow. "Thank you. For helping."

Thang you. Fa haping.

"Whatever, shut up, don't fall out of airplanes."

I grin. "Be kind, Samy."

"You shut up too, Chase. My legs hurt. Shoulda let me die."

"I wish I woulda, now."

"Shut up again."

Ai tells me, "I see you in the news. I think, maybe I meet him someday."

"How nice for you, meeting your hero. But you know what they say about meeting your heroes," growls Samantha. "It always sucks, that's what they say. Aren't you a doctor? Fix my legs."

"I did. Bones reset and they knit together now. Just have to wait. Few days."

"Fix them again. Make it faster."

I change the subject. "Tell me about the cure, Ai."

"I find it a year ago. I call Carter and tell him—"

I interrupt her. "How'd you know Carter?"

"He visit me, years ago. Gave me number. So I call him, about the cure. He tells me, don't tell anyone. We keep it secret. He would come see me soon. But then, not long ago, police take me. Take my lab, take my research. The President of your country, she try to get me. But Carter arrives. And he..." She stops and shakes her head, still watching me with bottomless eyes. "I wish I had not called him. He is not who I thought."

"Tell me about the cure."

"Is complex. I know much English medical jargon, but you might not."

Samantha barks a laugh. "She's saying we're stupid."

I nod. "We are."

"Yeah but she shouldn't affirm it."

"Disease is unknown to science. Like protozoa, but not exact. Housed primarily in lymphatic system. Turns macrophages against the body. Causes anomalies to testes, thymus, adrenal glands, frontal cortex, you understand? Immune system is hyperactive, usually to fatal degree. Over produces cells, like bone and muscle tissue. Causes telomere shortening, and overwrites the genome."

"Nope," says Sam, chattering. "Not a word did I follow."

"Means nothing to us," I say. "Can you fix it?"

She pauses. Nods slowly but looks uncertain. "I have, yes. In some cases."

"Only in some?"

"Depend. It depend on whether genetic code has been altered. Here in America, you have so many patients. The mutants. Some are insane, yes?"

"Yeah, we noticed," I say.

"Because their body reject new genome. Their body fight it. You and me, our somatic cells are overwritten at birth. And some other, like Queen Carmine, even later in life, the disease successfully integrate. But ones who present mental instability? Their genetic code is still pure. The insanity is result of the inner battle. The disease cannot fully integrate. Body is in constant state of infection and rejection."

"So who can be saved?"

"Patients exhibiting evidence of mental instability can be cured. I hope."

Samantha says, "So the crazy ones."

"Their mind isn't broken?" I ask.

"It is, but not irreversible. Human body is amazing. My mentor, Francis Collins, says we are designed that way on purpose."

"So," I say carefully. "I can't be cured?"

"No. Your changes are permanent. But the other, if the genetic code isn't permanently altered, gene therapy can restore sanity. Then we treat disease with cocktails I create. Similar to antiprotozoals."

"You've done it?"

She nods. "Yes, on three patients. Four total. Only one fail. Seventy-five percent success, so a small sample size."

Samantha and I lock eyes. There's a cure. She can do it. Already a seventy-five percent success rate. There's a way, without slaughtering thousands, to end the rampage. To remove the infection plaguing the middle of our country. Without their constant threat, the Resistance would be free to funnel resources elsewhere. Foreign countries could restore order inside their borders. The remnant of the Chemist's lingering scourge can finally be eradicated.

Katie would be released from her burden of maintaining the sanity of those who cling to her. She would be free.

"Won't be easy," mutters Samantha through clenched teeth. "Those bastards are hard to catch. How is gene therapy administered?"

"First step, an injection."

"Impossible. The mutants are hard to subdue even with electricity. Plus they're learning how to evade the Herders."

Ai tilts her head toward Samantha's gun, resting on the rock beside her. "Shoot them with it."

"Tried it. We can't produce a tranquilizer powerful enough."

"I can," says Ai simply.

Samantha perks up. "For real? No kidding?"

"Is not about power. Is about creativity and data. Your labs will create a solution to be injected. I will show them."

"And you'll put that injectable solution into a bullet?" asks Samantha, looking like a woman opening Christmas presents.

"Yes. Why not?"

I laugh. "I think Samantha discovered her purpose in life."

She whispers, in awe, "That sounds like fun. I want to shoot them so bad."

"We just need to keep you alive, Ai, and get you into the hands of the Resistance."

Samantha's phone rings, shattering our quiet conversation. Inside our sound box, the noise bounces back and forth, as if dozens of phones are ringing. She glances at it. Eyebrows rise. Tosses it to me.

"It's for you," she says. With a sneaky grin.

It's an incoming video call from Katie Lopez.

The Katie Lopez. Holy smokes.

My legs give out when I try to stand and my fingers tremble. The most perfect name I've ever read, right there on the screen. Calling.

"What's the matter, dummy? Answer it."

"I'm trying," I say. But I'm not. I can't. My thumb refuses to budge.

"No you're not, don't be a coward. You recently jumped out of an airplane. *Two* airplanes, actually. Answer the stupid phone."

"Who is it?" asks Ai.

"His girlfriend, Katie."

"Queen Carmine? But she is dead. Two years ago, yes?"

"No, shut up. Chase, answer it!"

"You answer it," I say.

"The mighty Outlaw," she cackles. "Afraid of his girlfriend!"

"Okay, fine," I say over the ringing. My voice only cracks a little. "Don't listen."

"I'm going to listen."

"You're the worst."

"Answer the phone!"

I do. As I walk away from the campfire, the screen blinks. Goes black and then an image appears. The girl of my dreams materializes. Her hair, the color of chocolate, is longer than I remember. Her green eyes brighter. The rest is exactly as I imagined for the past seven hundred nights.

A light on Samantha's smartphone clicks on, illuminating my face with a warm glow.

She makes a gasping sound. But she doesn't say anything. Neither do I. We simply stare, as though each of us is inspecting a photograph.

I sit on a stone near the Colorado River and watch her. She's in a bedroom I recognize—the room where Carmine slept, in a Los Angeles skyscraper. Two electric lamps burn on the side of her bed. I can tell by her eyes, she's searching my face. Looking at my hair. At my eyes, which brim with tears.

"Say something," she whispers.

"I still love you, Katie."

She smiles and it's like being warmed by the sun. Then she covers her mouth and fights down a sob.

"And," I continue. "I don't care if you're with someone else. I think you and I should get married."

She laughs and wipes her eyes. "Married?"

"Yes."

"You haven't even proposed."

"Well—"

"And you cannot propose over the phone, silly. Everyone knows that."

My heart nearly bursts. A sudden rush of happiness so piercing it's painful. This isn't the voice of Carmine; these aren't the warrior queen's words. I'm listening to Katie Lopez—she is truly back.

She says, "I love you, Chase. Ask me again when we're together. I'm still coming to grips with the fact that the only man I ever loved died two years ago, but now he's back."

"Yes. Sorry about the miscommunication."

"I am too." She rubs at her face with a sleeve and sniffs. "The worst failure to communicate imaginable. It's *so* good to see your face. I think you've grown more handsome."

"Probably."

"You've been on a boat the past two years? Why a boat?"

"It brought me peace. My heart was broken, you know. I got to fish."

"Chase Jackson hates fishing."

"Not anymore. It was a way to feed people," I say.

"Which people?"

"Caribbean islands. Helping them get back on their feet, after the crash. I hear you've been hiding on remote farms?"

"Yes. I've been feeding people too. I seem to pick up stragglers wherever I go," she says with a wry smile, still wiping her eyes. "Wish I could've been there with you, on the boat. I bet your views were better."

"I'm talking to Katie Lopez, I can tell. Not Carmine. She didn't care about pretty views."

"Carmine doesn't cry over cute boys. She's still around, though, inside my head."

"So your memories returned."

"The Infected warlord Russia almost killed me in San Diego and it jogged my brain. When I started to remember, my alter ego Carmine was no longer necessary. She's still here, trying to get out and kick everyone's butt."

"I liked her," I say. "She was fierce."

"I like her too. She kept me alive. One day soon I might let her kill Walter."

"No. You stay away from him. Let me deal with Walter."

"He's already here. Somewhere close. Los Angeles is a mess. There's fighting all over the city, and I'm exhausted from putting out fires. We drove Walter out, but I have a bad feeling. A premonition this is only the beginning."

"What do you mean?"

"There's a final showdown coming. Walter's not fleeing north, like he has in the past. Our water's cut off and we can't get it started again. Walter's entire army is here, fighting General Brown's....it's a mess, Chase. This can't go on. We've got to end this or die trying."

"The girl from China has a cure. Specifically for the insane, like your Variants. And Walter's freaks," I say.

"That's fantastic." She smiles but she's too tired to put enthusiasm into her words. "Really great news. But I'm not sure it'll be in time. We don't have long. PuckDaddy says you're in the Grand Canyon?"

"Essentially."

"Such a bizarre coincidence. When I last saw Tank Ware, that's the direction he was headed."

I roll my eyes and groan. "That dork is still around? What's he doing out here?"

"He's chasing the wolf man."

"The *wolf* man?"

"He's the scariest, Chase. He's a man who looks like a wolf and can control them."

"How's he do that?"

"I dunno. He's super gross. He has thousands of wolves under his control."

I glance up at the canyon we're in, which could suddenly turn into a prison. "They're both headed my direction?"

"I imagine you won't meet. The Grand Canyon is vast. But that is a curious accident, isn't it. Providence, perhaps? By the way, Tank can control animals now, too," she says. "Mammals, mostly."

"Tank can control mammals," I say in a flat tone. "Like mountain lions?"

"Yes, he has a pack of those."

I scoff. "Of *course* that ugly ogre can control animals. Why not? Nothing else in the world makes sense."

"Are you with Samantha?"

She shouts over my shoulder, "Hell yeah he is! And he broke my legs!"

Katie grins. "You broke Samy's legs?"

"She meant to say, *saved her life*, but she used the wrong words."

"Oh gosh, I miss you. Hearing your voice is everything. I'm in my twenties. Does that mean I'm too old to call you my boyfriend?"

"I don't think so."

"Yes!" calls Samantha. "It's weird!"

Katie covers a laugh with her fingers. "You know who else doesn't like it? Carmine. She's irritated somewhere between my ears. She has no time for trivialities such as this."

"Listen, Katie, Samantha's battery is running low, so I have to hang up soon. But there's something you need to hear first. We got Ai off the plane but I ran into Carter. Remember him?"

"Of course."

"Remember those kids you saved? The Inheritors? Carter took them."

For a moment, I think our connection is frozen—she's not moving. Her eyes are wide and her mouth hangs open. But finally she blinks and says, "That's not possible."

"He's got them stashed in Hawaii, he says, and that the kids need guidance. They'll be, what? Five years old by now?"

"I thought the Navy had them."

I shrug. "I don't know the whole story. He didn't tell me much."

She groans and rubs at her eyes. "Okay. I'll look into it. Thank you, Chase. Now hurry up and get here."

"For you, Katie, anything."

"Isn't it ironic, both of us reached this breaking point simultaneously, where we couldn't take anymore? Both of us received word the other had died and immediately went into hiding? And that the comedy of errors lasted two years?"

"Ironic and terrible."

She says, "I love you, Chase," and hangs up.

I sit for a long time, staring at the dark phone. At the afterimage of the girl I love. The *woman* I love. After her 'death,' I'd been suicidal. Couldn't find many reasons to carry on. Each morning the sun came up, baleful and harsh, bringing new light to my misery. It took months for the color to return, and even then the world lacked its previous vibrancy and chroma. But now, as her voice floats through my memory, *I love you, Chase*, I know it was worth it. Worth enduring the misery. I'd wait a hundred years, if I had to, for that phone call.

I need to get out of this canyon.

I need to get to Los Angeles.

I need to get to Katie. She's right, there's a showdown coming. The forces of this world, good and evil, are accelerating; I see it, feel it. Nature is fighting to restore order. Nature and maybe the Almighty, the man upstairs. I wouldn't blame God for watching us with disgust as we screw all this up.

Half an hour passes before I return to the struggling campfire. I don't need the light, though—I see fine without it.

To my surprise, Samantha is sitting up, staring to the west. Searching the black. A gun is gripped in her right fist.

"What's going—"

"Shhh," she says.

Suspiciously I follow her gaze. I'd been too preoccupied inside my own head to notice the world around. I squint and strain to hear.

There—movement. Someone's with us. Samantha must've detected it, and now she's trying to pinpoint the danger.

Surreptitiously I lower and retrieve my Thunder Stick. The tip scrapes quietly against the stones.

Ai's eyes are closed. She whispers, "I feel it. A person. A boy."

I nod grimly. I detect the sharp scent of a wild animal. A human being, but only barely.

"He is one like I told you," says Ai. Her head is tilted, testing the world with her senses. She's only mouthing the words, but we hear the movement of air she produces. "You can tell? His body fights the disease. He is mentally unstable."

"Chase," says Samantha, a note of alarm in her voice. "It's him. He's here."

"Yep," I say. My mind churns furiously, looking for options, looking for an escape, looking for hope. There isn't much.

"What do we do?"

"I don't know," I admit.

"That's not much help."

I say, "No sudden movements. Everyone stay calm." Outside the faint glow of our fire, the darkness shifts. A shadow moves closer. The scent of madness. "He's here."

Samantha swears softly, sweat beading on her forehead.

Into the light steps Andy Babington. He's hunched, catching himself every few steps with his hands as he trips. He's entirely naked, not even wearing shoes. The skin at his ribcage is red and inflamed, especially around the metal which forms part of his skeletal frame. On his back, a nuclear bomb blinks green. Blink, blink, blink, over and over and over.

"H-help," he whispers, coming closer. "Help me. I cant...I can't h-hold it much longer."

Katie Lopez

Early morning.

I stand in the tower's War Department looking at monitors. The majority of the screens are dark. We have fewer resources than we did two years ago—fewer working antennas, more dysfunctional satellites, and less electricity. I ordered a moratorium on all electric devices other than the essential—we don't want to drain our batteries too quickly (much of our power comes from water turbines, which aren't turning).

The citizens of Los Angeles are trying to consume two bottles of water a day only. There must be a solution to the water crisis. There *has* to be, but everyone who'd know the solution is either captured or dead.

It's gratifying and surprising how quickly the citizens adopted my leadership again. Even after two years, they still call me queen. My dramatic entrance, nearly taking Walter's head off with a motorcycle followed by the victorious roar, helped my cause.

On screen in front of me, video plays of General Brown's forces hammering Walter's in northern Los Angeles. We're losing, being driven back. Without Tank's help, and without the support of all those he took with them, we lose ground hourly to Walter's mutants.

I need to join the fight, today or tomorrow. I'm delaying the inevitable. Delaying because I'm not a fighter; that was Carmine. Carmine was the warrior queen, the woman who stood face to face against Walter and told him he couldn't come in. On the other hand, I'm Katie Lopez. Valedictorian and book nerd.

No, whispers Carmine. I know it's my inner dialogue and logic battling back and forth, but I swear she comes through as a voice. **You are more. You must be.**

I sure hope so. Otherwise the Guardians will be following an ineffectual leader into combat. If I can ever work up the nerve.

On a different screen, CNN wonders where the President is. Blue-

Eyes has vanished. Still in her mountain retreat, perhaps? But I doubt it. Her absence portends poorly for Los Angeles. She's long had her eyes set on this city. She's coming. Or perhaps she's already here.

Argh. I need more information.

Which reminds me, I have work to do.

I pass Kayla in the hallway. She looks ready for a bridal catalogue shoot or a movie set, and she smells like flowers. "Morning, love."

"Love?" she gasps, looking up from her phone. "I *adore* that nickname! You may call me it forever. And also, you are a darling dresser! So much more classy and trendy than Carmine."

I inspect my outfit. "I'm wearing jeans, a t-shirt, and sneakers."

"Which goes to show how much of a mess Carmine was. And also? The shirt you picked out is by Stella McCartney. Not too shabby. It used to cost three hundred dollars."

I feel woozy and I think my face pales. "Three *hundred* for a t-shirt?"

"Sure!"

I put a hand on the wall to brace myself. "Think I'll go change."

"What! No! You look darling. Personally I'd like to see those legs in a skirt and heels, but this will do."

I suppose the monetary value of clothing no longer matters, but the price tag is still jaw dropping.

She says, "Carmine always dressed in active wear. You know, cause she worked so hard and she was always gross."

"I looked through her outfits, but they're a little...form fitting."

"Right?" She beams. "Good thing you've got a perfect form!"

"Carmine didn't care what people thought about her, but I do." Somewhere between my ears, Carmine scoffs and tells me to dress like a hard worker and people will treat me that way. "I'm a little more...modest, I think."

She squints at me, cocking her hip. "I don't get it. You're still *you*, right? It's just...another side of your personality?"

"Basically. I don't get it totally either. Long story short, I'll be wearing fewer form fitting items."

"But you've got a dynamite tush! Everyone says so."

I clear my throat, certain my face is red. "Alright, that's enough. I need to go."

"How're your joints? Do they hurt?"

"Just my elbows and hands today."

She nods her head, pleased. "Perfect. I thought you needed a spot of color. I'll wrap them in red silk before you go."

"Kayla—"

"Ooooh, and let's look at earrings too!"

In the garage under the tower, I bypass my Land Cruiser and head for a hybrid Honda Ridgeline—a big powerful truck. Travis is already there, waiting for me. He's wearing pants specially sewn for him and his sword Hurt hangs from a scabbard strapped to his back. As always, I'm a little unnerved being around someone three times my size, thick with muscle and unbridled enthusiasm and prone to clumsiness.

"**My queeeeen**," he calls with an enormous smile on his face. "**Reaady?**"

"Let's do it, Travis."

I slide behind the wheel and Travis steps into the truck bed. Nearly fifteen feet tall and weighing over five hundred pounds, he fits into very few places. One of them, though, is kneeling in the bed of a truck, holding onto the cab's roof. He loves it, like a dog would.

I'm forced to carefully ease my way around Guardians on alert outside the tower—mutants either off duty or refusing to work with General Brown at the battlefront. They watch me go, trot in the wake of our Ridgeline, and then the Leapers take to the skies when I hit the gas. Desperate to stay with me. More and more I realize that these poor souls have minds which aren't healing. Even if I'm around, it's a temporary salve, an addict getting a fix.

I say a short prayer in the hopes that Ai can deliver on her cure. We need it in a bad way; Los Angeles is spinning out of control.

Our Guardian pursuers give up when I hit old Interstate 10 and accelerate to eighty miles per hour. Travis laughs and bangs on the roof, creating dents, and I can't help laughing with him. "**Faster!**" he shouts. I swerve between lanes and he hoots and I roll the windows down. After all these years Los Angeles still carries a familiar scent, the West Coast flora and fauna redolent in my nostrils. Unexpected bliss. The whipping wind and pure sunlight decontaminate me, washing my worries away. For twenty minutes I'm back in high school, driving through Los Angeles carefree. There is no Walter, no blue-eyed terrorist president, no battle in Sylmar, no eminent water shortage. Just me and the universe.

As we motor into the hills of Bel Air, the yoke of responsibility returns. The muscles in my jaw tighten again. Little girls live in this city, little Katie Lopezs, and they deserve the same chances I had, the same promise of a future without war. Unless we somehow manage to right the ship, those little girls are doomed.

I can't let that happen.

I park on one of Mulholland Drive's crests, offering an oversight view of northwest LA. Of Sylmar and Granada Hills and our former water treatment plant. General Brown's war machine is obvious— rooftop machine gun nests, arrayed missile launchers, marching columns of men. Despite the distance, I can zero in and make out details.

Trouble is, Brown isn't fighting a standard military force. He's engaging small squads of mutants his men can't target. Walter's goblins move too quick, climb too fast, leap too far.

You need monsters to fight these monsters. And I'm their queen.

Carmine roars somewhere inside. She wants to fight. To deliver Los Angeles this very minute. Her emotions surge into my veins, activate my amygdala, trigger my hate.

I press against my back, working against the accumulating ache. Nearby, Travis stomps into a house and begins playing with furniture. I hear glass break and wood splinter. Behind me, coming up the road, I *Sense* my two omnipresent tigers. Following protectively at a distance.

General Brown radioed me last night about a bizarre plane crash.

A small private jet hit in Northridge and we don't know why. I scan for the wreckage, for signs of a scar ripping through the neighborhoods. Soon my gaze settles to the north, where our water is blocked. Somewhere inside that shimmering haze, the enemy lays siege to our resources. But what to do about it?

I watch and think for hours. I'm deep in thought when I hear a sound from my youth—a noise I've heard thousands of times but not recently.

An airborne engine.

Another plane? I turn my gaze east, searching the blue. Two planes in two days? What are the odds. There, barely clearing Mount San Antonio. A fat aircraft, like a transport. Military green. Smoke billows from the tail—is it damaged?

For whatever reason, it's going to land in Los Angeles.

I radio for General Brown, and two minutes later his voice comes over the speaker.

"Good morning, General. Got my eyes on the cargo plane. One of yours?"

"Negative, not ours. Radar picked the bogey up and we radioed for identification. Pilot replied with our authorization codes, so must be a friendly. We called Resistance for confirmation."

I lower the radio and watch the fat plane rumble overhead, rattling nearby windows and disgorging oily smoke into the atmosphere. It's a Boeing with no telltale identification markings, diving toward an airstrip—not the big international Los Angeles airport though. Now that it's past, I can see the loading ramp is lowered. In mid-flight? Is that common?

The noise passes, I radio again. "The aircraft is landing at the old Santa Monica Airport."

"I'll get on the horn again to Texas, and send a squad to meet the bird at Santa Monica."

"No need, I'm only a couple miles away. Can be there in five minutes."

"Roger that. Keep me posted."

I grin. Good ol' General Brown. I missed him.

"Let's go, Travis! Need to welcome a Resistance plane."

He bounds out of the house, breaking apart the doorframe, and we motor south, leaving the hills behind for the flatland of Santa Monica. Although thousands live here, raising livestock, cleaning rubble, repairing the old world, this part of Los Angeles feels empty. In a city made for hundreds of thousands, the current residents are mere drops in an empty bucket.

Santa Monica Airport hasn't been used in over four years. Travis breaks open a locked gate next to the abandoned terminal and we weave through a rusted graveyard of carts and trolleys before hitting the open tarmac. The Boeing powered down at the far end, near the security fence. It's large enough to defy description. The pilots sit high enough to be on a third story.

I park near the tail. This was not an ordinary or scheduled flight, that's obvious. The ramp's down and the tail drips oil. This Boeing was forced to make an emergency landing. System malfunction? Busted engine?

Travis and I cautiously walk up the long ramp, nearly ripped off during landing. Military pallets line the sides of the cargo bay, but that's all we see; no one's here. Our boots echo hollowly against the fuselage. I find the source of the Boeing's belching smoke—a ragged hole is gouged in the starboard side of the cargo bay. Looks like a minor explosion.

We reach the cockpit ladder. Travis is far too big, so he waits below as I ascend.

"Hello?" I call. "Anyone need medical attention?"

In the cockpit I find a pilot. He's wearing flight gear adorned with an American patch.

American. My pulse quickens.

This isn't a Resistance aircraft.

The pilot's dead. Killed recently, based on wet blood soaking through his gear. With shaking fingers I close his eyelids. Carmine screams for action.

Someone was recently in the co-pilots chair. Unless my nose deceives me, I detect cologne—a scent I recognize but can't place. I drop back to the cargo bay deck. My giant companion watches me with alarm, absorbing my emotion. Only now do I spot the bloody bootprints. Fresh and sticky. Someone's still alive. The boots are large —a man. Has to be the same man who killed the pilot. I crouch and follow the crimson trail leading out of the Boeing through a forward hatch. The person is injured, based on his prints. A limp, one of the legs scrapping. And...I squint and scrutinize the tarmac, looking over the patterns in the dust...there's a second person. Two sets of boot-prints, but only one of them is injured. The trail runs into the grass and through a hole torn in the security fence.

The killers, whoever they are, can't be more than a few minutes ahead.

Find them, says Carmine. **Justice must be swift.**

"Travis," I say.

"**Yes, queeen,**" he whispers like an avalanche.

"Get Hurt ready."

The Outlaw

Andy Babington is starving. He's lived off the land for the past twenty-four months but forging's hard in the canyons. He's dangerously malnourished, his fingers trembling.

Samantha's trembling too, from pain and lack of calories; her body is healing itself and demanding supplies. She scoots to the water at first light and shoots two bass. I do my best to clean them, extract the bullet, and cook them over the small pale fire. I end up burning the fish and covering them with ash because my small roasting sticks keep breaking, but Samantha and Andy gobble them down anyway.

I don't know how close he is to death, or how close that bomb is to detonation, but he doesn't look good. His ribs and joints and tendons are all apparent, and his face looks pale and green. Maybe the fish buys us time.

"I can't," he mumbles, staring into the flame. He shifts and the metal cage bolted to his spine scraps the stones. "Can't f-find her. I got close, but...she ran. Won't wait m-much longer. I can't. So tired."

He can't find Katie. Keeps mumbling about finding Queen Carmine and ending his mission.

Puck texts me. Finally.

>> **aight homie**

>> **need u 2 head west**

>> **helicopter is close, but can't land**

>> **3 miles west, there's a place along the river called Lower Granite Gorge. Big flat place.**

>> **chopper will grab u there**

I glance at Samantha. She's getting the texts too. She nods. We can do that.

Okay, I reply.

Any thoughts on our nuclear predicament?

>> **general anderson put tranquilizers onboard the chopper**

>> **even if they can't fully stop him, it'll slow him down**
>> **long enough for you to escape**

I don't like it. Too risky. Plus, he'll keep chasing Katie.

Samantha whispers, "If we try to give Andy a tranquilizer, it might anger him. And I got a feeling that bomb is ready to blow. Plus, if he falls asleep, he's so sick...it might go off."

I nod agreement. But I don't know what else to do.

Ai watches us expressionlessly.

"M-maybe," Andy says, ignoring us and talking to himself. "Maybe it's time. To end this. Here with m-my old pal, Chase Jackson. Jackson, the rookie."

Andy and I went to high school together. I haven't thought about football in years, but he and I were on the same team, both played quarterback. Our rivalry was not friendly.

He turns miserable eyes on Samantha. "And y-you. Just the kicker. Always hated you."

"Likewise, dumbass," she says. "And put some pants on, for Pete's sake."

"Maybe it's time," he repeats.

The blinking green light on his back increases in pace. That can't be good. The nuclear bomb is armed and supposedly he can detonate it at will.

"It's not time, Andy," I say using a soothing tone, like talking to an angry dog. "Not yet. Trust me. Just relax, because it's not time."

"W-why?"

"Because..."

"Because what?"

"Because...you haven't found her yet."

He lowers his head to his knees and whimpers. He's about twenty-three months past due for a haircut. "C-can't find... She made me. Told me I h-had to, and I've looked everywhere. But..."

The green light flashes twice as fast as it did sixty seconds ago. Blink-blink. Blink-blink. Blink-blink.

"I know where she is. Okay, Andy?" I blurt. "I know. I'll take you there. To Katie. To Carmine."

Andy looks up. Stares at me through his grungy hair. "Where?"

"She's close. That way." I point north. "But first, I need to get my friends onto a helicopter. They're hurt. And then, me and you, we'll go there. To Katie, in the Grand Canyon."

"Together?"

"Yes. Together."

Samantha makes a groaning noise. Mutters under her breath, "Oh good grief."

I glare at her—you got a better idea?

Andy nods to himself, processing this. "Okay," he says and he licks his fingers, enjoying the fish remnants. "Okay. I can w-wait. Just a little longer. We go together."

"Everyone up," I say. "We need to hike west. Samantha—"

"Don't even say it, Outlaw."

"You can't walk."

"The hell I can't."

"Both your legs are broken."

"A mere aggravation."

"Which means—"

She cocks her gun. "I'll shoot you. I will."

"—you need to be carried."

"I would rather die," she snaps, "than be carried."

"On my back. Or in my arms. You choose."

"I choose death."

"Then I pick. I choose in my arms. That way we can look at each other as we walk."

Ai's lips, usually in a perpetual and firm line, turns up at the corners. She looks back and forth between us and covers her mouth. She makes a giggling noise, almost childish.

I take a step towards Samantha.

She snaps, "I'll bite you, Chase. I really will, no bluffing. If you carry me in your arms I'll pull chunks out of you with my teeth."

I bend over and snatch her before she's ready. Sling her over my shoulder, so her arms wrap around my neck. She yelps and sweats. I shrug and get her high, like a backpack.

"If I wasn't so extraordinarily tough," she says through clenched teeth. "I would tell you that hurt a lot. And to be careful with my cracked femurs."

"Wuss."

"It's no fair how fast you are. And your stupid rod of death is in my face, poking out the back of your collar."

"Wow," I groan. "You are super fat."

"I am not."

"Shockingly heavy."

"Shut up. It's all muscle and will power."

I trudge west alongside the river, calling for Ai and Andy to follow. We've got a long way to go.

Got a bad feeling our motley crew will be slow movers.

The three miles takes us three hours. My shoulders and arms and back are screaming when we reach the flat rocky expanse. Puck's aircraft is already here waiting, an army green V-22 Osprey; the airplane which can takeoff vertically with swiveling rotors.

The crew doesn't come greet us. They've been warned—stay away from the skinny guy, he's got a nuke. As we approach, they stare wide-eyed at me, the fabled Outlaw emerging from the canyons. Not looking so hot, I bet.

I slide Samantha through the open cargo bay door and the engines whine, the blades beginning a lazy rotation. Unexpectedly, her eyes well with tears.

"I should be with you," she says.

"Don't break your legs next time."

"I got a feeling, Chase. It's all about to hit the fan."

I nod. I feel it too. So does Katie. Eminent calamity, invisible and looming over our heads.

Samantha grabs my vest. "You don't die here," she says and wipes angrily at her cheeks. "Understand? Not here, not because of him.

You get far away from that nuke, soon as you can. Stay alive. I only need a couple days to recover. Maybe less."

"You got it."

"And...thanks for jumping after me. I owe you."

I grin. Takes a lot to get Samantha emotional and appreciative. Must be in extreme pain. I help Ai board and they both strap in. Samantha finds a survival kid from General Anderson and tosses it my way. Inside I see apples and granola bars and bottled water.

I point at Ai and call over the increasing din. "We need a cure. Fast. Get on it."

She nods. No expression.

Overhead, the rotors howl. Time to go.

I salute Samantha and jog back to Andy, who's cowering behind a rock. He's not used to people or machines.

The Osprey throws itself into the sky, anxious to flee the potential blast radius. Andy and I watch it ascend to safety and dart beyond the cliff walls, gone. All of a sudden, I've never felt so alone and hopeless.

I toss Andy an apple, and wonder—what the heck do I do now?

He bites it and smiles, the juice spilling down his chin. "Take me to her."

I nod wearily, longing for the peace of my boat, the simple life of a fisherman.

"Now," he says.

"Let's go."

"Where?"

I point north and west, a direction I know for a fact leads away from Katie.

"Where?" he asks again, a little angry. "How far?"

"Good question," I mumble.

We return to the shadow of the canyons, walls rising like temple pillars around us.

Katie Lopez

The bloody trails plunges into Penmar Golf Course, where it's obvious I'm chasing two men—there are two paths pushed through the tall grass. I send Travis north to circle around; he's too tall and noisy, and I'd rather him flank the men. For the moment, I'm alone. Carmine's pleased, reveling in the solitary hunt.

The men move quickly. Their trail leads straight through the overgrown golf course and into the neighborhood beyond. This section of Santa Monica is deserted and dilapidated; roofs are caving, cars rusting out, some houses are burnt to the ground. I'm always amazed how quickly nature subsumes untended civilization.

No birds chirp here, an eery silence. I still get wafts of the cologne, and someone else too.

I'm cautiously making my way down Glyndon Avenue through the once sprawling suburbia when a truck starts directly ahead. An old Tahoe, somehow able to still turn the engine. Its pistons and rotors scream, but it drops into gear and packs on speed.

Don't they know I can outrun an old junker? I set off at a jog, hugging the houses so they won't see me.

I don't realize my mistake until it's too late. Keeping my eyes on the Tahoe, I run past an ancient van. A man stands there; a trap! He releases the power of his weapon—an electroshock baton, the kind used by Herders. The load discharges into my body on contact.

The world ruptures. My sanity flees and my vision turns white. Feels like I'm inside a hurricane, like I'm inside the jaws of an alligator and being shaken to death. Pain unimaginable. Time and space spin and swirl like a snowstorm. I scream but nothing happens.

Wild memories flood past. Cleaning my room so Mamí wouldn't ground me. Applying lotion to my hands and arms and legs because I knew Chase was coming over. Passing notes in English class. Homework with Hannah in the library...

Slowly the world coalesces. I wake up inside the nearby house, a man dragging me by the heels into the grimy entryway. Above me, much of the roof is gone, surrendering to the elements of the past four years.

The man darts back outside and returns a minute later, muttering to himself about his friend who took off in the Tahoe. "Bastard left me. *Me.* After all I've done, he just...left me here. We shall see about this hypocrisy."

I'm twitching, no muscular control. I'm also weeping, the electricity having overridden my emotions. I don't cry about the pain or about the fear, but because I can't help it. Like my passions are still being electrocuted.

The man stands at my feet, texting on his phone.

"Leaves me," he scoffs. "After I keep that apostate alive. After I hand him the world on an alter. The judgement will be swift. Oh yes. Retribution shall be holy."

I'm able to blink. So I do, trying to focus on his face. A handsome guy. Maybe pretty is the right word, almost feminine. His hair coiffed and held with gel. His features sharpen, the blurriness fading...

"P-P-Priest?" I stammer.

"Yes, hello my *queen.*" He sneers the word. "Lovely to be back."

I haven't seen him in two years, not since he betrayed the kingdom and sabotaged our defense systems, costing us hundreds of lives. He's a religious zealot who believes the world's current dystopian state is God's judgement, and he a prophet helping the Almighty in his reaping.

"He wants to abandon *me*?" he mutters to himself, still texting. "Very well, I'll sell my prize to the highest bidder. Blessings rain down in many forms."

I'm able to wiggle my fingers. "W-what are y-y-you doing here, Priest?"

"I'm surprised you haven't divined that already, *queen*. Perhaps your eyes are blinded due to lack of faith. You thought you could keep Los Angeles forever? Punishment tolls for thee." He smiles at his phone and puts it away. "Oh yes, there will be punishment. And he's almost here. I'll sell you, a heretic, to another. She who lives by the sword, am I right?"

"Priest." My left shoulder is badly burnt, already blistering. With an extreme effort, I prop myself up on both elbows. Like doing it with a remote control and low signal strength. The Priest isn't injured, which means it's his friend who's bleeding profusely. But who is it? "You were in the p-plane? With who?"

"Don't be a hero, queen." He pats the electric baton resting on the stairs. "You aren't a god. I've got two more charges and I will sacrifice you if I must."

"Who are you w-working with?"

Carmine screams at me. **Who CARES who he's working with? Get UP!**

He says, "Everyone and no one, of course. All of these villains utilized to bring judgement, they betray one another on a daily basis. The powers above choose strange vessels, Queen Carmine. Unfortunately for you, it appears you are no longer one of the chosen."

I can flex my feet. "What's your plan, Priest? W-why're you here?"

He picks up the baton and holds it near my face. I can smell my charred skin. He says, "Simple. We're reclaiming Los Angeles. Time to bring the kiddies home. The kiddies and the President. She wants to live here. Don't ask me why."

"The kiddies? From Hawaii?"

"Enough questions, girl. You defiled this holy temple long enough."

Keep him talking. Get to your feet. Where did that giant kid go?

I ask, "The Witch wants to live h-here? Los Angeles? But Andy Babington is going to obliterate it soon with a nuclear warhead."

"The boy with the bomb, oh yes, he didn't find you quickly enough. His usefulness is at an end. The wolves will see to him."

The wolves? He must mean the wolf man.

Good grief, what a mess.

The wolf man was sent to kill Andy! To detonate the nuke. But Tank's with him!

My muscular control is returning, enough to let me wipe my eyes.

He says, "Stop moving," and clicks the button, and his baton activates. Power courses through the rod, crackling and making my hairs stand up. "Don't try it, queen."

"What will you do with me?"

"I'm not doing anything with you. Better to ask *him* that question."

"Him who?"

He smiles, sinister and selfish. Perfect white teeth. "Walter. I just notified him. He's almost here. I expect a public sacrificial service. An unpleasant one."

Walter.

My blood runs cold. My death approaches, with claws and gold teeth.

Get up and go. NOW.

I need help. Quickly.

I lay my head down on the tile. Close my eyes. Saul the Zealot wouldn't be happy with this trick, but I have no choice. I willfully slow my pulse and unclench my muscles. Almost impossible, ignoring every biological imperative screaming at me. Relax, Katie, relax. I breathe in deeply and cast myself outwards, a mental device I've mostly neglected for two years. My soul can link to others, joining a noetic network, like a hive mentality. I *Listen* and *Feel* and *Probe* and *Call*.

My awareness expands, the world unfurling.

I *Sense* my Guardians. I map and connect with them. They absorb my emotions like a rapacious sponge.

Danger, I warn. *I need your help.*

Radiance flares behind my lids, the network activating.They *Hear*. And they're coming. But I'm miles away, too far.

I open my eyes.

Walter is above me. Shirtless, wearing sunglasses. He crouches on the roof like a vulture, peering down through caved rafters. His claws dig into the shingles. He taints the world around him, almost a visible stain.

Go go go go!

Despite the glasses, I can tell he's squinting at me, holding his head like it hurts. He feels it too, I realize. I broadcast with such power that I rattled his brain. I know the feeling, strangers trying to force their way in. A disorienting sensation, and Walter's shaking it off. I jarred his concentration.

My muscular control has mostly returned, but the cattle prod's still in my face, and Walter's faster than me.

Katie, you need to run. You...

We feel the earthquake simultaneously. The ground inexplicably shakes. Bouncing vibrations. It's not Walter—he's as confused and suspicious as the rest of us.

The Priest turns in a circle, glaring at the entryway floor. "One of the infamous southern California quakes? God's judgement, no doubt. Ready to swallow your pride and hedonism and sacrilege, once and for all!" He cackles, delirious with righteous fervor.

That's not it. I breath, "Oh no..."

A colossus bursts through the living room wall. The timbers, weak with termites and water damage, shatter. Travis stampedes through the house without thought, without harness on his momentum. Bull in a china shop.

His shoulder lowers and he catches the Priest in the face. Like an enormous football player plowing over a scrawny pre-teen. The Priest collapses and Travis stomps on him twice before he's able to halt himself. The Priest's body, thin and weak compared to ours, breaks under the five hundred pound rampage. A sound I'll never forget, like watermelons bursting under sledgehammers.

The electrified baton bounces harmlessly into the other room.

"Travis, look out! Above you!" I scream.

Walter drops like a nightmare. He's faster than gravity, faster than thought. Travis swings Hurt one time before Walter wrenches it from him, like a parent discipling a toddler. Walter is no mere mutant, he's pure-born. He laughs like a demon, haunting the house. In his fists, Hurt sings through the air and bites into Travis's flesh. I can't look away.

Travis's abdomen separates from itself. Walter cut him in half just above the hips. His face looks confused and then the muscles slacken.

The madman howls and watches Travis fall in two pieces. The evil inside him revels at the carnage, insanity pitched hot. He dances and laughs.

Katie, get UP.

I can't. I can still barely move.

You've got to try!

At this moment, blind aggression or panic gets me killed. Patience keeps me alive. I lower to the floor again, fully prone and pretending to be immobile.

Don't look at Travis, Katie. Don't look. Don't think. You can react later.

Carmine screams between my ears, enraged.

Walter turns to me, slowly twisting at the hips. With one clawed hand, he pushes the Ray-Bans onto his forehead. He grins, exposing dirty gold. He's entirely uninjured, so he wasn't the bleeding man on the airplane either.

"Lawd have mercy." He lowers to his haunches and rubs fingertips along my calf. "Priest zapped yo ass good, huh."

"Don't do this, Walter," I say, unable to keep a tremor out of my voice. "Don't give in to Blue-Eyes. You can resist her."

"Right now, little girl, at this moment, it ain't her you should be worried about." He jerks his head, indicating the mess behind him. "Sorry 'bout your friend."

"His name was Travis. I needed him. The world needed good men like him. You *have* to stop this destruction. Soon there'll be nothing left."

"It was me, you know. Who captured you. That night on the beach, what, four years ago. Pretty little thing, almost kept you for myself, instead of giving you to the Chemist. Should have. Saved myself a lot of trouble." He grabs my ankle and stands. "Oh well. Never too late to do a job right, ain't that the damn truth."

"Walter, stop!"

He walks out the front door, dragging me after him. "Stop? Oh no, the fun about to begin."

Walter is already here, I call with my mind. *Stay away! Come no closer.*

There's a response. Not a voice, but rather an emotion and a picture. Yet the meaning is clear.

We are coming.

The Outlaw

Andy and I scale the shortest cliff I can find, egressing from the basin and putting distance between us and the Colorado River, just in case a nuclear eruption could contaminate the water and kill those downstream. We head north for hours through desolate grays and browns. We're miles west of the Grand Canyon proper, and the land here is mad. The ground suddenly drops in dizzying gulches or rises like knives in sharp ridges. Hardpan crunches underfoot and temperatures swell—I'm soaked with sweat. The sun scorches Andy but he's beyond caring, beyond pain. His skin is tough leather, no longer able to blister, as his feet are no longer able to be cut by rocks.

He's delirious. Jabbering about Queen Carmine and about his old life. He staggers along with his eyes closed for minutes at a time. My heart breaks for him. Seems excessive punishment for a kid who made the simple mistake of bragging and lying on social media, drawing the attention of monsters.

Puck keeps me updated with text messages about our location; Andy and I are entering a vast reservation owned by the Hualapai tribe. We crest a rocky rise and an expansive flatland opens before us, stretching north beyond the curvature of the earth, carpeted with pines and oaks, a welcome site. To the far east and west, canyon walls. Puck texts that this part of Arizona is called Oak Grove, and it's abandoned as far as he can tell.

Puck's overworked. He's strained near breaking—too many moving parts to track, too many people depending on him.

"She's not here," Andy croaks. He's panting and rubbing at his eyes. "You lied to me, Jackson. Never liked you. Never will."

I point at the tree line, only a mile ahead. "Let's reach the trees, Andy. We'll find shade and we can talk."

We slide and crunch our way down the desiccated hill, careful for sudden and breathtaking canyons that appear like mirages. Two water bottles are drained, leaving one more. At the base of the rise, on the floor of the Oak Grove flatland, we find scrubby grass. It has to be my imagination, but this ground hurts my feet less.

We reach the shadows cast by pine and oak trees, the very shade of Xanadu it seems. Andy slumps to the ground face first and moans. I turn in a circle, glaring all directions. The trees cut off my ability to see in the distance. The shade is bliss, but it's accompanied by a nagging sensation that we're vulnerable. Our enemies, if we have any, can attack undetected.

I shrug my shoulders, trying to dislodge the warnings.

Andy talks into the pine needles below his face. "You lied, Jackson. Sh-shoulda known. Admit it. You lied."

I lower to the ground next to him. Pull the Outlaw mask from my pocket and dab at my forehead. Only one bottle left; I set it beside Andy. "I admit it. I tricked you."

"W-why?"

"Had to get you away from innocent civilians."

"Why?"

"So the bomb on your back wouldn't kill them."

He raises his head to stare at the water bottle. "I wouldn't kill them."

The light on his back flashes green. Over and over and over. "If you detonate that thing, yeah, you would have."

"It's only for Queen Carm-m-mine."

"Doesn't matter. You'd still destroy others."

"Jackson," he says in a whisper. "Chase. I don't want the water."

"Okay."

"I just want...I want to be done. So tired."

I nod and pat his shoulder. He flinches, but then rests his head on my hand. At that moment, he's no longer a walking death device, but a little kid, tender and scared. I ask, "Would you let the medics and bomb techs at the Resistance base look at you? See about unhooking that thing?"

"No."

"Why not?"

"It's part of me. They c-cant. I think, maybe...I just need to let go."

I try to swallow, but my throat's too dry. "But what if—"

"Glad you're here, Jackson," he murmurs. "Jackson. Good ol' Jackson. Always hated you. T-took my job. But now you're here. When no one else is. At the end."

"The end?"

"Jackson. Let's r-rest. Only for a few minutes."

"Okay. Just...don't give up. Not yet."

"Maybe. Little longer. Then I don't know."

I don't know either. I keep my hand on his shoulder, and he falls asleep in three heartbeats. Shuddering breath, then normal rhythm. The green light blinks. Long pause. Another blink. Longer pause...blink.

My heart rattles in my chest. Being this close to a nuke's got me unhinged. Poor Andy's been living with it for years. I understand why he seeks the peace of an afterlife—this world's been hell on him.

Should I bolt? While he's asleep, quietly run like heck for the canyons? Might be my best chance. What if he wakes up angry? What if he wakes up, finds me gone, and decides to continue his quest for Katie?

God, I pray. I'm in trouble. I don't know what to do. If you haven't given up on this world yet, send help. Tell me what to do.

Andy shifts and emits a soft moan. Rubs his scruffy face against my fingers and smiles. Maybe he'll have good dreams for the first time in forever. Maybe physical touch protects him, the same way Katie used to protect me.

I can't leave. If I abandon Andy I'm no better than the Witch who inculcated him in the first place. I don't know why I'm here, nor how this thing will end—but however it does, I think my role should be to help ease the pain of others. Maybe that's the best I can do, bring little pieces of heaven to earth as often as I can. Like Carmine tried to do, with Los Angeles.

So I squeeze his shoulder. And I stay.

Someone approaches.

I can *Feel* it, somehow.

Judging by the sun, falling to the west, I've been asleep two or three hours. My hand's still pinned between Andy's cheek and shoulder; I pull it loose and shake the fingers to restore circulation.

He sits up and yawns, the cage on his back clanging against a tree root. He stretches, shifting his muscles but unable to find comfort. "You're still here."

"Yep." I get to my feet.

"Thought you'd l-leave."

"Not until you're safe, Andy."

He smiles. "That's...nice. I didn't want to die alone."

In every direction, all I see are trees. Yet somehow I know, we're not alone.

"Wait here," I tell him, and I ascend a tall nearby oak tree. Two jumps and I'm up, thirty feet high and swaying. Below me, the forest ripples; above me, wisps of clouds scrape the blue. In that moment, I'm struck with longing for my boat and the tumultuous waves and the towering mast—miss it so fiercely my breath is stolen. Somehow the world seems to spin less quickly on the water.

Focus, Chase.

I glare to the west, against the sun. From that direction...

...I feel...

...something...but what?

A lone sound startles me. A strident call issued from inside the wide forest, a quarter mile north. It's a wolf howl, one of those eery wails to chill the bone.

A wolf, here for us. Has to be. He was sent ahead to search, and he found us. The wolf is a scout and he summons his pack.

The wolf man. Katie told me about him.

To the west, his pack responds. An answering call, thousands of them. Howling like a rainstorm, voices beyond count. These don't chill the bone—they shatter courage and hope. As I watch, shapes begin pouring out of a canyon under the molten sun. First a trickle, then a flood. A great stain, numbers unending.

"Andy, we gotta go!" I release my hold and plummet, snapping branches the whole way. "They found us!"

He raises wearily. "W-who? What?"

"Wolves. They're coming."

"Wolves? You mean...I know him. He wouldn't..."

A wolf snarls. The nearby scout comes through the trees, teeth barred. He weaves through trunks with twitchy lupine muscles and lunges for Andy's jugular. The wolf ignores me completely.

I catch the animal by the throat, inches from Andy. The wolf is male. He squeals and scratches at me. A killing machine with gray matted fur.

"The wolves are here for *you*, Andy," I say. "We need to run. Stay with me."

"But..."

The green light flashes faster.

I squeeze and the wolf dies. I steer Andy to the east and we run. Well, I run. He trots and moans and falls. This won't work.

He pants, pushing hair out of his face. "We can fight him. Fight h-him and his wolves."

"There's too many." I haul Andy to his feet.

"How many...are there?"

"All of them. Keep running. Stay with me."

He does his best, but it's not even a jog. The wolves will eat him alive. So I sling him onto my back and increase my pace, but I move awkwardly. Carrying him isn't a life-saving solution.

"Maybe," he wheezes into my ear. "Maybe you should leave me."

"Not if I can help it."

The howls are rejoined behind us. They found the executed scout.

I don't know whether it's better to fight them in the trees or try for a canyon. Probably the forest, where there's less chance of the pack overwhelming us.

Shadows flit past. Loping wolves cutting off our escape.

What are my options? Kill ten thousand wolves. Any others? Not that I see.

Without warning him, I toss Andy upwards into an oak tree. He gasps and snatches the lowest branch with feeble fingers. Sits astride it. "Climb," I order. "Get high. Any wolf gets near you, you kill it."

"Jackson," he says and his voice trembles. "Listen...listen to me. You should run. I'll t-talk to the wolf man."

"Rabid animals can't be reasoned with. Stay up there."

"I'm ready. Ready to be done with...everything."

"Not like this. And not alone. Now climb."

He smiles. Nods. Turns his face upward and reaches for the next branch.

The forest through which we fled thickens. Patches of light clot with fur and bodies. So be it, we'll make our stand here. I wrap the Outlaw mask around my face, and tie it behind. I tug the Thunder Stick from my vest and it swings easily, fist to fist. My muscles swell, pressing against the outfit. Bones harden into hammers. I spent years in combat, and years more fighting the ocean. I don't die easily.

They come. They leap along the ground; they bound overtop one another; they claw and climb the trees, a sickening marvel to watch.

My weapon whistles and breaks apart the avalanche. Their bodies pulp and shatter against me, and I fling them aside with each swing. Their teeth crack and bones fracture. Carcasses land in heaps around me, still hot. I wield death in one hand and punishment in the other—my fist is almost as hard as the rod. These aren't mutated animals; they are meat and blood, and I could withstand hundreds of them. Maybe a thousand. In a fight, I am an unholy terror, nothing the planet's ever seen before, more destructive than lightening strikes. But more than a mere thousand wolves throttle the forest. The pack is ten thousand strong, at minimum. Maybe a hundred. And they aren't after me; I'm an afterthought. It's Andy they seek.

The beasts climb the mounting pile of bodies and leap over me, scrabbling for purchase on Andy's tree. The bravest scale nearby pines and jump for Andy's oak. The first fall short but that won't last, as their blood thirst builds.

Soon I have nowhere to step, so many animals lay dead at my feet. I'm killing two with each hack, but four take their place. The bodies climb higher, providing a ramp for our attackers, and soon they swarm the oak. Dozens in the tree, scratching higher and snapping at Andy's heels.

Through the confetti of fur and falling needles, I spot the wolf man. He lopes on all fours, snarling on the fringe of the battlefield. What happens if he dies?

"Jackson!'" cries Andy. The wolves reach him—he can't climb fast enough. He'll be shredded in seconds.

"Get ready to jump!" I roar. "To another tree!"

I use the Thunder Stick to crush his oak at the base. One mighty chop and his tree is felled. The wood splinters, spitting sap, and the trunk groans. I push the oak in the right direction and it begins a slow fall.

"Jump, Andy!"

He does, leaping into a neighboring pine. But he's lower to the ground now. Pouncing from below, wolves almost reach him. Andy doesn't have calorie reserves to burn, not enough muscle tissue to continue for long. Time has ground him down.

The green light flashes—blink-blink-blink, blink-blink-blink.

"Jackson! I can't...can't wait...much longer..."

"Hold on! Don't give up!" I bolt into the woods, cleaving aside beasts flinging themselves at me. The wolf man spots me coming and darts to the side, running on all fours with the pack, circling. It's like chasing a shadow, impossible to catch. His hairy entourage hurls themselves at me, protecting their alpha. "Wolf man! Face me!"

But he won't. He knows I'll break him, and he hides within his ranks. Andy will be long dead before he's caught. And when Andy dies...

"Climb! Andy, climb!"

He's trying. But wolves have him by the feet. Dragging and chewing. The trees swim with them. I haven't made a dent in their numbers, and still they swarm from the west. They cover the forest floor. They crawl hideously through the branches, blotting the sun.

We are lost. There is no hope for saving Andy. Again I'm pressed by the question—do I run? Do I abandon Andy and his nuclear weapon to inevitability? Because of Katie, I think the answer might be Yes... And yet, something within me resists. A still small voice. Counter-intuitive whispers.

Stay. My place is here.

I'm cut off from Andy's tree. A hundred savage wolves bar my path, and he's being slashed to ribbons.

As though an answer to prayer, the treetops part. Only for an instant. A strong gust of wind allows a glimmering shaft of sunlight to pierce our gloom. So powerful I wince. Thousands of eyeballs swivel, caught by the light. There, spotlighted by the cone of brilliance, charges a golden mountain lion. Heavier by far than the mangy wolves, muscular and graceful. Am I seeing things? A hallucination? It leaps above the fray. Catches a wolf between its jaws and picks the animal clean off Andy's pine tree.

Through the fur and blood, another mountain lion streaks. Then another. Dozens, strong and powerful, waging war with the startled pack. Somewhere, the wolf man howls with fury.

I fight my way to Andy's tree, but without warning a bear blocks my way. A *bear?* An enormous Kodiak, bellowing hate. Its growl is deep and gravelly compared to the high snarl of the wolf. I don't have time to fight this mammoth.

I *Jump* over the animal, to the base of Andy's tree. Desperation gives me strength; I grip the trunk at the base and heave. The roots complain and break, and suddenly I'm holding the entire thing. I shake the pine to dislodge Andy's attackers. They fall gracelessly, landing hard. Andy jumps the distance into an oak, easier to climb. His legs are a bloody mess.

"Don't give up yet, Andy," I tell him. "Stay there."

"Okay," he pants. He's exhausted. Barely conscious. "I don't want... don't want you to die."

"Makes two of us," I mumble. I throw the pine tree like a spear, mowing a path through the wolves.

More cougars and bears enter the fray, fighting against the tide. A vicious riot of claws. A herd of bison thunders past, stomping and kicking the wolves. I stare in disbelief, this new phenomenon too much to assimilate. The bison look as though they weigh a ton each, an avalanche impossible to stop. Wolves scream and die underfoot.

A wild battle, nature versus itself. The animal kingdom rising up against the hateful wolves, who allied themselves with evil. As though the very land is groaning, ridding itself of the plague.

I stare too long. Fascination making me vulnerable. I'm hit from behind—a crushing blow to my back that sends me reeling, head over feet. I bounce off two trees before coming to rest upside down on the back of my neck.

A giant crouches next to me and chuckles. Deep, like an earthquake. My least favorite voice.

"Don't take that personally, pajamas," says Tank. He grins with that big stupid face of his. "Been waiting to do that for years, a good clean sucker punch."

"Glad I could help," I groan. "You're a real peach."

"Listen, pjs." He indicates the fight around us with his right hand. As always, he wears white gloves. Except they're dirty and ripped. Now that I look again, the rest of Tank doesn't look so great either. He has a haunted and lean appearance. "Don't think you realize the predicament you're in."

"Hey wow, good for you, Tank. Predicament, that's a big boy word."

"These wolves you're fighting, you can't win. This whole damn forest is stuffed with them, and they're still coming."

"It's worse than you think." I point to the tree over his shoulder, where Andy is feebly moving higher up the oak, away from hungry jaws. "That's Andy Babington."

Tank swears. One of the really bad words. "The kid with the nuke."

"Right. And he's going to die any minute."

"Which means we do too." He chuckles and pats my face. I try to bite him but miss. "Me and you gonna die together, pajamas. Something poetic about it."

"Shut up. That's not poetry, and I'm not ready to die."

"You're not?" He's genuinely surprised. He asks it like a man who thinks a lot about dying. "You don't feel it? The planet's about to blow. We're on this trajectory with death, and none of us escape."

"I feel it. But I'm not giving in. Not while Katie's in danger."

His smile drops. He looks down at his hands. "Katie..."

"Right."

"You love her."

"Always."

"And...she loves you?"

"If we live through this, we're getting married."

His eyebrows rise. "You asked her?"

"Basically."

"She said yes?"

"Sure. Kinda. Well, maybe. Not in those words..." I glare at him suspiciously. "Why? What'd you hear? Did she say something about it?"

"You're an idiot, Jackson."

"I know this."

"You don't deserve her."

"I know this too."

"Neither of us docs."

"Perhaps we should focus on our more immediate problems."

He stands and surveys the madness. Even enervated, he stands like a Greek god. "I'm here to kill the wolf man."

"Be my guest. It'd be the first helpful thing you've ever done."

He looks down at his feet. A muscle in his jaw pulses. "I owe a debt. And besides, I want to do something good. Just once. For my soul..."

I am skeptical. And I don't respond. This doesn't sound like Tank.

He chuckles. "Bet you're thinking I don't have one of those. A soul."

"What? Me? I would never think that."

"Yes you were."

"Nah."

"Admit it."

I shrug. "You *did* almost break my back just now, and brag about the sucker punch. Not very soulful."

"Maybe our paths didn't cross by accident. Maybe we help each other."

"How?"

He points with a gigantic finger. "I'm killing the wolf man. You see him, you herd him my direction."

"Meanwhile, I'll keep Andy alive," I say and I climb to my feet. Every vertebra cracks. "Or die trying."

- 21 -
Katie Lopez

I am dragged by my heels for three blocks, scrapping my back raw until we reach a black truck. I'm only pretending to be immobile; I could kick and run. Walter would catch me, though. At the moment, I have no recourse.

Carmine rages.

"Blue-Eyes is coming," I tell him, unable to keep fear out. "She'll trap you. We can't stop her separately. We need to work together, Walter."

He grins over his shoulder. "Got me a plan for the blue-eyed bitch. Me and the old man, Carter, we tired of hiding. Past time for her to go. She gets here? She's dead."

"The Priest was right. You monsters betray one another on a daily basis."

He crouches at the truck's rear bumper. Ties a rope to the hitch and the other end to my ankle. "I'd tell you this ain't personal. But that'd be a lie. This as personal as it gets. Gonna drag you through Los Angeles till there ain't nothing left. Till everyone lives here gets a good look. Till we on every news station on the planet, watching the warrior queen get ground down to nothing." He pats my foot. "Too bad the Priest ain't here to enjoy. He the one shocked you."

"Walter—"

In my mind, a whisper.

We are coming.

Walter grins again. Full of malice. "I had more time, I'd enjoy you first. But I don't want those pretty little muscles working again. So long, queen. This a better death than you deserve."

He thinks I'm still paralyzed.

He gets into the truck. Fires the engine.

Now, screams Carmine. **Now now now!**

The exhaust coughs in my face and the tires squeal. The coil of rope whistles as the truck roars forward, using up slack.

I bolt upright. My razor-sharp nails slice neatly through the rope.
Move!

I grasp the loose end of the rope with both hands. Close my eyes, grit my teeth, dig in with my feet...

The rope snaps taut between me and the truck. My hands clamp. The impact jerks my arms out of socket, nearly fractures my spine where it connects with my hips. But I hold fast. Refuse to budge.

The truck, accelerating past forty miles per hour, crashes to a halt. The front wheels buck upward. Something metal underneath breaks, an ear-piercing sound. Walter bursts through the windshield, his claws shredding the airbag. He and the front tires land at the same time, and then the wedges of glass.

The top goes slack. My shoulders, freed from the strain, pop back into socket. I nearly blackout.

We are coming.

He bounds up. Snaps off his glasses.
Run!

"Cute trick. You wanna play now? That was a helluva mistake, queen." He advances on me. Theatrically cracks his knuckles. But he pauses. Clenches his eyes and shakes his head. Bends over, as if struck by an intense migraine. He growls, "Damn headaches. Every day. Breaking your legs might make me feel better."

He's not looking. Do I run?
Yes! Or kill him!

My head buzzes. Voices, stronger than a whisper...

We are here.

Walter never sees the tigers. Nearly as big as his truck, they descend on him from behind. A storm of orange fur and pearlescent fangs. No time is wasted with fighting or claws. They sink their teeth into him; the male bites Walter's torso, the female his legs. They tug and pull. Walter is separated from himself and consumed in under five seconds.

It's too much. All of it—the Priest, Travis, and now Walter. I bend over and vomit. Human eyes weren't created to watch such things. At least not the eyes of a girl raised in southern California. My hands shake. So does the rest of me. I cover my ears and empty my stomach again.

When I look up, wiping my mouth, Walter is entirely devoured and my tigers watch me placidly.

We are with you.

I lower to a sitting position. Hug my knees. My shoulder is blistered, my back bleeding, my joints throbbing, head pounding...but I'm alive. In this savage land, that's an improbable feat.

Travis. He deserves a proper burial.

But not today. And not by you. Gears turn. You are needed elsewhere.

Leave it to Carmine, reminding me there's more and more and more work to be done. The sun will set in a couple hours. Yet there's no strength left to get me home.

I feel the Guardians arriving, but I can't greet them.

I can't even stay awake.

I can't...

The man called Nuts wakes from his nap in the early evening. He despises naps and scorns those who take them. He goes for days without sleeping; there's too much to be done, a world full of broken systems waiting for him. What's the old saying, he'll sleep when he's dead? A foolish sentiment—how can one be productive in death while sleeping? Anything worth doing is worth doing right, and that includes being dead. Yet, for the past week, he's decided napping is the wisest way to pass the time. It's better than lying still, going crazy. The naps preserve his sanity.

He blinks, instantly awake. Something woke him. More sounds of warfare? General Brown must have his hands full, fighting these drooling freaks. A stout and trustworthy man, that one. Hard working and determined, as a man ought to be. But what—

Outside his tent, someone shrieks. One of the goblin-like Variants, by the sound. He wails, and he's rejoined by others. A battalion-sized scream. The sound warbles and dies, then ratchets up in intensity.

The guard in his tent, one of the more lucid Variants, stands. Nuts twists to inspect his captor. The kid (he's not more than twenty-two—an infant, compared to Nuts' vaulted lifespan) takes a step and nearly falls. His eyes are shot wide and he's pale.

"He's gone."

"Who's gone?" demands Nuts. "Tell me, boy, what's happened?"

"He's just...gone."

Nuts sits up, frustrated. He uses his foot to part the tent flaps. The dusk is crimson and gold. Outside, the army of mutants spasms. He sees Variants rolling on the ground, crying. Others stand still, too shocked to function. The rest scream and *Leap* and pull their hair and beat their chests.

Nuts snaps, "Tell me, son. Explain this mess."

The boy falls to his knees and groans. Starts crawling for the tent's door. "He's gone. I don't... What do we do now?"

"Who's gone? I don't have patience for riddles."

But the boy can't. He cries from sudden grief and hopelessness. He stands. Wobbles. And ducks out of the tent.

"Can't ask a millennial to do anything," grumbles Nuts. His hands are still tied at the small of his back, but he slides the razor out from his belt where he's gingerly kept it hidden the past two days. "Not even explain his own mind."

Nuts begins sawing through his binding. Maybe he still has time to see about that water reservoir.

The Outlaw

My Thunder Stick hums through the air, tomahawk style. The heavy metal blasts two wolves off of Andy, and imbeds itself into a neighboring trunk. He sees the protrusion and jumps for it, transferring again to a nearby tree, another escape from the jaws.

I'm exhausted. The sun sets in the west over the Arizona desert. Feels like we've been fighting for hours. For days. Years. I'm soaked with blood, scratched and torn to shreds.

Still, there's no end to the wolves.

Tank's animals are dying. Despite the skill of his mountain lions, the bulk of the bears, the nobility and strength of the bison, they face evil unending. There are other animals here—eagles above, squirrels in the trees, cats scampering about, but they can't contribute. He says he has giants outside the forest but they won't enter—they're too big, and the trunks and branches are like spikes and spears. Soon his army will be decimated.

He finds me under Andy's tree. He's shredded to pulp, like us. He supports himself against the trunk.

"Can't catch the little freak," he pants.

Andy watches from above. His eyes are hollow and lifeless. The light on his back flashes so quickly it's almost permanently green.

"Dunno if this battle can be won," says Tank. "Too many wolves."

Andy's voice is a whisper. "I know a way to kill them all..."

Tank's face pales. We both know what Andy means.

"I can't hold this any longer," he whimpers. "It's time. Time for you to run."

"No," I say. "There has to be another way. I refuse to let you die alone."

The wolves find us again. Creep closer, eyes shining in the shadows. Tank's army bought us time but we're almost out. My Thunder Stick twists free from the oak and lands with a thunk in the soft turf, but I'm too tired to pick it up.

"Outlaw, go."

"No, Andy," I snap. "I refuse. We can do this. Friends don't let friends die alone."

"Please..."

Tank asks, "You remember the Zealot, Jackson?"

"Sure, I remember Saul. Never heard what happened to him, though. But, is this the best time to—"

"He saved my life. Wouldn't let me die alone. Said he bought my life with his blood, and gave it to God," says Tank.

Andy listens intently, climbing down the tree. He's too weak, though, and he slips. Tank catches him and sets him down, leaning against the trunk.

Andy's weary eyes close and he says, "Yes."

Tank lofts my heavy bat and tosses it to me. He repeats, "Bought my life and gave it to God. Craziest stuff I ever heard. So that's what me and the quarterback are gonna do too, Jackson. We're buying your life with our blood."

I frown, confused and uneasy. "You're not making sense."

"And I'm giving you to Katie. As a gift."

"Tank..."

"I'm staying with the quarterback," he says. "He and I, we die together. Not alone. And we won't die in vain. And we'll take the wolf man with us."

Andy nods. "Yes."

"I'll keep the quarterback alive. Got enough strength left for a few more minutes," Tank says.

The wolves encircle us, darkness within shadow.

"I can't leave you here." Emotion chokes my voice.

"Yeah. You can. For Katie."

"Jeez, Tank," I say through a sudden sob. "That's...that's..."

"The Zealot said I belong to good now. So that's what I'm doing." Tank sticks out his hand to me.

For some reason, the wolves don't advance. In fact, the growls die in their throats. Nature making time stand still.

"This is too much," I manage to say. "A gift impossible to accept."

"It's ain't for you, pajamas. Accept it for her."

I pull my mask off and use it to scrub my eyes. "Okay. I can do that. For Katie."

Andy breaths a sigh of relief and he smiles. "Please...hurry."

I shove my hand into Tank's, and we shake. His grip nearly breaks mine. "Tank, thank you."

"You're welcome. Marry that girl, Jackson. And if you have a boy? Keep Tank in mind for a name."

I laugh and sniffle. It's one of those indelible instants in time where my fate abruptly changes direction; a moment I'll never forget, but right now I can't get my arms around it. Doesn't seem fair. But what about life is fair recently?

The wolves snarl and advance again. Our time is up.

I shake Andy's hand. He's beaming, like his vision has focused on something far better than the world around. He's already moved on to some place good.

"Thank you, Andy."

"Run," he whispers. "Run, Outlaw. The world needs you."

The light on his back turns solid green. Then an angry red and the device buzzes.

Holy smokes.

I *Run*. For Katie. I bolt beyond the immediate ring of wolves in a flash. Moving through the trees so fast I barely touch earth. Behind, a burst of noise—Tank wages his final fight.

Andy has minutes. Maybe seconds. I'm fast, but not faster than a nuclear blast. It's a race to clear the radius of destruction. A race I don't know if I can win.

Animals flee nearby. The mountain lions and bison stampede for the distant borders of the forest. They know this part of the planet will soon be a crater.

I *Leap* over the wolf man. He raptly follows my flight, alarmed.

The trees surrender their grip and I'm in the clear, pounding across desert sand. In the distance, I spot giants running. Animals everywhere. Dogs and cats and rabbits and elk and chipmunks, and I outrun them all.

Run faster, faster, go, go...

A sudden flash. So brilliant my retinas partially fry, brighter than daylight. My silhouette is cast before me in sharp relief. The silvery flare intensifies and then yields to a steady scarlet glow. Eerily, I hear no sound yet.

A nuclear blast, unreal. Andy's gone. Tank's gone. The wolf man's gone.

Katie...

A sharp crack shatters my ears. Thunder so loud it's not really a sound but a rip in reality.

Intense pressure. Agony.

The crust of the earth jumps as the first shock wave passes. Sand for miles kicks upward in a swelling circle. I'm seared by sudden heat. Too much dirt in the air, I can't see. A second wave of destruction crashes and heaves me forward.

The atomic blast consumes the trees, the forest, the animals, the entirety of Oak Groves, the very air I breathe...

The world in torment.

All is lost.

I wake up in the passenger seat of a Land Cruiser. Don't remember getting in. Sean drives. He looks leaner than a week ago, haunted and scared. Poor guy, he's gotten more than he bargained for when he left the farm in Idaho.

We're almost to downtown, motoring quietly along a deserted interstate. Two of my Guardians sit in the back seats. Two more crouch on the roof. Night has fallen.

I pat Sean's arm. His face glows from the dash lights. "You doing okay?"

I startled him. He chuckles and nods. "I been better. We're in a war. And you almost died."

"Thanks for coming to get me." I rub my knees and my wrists, pressing at the soreness.

"Your..." He jerks his head to indicate the Guardians in the back seat. "Your *friends* knew you needed help. How'd they know?"

"I told them." Sean's phone sits in the cupholder between us; mine was short-circuited by the Priest. I use his to text Kayla, asking for an update.

"Yeah, but...*how?*"

"I'm not entirely positive how it works, Sean."

"Something like telepathy?"

"Yes. Although, more like shared emotions."

He makes a low whistling sound. "When I first met you in Idaho, I thought you were just this cute Hispanic girl."

"Didn't realize what I mess I am," I say with a tired laugh.

"Right." He winks at me. "But I think you might be worth it."

"I totally am."

"When I got into the car with you, at the farm, a thousand miles and a lifetime ago it seems, I thought maybe you and I might...you know." Sean squirms and snickers awkwardly. "Get together."

I nod and my cheeks burn. I don't know how to reply. So I text Kayla again. It's been thirty seconds with no reply, an eternity for her.

"But," he says. "I'm figuring it out. You and the Outlaw, you're an item. Right?"

"We are." Feels strange, acknowledging it out loud. Strange and perfect. "In Idaho, I didn't know he was still alive. It's been a long and revealing thousand miles."

Sean turns onto Figueroa and stops at the base of my tower. Lanterns at the intersections are being lit. He turns to face me, one hand resting at the top of the wheel. Feels like the Land Cruiser's cabin shrinks.

"But if the Outlaw hadn't been alive...what then? About me and you?"

I grip his hand tight for an instant. In what I hope is a reassuring, affectionate, and platonic way. "Let's say, your chances were much higher while Chase Jackson was dead."

"And now?"

"You're sweet, Sean. An angel when I needed it. But I'm in love with my ideal perfect man. And every minute, I think about him, hoping he shows soon."

"Yeah." He nods, a wry twist to his lips. "The Outlaw is kinda badass."

"In every way." I wave his phone. "I need to go. And I'm taking this."

"But—"

"Have you heard from Kayla recently?"

"The crazy hot girl? Why would she talk to me? I can't even think when she's around. But for real, can I have my phone back?" he asks.

"Yep. Soon as I get a new one. Thanks, Sean."

I close the car door behind. The Guardians exit and follow me into the 717 Olympic lobby.

Why isn't Kayla responding? Who could she be with? Not many of us are left. It's a sad and startling moment to realize most of the friends you rely on have died. Travis, Dalton, Becky, Mason...who's next?

I grab the closest Guardian. It's Renee, the girl who helped run our farm in Idaho. I squeeze her shoulder and she beams. "I need a favor. Take a friend and return to where you found me. Find Travis's body in a house on Glyndon Avenue and give him a good burial. Then tell me where. Okay?"

"Yes Queen Carmine," she replies breathlessly. She glances up at the ceiling, then back at me. "Of course."

"Take Sean. He's outside with a car."

She nods and leaves.

Sean and Renee. They'd be a cute couple.

I ask the rest, "Has anyone seen Kayla?"

No one answers. They shuffle. Glance at me, then glance to the ceiling. I order them to remain in the lobby, and I call for an elevator. I take it up, lost in my thoughts. Oblivious to the world.

I should have noticed the Guardians were acting weird. They were standing rigid, staring upwards. Very unlike them.

I should have noticed bloody bootprints on the hallway carpet outside my room.

Should have noticed the hairs on my neck were standing up.

Should have been more alarmed at how strange it was that Kayla wasn't returning my texts.

That the air held a familiar scent—a waft of power, and also madness. Should have noticed the disease swirling through my living room...

But I'm lost in thought. Thinking about a shower. About contacting General Brown. About Chase. Wondering how Walter's Variants will respond. Longing for sleep. About...

I trip over a body and nearly fall. It's my Devotee. Face first on the ground. His neck's broken.

The day rushes back. I forgot about the injured man, the one I tracked off the airplane. The one who left the Priest behind, rattling off in the old Tahoe. I forgot him and now it's too late.

He's here.

In my bed.

Carter.

An unlit cigarette is pinched at the corner of his mouth. His bald head reflects the lamp's naked bulb. My sheets are bloody. His shirt looks like he's the one who got mauled by a tiger. He leans against my headboard, legs straight, boots crosses at the foot of my bed.

He has two girls in the bed with him. An arm around each.

In his right arm, Kayla. She watches me with eyes like twin moons, terrified. Around her neck is a collar I recognize; the same kind that Blue-Eyes once fitted Chase with. The collar was built with minor explosives along the interior. Carter holds the trigger, pressed against Kayla's shoulder. He compresses it and her head will be blown off.

The second girl he's holding makes my blood run cold. The Cheerleader. A friend of mine from high school, Hannah Walker. She's still eye-catching and beautiful, but like a mannequin. Plastic and fake. Her blonde hair is long now. She rests on the bed, asleep, cuddling against Carter like a little girl. Gasoline, that's what I smell.

"Hello, Katie," says Carter, voice full of magma. His breathing sounds wet. "Been a long time. Got a light? Can't seem to find one."

I don't reply.

Carmine rages. She tries to take control of my body, to attack him. I fight her down.

He chuckles and coughs. Specks of blood spatter his chin. "Not a very warm welcome."

Kayla speaks in a whimper. "Carmine, what—"

"Shut up."

I tell her, "It's okay, Kayla. Right now, we're going to do everything he says."

"Damn right you are. Where's the Priest?"

"Dead."

"And Walter?"

I say, "Even more dead. Dead and gone."

Kayla makes a gasping noise. "Really?"

Carter's mouth turns into a hard line. "That's why his army is going berserk."

"Let the girls go, Carter. You're outnumbered."

"It's not me you should be worried about. Like your boyfriend, you aren't thinking far enough into the future."

Carmine fumes. I know the feeling; Carter's not worthy of even speaking Chase's name.

He says, "Now, you're gonna do three things."

I cross my arms. "Which are?"

"First, find me a lighter. I would kill someone for a smoke."

"You think fire around her," I say, indicating Hannah, "is a good idea?"

"What's life without a little risk? Second, get the Resistance on the phone. They have someone who belongs to me, and I need her back. By tomorrow."

He means Ai, the girl from China. "And the third?"

"Get a sewing kit." He indicates his ravaged torso. "Need you to stitch me up. Turns out, grenades are hard things to survive."

"I'm not a surgeon."

"Better hurry and learn." Her face darkens. "Because she'll be here soon. And she's going to kill us all."

PART III

"Those were the stories that stayed with you. That meant something, even if you were too small to understand why. But I think, Mr. Frodo, I do understand. I know now. Folk in those stories had lots of chances of turning back only they didn't. They kept going. Because they were holding on to something. That there's some good in this world, Mr. Frodo. And it's worth fighting for."

-JRR Tolkien, *Return of the King*

Katie Lopez

I sleep on the floor of my bedroom. But not well and not for long. My joints ache. Carter stirs and grunts all night and Hannah Walker talks in her sleep about her lost boyfriend and Kayla whimpers.

The worst roommates imaginable.

Carter's enhanced body is fighting a fever and slowly repairing itself. His chest and stomach will never look normal again, though. Not after my botched attempt at stitching him up. Needles kept breaking against his tough hide and I couldn't force the torn remnants of flesh to properly connect. Half of him looks like a Halloween horror movie, and I can clearly see one of his lungs.

But he'll live. An hour after I finished, his skin cells were already regenerating.

It is not his groaning which wakes me up, though. Nor fear over him accidentally blowing Kayla's head off, nor the Cheerleader engulfing the tower in flames. What wakes me up is the silence.

I stand and rub my elbows and listen. Wish I could change out of this t-shirt and jeans outfit. Maybe Carmine had the right idea—all active wear, all the time.

Kayla, unable to sleep and still locked in Carter's arm, watches my every move. Hoping I'll think of something brilliant to save us. But I got nothing at the moment. Neither does Carmine.

After days of listening to the sound of distant missile strikes and growling tanks and howling Variants, the absence of noise unnerves me. Did the battle just...stop? I step onto the balcony. In the open air of Los Angeles, the silence feels even more profound.

Guardians perch all over Olympic and the nearby skyscrapers. They sit like gargoyles keeping a watchful eye, but not all of them are watching me. Many have their eyes closed, or they stare north. Others to the east. Usually energetic, overflowing with adrenaline and emotion, they form a quiet host of spectators. Darren is the closest. He still holds the spear he carried in Idaho.

Behind me, Carter sits up in bed, grunting and sweating from the effort. "What? What is it?"

"I don't know. All the noises stopped."

"This is your damn city, what's wrong?"

I snap, "Let me go, or give me a phone, and I'll find out."

"No deal. Why don't I hear Walter's mutant army? Last night it sounded like they were about to end the world."

"Wish I knew."

Carter's phone rings. We all jump. Hannah Walker murmurs sleepily. She's going to wake soon, a realization which fills me with dread. Carter answers, puts it on speaker phone.

He says, "Anderson, I'm done being toyed with. If you don't have good news, I execute one of my hostages."

A voice I recognize as General Isaac Anderson comes over the speaker. I'd bet the entire city PuckDaddy is on the line too. He says, "I need proof Queen Carmine and Kayla are alive."

Carter nods at me.

I loudly say, "I'm here, Isaac. Kayla and I are fine."

"*Fine?*" she squeaks.

"Good. You two stay that way."

Carter says, "They won't be for long, Anderson. Not if I don't see Ai very soon."

Hannah Walker rubs at her eyes and sighs.

"She's inbound on a chopper," says Isaac Anderson. "I've given orders to General Brown not to shoot it down."

"How long?"

"She's flying from Arizona. It'll be a few hours."

"I need her faster."

"That's not possible. We've given in to your demand, Carter, but we expect to receive both Carmine and Kayla alive. I have every satellite and missile at my disposal aimed on your position. I don't care if you're a fast mutant, I'll obliterate you if we don't get your hostages."

Carter growls, "Where's the Outlaw?"

My heart quickens. I wondered the same.

A pause. Anderson waits two heartbeats before answering. "We don't know."

"Don't lie to me! You've got him. He saved Ai's life."

"No, Carter, listen...Carmine, this may be hard for you to hear."

I step closer to the phone. "I don't care. Where's Chase?"

"A nuclear bomb went off in the desert, and—"

"Did it?" Carter chuckles. "About time. You have proof?"

"Ask General Brown. His systems should've registered it."

My head swims. Andy Babington died. Has to be. The wolf man found him? What about Tank? What about...

I ask, "Isaac, was Chase with Andy?"

Another pause. "Maybe. We lost track of them, and...and now we don't know. We're searching."

Searching. He means, sending teams to the site of the blast to look for bodies.

I should be crushed. I should be freaking out, screaming over losing him *again*. But I'm not. Chase is alive. He didn't come this far and fight this hard to die in the desert.

Carter doesn't look convinced either. An absurd notion, us assuming a nuclear bomb isn't sufficient to kill the Outlaw. But those of us who know Chase learned never to doubt him.

Carter says, "If that chopper doesn't get here today, or if it doesn't have Ai on it, I'm killing your precious girls and you'll never see me again. Then watch this city tear itself apart."

"I sent the flight plan and aircraft identification to General Brown. He'll keep you updated with progress. I've done all I can."

Carter punches the phone with a finger, hanging up. His abdomen has him in agony.

Kayla, the innocent babe, is genuinely worried for him. She asks, "Carter, that wound is so yikes. Are you sure you don't want medicine?"

"Won't work. At least not well."

My fists are on my hips. "What are you gonna do with Ai, Carter?"

"Kill her if I have to. Should have on the plane. Things didn't go as I intended." He closes his eyes, perspiration beading on his forehead.

"You could have killed her in China."

"I said, if I have to. Plan goes right, she'll work for me. Develop an immunity to Blue-Eyes. She's only dead if she can't. Or won't."

I throw up my hands. "But she knows a cure. A *cure*, Carter."

"Exactly why the Resistance can't have her."

"Our world is heading to the stone ages. And the Variants are a big reason why. Don't be a fool. Get up and look outside. Hundreds of them are on the roofs, clinging to walls, killing machines on the verge of frenzy. We could fix that!"

"Don't you get it?" He gently prods his abdomen and chest. Winces, but he appears pleased. "You're a queen now. A *queen*. I first met you, you were nothing. A bashful little nobody with her nose in a book. Now? One of the foremost leaders on earth. You command armies. Control the western seaboard, for all intents and purposes."

Kayla whispers, "The second-most searched woman on Google."

"All because of the disease. Fate delivers fortune and fame to very few. We are the chosen, Katie. The future *belongs* to us, as decreed by nature herself. And Ai wants to disrupt that."

I shake my head. "Victors always believe they conquer because of God's blessing."

"Exactly."

"But sometimes they conquer because they are the most cruel. And it's nothing to do with fate or nature, and everything to do with hate and greed."

He shrugs and grins. "Guilty as charged. Ambition is the engine that drives progress. I am unashamedly ambitious."

"Ambition killed five billion people during the previous three years."

"Only the strong survive. Aren't you living proof of that, kiddo? Haven't you earned the right to rule?"

"I led out of desperation. We had no choice. Only tyrants believe it's their right. Only tyrants seek to capitalize on the misfortune of others. Madmen such as yourself consolidate their power by eliminating innocents. Like Ai."

Hannah Walker sits up. The rest of us lean away from her warily. She gets out of bed and blinks at the pale sunlight.

I point at her outfit. She wears a scanty red and black Hidden Spring Eagles cheerleading uniform. "Are you kidding me?"

Carter shrugs. "She showed up wearing that. I didn't call her, she just...got into bed. Not that I mind."

"You two talk quieter," whimpers Kayla. "Before she kills all of us."

"I know you," Hannah whispers. Rubs her eyes and seems to float across the room. She takes my hand and squeezes my fingers. "Yes. We're friends. Aren't we?"

"Hello Hannah." I throw as much affection into my voice as I can muster. Carmine is freaking out, big time. "It's me, Katie Lopez. From high school?"

"I knew it!" She hugs me, a breathtakingly strong embrace. Once upon a time, she'd been the taller of us. But the disease lengthened me. I hug her in return and pat her hair. Immediately the pungent aroma of gasoline invades my nostrils. It's stronger than a mere scent, more of a physical force. I think the very air around her is flammable. "Katie, have you seen Chase?"

"I haven't."

"Don't lie to me, Katie. We're friends."

I release and step back. She grips my fingers tight. Her bright blue eyes have trouble focusing. "Honestly, Hannah, I haven't been with him in two years."

"I wish I could find Chase. I need him."

"Why do you need him?"

"He must transform." She smiles happily. "Reborn with fire. And become like me."

I gulp. She wants to burn Chase alive so they'll be the same. She doesn't realize how much work the Chemist put into bringing her back to life. I change the subject. "Are you hungry?"

"Yes. Very."

"Me too," says Carter. Hannah stares at him. Sniffs. Then forgets him immediately. He gets out of bed and pats his stomach. "Used up my calories healing. Feeling better already. You did good, kid."

"But it looks so *ew*," says Kayla.

"Shut up," snaps Hannah Walter, glaring at her. "I don't like you."

Kayla gasps. "What'd *I* do? I'm so nice!"

Hannah flicks her fingers. A motion that causes her thumbnail to scrap across the nails of her other fingers. A spark and then a small flame appears in her hand. She takes a step across the room. "Don't speak. I hate it."

Kayla pales. So does Carter.

I grab Hannah again. Press both of my hands against hers, extinguishing the flame. "No, no, Hannah. That's just Kayla. She's silly. Ignore her."

"I don't like Kayla. I don't like what her voice does."

"C'mon, let's check the kitchen for food." I pull Hannah out of the room. She heads for the stool at the counter, stepping over my dead Devotee. I stick my head back in the bedroom and hiss, "Kayla, what'd you do?"

"Nothing!" she squeals. Involuntarily she pulls at the macabre collar around her neck. "I don't think she likes my voice."

"Well, stop it!"

"Stop *what*?"

"Everything!"

I find oranges and granola in the kitchen, which I slide to her. Carter helps himself. There are eggs, but I don't know what heat source the Devotee used to cook them. And I'm too frayed to figure it out. I feel raw, like I'm coming apart—the red sunlight ricocheting off the skyscrapers hurts my eyes, and I ache with dread. I bet prisoners on death row wake up feeling worse on their final day, but I'm not far behind.

Hannah hums. "Do you know what today is?"

"What?"

"It's my birthday," she says. "Today is going to be magical."

I gulp down fear. "Is it?"

She nods and smiles.

Carter sets his phone on the counter. Shoves it my way. His other hand holds Kayla's trigger. "Call General Brown."

"Why?"

"I want updates on Ai's helicopter."

"Carter, I'm tired—"

"You still don't get it. The battle for Los Angeles and the entire world begins today. *Today*, kid."

"Yes, today!" Hannah chirps happily. "It all happens today."

Carter glances uneasily at her, says, "We're out of time, Katie. Blue-Eyes will be here soon, and unless we're ready, she'll kill both of us."

Hannah delicately peels an orange. "Who?"

I say, "Blue-Eyes. You met her, Hannah. She's the president now."

"Oh yes. I remember. I did not like her. She tried to take Chase."

I nod. "That's right, very good. She did."

"Call him. Now." He waggles the trigger.

Hannah nods, pleased.

This is so wild. All sense of normalcy and any ability to predict the future is long gone. I punch in a number from memory. Brown's direct line.

He answers the third ring. "Yes. Who is this?"

"General, it's Katie. Err, Queen Carmine, whatever you want to call me. You received information about an inbound chopper?"

"Yes."

"Great. Send updates to this cell phone, please."

"Where are you?" he demands.

"My apartment."

"We need to meet. Now."

Carter looks at me suspiciously. I shrug. "Can we talk over the phone?"

"No. In person."

Carter whispers, "You aren't leaving this tower."

I say loudly, "How about the War Department, here at Olympic?"

"How soon?" asks Brown.

"One hour."

"Affirmative." He hangs up.

Carter says, "Strange. He always like that?"

"He's running on no sleep, trying to get our water turned on, and fighting Walter's Variants. Probably wants to know why everything's gone silent," I say.

I don't care what Brown wants. I need another ally here, help me figure out what to do. I can only stand being an obedient hostage for so long.

Carter growls, "He didn't say anything about the helicopter."

"Ask when he gets here."

"Call him again."

"Carter, no. He's en route."

The bald man gets up from the counter. Finishes eating an apple. Fishes a cigarette from his pocket and lights it. Breathes in. Holds it. And exhales a blue cloud.

"Got a feeling," he says to himself. "You're going to die today, Katie Lopez."

Hannah yawns. "I hope not. It's my birthday."

I am overloaded with things to get done. Walter's Variants are apparently going berserk and destroying northern Los Angeles with their bare hands. Or at least they were until the sudden silence. My Guardians are spooked, acting weird. We still have no water, and our water bottle supply runs dangerously low. Nuts is missing. Farming and agriculture grind to a halt because of the unrest. The citizens of our city need communication and comforting.

This list goes on and on.

Yet here I sit in the War Department, held hostage because I don't want my best friend to lose her head. Kayla stays near Carter because he told her that if she distances herself from the trigger the collar automatically detonates. I feel profane, watching one of the most beautiful and intelligent and kind women on earth follow Carter around like a dog.

Hannah Walker is wrapped in a blanket in the corner, asleep again. Otherwise we're alone—I sent the techs away.

Carter jumps around the room, bending and wincing.

"Amazing what our bodies can do, given a little help," he says. He changed out of his bloody clothes, only keeping the boots and trench coat. Everything else once belonged to my Devotee. He *Leaps* across the room, stretches, and examines his sutures again. "Last night I thought I might die. And now? Almost good as new."

"I can still see the bones of your ribcage."

"Not for much longer. Few minutes ago you could see my lungs. This is progress."

General Brown should arrive ten minutes from now. So we wait.

A thought's been nagging at me. At this very minute, it's not one of my pressing concerns. But it matters, long term. "Carter, did you take those kids?"

"Kids?"

"The Inheritors. Those infants the Chemist infected before dying."

"Ah. No, I did not." He flicks the dead butt of his cigarette across the room and clamps his lips around another. Lights it. "The Priest took them. Brought them to Hawaii. I merely assumed possession and responsibility for their care and well being."

"And for their brainwashing."

"Naturally. What good are weapons if they're unaimed?"

I ask, "How many are left?"

"Hell, I don't know. Most. You gonna cry about this too, mate? They're alive. So are the mothers. Fed and safe. Living in paradise with no worries. Admit it, I provide them a better lifestyle than you ever did."

"They need to be with the Resistance. You must let Ai look at them."

"With proper training, those children grow up to be the most powerful warriors this planet's ever seen. And the hand that rocks the cradle?" He jerks his thumb at himself. "Rules the world."

"That's madness."

He snatches the cigarette from his mouth. Smoke secretes from his nostrils and the corners of his mouth. Even from his ears. And... good grief, from a gash in his chest that hasn't closed yet. "What I'm doing is the same thing you did in Los Angeles, *queen*. Build something from the ashes."

"I didn't cause the ashes. You want hell on earth. I want the opposite."

He snorts. "The kingdom of heaven?"

"Absolutely."

"Delusions of grandeur."

"You're one to talk."

"You're *done* arguing with me. Keep your mouth closed."

Kayla's at the window, peering behind the heavy blackout curtains. "They're *all* here."

"Who?"

"The Variants. Like, thousands of them. They surrounded our tower. Staring. *Super* creepy."

Carter joins her. Pulls aside the curtains. The morning sun makes a halo around their silhouettes. I can't see beyond, but Carter's speechless for a full thirty seconds.

I position myself behind him, ten feet distant. If this meeting goes wrong I plan on plowing him through the window. I think his trigger proximity warning was a bluff.

He whispers, "What are they doing?"

"They're not normally like this. This is yikes."

"So many freaks. Such power. It's absurd you haven't conquered the world yet."

I say, "They aren't weapons. They're people."

He glances at Kayla. "Tell me. Why are they gathered out there? Waiting? For what?"

"Let me have my cell and I'll find out," she says hopefully.

"No chance."

"*Please!* I'm dying without a phone!"

Outside in the hallway, an elevator dings. The General's early, as usual.

Carter says, "I do the talking."

He moves away from the window; I shift, keeping him in line. I'm not strong enough or fast enough to kill him. But a fall from this height would.

General Brown enters the room, dressed in army fatigues. He looks a year older every time I see him.

"Queen Carmine. You're here," he says loudly.

I nod at him. "General."

"Carter, you're here too."

"We've got a lot of work to do, General," says Carter. "For starters, I need access to the medical labs in the basement of—"

"And Kayla is here. Other than that, the room is empty," calls Brown. Like we're hard of hearing.

Carter opens his mouth to reply. Stops. He and I both realize it at the same time; something is horribly horribly wrong. He's shouting for the sake of someone else.

The door to the War Department opens farther.

The Blue-Eyed Witch enters, being pushed in a lavish wheelchair by a Secret Serviceman. Her legs are covered with a cashmere blanket. Her blouse is extravagant silk and scandalously revealing. Even sitting, she's beautiful beyond comprehension. So attractive I'm shattered on the inside.

"Hello my darlings," she purrs.

Her voice melts my ears and heart. Her enchanting disease is unstoppable. I'm instantly snared.

Carter roars, "No!" He snatches the heavy revolver from his holster.

General Brown steps in front of the President, fumbling for his sidearm. A human shield.

Carter gets a shot off. He's *so* fast. The report nearly deafens me, loosening my obsession with the Blue-Eyes for a nanosecond. Hannah Walker is startled, waking up abruptly. The round catches Brown in the shoulder, spinning him in a full circle.

"Stop, please, my love," says Blue-Eyes calmly. "Lay down your gun."

I don't have a gun. If I did, I'd set it down.

Kill her! Don't listen to her words! No!

Carter falls to his knees. Groans on all fours. Tries to cover his ears, but he can't.

"Oh Carter, my old friend," she says, leaning forward. "It's been so long since I've seen you."

He slowly raises the revolver. The barrel quivers.

"Drop it. Now." A direct order from Blue-Eyes.

The gun lands with a thud. The trigger to the collar stays in his left hand.

"And you, pretty little thing," she says, pointing a finger at Kayla. "I admire your collar. Don't open your mouth. Not once. Understand? As they say, this town isn't big enough for both of us."

Kayla nods, tears leaking from her eyes.

Blue-Eyes leans back in her chair and swivels her eyes to me. I'm so hopeful she'll speak to me, I can barely breathe.

What's the MATTER with you? Fight it!

"And the lovely Queen Carmine, back from the dead. Or do you go by Katie now? I'm glad your charade is over. Without knowing where you were, I was afraid to take the city."

I nod and try not to cry, I'm that happy. "Yes, mistress."

"So." She crosses her hands, lays them in her lap. I wish she'd touch me. Hold my hand, anything. "Let us talk. There is much to be done in Los Angeles. Oh yes indeed, my beauties. But first, General Brown tells me the girl from China is being flown here. How perfect."

The General is on the ground, tying a bandage around his shoulder. The blood loss is significant, and he's no mutant. It'll take months to heal.

Blue-Eyes is everywhere. She's all I see. All I hear. I breathe her in like oxygen. I'm hopelessly enamored. All the love I possess for my mother and for Chase and for Kayla and everyone else, all rolled into a single person.

No...not like the love I have for Chase. I love him more.

Do I?

I can't think clearly.

"Do you know what we'll do with the cutie from China?" she asks. "We're going to kill her. And then? We'll kill Carter and the queen, too." She glances my way. "Publicly. Private deaths leave too much room for unconfirmed rumors. It's better this way, don't you think? We'll let the freaks watch. We'll let the citizens of your fine city witness. That way, the world will know that I won."

Carter nods, breathing heavily. One of the strongest and most influential men to ever live, laid low by a beautiful woman.

She's going to kill me? Dying for her sounds like something I would very much like to do. Carmine screams between my ears. I ignore her. It's all going wrong. It's falling apart and I can't stop it. Nor do I want to.

Hannah Walker rises to her feet like a soundless phantom. Blue-Eyes hadn't noticed her in the corner and she gasps. Her face pales and she leans away. "The fire girl! The...*cheerleader*. What...what are...get *out!*"

The President knows what we all do—the easiest way to kill us is fire. But I would never let that happen.

Hannah tilts her head and doesn't budge. "I remember you."

"Get OUT."

"I don't like your voice," says Hannah. "Or your face."

Blue-Eyes is panicking. She taps the Secret Serviceman and says, "Kill her. Use your gun."

"No!" cries Kayla. "You might set her on fire!"

"Yes, mistress, you must be careful," I say. "I'll remove the cheerleader."

Hannah glares. She's gone a little red in the face. "I remember. You tried to take Chase from me. I hate you. You can't have my boyfriend."

I grab Hannah's hand. She ignores me. Blue-Eyes rolls away from the door, breathing heavy.

"Get her out," she tells me. "Far away. What a nightmare she is."

"You can't have Chase."

"Chase is dead, you little bitch," says Blue-Eyes. "Now *go*."

"Dead?" Hannah asks.

"Dead?" I ask. That can't be. I know that isn't true.

"Yes, dead," says Blue-Eyes wickedly. "In the Arizona desert, not far from Las Vegas. Maybe you should go there, freak."

Hannah makes a strange choking noise. Closes her eyes.

"That's not true," I say. "He's not... You're lying."

Blue-Eyes is startled. She's not accustomed to being defied. She snaps, "I watched it happen through the eyes of my servants. A great fight in the desert. Even the giant man-child was there; Tank, somehow controlling bears and such. He fought heroically, the Outlaw, but in the end poor Andy Babington wasn't up to the challenge. And when he died, so did your beloved Chase Jackson. You see..." She smiles, savoring our pain. "...he refused to leave Andy's side. I listened with a thousand ears. Isn't that delicious? What a worthless sacrifice."

"No," I say. Somehow, someway, I know it's not true.

"Don't speak again, queen, or I'll be displeased."

"Yes mistress," I say, bowing my head. But I know she's wrong. And...I'm conflicted.

"Chase..." moans Hannah. The aroma of gasoline intensifies. "...*dead?*"

"Carmine, take this freak away. Now, before she—"

Hannah releases a scream. A blast of pure wrath, the sonic embodiment of insanity. We grab our ears and cower. I've seen her catch fire, and we won't survive it.

"Chase!" she bellows from a throat that never fully healed. "CHASE!" But she doesn't ignite; she bolts from the room. The stairwell door crashes open. We hear howls for several minutes, so loud we cannot talk over it.

Finally, silence. She's gone. Who knows where.

"Well now," says Blue-Eyes. "That was horrifying. Where were we? Oh yes. Your deaths."

Katie Lopez

Blue-Eyes requests I push her. It's the greatest honor of my life. We exit the tower's lobby and turn north on Figueroa.

I ask, "Where to?"

"I used to watch your videos, you know," she says. "I was as fascinated by the warrior queen as anyone else. How was this little girl *doing* it? Rallying the homeless into a working force? Harnessing the wild Variants? You gained followers at a startling pace. I have to use my enhanced abilities—my looks and my voice. But you? They seemed to follow you...willingly."

"Yes mistress."

"One video in particular, I remember. It was judgement day. Do you remember, love? Your security force brought prisoners to a ball field, where you personally slit their throats."

I remember. Kinda. Carmine was a tough leader. I watched through her eyes, watched my hand dispense discipline. "Yes, I remember."

We are not alone. She has an escort of Secret Service—men who adore her. Carter and Kayla walk behind. So does General Brown. But there's more than just us. The streets are lined with mutants. They cover sidewalks and the facades and the rooftops like a fungus. Thousands, more than I knew existed.

Not just mine perch above. Walter's abandoned army also stares. They're barely recognizable as human. They move on all-fours or walk stooped. Their faces are twisted. Bodies covered with scars and burn marks. They wear beaten metal as armor and hold spears and knives. Rabid animals, quiet for the moment, side by side with my Guardians, only slightly less rabid.

One of the goblins detaches from the crowd at her beckoning. He's the tall goblin king I saw previously. Walter's right-hand man. Errr, beast. He glares at me, and he smells rancid.

A handful of giants mix in with the crowd. I spot my tigers on a distant street, lounging in the sun. I love Blue-Eyes, so they do too. They are at peace. Everyone is...

That's why the sounds of warfare suddenly went silent, I realize. The Variants began obediently trailing Blue-Eyes as she moved through the city. And then she indoctrinated General Brown, and the military ceased firing.

They're bound to her now, groans Carmine. *She's the alpha. Humanity is lost.*

Not yet, I think to myself. The mutants get worse over time, even with an alpha. Besides, she can't stay near them for the rest of her life. They need healing. To learn independence again.

And besides, the Outlaw is still out there...

I blink. Shake my head. I shouldn't be thinking about him. I should focus on Blue-Eyes.

I can tell she's in discomfort. Her paralysis bothers her, causes pain. As we move, her spirits darken. She shifts to different sitting positions. She's gone from jubilant to brooding, and she inspects the mutant army with no joy.

"Mistress, are you sad?"

"I'm being *pushed*," she snaps, and I flinch. "In a wheelchair. What do you think?"

"Would you like—"

"What I would like..." She pauses. Closes her eyes and tilts her head back to the morning sun, now streaming down. There'll be no rain today, no relief to our water shortage. "What I would like is to start over."

"I don't understand."

"This was supposed to be fun. Martin promised the world. You remember him. The Chemist? He said we'd be kings and queens with his new technology and medical advances, and..." She tilts her face down and opens her eyes. Indicates the mutants we pass. "And look. We have monsters and decay. Martin is dead. So is Minnie and Carla, and the beautiful Mitch. Even Walter. Caleb's been gone for years. And...and I'm alone."

"You're not alone! I'm—"

"Quiet!" She takes a deep breath and continues. "The President killed himself. Carter wishes me dead. Samantha paralyzed me. I mean, look at yourself, Carmine. You're battered and bruised and bloody all over. Each of us is missing pieces. All broken. This wasn't what I was promised. This is no fun. What I want? Is to start over and try again. Find a future where I'm not in a wheelchair. Find some meaning in this miserable machine of a world."

From behind us, General Brown calls, "Madam President, I received an update. Ai's chopper is an hour out."

Blue-Eyes nods to herself.

We walk in silence for several minutes, as forlorn as a funeral procession.

As we exit the downtown tower cluster, she points northwest to Dodger Stadium. "You asked where we're headed," she sighs. "To the ball field. For judgement. Maybe the poetry and symbolic spectacle of your death will bring joy to my life. For a few hours."

Katie Lopez

General Brown and I video conference with Ai. Blue-Eyes insists it will ease any Resistance misgivings. Ai's on a chopper, wearing a headset, sitting between two armed guards. The phone connection is bad and rotors prevent any real communication, but we do our best. Ai looks frightened.

Afterwards, Isaac Anderson texts Carter. Tells him he monitored the call, and if the hostage exchange doesn't go well he'll destroy Dodger Stadium within seconds. A bluff? I truly don't know. I doubt that's possible.

One thing is for certain—the Resistance doesn't know Blue-Eyes is here. Ai's being flown to her demise.

Brown, Carter, Kayla, Blue-Eyes, and I pause in a tunnel, under the seats. The stadium's lower seating fills with mutants as we watch, forcing any curious civilians to take the higher sections. The goblin king directs his minions but its clear they prefer taking orders from Blue-Eyes.

She instructs Carter, "The helicopter will land in centerfield. You receive the girl from China. Then tell the pilot that the hostages are chained in the parking lot. As soon as it lifts off again, clear of the stadium, General Brown will shoot it down."

Carter nods. His shirt is soaked with sweat and blood as he fights an inner battle, trying to resist her. But he can't.

She continues, "General, if the helicopter does anything suspicious, destroy it. I'd prefer to speak with Ai, but let's be safe rather than sorry."

"Yes, Madam President."

"I remain hidden by umbrellas until the aircraft is destroyed, either way. After that, we begin with the judgement."

We all nod and agree.

Carmine is so angry she's almost crying.

We follow Blue-Eyes onto the field. I push, as she demands.

There's an old wooden platform we once used in our first meeting with the Outlaw. She pauses near it and signals for her servicemen. They crowd around her and raise black umbrellas, shielding her from the sun and any prying satellites.

"Carmine, be a dear and get on the platform."

Don't go up there.

I pause. Carmine interfering with my obedience.

I open my mind to the Variant network, that strange supernatural dimension where we can connect. Saul the Zealot taught me to keep my borders blocked, but maybe if I link with the thousands of nearby mutants...

My spirit is immediately repelled. Instead of willing interconnections, I find a throbbing cancer. The network feels hot and angry. They *love* her. A blind allegiance beyond logic—mob mentality. She fears me, so her followers hate me. Blue-Eyes's power is overwhelming; I feel it secreting throughout their minds.

She's the reason we all felt anxious, as though a disaster was imminent. She's the reason for our looming anxiety. Through this hive mentality, we sensed her plans to strike.

I'll find no help from my former Guardians. I didn't solve their critical dependence quickly enough. They're addicts desperate for a fix. For an alpha. And they think Blue-Eyes will fill that gaping need. Little do they know...

She glares at me. "Now, *please.*"

"Yes mistress."

I step onto the raised wooden dais. No one else does.

"Carter, take the jugs of gasoline," she says, indicating a cart pulled by one of her government servants. "And cover sweet Carmine and the platform, please. Soak her thoroughly."

Carter takes the heavy canister from the cart. The contents slosh inside. He stalls by the platform.

My muscles quiver. I shouldn't let him drench me with gas. But...I have to obey her.

Carter asks, "Just her?"

"Yes. Only drench the *queen*," she purrs and nods.

"Is this necessary?"

"Indeed. She's caused me trouble for years, and must be made an example. Besides, I sense within her...opposition. She's fighting me. Somehow. So, even if nothing else goes right today, it's imperative that she dies. And the world knows it. I'm holding a leadership summit here next month, and it would ease troubled minds to know she's gone."

Carter nods. Looks at the canister. Looks at me. He says, "Sorry, kiddo. Gotta do it."

"Oh, Carmine," she calls. "Get on your knees."

No!

"No," I say.

"Yes. *Now.*"

My knees mutiny and bend. I have no choice. I love her more than I love myself or my own survival.

Carter steps onto the dais and walks around, sloshing the liquid out until the wooden fibers are sodden. He chucks the empty canister aside and fetches the second. This one he turns upside down over my head, drenching me. The oily gasoline soaks my hair, seeps into my shirt and socks. Puddles in my shoes. My eyes burn and I spit the stuff out.

One spark would do the trick.

Dodger Stadium, packed over capacity at sixty thousand, collectively gasps, watching.

He steps back, looking troubled. Like he's genuinely remorseful. Kayla weeps, forlorn and plangent, even after Blue-Eyes tells her to stop.

So we wait. Me on my knees, getting high on fumes. Ready to die. I can't help remembering years ago when the Chemist's men punctured gas tanks near Compton, soaking the interstate for miles. I escaped the blast, but Hannah Walker didn't. Today the situation is reversed.

General Brown accepts a phone call from Isaac Anderson and acts natural. Plays it perfectly.

He hangs up and calls, "Chopper's here. Coming from the east."

"Where?" demands Blue-Eyes, shifting in her chair. "I can't see it."

"Flying low. Stadium walls obstruct the visual."

"I can't hear it, either. Carter, run up to the top and tell me what you see," she says.

Carter *Leaps*. He can't soar like the Outlaw, but he reaches the rim of Dodger Stadium in four jumps. He grunts as he does, ripping sutures. The multitude watches him. He reaches the top and searches the wide horizon.

He calls in an unnaturally loud voice. "I got it. A mile out."

Poor Carter, I almost feel bad for him. He worked so hard to secure Ai and her understanding of the disease, and now she's being taken away from him again.

"Only one chopper," he shouts. "Southeast. Transport, not attack. Just as I asked."

Blue-Eyes breathes a sigh of relief. "Good. Maybe, perhaps this one time, everything will go as planned."

The beat of the blades becomes audible. Heavy whomping.

"Less than a mile, now!" His voice is heard by all of us, as if he has a megaphone. But he doesn't—just a disease.

She smiles. "Yes. I think, at last, today will be—"

"Wait...something's wrong."

We all stop. Focus on him. Sharpen our hearing. What is it?

He says, "There's something... No, someone is dangling below the chopper."

"Dangling? Who? Ai?" asks Blue-Eyes. Despite the distance, despite using a normal voice, the sound carries easily.

"No, a man. It's..." He swears. "General! Shoot it down!"

"Why? Who is it?" screeches Blue-Eyes, gripping her armrests with white knuckles. The blades are loud now, very close, a violent staccato caroming inside Dodger Stadium.

Carter cups his hands around his mouth. "General! Now! Shoot it!"

Brown looks calmly at Blue-Eyes for confirmation. "Madam?"

She deflates. Her glorious day ruined, and she doesn't even know why yet. She nods. "Do as he says."

Brown raises a radio and speaks into it. "Control Two, this is Brown. Take it out. That's a hostile. Repeat, take it out."

We're all wondering the same question—what did Carter see? Why the sudden—

The helicopter roars into view, mere feet over the stadium walls. Someone clings to the landing gear. Behind the stadium, rockets hiss and flare. Scarlet streaks.

The little chopper shatters, the detonation shaking Dodger Stadium to its base. A disaster directly over our heads. Those higher up will have broken ear drums. The helicopter was moving fast before impact, and the streaking rockets punch it it farther west. A ton of chaotic metal. Fragments of steel hurl at the horizon. The eruption showers us with fire but the wreckage summersaults across the sky and falls safely into a nearby parking lot.

Flaming shards of debris land dangerously close to my platform.

I can't hear. Head pounds and ears ring.

The man lands in the seats, only a few rows back from the field. I don't get a good look. Surrounding mutants draw back in fear but then crash like a tsunami. They scream and rampage. Clawing to get closer, to slash and rip and destroy.

I know who it is. We all do. Only one man would hang from a helicopter and let go at full speed. Only one man willing to plunge into a stadium full of his enemies. Only one who creates this strong a reaction from the mutants.

They descend upon him. Hundreds. He is buried at the bottom of the pile, completely lost from sight.

"Capture him!" shrieks Blue-Eyes. "Don't let him escape! Carter, bring him here!"

Carter fights his way through the mob, shouting orders. Could anyone be alive at the base of that mountain of bodies? The savages refuse to give up their prize, each wanting to personally disembowel the long despised hero. Several minutes pass of snarling and fighting before Carter finally reappears from the melee.

With him is the Outlaw. Dressed in the notorious vest and red mask. Tattoos glint on his muscular arms. He's not like the mutants.

He looks like a demigod ripped from ancient lore. The peak of mankind, potential fully realized and pushed beyond by the disease. I haven't been with him in two years but I'd recognize him after a thousand. I know those shoulders. I know that color of brown hair, even if it's longer and tinged with sunlight. I know those lips.

"Chase!" I scream.

He wears the crimson mask. His vest is torn. Blood pours from scratches and bites. Carter has him in a headlock, revolver pressed against his temple. Some of the more sane Variants keep his arms locked in theirs. It takes six total, including Carter, to subdue him.

What is he *doing* here? This can't be going according to plan.

They bring him before Blue-Eyes. Her eyes are alight with pleasure. He towers over her, power overwhelming meets beauty beyond reason.

"Look at you, flawless angel," she says, her voice sensuous and smooth. "If possible, you're more desirable and handsome than ever, my plaything. Bow. On your knees, at my feet."

Something inside me panics. No...this can't be happening. That can't be Chase. This is a trick. That's someone else! She can't have him!

Cautiously, Carter and the others release their hold. Ready to pounce. Carter keeps the gun pressed firmly against the Outlaw's head.

Chase drops to his knees, panting. He bends over. "Yes...yes mistress."

No!

"No!" I scream but I can't move. Gasoline spittle flies from my lips. If she truly has him, we can't win. It's over.

But this is a trick. A horrible joke. That's not him, it can't be!

Blue-Eyes bends over. Takes the red mask between her fingertips, and pulls it off inch by inch.

My heart nearly dies. Without the mask, we all clearly see— Chase Jackson. It's truly him, the love of my life.

She has him. And all is lost.

4

The Outlaw
Seventeen hours earlier

THE WORLD BOILS.

The atomic blast consumes the trees, the forest, the animals, the entirely of Oak Groves, the very air I breathe...

The swirling sand blinds me and I'm staggering off balance from the shockwave. The heat intensifies. Disorienting pain. My clothes smolder. The air I suck down scalds my throat. My skin's about to blister.

These are mere shockwaves. I won't survive the oncoming might of nuclear wrath.

Just when I think all is lost, I fall. A direct plunge into a canyon— a chasm I didn't see near the base of the hills. I spill down the steep decline, crashing through blessedly cooler air. I don't stop bouncing until I splash into the creek at the bottom. Searing heat washes over the chasm but doesn't descend. I'm going to live! Maybe. At least until the radiation kills me.

The water isn't cold like rivers cascading from mountains, but it's cool enough. It soothes the thousand bite marks covering me. I'm torn—I want to laugh and splash and thank God I'm alive; but also I want to cry for Andy and Tank and question why awful things happen.

I compromise; I run. I don't know where I am, but I know I need to get away from the detonation. And the rocky canyon doesn't give me a lot of choices, forcing me south and west. Towering in the dusk over my shoulder, a mushroom cloud swells. The second America's seen in under three years.

Such a surreal notion, me fleeing and splashing along a desert canyon, alone, nearly torn to pieces by wolves, outrunning nuclear fallout. I bet Batman never had to do this.

~

HOURS later I'm trudging in absolute night. An eternity of black. The cloud of ash and sand wiped out the stars, and now falls like snow. My feet kick up the stuff with each scuffle.

My eyes and ears haven't healed yet from the overload. I can't process the enormity of what just happened. Can't force my brain to absorb the dreamlike reality of wolves and cougars fighting, and Tank and Andy dying, and atom bombs detonating...it's too much. Instead I blindly shuffle and follow the faint glimmer of water. Where am I going? I don't know. There's nothing for hundreds of miles. Is anyone looking for me? Doubtful; they have to assume I died in the blast. Is it super creepy alone in the canyons? Yes, major creepy, and I hate it. Am I going to die here? Almost certainly. Probably not from radiation though, because my cells regenerate so rapidly. So something else will do the trick. Starvation, maybe.

But I keep thinking, Katie's safe. Her nuclear threat is gone. Katie's safe.

And that's enough.

I want to sleep. I *need* to sleep. Close my eyes and forget. Feels like an eternity since I stood on my boat; I didn't sleep well there either but it was a safe slumber, and usually I got to pick when. Every rock I pass looks like a fluffy pillow. Every shallow pool a water bed. But I can't stop, not yet. Need to find a phone that isn't short-circuited, need to contact Puck, need to hear Katie's voice, need to...

Gradually the rim of the canyon wall ahead of me is becoming visible. A distant illumination highlights the ridges. At first I think it's the moon penetrating the murk, but the angle's wrong. And the light source is approaching; a manmade light.

A plane?

Wearily I *Leap* across the river to the southern shore and climb the sheer face. The forty-foot ascent is almost too much. I'm groaning and verging on surrender as I claw onto the upper crust of Arizona. My breath disturbs the unsettled sand and ash, but I make it.

Noise explodes. A powerful spotlight sweeps back and forth from a thundering Black Hawk helicopter, only a quarter mile distant.

Salvation. Gotta be a rescue from General Isaac Anderson.

Detritus flings in my face as I run to the....as I *hobble* to the chopper. The spotlight snaps onto me and the Black Hawk lowers. Wheels touch. Its starboard gunner door is already open, and I slide in.

I pant, eyes closed, and shoot a thumbs up. The deck lurches beneath me and the engines roars. We're up.

To my surprise, the passenger bay is empty. I clamp on a headset and position the mic above my lips. "Thanks for the lift."

"Don't thank me yet, Outlaw." The voice of Samantha Gear fills my ears. "We got work to do."

I sit up. Peer into the gloom of the cockpit.

"*Sam?*"

"Yeah baby. Strap that ass in, we're in a hurry."

"But..." My head swims. Below, dark shapes flash by as we climb. I force myself up and into a seat. "But...your legs are broken."

"Correct, genius."

"Shut up. How are you flying a helicopter?"

She turns on the cockpit light and pats her thigh. She wears a cast on both legs. Pink, of all things. "The plaster had just finished drying when we heard about the bomb. During the commotion I found a pair of crutches and stole the chopper."

"A helicopter can be flown by a pilot wearing casts?"

"Not easily. I had to break the cast at the knees. It hurts like hell. I've almost crashed twice, so Puck's helping remotely."

"Thanks, Sam. You're the best."

"Thank Puck and Lee, too. They put a transmitter into your vest to track you. It's been short-circuiting but Puck was getting an intermittent signal, enough to guide me in," she says.

"A transmitter? What a colossal invasion of privacy."

"You have the habit of disappearing. Seemed like a good idea."

"Yeah, but," I say, and I point at her cast. "Pink?"

She snaps off the light. "I hate you. The doc was hot and told me I'd look good in pink, and...it just happened."

The helicopter banks suddenly, and I grab a safety loop to keep from falling out.

"Maybe you should focus," I tell her through the mic.

"Maybe you should shut up. This is hard. My legs are broken."

"Where are we going?"

"Get three hours of sleep and then I'll tell you," she says. "It's four in the morning and you look like hell. Eat some food back there, sleep, and you can fill me in about what happened in the desert."

"Is Katie okay?"

"Katie's okay," she says but I know there's more to the story. "We're going to get her."

I yawn and latch a belt around my waist. "I like that plan."

"Good. Your Outlaw suit is a mess. Like you're wearing rags. You can take it off, I won't watch. Okay? Chase? Hellooo?"

My headset is off and buzzing next to me. I'm already asleep.

5

The Outlaw

"OKAY, DUMMIES, GOT SOME NEW INTEL," says Puck into our ears. Samantha and I just switched helicopters at an outpost. Now we're in a Little Bird, less than an hour outside Los Angeles. We're flying in under the guise of being Ai's escort, in exchange for Katie and Kayla. Little does Carter know, Ai won't be in the chopper—we will. Meanwhile, Ai is flying around in a dummy chopper because Carter keeps demanding to video conference with her, and we need to keep up appearances. "Life just got more complicated, and we need a new plan."

"But we just came up with *this* plan," I groan.

"Our plans never work," says Samantha.

"Katie just video conferenced with Ai again. Afterwards, she didn't hang up. She let the video keep rolling, so I could spy."

Samantha nods. "Atta girl."

"Guess who I saw?"

I share a glance with Sam. My heart sinks. "Gotta be Blue-Eyes."

"Bingo. She's there. And got everyone under her influence."

"Carter and Blue-Eyes together." I whistle. "This is going to be a doozy."

"We're screwed," says Samantha. "So screwed."

"So Puck, what's the plan?"

He says, "Yo, PuckDaddy got no idea. That's up to you two."

"Dang it," I say. "I hate when it's up to me."

"Too bad Katie's there. We could just have Isaac Anderson drop bombs on them."

Puck says, "She's got General Brown under her influence now. The missile shield is intact, protecting the bad guys. Also, all the Variants are following her now, too."

"So, in summary, Blue-Eyes now controls Carter, Katie, Katie's army, and also Katie's Guardians," I say.

Puck replies, "And all of Walter's. Essentially, she's queen of earth now."

"Not if we kill her."

"Oooh, I like that plan," says Samantha. "How?"

"She doesn't know we're coming. She thinks she's about to get Ai. We have the element of surprise."

She scoffs. "So? She has Katie and Carter and Brown and legions of mutant freaks."

"But all we need is one shot," I tell her. "You put her in the wheel-chair before. Now it's time you finish the job, while I distract her."

"I can't shoot well from the helicopter. I've tried; it's hard. I'll miss, and we'll have blown our opportunity."

I grin. "You're not going to shoot from the chopper. You'll fire from a rooftop."

"They'll see us if we land!"

"We won't land. We'll barely reduce speed.

"Then how—"

"You're going to jump out, obviously."

She glares at me. "With broken legs."

"Yes. They'll probably break some more. But that's a risk I'm willing to take."

"I wish the nuke had killed you."

Puck grumbles, "Our plans are the worst."

6

The Outlaw

WE COME in low from the southeast; a weird direction, but we need a tower for Samantha to shoot from. The Los Angeles Department of Health is the closest—still a half mile from Dodger Stadium. It'll be a heck of a shot, but she's confident she can do it. Puck assumes control of the chopper remotely while Samantha sits on the landing strut.

"How fast are we going?" she shouts over the wind.

I glance at the dials. "Eighty miles per hour."

"Slow to fifty! Or I'm not jumping!"

"Wimp," I call.

"Fifty!"

Puck can control the chopper's altitude and speed, but I have to keep it pointed in the right direction, which is the limit of my helicopter-piloting abilities. Using my headset, I tell him to reduce speed to fifty.

We're approaching the tower in a hurry, buzzing near the downtown spire cluster. I missed this city. Even haggard, it's still the City of Angels.

I eyeball the roof and tell Puck, "Drop ten feet. We need to be close."

"Roger that, homie."

"Lower!" shouts Samantha. "And slower!"

"Get ready to jump! And stop complaining!"

"Lower and slower, you morons!"

"Wow, she must be freaked," mumbles Puck in my ear. "I can hear her through your mic."

I call to her, "Okay, we're going fifty!"

She groans. "We're going too fast. I'm going to die."

"Get ready! We're on approach."

"I can see that! And shut up!"

"Drop five more feet," I advise. I want to be so close we nearly skim the roof; if Samantha is too injured to shoot, we're toast.

"Roger that. Also I love saying roger."

I take off my headset and reach behind my seat for her gear. Two duffle bags, full of firepower. I hold them tight, leaning out of the cockpit and into the rotor wash.

The tall building, formerly home to the Department of Health and one of the city's bigger libraries, swells to monstrous proportions and suddenly flashes underneath us.

Samantha and I shout "Good luck!" to each other simultaneously.

I drop the bags. They fall fifteen feet and land hard. Skidding and spinning across the roof until colliding with an old A/C unit.

Samantha essentially does the same thing, except she ricochets off the A/C unit and slams into a security rail. I wince. Looks painful. Would kill a normal person.

I grab the mic. "She's on! And alive! I think!"

"Puck is freaking out," he mumbles.

I make a course correction, aiming for Dodger Stadium. Center-field. "Let's finish this." I tie on the Outlaw mask.

"Okay." His voice pumps straight into my ear now. "Okay, okay. PuckDaddy bringing you lower. You think Shooter's good? Holy moly, I'm stressed."

The Little Bird pitches down as Puck awkwardly tries to wrangle the altitude. I'm easing myself out of the co-pilot chair and I slip—my foot misses the landing strut. I flail but find no handhold. I'm falling.

Time slows down just enough for me to twist and snag the landing gear with one hand. I swing underneath, like a monkey in a tree. I concentrate all my attention on my fingers not releasing.

Terrain streaks by below. We're almost at the stadium.

Puck says, "You ready, Outlaw?"

"Maybe," I gasp.

"Hang on...getting radio traffic. They see you!" he blurts. "Missile's fired! Inbound! Let go *now*!"

This happened too fast. I take a deep breath. And release, falling toward the bleachers.

Katie, I'm coming.

7

"Isn't this fun," says Blue-Eyes, examining the Outlaw at her feet. "After these many years, finally, gang's all here."

"Yes, mistress," he pants.

I want to scream.

Fight her, Katie!

She turns her withering gaze onto Carter. "I should have known your plan to get the girl from China wouldn't work. A preposterous hostage swap."

Carter closes his eyes and grinds his teeth. He wants to fight her but can't. I know the feeling.

"On one hand, Carter, you ruined my perfect day." She leans forward and pushes Chase's hair out of his eyes. It's long enough for some to stay tucked behind his ear. I should be the one doing that. "Yet, on the other, your bungling idiocy brought me the perfect prize. The boy I've longed to get my hands on. Sink my teeth into."

Carter doesn't reply. He fishes a cigarette from his trench coat pocket, clamps it between his teeth, and lights it with a silver Zippo. Even in obedience, some things remain true.

"You're smoking? Who smokes, these days?" she asks, her nose wrinkled. "How old are you, Carter?"

"Hundred and fifty, maybe."

"Too old."

"Yes, mistress," he says in that deep gravel.

"Chase Jackson, my love," Blue-Eyes purrs, and I want to gouge her eyes out. "Kill Carter."

Chase stands. "Yes."

Carter's eyebrows rise. His hand goes to his side, to the holstered revolver she let him retain. "Mistress...this isn't necessary. I won't disappoint you again."

"He's going to kill you, Carter," she says with a wicked cackle. "Unless you kill him first. Yes, I like this, entertainment for our audience! Who shall prevail over—"

Carter's pistol flashes out. Three blasts, startling me. Even with my ears ringing, the gunshots are violent and loud.

The Thunder Stick sings in Chase's fists, deflecting the rounds. He leaps into Carter. Carter meets him halfway in midair. An elemental collision of the gods. Like rocks breaking.

Carmine holds her breath.

I often wondered who would win this fight. Carter with his body hardened by age, with his cunning, and his firepower. Chase with his strength, quickness, and youth. Both are in bad shape. Carter's chest is only half healed, and Chase looks as though he's been through a blender.

The collision gives me chills. It's like they're dancing, too fast for my eyes to follow. Carter fires three more times. The Rod of Death, or whatever Chase calls it, whistles. More cracks like lightening, and the two men touch down onto the dirt near second base. The Thunder Stick thuds nearby, driving into the ground like a spear. Near my platform, the silver Zippo bounces.

Chase lands victoriously; his opponent is slammed down, face first. His knee presses into Carter's neck, near to breaking. His left arm encircles Carter's, ready to snap the old man's elbow. A submission hold.

The mutants in the audience bellow with disbelief and outrage. The civilians higher up cheer, and applause cascades down. I remember, long ago during a simpler time, watching fans cheer for Chase on a ball field. He'd been playing for his high school, though, not fighting for his life.

Blue-Eyes claps too. "My my, that was fast. I must say, I'm a little disappointed."

"He's stronger than me," says Chase through gritted teeth. "But he relied on the gun. A mistake. What do I do with him, mistress?"

"Chase, no..." I groan. I hate hearing him call her mistress. Why'd he come here? He had to know this wouldn't work.

Katie, you're out of time, you've GOT to break free.

Blue-Eyes turns in her wheelchair and beckons the goblin king. "Help the Outlaw bring Carter to the wooden platform."

The hulking giant lumbers forward. He grabs Carter's other arm and he and Chase haul the old man together. Carter kicks and bucks like a wild man, until Blue-Eyes says, "*Enough,*" and he stops. Chase pins him to the gasoline-soaked dais, beside me.

I'm close enough to touch Chase. It's been two years since I have. My hand twitches. His face is cut and his ears bleed. Some of his beautiful hair is torn out. His vest is shredded.

I realize Blue-Eyes is calling my name, and I haven't been listening. "Oh...yes? Sorry, mistress."

"Were you not listening to me?"

"I was wondering why our world is so cruel, mistress. Why good men like Chase must suffer so?"

She scoffs. "Who says he's good? He's no more committed to his cause than I am to mine. Who decides what's good and what's not? Is God the judge? Because clearly I have His blessing. I've won, after all."

Chase shakes his head. He mutters, "That's not...true, mistress."

The witch in the wheelchair glares at him and then me. "You two beautiful simpletons befuddle me. I cannot be resisted. Why do you try?"

"Sorry mistress," I say.

"Resistance is a tumor, you know. It must be extracted. It's a shame, really. I think it best if you both die."

"Yes mistress," says Chase.

"Katie, be a dear and fetch the lighter in front of you," she says. "Speaking of God, let's make him a burnt offering, shall we? A human sacrifice. My first fruits."

I step down from the platform and pick up the Zippo. My shoes are so full of gas that they squish. I can't stop. I'm trying. Carmine howls between my ears. But my functions obey Blue-Eyes blindly.

Using my thumb, I pull the back the Zippo's silver lid. Ready to flick. I return to the wooden dais.

"Any final words?" calls Blue-Eyes. Behind her the goblin king smiles.

"No mistress," grunts Carter, pinned.

Chase's eyes are closed. His whole body shakes. He won't respond. WHY did he come here?

"No mistress," I say. I begin to cry.

Her words swell with passion. "Very well. Queen Carmine, your reign over this city is at an end. Please do the honors and—"

"Katie." Chase interrupts her with a voice surprisingly clear. I glance down. He's watching me with bright blue eyes.

"Yes?"

"Marry me," he says.

His voice carries. The crowd of sixty thousand gasps, even the Variants.

Wow. Didn't see that coming.

Me either.

For once, Blue-Eyes is speechless.

"Please," he continues. "Say you will, before we die."

Carter makes a snorting noise.

A growl rises in the throat of the goblin king. Kayla, standing behind him, hops and claps.

"Chase..." I say.

"Yes."

"I've been waiting for you to ask me that since middle school."

He smiles. Wide and beautiful, and my heart dissolves.

"Do you have a ring?" I ask.

"I do, I do, I do!" calls Kayla, waving her hand. Her sinister collar bounces. "The Outlaw gave it to me to hide, two *years* ago! He was gonna propose before everything went all blah and you two died. I still have it!"

"This is kind of lovely," says Blue-Eyes. "A poetic end; the queen finally getting her prince. How nice. Truly, I'm happy you get to die together. But anyway. Carmine, dear, light the fire."

My thumb pushes the Zippo closed. I toss the lighter into the grass.

The crowd murmurs. Carter ceases struggling, and he watches with interest.

"Carmine," snaps Blue-Eyes. "Or Katie, whatever you call yourself. *Pick. Up. The lighter.*"

"No."

8

The Outlaw

"No," says Katie.

"Oh man," Puck whispers in my ear. "Did she say No?"

Too many voices in my head! Anytime the Blue-Eyed Witch speaks, it consumes me. Can't focus, can't concentrate. But if I keep my eyes on Katie, the world makes more sense.

"*No?*" screeches Blue-Eyes. "You can't tell me *no!*"

"Yes, I can. I love him more than I love you," says Katie. "I have to choose one. And I don't choose you."

"*Sit down!*" says Blue-Eyes with such authority that I immediately drop onto Carter's back. Kayla and everyone in the audience also sits. Katie fights it. Blue-Eyes indicates the goblin king with her chin. "Enough games! Light them. *Now.*"

The goblin king takes a step.

Puck mutters, "C'mon, Shooter, now's the time..."

9

Samantha Gear, laying prone on the rooftop sheet of synthetic rubber, ignores her fractured legs. In fact, despite the pain and grinding teeth, she grins. Blue-Eyes is rock steady in her rifle scope; the woman's in a wheelchair, after all. A sitting duck.

Samantha takes a breath. Lets half of it out. The atmosphere between them is a map, swirling winds like a terrain, easily read and maneuvered. Minute adjustments. Her right hand tightens on the grip.

She whispers, "So long, Madam President."

Slowly she squeezes the trigger.

The man called Nuts surfaces from the overflowing Van Norman reservoir. He treads water, sucks oxygen, and wipes his eyes. He can hold his breath a powerful long time, longer than anyone has any reasonable need to. And yet, not long enough.

He's entirely alone; Walter's forces fled yesterday evening, called south. Nuts felt the siren call too, but he ignored it. He has work to do.

Trouble is, for the first time he can remember, he can't fix the problem. A mess, that's what he's got. A damned mess. And he helped create it. In his haste, years ago, he shut down the other aqueducts, he rerouted the rivers here, he rewired the systems, and he failed to fully plan for eventualities. And now the rivers plunging from the Sierras keep churning through the open channels until reaching this reservoir, where the water is stoppered. Walter's forces clogged the point of egress with startling efficacy.

With a dozen men and with the right tools, this could be done safely and properly. Trouble is, he's got neither.

He climbs up the bank, which spills over with cold water, and glares into the depths. At the bottom, the massive drain. But the valve is closed. Without power, he can't safely open it. He tried rewiring it, tried attaching a remote detonator, tried half a dozen things. And Walter, fool that he was, blocked the underground access. Nuts would need dynamite to blast his way in. Who in their right mind would do such a thing? Did Walter really believe he'd never need running water after his siege worked? The man demolished his own supply chain.

Give evil enough time and it'll always destroy itself.

But Nuts doesn't have time. And he doesn't want the good people of Los Angeles to be destroyed.

There is another option. He can manually open the drain with a hand crank. It's simple, for someone who knows how—he swims down, turns the crank, and water begins flowing again.

Simple but deadly. The valve is damaged and the reservoir is far

over capacity. The hand crank is meant to manually open the drain
when the basin is *empty*. Not full. Once he partially cracks the valve,
it'll break. And hundreds of tons of water will pour through. A devas-
tating rush. That amount of power stretches imagination. The water
pressure will rip through homes, burst pipes in sky scrapers, flood
the sewers, almost certainly kill anyone fiddling with their toilet
or sink...

...and it's all his fault, because he personally disengaged the safety
measures. They were part of an old system and he upgraded it, but
the new safety valves operate remotely with electricity. And at the
moment, he has no power. No way to control the water pressure.

On top of that, once the valve is open, the person operating the
hand crank will be immediately sucked down the pipe. No chance for
survival.

Nuts tears his eyes away from the valve and its hand crank, and
gazes southeast to the downtown tower cluster, visible through the
distant haze. He knows the forces of good and evil are clashing. Five
minutes ago, during his last break for air, a helicopter disintegrated
and fell out of the sky.

But he can't do anything about that. Only a fool worries about
problems he can't solve. He can only focus on one problem at a time.
So he again examines the reservoir.

And wonders, for the first time, if it's time he hangs up his tool
belt. Makes an ultimate sacrifice and heads for the great workshop in
the sky. Finally get some rest.

He rubs his bald forehead with knobby fingers.

That doesn't sound so bad. Not bad at all, come to think of it.

The Outlaw

Blue-Eyes indicates the goblin king with her chin. "Enough games! Light them. *Now.*"

The goblin king takes a step. Who is this monster? I can't think straight. The pungent gasoline fumes I'm breathing in don't help.

In my ear, "C'mon, Shooter, now's the time! Chase, dude! You've got to go, homie! You can't listen to that crazy witch! Go go go!"

The monster bends down. Picks up the Zippo. Smiles with broken teeth. A grisly sight. He places a thumb on the flint and flicks down. A small yellow flame appears.

My muscles quiver and shake with exertion. I'm so close to getting control again...

Despite the terror and horror, I'm still borderline in a good mood. Because I asked Katie to marry me. And she said yes.

Well, kinda. Basically.

I hope.

And I'm just going to sit here and let her die? That doesn't sound right. I shake my head, trying to repulse Blue-Eyes. She's everywhere. All I see, all I hear. But...Katie's about to die? Can that be true?

Of course not. The President wouldn't do such a thing.

Would she? Maybe...

Puck buzzes in my ear. Gasoline pierces my nose.

Argh, can't concentrate. I need one truth, one single thing to cling to. And that is...

And that is, I love Katie. Nothing else matters.

Two things happen at once—I stand up, temporarily breaking free from the mind control; and Blue-Eyes is hurled backwards.

I see it happen in my periphery. Her silken shirt puckers at the stomach. She's violently knocked over, as though crushed by an invisible hammer. Her chair lands on top of her. The earth around kicks up in tufts.

Supersonic rounds. The bullets arrived first, followed by reports.

Four blasts. Samantha finally found her target, with at least one round.

"Atta way, Samantha!" hoots Puck in my ear.

Blue-Eyes begins screaming.

An explosion of instant activity. Mutants in the stands freak out, as though *they've* been shot. Many of them clutch their own stomachs and collapse. The rest charge the field. Carter, Katie, and I shake loose from her mind control. The spell is broken. Katie reaches into Carter's pocket and comes up with a remote control device. I grab her and haul her off the wooden dais, away from the monster with the fire. I want to take her far far away, where she'll never be hurt again. But I can't. Yet.

We're instantly surrounded by howling Variants, surging to protect their queen. I lose sight of Carter and Kayla.

Blue-Eyes is lifted by dozens of hands—some of them Secret Service and some mutant. She screeches in pain and the mob bears her away from the field. Away from the invisible sniper.

Katie grabs me by the ears and pulls my face to hers. Our noses almost touch, her eyes so large I could drown. "Chase. You're the most beautiful man I've ever seen. But don't kiss me yet," she says, flushed and angelic. An angel of wrath.

"Why the heck not?"

"Because this isn't over yet. I'm going after her. She can't escape again. This ends today."

"But—"

"Find Carter. Kill him. I'll handle Blue-Eyes."

"She has an escort of a thousand guardians," I point out.

"Which is why she has to die."

"I'm coming with you. You don't get out of my sight."

She smiles. "Fine. Unless Carter intervenes." She fiddles with the remote control device until it beeps. "There. That should deactivate Kayla's collar."

Mutants form a circle around us. These belonged to the goblin king, twisted and evil. They creep closer, dressed in macabre armor like orcs, eyes aflame.

I raise my hand to them and shout, "**Get back.**"

They screech and rear away, as if scalded. Katie and I bolt through. We *Leap* into the stands above first base and charge through the throng of civilians.

All is chaos. Thousands of mutants are ripping the stadium apart with bare hands. Soon they'll turn their fear and wrath on innocent people. General Brown and Kayla huddle near the visitor's dugout, looking as though they've broken free from the influence of Blue-Eyes. Brown has a radio to his mouth.

I shout, "Puck, where are they taking the witch?"

"Are you talking to PuckDaddy through bluetooth?" Katie asks. "Tell him I said hello."

"Maybe you should focus."

Puck replies, "Tell Katie I say What's up. Blue-Eyes is being carried out of the stadium by a pack of wild idiots. South, through the parking lot."

We reach the rim of the stadium and Katie points to our right, to the flowing mass of bodies bearing their queen away. She's in the middle, held over their heads.

"They're taking her downtown," says Katie. "Why?"

"I bet her Secret Service stashed a small emergency chopper on a roof."

"Oooh, very sneaky," mutters Puck.

Katie asks, "Was that Samantha who shot her?"

"Yep. And she needs to work on her aim."

"Be nice. I'm sure she tried her best."

Puck asks, "Is Kayla okay? Haven't heard from her recently."

"She's alive. And unharmed," I say. "I'm surprised you haven't been spying on her through phone cameras."

"Been a little busy."

"Doing what? You seem more overwhelmed than usual."

"I'll tell you when this is over," he says. "Maybe you need to focus."

Katie says, "We're out of time."

Hundreds of Variants swarm up the stadium after us. We can't fight that many, and if we try Blue-Eyes will get away. She might not live through Samantha's gunshot, but I want to guarantee it. I still hear her angry shouts.

We *Jump* down.

The witch's horde runs up the ramp onto the 110. Katie and I shadow parallel on Bunker Hill. Mutants have taken custody of her body, outrunning the Secret Service men.

They pour onto Figueroa, like a stain.

The raving clan of goblins spills out of the stadium, chasing us. They aren't giving up. The witch wants us dead so they do too. We can outrun them, or we can keep an eye on Blue-Eyes—we can't do both.

I say, "I'll deal with these idiots and find you in a few minutes. Puck will tell me where you are."

He mutters, "Puck will try. Lot going on."

"Don't die." Katie grabs my hand and squeezes. "I just got you back." She keeps running parallel to Blue-Eyes and her mob.

I turn and face our pursuers. Hundreds. Drooling. Gnashing. Spitting. I sidestep chucked spears made from rebar. Over their heads, I see giants ducking out of the stadium and headed my way.

"**Stop,**" I order, using the voice I've learned deflects them. "**Turn back!**" The first rank of the horde falters, but they're overtaken by others. Too many. Can't reason with rabid animals.

I jump into their midst. My body's trained to speed up my reflexes and strengthen my synapses in fight-or-flight situations, and the mutants move in slow motion. I dance through them without breaking stride—spinning and wielding the Thunder Stick. I'm gone before their claws dig in. I'm above them before they're ready. I'm behind them, grinding them into the street. I am the sledge hammer, and they are like thin boards sundering. Dozens break. When the melee gets too thick, I quit the dance and cleave wide swaths through them. They scream and duck. The wiser Variants flee from the awful rod; the less wise die. A wave shattering against a cliff.

They verge on breaking. Ready to retreat.

Then there is Carter. He blasts me from my blindside, a thundering kick to the head. The lights of my eyes flicker. The world spins dizzily. I bounce and skid to a stop, come up disoriented. He aims the heavy revolver, freshly loaded. Fires. The round punches me in the chest; my ballistic vest prevents penetration but I'm knocked off my feet again.

"Happy, hero?" he fumes, voice a volcano. "It's all falling apart. We should be gods over the entire planet, yet here we are. Bickering. Killing each other."

"She's never going to share power with you," I wheeze.

"I should have Ai, but you interfered." He fires again, but I'm rolling across the street and he misses. "I should have an immunity, but you meddled." Another gunshot, nearly taking my ear off. "I should—"

I interrupt him. "Carter."

"What," he growls.

"Shut up." I push off the ground with my hands, springing into the air. The mutants watching our interaction draw back and hiss.

"I rely too much on my gun, huh," he says and he tosses it aside. "Fine. Fight me like a man."

We crash at the intersection of Figueroa and Sunset. He's a demon—moving at an unholy speed. He's faster than me, his body harder than mine. But I have a suspicion; I've grown stronger than him. Two years on a boat, eating lots of protein from fish, working and sweating all day, while he's been hiding in paradise. I can't outfight him, but maybe I can outmuscle him.

My body nearly cracks on impact. He's steel. I grip his hands. Our fingers interlock. A contest of strength; whose bones will break first? I push against him and he shoves me back. Neither of us release. There will be no quarter.

The mutant audience bellows.

Sweat rolls down his forehead. "Shoulda stayed on your boat, kid."

He's pressing me back. The blacktop under my feet gives a few inches. I'm suddenly on the defense, every sinew straining.

His breath smells like ash. He grunts, "You're good. Coulda been great. But you're not ready to wrangle with me. Need another half century, Outlaw."

My voice comes out in a strangled groan. "I was wrong."

"About what?"

"You're stronger than me." And he is. Nature and the disease turned him into a colossus. His power dwarfs mine.

His head is almost touching mine and he tries to break my hands, thrusting me back. "Finally, you got something right, mate."

I laugh; it comes out as a whisper. My entire body shakes with exertion. "But I'm still gonna win."

He pauses. Like a man wondering if he's fallen into a trap. "How's that?"

"You have nothing to live for, old man."

"So?"

"I have Katie. She makes me desperate. You only have arrogance, and it makes you overconfident." I release the power in my arms. He staggers forward, meeting no resistance, and I head-butt him. A crisp blow to his nose. He roars. I hit him again, breaking his nasal and temporal bones. He tries to rear back and retreat, but I hold tight. All the muscles in my hands contract—muscles accustomed to the brutal work of taming oceans. He's unprepared for the squeeze. Bones in his left hand fracture. He howls and yanks free before I crack the right.

He cradles the busted hand. Blood pours from his face.

"I win, Carter." I retrieve the Thunder Stick from the street. It sparks against blacktop. "And it's time to end this."

"Oh yeah?" He snarls. "They disagree."

"They who?"

Suddenly I'm swarmed. The mutants—forgot all about them! Don't even have time to jump. No! Dozens of them get their hands on me. My weapon is wrested away. My arms pinned back, feet hoisted, and then I'm slammed to the road. Buried under a mountain of madness. The stench is brutal.

Gingerly he bends over and picks up the revolver with his good hand. "Who's over-confident now, hero?"

"I beat you, Carter," I snarl. I can't even pick my head up, because three of them are forcing it down. No way to get leverage. "Call off your dogs."

"You think there's any honor in war?" He walks to where I'm pinned by at least ten Variants. The rest leap on all fours and shriek. "No. It's kill or be killed. And I've thought about killing you for a long time."

"Coward!" I shout. "Let me up! You lost!"

He waggles the gun. "Three bullets left. Three headshots. But first." He holsters the revolver. Fishes a cigarette from his jacket pocket. "When I pictured this, when I finally kill you, in my head I was always smoking a cigarette."

"Let me go, Carter. Katie needs help."

"Can't rush this. Need to savor it, mate. Kill you and flick the ash onto your corpse." He pats his pockets. Comes up empty. "Hey kid. You got a light?"

A car honks. No, it's not a car, it's a bus, and one of those deep-bellied horns. Neither Carter nor I paid attention to the road behind him, to the bus racing to our intersection. It's electric, producing no engine growl.

Carter half-turns to inspect the horn, and the bus hits him. The nose catches him full; his skull splinters the windshield. I hear both the glass and his cranium break. He's thrown ten feet. The bus's trajectory shifts slightly—the driver aiming. Its wheels turn enough to run over Carter's body, still rolling. Brakes lock and squeal. Carter is pinned and smeared underneath the front passenger tire. Never to rise again.

The mutants holding me lose their minds. They shriek and flee, startled by the sudden appearance of the vehicle. It looks like a space-ship on wheels, sent from the future on a rescue mission. Windows and antennas and even a remote controlled machine gun on the roof.

The driver of the bus raises his arms. I see him clearly despite starburst designs on the windshield. PuckDaddy calls in my ear, "I got him! Is he dead? Oh please tell me he's dead."

"Puck!" I laugh. "That's you in there, driving?"

"Heck yeah it is! I moved all my computer terminals to the dash. I even steer with a keyboard. Dude! Is Carter dead? That guy terrifies me."

"Yeah." I nod, breathing an enormous sigh of relief. "You got him. He's toast."

Puck pumps his fist. "Woohoo! Suck it, old man! You take my legs? I mow you down!"

Wearily I climb to my feet.

"Puck, where's Katie?"

And that's when the ground begins to shake.

The man called Nuts makes his peace with God. Apologizes for all the foolhardy stuff he's ever done and all the profitable things left undone. Asks forgiveness for never reading the Bible, and tells the Almighty, from the stories he's heard, he thinks Jesus was probably the finest man who ever lived.

He takes hold of a heavy wrench. Looks at the infinite wild blue and decides this is a fine day to die. Yes sir, this is how he wants to go out—fixing one last problem.

Nuts dives into the churning reservoir. The wrench drops him quickly to the bottom, which is already littered with other tools. The reservoir is deep, after all. His ears nearly burst.

He takes hold of the hand crank. It's old and partially stuck, but Nuts's powerful forearms won't be denied. He emits a stream of bubbles, straining, and the crank twists. Through the water, he hears a squeal. Another twist. And another. The valve opens like a great iris.

The pressure and weight is too much. The valve groans and breaks. Suddenly, after a week of frustration, the pent-up water has someplace to go and it gushes in. A handful of underground pipe seams rupture as acres and acres of water rush through. Like an entire mountain liquified and blasted through a hose.

The foaming runaway freight train of water roars by all cutoff valves. A half mile downstream, water pressure shatters a porcelain sink and throws the toilet through the roof. Then obliterates the next house. Entire neighborhoods spout water.

Minor streams of the flood are bled off at diverging branches, but the main thrust of the torrent continues unabated, heading towards Downtown and its towers and hospitals.

The man called Nuts, his sacrifice complete, is gone.

Katie Lopez

The Blue-Eyed Witch is still alive and issuing orders. But for how much longer? I'm no executioner but I won't accept the chance that she'll live. If Samantha hit her a few inches higher, this would be over. I no longer fear the witch nor her voice—I was trying to resist her with hate. Trying to drive out the dark with darkness. Yet it was love that set me free. I choose Chase and love and light.

But that doesn't mean she gets to live.

I'm on 2nd Street, keeping out of sight. As soon as her guards see me, they'll attack. We pause at Broadway, near a small condominium tower. I know this place. Haven't I been here before? I'm sure I recognize it.

Blue-Eyes screeches as the goblin king picks her up in a fireman's carry, and he begins scaling the wall, using bricks and windows for purchase. The rest of the mutants climb adjacent structures, keeping watch over their beloved alpha.

The condominium building is connected to a few others. I retreat one block and scale an old bank. Scoot across the roof, staying out of sight.

Where is Chase? He should be here by now. I need a phone.

I reach the condo tower. Not really a tower—only five stories tall. I swear I've seen it before. I creep along the adjacent building, on the second floor. There's a fire escape system of landings and ladders, and I silently ascend. My shoes squish with gas, my hair and clothing still sodden.

The goblin king reaches the roof the same time as me. He's panting and tired from the climb, carrying the witch. Her blouse and pants are dark with blood, her face pale. He turns to the far corner of the rooftop. I spy a small helicopter, hidden behind the penthouse. The aircraft's only meant for two, and only for short distances. Her emergency escape plan.

She spies me and shrieks. "You! How do I get rid of you people? Sit *down!*"

Her powerful voice crashes into me. I almost sit. Nearly collapse with the effort of resisting. But I focus on Chase. Keep his face fixed clearly in my mind's eye. I love him. Not her.

The wave passes and I'm still standing.

Way to go, Katie!

"Set her down," I tell the goblin king.

In response, he chuckles.

Good grief, that's an ugly guy.

The goblins on surrounding buildings climb high enough to see me. They witness their alpha in trouble. They scream and nearby windows shatter with the noise.

The goblin king carefully sets Blue-Eyes into a cast iron chair. She gasps, close to fainting.

"Kill her," she whispers. "Cut the *queen's* throat and throw her off the roof. I...I hate her. And hurry, my disgusting pet. I don't have long."

The goblin king removes a wicked knife from a sheath on his thigh. More of a short sword, hooked and jagged and black. He issues a noise like a snake. I edge backwards, unsure if I can beat him.

A new voice. "Katie?"

We're stunned. The noise is so out of place I almost don't register it. Who?

Hannah Walker steps from the stairwell. Despite myself, I shiver. Her eyes are red from crying. Tears of gasoline?

"Hannah?"

"Katie, why are you here?" she asks in a raw, scratchy tone.

I say, "The better question is, why are *you* here?"

"This is where I live."

The goblin king glances between us, not moving. He knows enough to fear the Cheerleader.

I ask, "You live *here*? For all these years? Why?"

"Because..." She stops to suppress a sob. "This is where I found Chase."

"Found? What do you mean?"

"I smelled him. He used to come here, I think. A long time ago."

"But, Hannah, you're all alone," I say.

"Yes. All alone."

"You could have come to live with me."

She wipes her eyes. Stares at me but has trouble focusing. "Really?"

"You shouldn't live by yourself. We can figure something out."

"Thank you, Katie." She sniffs. "We've been friends since high school. I remember."

"Oh shut *up*." Blue-Eyes groans in pain. Her hands, clutching her stomach, have begun to tremble. "This is like some awful high school soap opera. And here I am, President of America, leader of the world, shot. And listening to you two twits."

"You." Hannah turns to Blue-Eyes. "You're unkind to Katie. You killed Chase."

"No, sweetie. You crazy idiot. I didn't. I said someone else did. But in fact, he's still alive. So go back downstairs and die alone, kay? I'm bleeding to death and you're in the way."

"You're a *liar*." Hannah's face twists in hot fury. Blood pools out of her eyes and she quakes. I take a surreptitious step away. "You lie, and I hate your voice, and you killed Chase."

"*No*," shouts Blue-Eyes through a groan. "I didn't. I command you, *throw yourself* off this building! You don't deserve to be alive, you *freak*."

Fire secretes from Hannah's pores. Small flames dot her face and neck and under her arms. Strands of her hair catch. Tendrils leak from her nose and ears. She screams and flexes, and the rest of her lights up. One second, she's the Cheerleader. The next, she's the girl on fire. Her body becomes a silhouette inside the raging inferno. Heat so strong that the goblin king and I duck away.

She descends on Blue-Eyes. Picks her up like a baby, except her right arm wraps around the witch's neck, instead of under her head. Blue-Eyes's neck snaps audibly.

"Hannah!" I scream, as she nears the edge of the tower. "Be careful!" The Cheerleader turns to look at me, but I can't see under the flames. She *Jumps* into the sky, carrying Blue-Eyes with her, the pair of them smoldering.

I crouch on the roof, watching them sail like a shooting star into the distance and fall out of sight. After they're gone, I still hear Hannah's angry wail.

I hope she's okay. Hannah didn't deserve her fate. I raise to a sitting position, wondering if the fall killed her.

Katie, move! The goblin king!

The monster stands above me. In his left hand, the knife. In his right, the silver Zippo lighter. A small pale flame dances on the wick. He makes a gurgling noise and whips the knife down. I spin away.

I worry more about the lighter. I catch his large wrist in my right fist. He snarls, emitting fetid breath. I strike. With the fingernails on my left hand, I open him from groin to ribcage, like unzipping a bodybag. My nails slice cleanly and deep.

He gasps and releases the knife. Grasps at his abdomen.

He also releases the lighter. I fumble for it, but our hands tangle. The Zippo falls in slow motion. Past my searching fingers. Bounces against my shoe. The pale flame touches the Nike's fabric. My shoe and my sock, sodden with gasoline, ignite.

My jeans are saturated too. And my shirt and hair.

I go up like a torch.

- 14 -
The Outlaw

"Katie!" I scream, running through northern Downtown. She's nowhere. Puck can find neither her nor Blue-Eyes. "Katie!"

Behind me, a shattering spray of water bursts through the glass storefront. That's the third one in the last sixty seconds. What is the *deal* with the plumbing? Nozzles are being blasted off fire hydrants. It's like the whole ocean is trying to spurt up from the ground. Some streets already hold standing water.

"Katie!"

I turn onto Broadway.

Suddenly there are goblins everywhere. Walter's mutants, clinging to walls. A group of them spot me and jump down, howling. I'm in no mood to fight—there's no time.

Hey, I know this place. That's Natalie North's old building. The tower where I fought Tank.

The road rumbles. I feel it in my shoes, and the nearby manhole cover rockets upward. The projectile goes *through* one of the oncoming mutants like a frisbee, and the jet of water spears the rest. Across the intersection, the street cracks and water roils from the blacktop. Who knew water could be so strong?

Above me, someone shrieks. Further fraying my nerves. It comes from the roof of Natalie North's tower. Katie? Doesn't sound like her.

Someone steps to the edge of the roof. Someone on fire! Two people actually, one cradling the other. Has to be the Cheerleader.

What is *happening* up there? I border on the verge of hysteria, unable to process anymore mind-boggling surprises. This day is madness.

"Katie!" I *Leap,* leaving craters in the blacktop. Climbing to Natalie North's roof used to require half an hour, and now I do it with a single jump.

The Cheerleader jumps too, away from me. An impressive leap, sailing far to the north. Her screams rattle my ears.

I reach the roof in time to witness a bad dream.

I flash back to finding Tank here, Katie his captive.

But today I see the goblin king. He and Katie are grappling. As I watch, the love of my life turns to fire. A whoosh and she's engulfed.

"Katie!" My Thunder Stick whistles and catches the goblin king at the base of his neck. His head bursts upwards in a messy spray, separating from his shoulders.

I don't watch. I don't slow. I take one step and scoop Katie into my arms, cradling her. One arm under her knees, one arm under her neck. She's aflame and strangely silent. My skin sears, and my ragged vest catches. Another step and we're over the ledge and falling. Tumbling out of the sky.

How long does a person have when soaked in gasoline? I don't know. But I bet it's short.

Don't die, Katie, not now!

I watch the oncoming ground, calculating our spin with a keen and focused attention. We plummet for three seconds, an eternity when someone you love is on fire. Right before impact, I rotate us so I'm on bottom. Spinning.

My left hand I put behind my head. Curl into a ball, Katie held on my stomach.

I hit the ground like a boulder. My body is hardened almost to rock. Even so, most ribs break. Katie lands on my chest, driving the air from my lungs. My left hand is broken between my skull and the street. The blue sky above darkens for a moment. The jarring impact feels a bit like being electrocuted.

We're awash. Underground pipes are pumping cold foaming water through sewers and faucets, and it's ankle-deep. Katie rolls off me and splashes, turning over and over and over. The water washes her clean. Oily puddles slide off her, flame for a moment on the water's surface, and then extinguish. She's safe, although her hair still smolders and her clothes are singed.

She coughs and sputters. "Where'd *this* come from?"

"Providence from above." My words come out in a wheeze.

"Chase!" She scoots to me. Gently lifts my head into her lap, keeping me above water. "Talk to me. Are you okay?"

"Are *you* okay?" I rasp.

She pushes hair out of my eyes. "I am badly burnt. And it hurts. And I need medical attention soon. But most of the fire was burning the gasoline, not me. I held my breath and closed my eyes. Somehow I knew...I *knew* you would be there."

"Always. Is Blue-Eyes...?"

"She's gone. And Carter?"

"Gone. Forever."

She looks me up and down. "Is anything broken?"

"Yes. Everything."

"Oh no!" She gasps and covers her mouth. Tries not to laugh, but we both do. It's absurd. Our life is absurdly out of control. And it's either laugh or cry. So we choose the best of the two.

Nearby, mutants are returning to the ground. Guardians and goblins. But they've lost their savage instinct. They move slower and look forlorn. They feel it—their alpha is dead. Her fury is gone and so is their hatred. They sit on all fours and watch us from a respectful distance.

"Should I move you?" she asks.

"No. It's not so bad," I say with a wince. "Last time you broke my back, you forgot who I was. This is an improvement."

"I'll never break your back again." She's smiling and sniffing. "Chase, I will marry you. My answer is yes. It's been yes for years."

"Today?"

"Maybe not today. I require a husband who isn't bleeding from a thousand wounds. But soon. The very first second you're able."

"I love you."

She says, "I love you too," and she kisses me.

We stay that way a long time on 2nd Street, cooling off in the water. Kissing in the City of Angels and watched by expectant Variants. Under clear blue sky. Forgetting the painful past.

One thing is true. She's worth it all.

PART IV

There are far far better things ahead
   than any we leave behind.
      -CS Lewis

- Finale -
Chase Jackson

Katie and I sit at a table in Hidden Spring High School's cafeteria. Across from us sits Samantha Gear and Lee, my best friend from our halcyon days. I haven't seen Lee in four years. He's still a bundle of energy with a shock of black hair, but more of a man now. Or maybe he only looks that way because he wears trendy reading glasses and a groomsman vest.

"How long have you worn glasses, Lee?" asks Katie. Her hair is done up with fresh flowers and she glisters like pure sunshine. I sneak glances at her as often as I can, obsessed. She is the Katie of my youth, but more. She wears bravery like jewelry, confidence like a tiara. Her eyes have seen too much, yet they still shine with passion. Every inch the Queen, a title she's set aside. She is rock wrapped in rose petal. She is both dainty and diamond.

"Not long. I don't need them, bro. They have no prescription. But they make me look mega hot." He glances at Samantha Gear and gives her a little nod. "Right, babe?"

Her green eyes intensify. "Call me babe again and you'll eat those glasses."

"Still playing hard to get? Okay, I feel you, I understand."

Next to Samantha is an open chair. We placed it there for Cory, our good friend who didn't survive the journey. He is deeply missed. We could fill the entire room with chairs for our lost friends, in reality.

The sun streams cleanly through the eastern wall of the cafeteria, which is good because all the lights are busted. The place looks grim, but I wanted to return here one more time. Close the story where it began.

"Look at you two kids," Samantha snorts. "Can't keep your hands off each other, just like in school."

"We got married this *morning*, Samantha," says Katie through a laugh. Her wedding and engagement rings flash in the sunlight. Her reception outfit, a gauzy top and jean combo, is by Rick Owens and cost over five thousand dollars, according to Kayla. "What do you expect?"

"Yeah, and also shut up," I say. And I scoot my chair closer to my wife.

Samantha grins. "I expected you to be on your honeymoon by now. You've been waiting *forever*."

Katie's hands tighten around my arm. "My thoughts exactly. He hasn't even told me where we're going."

"Yeah, dude," says Lee. "Ya'll go. Samantha and I need alone time anyway."

She groans.

From the end of the table comes the musical sound of Kayla's laughter. The cafeteria would stink if she wasn't here, but she makes it smell like cookies and fresh air. She sits sideways on PuckDaddy's lap, her legs crossed, her arms around his neck. Her head leans against his and she plays with his hair. For once, neither are glued to a screen. She's so happy I think she might be emitting light.

"I don't get it, homie," says Puck. He wears a groomsman vest too. "What's so special about this place?"

Kayla nods. "Yeah, you're not icky kids anymore."

"Well, some of us aren't," mutters Samantha, winking at Lee.

"Then turn me into a man, already!" Lee shouts. "How long I gotta wait?"

"Icky?" I frown. "I was never icky."

Katie says, "I wish you could have been with us at this school, Kayla. You would've had so much fun."

She beams. "Right? That would have been the *best!* Queen Carmine and me, sharing lockers! Err, I mean, Katie."

My knees bang the table. "I don't remember the tables being so small. I don't really fit under them anymore."

"That's because you used to be normal," replies Samantha. "I mean, a football player, but normal. Now you're a big masculine war machine."

"Still, that shouldn't shrink the tables."

"And Katie used to be this cute little soft girl," she continues. "And now?"

Lee makes a hooting noise. "And NOW she's like this exotic amazonian with crazy muscles and curves for *days!* Can't even believe she got hotter."

Her cheeks turn pink. "Thank you, Lee."

"I kinda miss Carmine," sighs Samantha. "She would pound this little twerp."

"She's still in here." Katie taps her temple. "And she doesn't understand Lee at all."

"Who does?"

"When do you leave, Sam?" I ask.

"Soon as this is over. Chopper's ready. I'm going big game hunting in the east, trying out Ai's new formula on the wild mutants. Just me and the rifle, like vacation. Give me six months and I'll have caught at least half."

"Legs are fully healed?" asks my wife.

"Good as new. I can outrun Chase, I bet."

Puck's smartwatch beeps. "Okay, dude. We gotta roll. Better wrap it up."

I stand. "You guys are my home. But this place is too. And I wanted to come here and thank you."

"Thank us for what, dude?"

Samantha says, "Shut up, Lee."

"Make me, baby."

"Thank you for everything." I raise my can of soda. "Thank you for believing in me, and for not giving up. For supporting Katie. For being my friends. And for the next hundred years."

"Not all of us gonna live that long, dude!"

Puck mumbles, "Thank goodness."

Everyone raises their drink and we toast. To the next hundred years.

∽

The hallway outside the cafeteria is stuffed with people. General Isaac Anderson is there, wanting a few more words with me about my future involvement with the Resistance and the country's eminent restructuring. We defeated Blue-Eyes and he wants us to tour the world, touting our newfound peace. Not a chance, General. Natalie North waits with him, resplendent and perfect, and she kisses Katie and me both. The Governess asks Katie final questions, and so does General Brown. They're nervous about running the place without her again.

Eventually I take Katie by the hand and pull her away. The military and Los Angeles and the world must learn to survive in our absence. We're out of here.

Our well-wishers gather in the school parking lot to see us off. My father and Katie's mother, here for the wedding, wrap their arms around each other and smile. Katie and I pull on helmets and get on my motorcycle, an electric machine Katie gave me from Carmine's private garage. The tires squeal and we zip from the parking lot and into freedom.

Katie undoes the middle buttons of my shirt and slips her hand inside. Lays it flat against my stomach like she used to, and we laugh like kids in love.

We streak through Downtown and Variants line up to watch. They aren't happy about us leaving, but rumors have spread of a new medicine that will make them feel better. Ai is hard at work inside Good Samaritan hospital, and her trials have been successful. Our hopes are high. In the meantime, goblins and Guardians alike will mope around the city and help clean up. Their inner fire is temporarily held in abeyance.

An hour later we arrive at the Pacific Ocean. I park at the deserted marina in Long Beach underneath a sun laying sheets of sparkles across the waves. The breeze carries the ocean scent I know she loves, and that I've been craving. Above, gulls cry and squawk. Katie says, "You know me well. I've been aching for the beach!"

I take her hand and walk her down the dock, passing hundreds of boats.

"It's a strange sensation," she says. "I can't feel any Variants. For the first time in...forever, they aren't near."

"Good. We'll keep our cellphones off too. At least for a while."

"Where are we going, husband?"

I point to the perfect catamaran bobbing at the end. The hulls gleam, freshly waxed. The lines and white sails are brand new and brilliant. The water tank is full, the electrical equipment was updated, our cabin holds a new mattress and sheets, and the coolers are stuffed with fresh food and drink. "There. My boat, named *Angel*."

She gasps. "It's gorgeous. Is that where you lived the previous two years?"

"Yes."

I help her aboard. She steadies herself and sighs, rubbing her wrists. "Like magic, my joints quit hurting."

"Something about the waves. It brings me peace."

She steps to the mast and hugs it, like an old friend. "You can pilot this by yourself? It's gigantic."

"Absolutely. I did it in my sleep on occasion."

"This is twice as big as Saul's sailboat."

I'm untying mooring lines and I pat the hull. "I love the *Angel*. She's fast and dry and sails close to the wind."

Katie slides on a pair of sunglasses and points to the north. "That looks like Minnie's yacht."

"Yes, *Amnesia*. I gave it to the crew, and they ferried my boat here. It's waiting for Kayla and Puck. As a favor to me, the owner is bringing them over in a month or two."

She grabs me by the shoulders and forces me to look at her. She's smiling. "Chase, bring them over *where*? You still haven't told me where we're going."

"Hawaii, of course. Nothing but the best for you."

She laughs and flushes with pleasure. "You *knew* I've always wanted to go! We can get there on this boat?"

"Traveling in style. It'll be the happiest week of our lives."

Her arms go around my neck. Her lips brush mine. "It'll be the happiest week, no matter where we are. I'll make sure of that, my husband."

Our third night out, we recline on blankets draped across the hammock netting. The sky is an inky blue and bright with stars. Our ocean is calm, like a mirror for the wide universe, a sheet of starlight laid on the Pacific. The moon hangs full on the western horizon. Breeze comes from the north and pushes us silently across the planet.

A realm with only us.

Katie murmurs, "You were right. This is the happiest I've ever been. Carmine hasn't spoken for days, which I think means she's at peace." She raises a glass and drains the fruity pineapple drink. "Uh oh, I finished it. I'll fetch you another."

"Not yet," I say. "I'm too content for you to leave."

"Okay. I'll stay."

Nearby, tiny sea creatures create bioluminescent patterns beneath the surface, and we hear whales breaching in the distance.

She says, "Do you remember that day you tried out for the football team as a junior? You were so nervous."

"Six years ago? Maybe longer. I remember throwing the football out of the stadium."

"Yes. You did. That was the start of it all." She twists on the blanket so she can lay her chin on my chest and look at me. "I remember watching the ball sail away. And I thought to myself, look what he just did. And I thought, one day we'll be mutants and get married and sail to Hawaii by ourselves."

I laugh. "You did? Wow. That's significant prescience."

She pokes me and smiles. "I have a favor to ask."

"Sure."

"After we're in Hawaii, and after we enjoy ourselves a while, I want to check on the children."

"The Inheritors," I say.

"Yes. I don't trust the government, even the Resistance. Isaac promised to have Ai look in on them, but somehow I consider them my responsibility. I think you and I should be involved."

I nod. "It was already on my agenda. With power such as those kids have, they're going to need a lot of oversight and attention."

"They worry me."

"Don't let them worry you for...at least another month."

"Mmmmm." She smiles. "Maybe two months."

"Deal."

"What do you think would happen?" asks my wife, tracing lines on my stomach. "If you and I have a child? We both hold the disease in our genes now, according to Ai. What would we produce?"

"Good question. Maybe Thor."

She laughs again, my favorite sound in the world.

She says, "But I don't want a child. Not for many years. I want you to myself. Okay?"

"For you, Katie? Anything."

The End

D^{ear reader,}

THANK YOU. Thank you.
   Thank you. Thank you.

WRITING THE CHASE/KATIE saga has been one of the great joys of my life. Thank you for reading through the ups and downs.

SPECIAL THANKS to Debbie and Teresa, two of my editors who did the work just because they are kind.
   More thanks for Sarah, for the love and encouragement.

THIS BOOK TOOK a long time to write, partially because Samantha Gear was supposed to die. She was supposed to perish saving Ai in the fall from Carter's plane. And then...she just wouldn't. The story floundered without her, and so did Chase. So, much of it had to be re-written. I'm very glad she found a way to survive. I like thinking about her hunting in wild America.

WHAT HAPPENS NEXT? I'm not sure. My initial intention was to write another series based around the Inheritors, and specifically around Chase's son. I also have a 'western' planned out that takes place in America after the events of this book. But I'm up to my ears in other projects, so I'm not sure if that will happen. But you never know.

ONCE AGAIN, thanks for coming on this journey with me.
   I depart with the permanent and deeply satisfying image of

Chase and Katie on the shores of Hawaii in matrimonial bliss. Free from responsibility, and happy ever after.

-ALAN

  1 Thess. 2:8

Made in the USA
Middletown, DE
27 October 2020